"A LOVELY,  INDIA."

"The pleasure of *THE PEACOCK SPRING* lies in the colorful bazaar that is Rumer Godden's India." —*The Sunday Denver Post*

"RUMER GODDEN'S CHARACTERS ARE DRAWN BRILLIANTLY AND SYMPATHETICALLY BUT WITHOUT COMPROMISE AND THE RESULT IS A FAST-PACED DRAMA . . . THAT RANKS AMONG HER BEST NOVELS."
—*Hartford Times*

"*THE PEACOCK SPRING* is Rumer Godden at her best. . . . At once somber and joyous, the novel will be wonderfully welcome after the long wait since *IN THIS HOUSE OF BREDE.*" —*The Anniston Star*

"THIS IS A SUPERB NOVEL ABOUT INDIA. . . . THE AUTHOR KNOWS INDIA WELL. . . . SHE USES ITS MYSTERIES AND CHARMS WITH DRAMATIC EFFECT TO PRODUCE A MEMORABLE STORY." —*St. Louis Post-Dispatch*

"Rumer Godden is a writer 'par excellence.' . . . Superb story-telling." —*Bestsellers*

"A BRILLIANT TRAGEDY OF COLOR, PASSION, AND VIOLENCE."
—*Baltimore Sun*

Fawcett Crest Books
by Rumer Godden:

IN THIS HOUSE OF BREDE

THE PEACOCK SPRING

ARE THERE FAWCETT PAPERBACKS
YOU WANT BUT CANNOT FIND IN YOUR LOCAL STORES?

You can get any title in print in Fawcett Crest, Fawcett
Premier, or Fawcett Gold Medal editions. Simply send title and
retail price, plus 50¢ for book postage and handling for the first
book and 25¢ for each additional book, to:

MAIL ORDER DEPARTMENT,
FAWCETT PUBLICATIONS,
P.O. Box 1014
GREENWICH, CONN. 06830

There is no charge for postage and handling on orders for
five books or more.

Books are available at discounts in quantity lots for industrial
or sales-promotional use. For details write FAWCETT WORLD
LIBRARY, CIRCULATION MANAGER, FAWCETT BLDG.,
GREENWICH, CONN. 06830

THE
PEACOCK SPRING

Rumer Godden

A FAWCETT CREST BOOK

Fawcett Publications, Inc., Greenwich, Connecticut

THE PEACOCK SPRING

THIS BOOK CONTAINS THE COMPLETE TEXT OF
THE ORIGINAL HARDCOVER EDITION.

A Fawcett Crest Book reprinted by arrangement with The
Viking Press, Inc.

Copyright © 1975 by Rumer Godden

All rights reserved, including the right to reproduce this book
or portions thereof in any form.

ISBN 0-449-23105-4

All the characters in this book are fictitious, and any resem-
blance to actual persons living or dead is purely coincidental.

Alternate Selection of the Literary Guild
Selection of the Doubleday Book Club

Printed in the United States of America

10 9 8 7 6 5 4 3 2 1

"*Do you know why the peacock gives those terrible screams?*" asked Una. "*He has looked down and suddenly seen his feet. He had been so busy admiring his train that he had forgotten he had them.*"

ONE

Ganesh, the old gardener at Shiraz Road was showing Ravi, the young gardener, how to sow the summer seeds.

"What, more flowers!" Ravi's expression had said. This Delhi garden was already full of them: turrets of roses, long beds of more roses, all now in their second flush: borders of delphiniums and lupins, snapdragons, petunias, dianthus, stocks; English flowers, most of them unfamiliar to Ravi, though he knew pansies and, of course, knew the creepers that flowered over walls, summer house and pavilion—scarlet bunches of clerodendron, blue trumpets of morning glory and, everywhere, bougainvillaea cream, pink, magenta, and crimson. Bowls of narcissi, growing in pebbles, were carried into the house for which, each morning, Ganesh arranged a score of flower vases. Pots of carnations were ranged on the steps and along the paths and, in the cut-flower garden, shielded by jasmine hedges from what Ganesh called the 'show garden,' were cornflowers, poppies, sweet sultan, sweet peas. Ganesh always gave these a double "s" like a hiss—"ssweet ssultan," "ssweet pea"; Ravi, who could pronounce them perfectly, did not name them at all; he worked mostly in silence. Now he was dribbling the seeds two or three at a time into the drills he had made in shallow earthenware pans. The seeds were nicotiana and portulaca to bloom in the hot weather. Ravi had not seen their flowers either but when they were sown he would lift the pans onto the slatted shelves of the seed house he and Ganesh had built last October, a small bamboo house on stilts; every evening its roof of mats would be rolled back so that the seedlings could have the cool air and morning dew; by day they would be shaded from the sun. Ravi had learnt how to water the minuscule plants by dipping a leaf in water and shaking it over them—the finest watering-can nozzle, Ganesh had told him, would give jets too strong.

It was oddly delicate work for such a big young man and Ravi's hands were not deft; Ganesh often frowned as he watched him at work. *"Beta*—son," he said. "You could do anything," meaning Ravi should do something else, but Ravi had paid fifty rupees to Ganesh—'tea money'—to get this post, and so he only smiled his absent smile, absent because his thoughts were far away. "You are educated." Ganesh said it almost as an accusation. "You are much educated."

"Am I?" Ravi did not contradict; nor did he say that the attraction of gardening was that he could be a gardener with his hands, his back, and strong legs, keeping his mind for his own. Ravi was the *'chota mali'*—'chota,' in his case, meaning not 'little' but 'lesser'; if he had been the *'burra mali'* or head gardener like Ganesh, he would have had to think, plan, decide, take responsibility; as it was, he could dig and weed unworried, squatting on his heels with the sun on his back—if he were alone in the garden he worked only in a loincloth—carry water, flail the dew from the lawns with bamboo rods so that the sun would not scald the precious grass. He would sow seeds that would grow, minding their own business, into their own beauty; a few would never quicken or would have their first shootings overcome; some would wither: "If they must, they must," said Ravi.

"But you must sow them as carefully as you can," said Hemango Sharma who was Ravi's best—perhaps now his only—friend.

Hem was always anxious. "Should you not," he had asked, "change your name?" But Ravi had only laughed. "I am Ravi Bhattacharya, good or bad. Let them do as they like."

"You do not know what it is they do," Hem had said roughly.

"I don't want to know," said Ravi.

"And I don't want to talk about it, but remember, young Indrajit and Prasad are both still in prison," and Hem had walked away to the lower garden among the baskets and hoses and humble earthenware pots which somehow calmed him.

Shiraz Road was one of the wide tree-shaded roads of New Delhi with spacious houses and flowered, fountained roundabouts; an oasis in the India of struggle and striving with which Hem was concerned; misery, privation, slums, disease—"Particularly disease," said Ravi—but in this protected world of No. 40 Shiraz Road and its like, if there were a drought the fountains still played, "Though only for a time," said Hem. "There will be an electricity strike." Though there was a famine in the country, the Delhi ladies still went to Connaught Place to buy cherry cake and canapés for their parties. "Again, not for long," said Hem. "There will be riots." "It has always been like this," said Ravi. "That's what makes it so peaceful here."

"Once you, too, wanted it broken."

"I know better now."

"Or worse." Hem gave a sigh. Then he said, "At least nothing—and no one—can interrupt you here," and, presently, when it is dark, thought Hem, you, Ravi, will stand and stretch your six-foot strength and go to your hut at the end of the garden—Hem always seemed able to see Ravi's every movement. You will wash at the courtyard tap, pouring water over yourself from your lota, then put on a clean loincloth, a singlet or muslin shirt, eat with your fingers those chapati—soft wheat biscuit-bread—and the vegetables and lentil sauce I insist you buy, then you can light your lamp and, if the writing comes to you, write. "If it does not come, never mind; it will come tomorrow," Ravi would have said. Hem often thought Ravi did not fret or despair enough to be what Hem thought of as a true poet, but there are poets and poets and Ravi would sit on the floor at his table, which was an old school desk with the legs sawn off, until he was tired, then sleep on his charpoy, the cheapest native string bed. "You need not be *quite* so simple," said Hem, but simplicity was the present fetish. "You make a romance of everything," complained Hem.

"Of course," said Ravi. Perhaps his poem would wake him in the night, perhaps not, but presently, in time, a poem whole and new would come. Even now, as his fingers pressed the seeds into their pit of earth—"Too deep," Ganesh would have groaned—words were beginning to form themselves in Ravi's head. Like a seed, a poem had a miraculous power of growth. "Except flowers are more certain," said Hem.

Ravi knew Hem gave him these pricks only to spur him on—and would not be spurred. *"Sust*—lazy," Hem would fling at him.

"Chulta purza—busybody," Ravi would fling back, then put his arm round the shoulders of his friend. I am so plain, thought Hem, so dark-skinned against your height and fairness—"Complexion of bright wheat," the admiring girls who had known him said of Ravi, said it usually to Hem. Ravi though had no use for girls. "I have never seen one that I liked. When I do . . ."

"Some idealized model of a damn Rajput princess, I suppose," said Hem.

"Come, make peace," said Ravi who could be irresistibly winning. "Cease teasing me and I won't tease you. What is there to worry about?"

"You may yet be dismissed," said Hem.

"Not very well," Ravi was calm. "This is a United Nations house. They might dismiss one of their own people, but not one of us."

"Unless you are as usual unusually foolish."

"Granny Hem," teased Ravi, but Hem was right; Ravi himself never knew when he might become restless. "To be at the beck and call of one man," he grumbled.

"Not one man," said Hem. "Four years ago it was the French delegate who lived here; last year it was the great Mr. Svend Ramussen; now it is this new secretary for the First Asian Common Market Conference, Sir Edward Gwithiam. Next year, who knows? No matter who, they cannot much interfere," and it was true Ravi had only seen the English Sir Edward as a small colourless man in the distance in the upper garden or on the veranda of the house. "The house is the United Nations," Hem insisted.

"And there is no *mem*," Ganesh would have added with satisfaction. Ganesh knew that *mem-sahibs*, Indian or Western, white, brown, black, or yellow, could disrupt even a nation; at present, No. 40 Shiraz Road was blissfully at peace.

Then, one day in late January news filtered from the house servants to the gardeners that soon there would be a mem—"A sort of mem," said Ganesh. Two Miss-babas, Sir Edward's children were coming from England. "They will play ball," said Ganesh in dread. "They will be noisy and ride their bicycles over our flower beds."

"These are not our flower beds." Another fetish was that Ravi did not wish to own anything.

"It is many years since we had babas here," said Ram Chand, the old bearer, and the house was in a ferment of excitement. Ravi did not care either way; the children of Sir Edward were nothing to do with him. He was cleaning out the pavilion lily pool and, now the fountain had been turned off, could see his reflection among the goldfish. Ravi's hair was long to his neck and he had stuck a frangipani flower in it, just behind his ear. "Are you a Santali maiden in the marriage market?" He could imagine Hem's caustic remark, but the effect of the deep cream petals against the well-oiled black pleased Ravi mightily.

Bonfires! Nothing but bonfires! Hal Gwithiam wrote in her diary. *Such a deal of wonder has broken out within this hour! The Winter's Tale* was much in Hal's head: the school was doing it for the end-of-term play and Hal was playing Perdita—was to have played Perdita, she corrected herself because *nothing but bonfires! Crackers sent for Una and me.* Crackers was their headmistress, Mrs. Carrington. *We have been back at school two days, only two days,* she wrote, *but he has written to say we are to leave at once and go out to him in Delhi—saved from this horrid old dump.* 'He' was her father, Sir Edward Gwithiam; the dump was Cerne, one of England's most distinguished schools—and one of the most expensive, as Great Aunt Frederica continually reminded them. "It costs Edward more than a thousand a year to keep each of you there." Yet money alone could not get a girl in. "There has to be *some* ability," as dry Mrs. Carrington said. Hal guessed she would not have qualified if it were not for Edward's name and the fact that he was abroad—"And his high position," said Great Aunt Freddie. It was also because Una was there, "And Una has brains." Hal did not say it enviously—and, too, Hal had no mother; "No mother at home," said Hal. Una had had another mother, Kate, who had died when Una was born.

At Cerne, though, Hal had won her way as she always did. Had she not been chosen as Perdita—*The prettiest lowborn lass that ever ran on the green sward?* She supposed she was lowborn compared to Una and she was certainly pretty— "Too pretty for your own good," said Great Aunt Freddie. Hal did not see why; so far it had done her nothing but good. Hal's real name was Halcyon. "Sir Edward must have his foolish moments," said Mrs. Carrington, "to saddle a girl with a name like that!" Yet Hal was not saddled; she was her name, with a nature that was halcyon, a warm insouciance that made her popular and charmed the most cynical of teachers. Now she looked down at her copy of *The Winter's Tale,* marked for the part of Perdita:

> . . . *When you speak, sweet*
> *I'ld have you do it ever: when you sing,*

I'ld have you buy and sell so . . .
. . . When you do dance, I wish you
A wave o' the sea, that you might ever do
Nothing but that; . . .

and Hal knew that fitted her as perfectly as it fitted Perdita.

Do they have sward in Delhi, she wondered? The post-cards Edward had sent—Why only postcards? There used to be long letters—showed carved red sandstone buildings, a blue-domed mosque—"The famous Delhi blue," Una had told her—or a frangipani tree—"The flowers have a heady strong scent." Una, as a baby, had been in India and could just remember it.

There was a postcard of a snake charmer: a cavalry soldier on a camel: another of a bullock cart on a dusty road and there was one of a peacock—*They abound round Delhi!* wrote Edward. After two years of Cerne, Hal ached to be abroad again. True, Edward had written they would have a governess; that was certainly the ignominious fly in the ointment but Hal hastened to reassure herself. *Of course she will only be for lessons which I suppose we must have . . .* and, *Nothing but bonfires!* Then Hal stopped writing.

Under the elms and chestnuts of the park where Cerne's own sward, kempt and smooth, was crisscrossed by gravel paths, a figure was walking alone in the January cold; she was wrapped in the long green cloak all the girls wore in winter when they went between their houses and the main school; this figure, Hal's familiar from her earliest days, was not going anywhere, but pacing, withdrawn, and so solitary that, even in her tumultuous joy, Hal paused.

When they had come out of Crackers' study, Una had been so silent that Hal paused before she rushed away, "To tell everyone," as she said.

"Una, you *are* pleased?"

"I thought I had three years," said Una.

"But . . . you are pleased."

"No."

"Oh Una! You must be. Think—Delhi and here!"

"I happen to like it here."

"You can't. Not compared . . ." Then Hal beseeched, "Una—why?"

"Here it's—orderly." Una could explain no more than that.

"You needn't go back to your classes," Mrs. Carrington had said.

"No, it wouldn't be much use now, would it?" Una had agreed and, "I'm going out," she told Hal.

Watching the solitary, pacing figure, Hal knew there was no feeling of bonfires in her sister Una.

"Write to him," suggested Mrs. Carrington.

"I did, but I tore it up."

It was not easy for a Cerne girl to see the headmistress; for most of them, Crackers was a figurehead, someone who, in her cap and gown took assembly, sometimes gave lectures to the seniors, and, on occasions, conducted the school orchestra; yet, mysteriously, Mrs. Carrington knew her girls, all four hundred of them. She was often met with in unexpected places, did unexpected things, which perhaps had given Una the courage to go to her directly. Una had first though to pass the secretary whose desk was in an alcove outside the study door.

"Please may I see Mrs. Carrington?"

The secretary had not been with Mrs. Carrington for sixteen years—longer than Una had been alive—without learning something of her ways and, "You are Una Gwithiam?" she asked.

"Yes."

"I think you may knock and go in."

Now, "You tore up your letter?" said Mrs. Carrington. "Why?"

Una's grey-green eyes did not baffle—did not deign to baffle, thought Mrs. Carrington—as did the eyes of most young girls; they were honest which was at variance with the half-mocking understatement, the shrug with which she usually hid her feelings. "Surely that girl is uncommonly self-contained," Mr. Rattray who coached Una in mathematics had said.

"So would you be if you had spent most of your life in suitcases—metaphorically and actually," said Mrs. Carrington. In her time, the headmistress had known and assessed perhaps ten thousand girls, she thought a little wearily, and now she looked carefully at the one opposite her. Una's face was too long for beauty, but fine-boned, with a high forehead, a fine thoughtful forehead. This girl, given a chance, thought Mrs. Carrington, might grow up to the nobility and integrity that, with a certain toughness, had made Sir Edward Gwithiam the notable diplomat he was; but perhaps, thought Mrs. Carrington, there was only room in one family for one Sir Edward. Yet she had always thought of him as an attached, even a doting, father; not six months ago he had been, proudly, she had thought, discussing Una's prospects of getting into University, though he obviously did not think as much of her quiet achievements as, for instance, he did of Hal's music. "I want Hal to study with Signor Brazzi."

"Such a little girl, Sir Edward?"

"Yes." He had been firm but now had come this sudden veer of mind.

"Your father will have to pay a term's fees," the other girls told Una and Hal. "A whole term's fees for nothing." Such an improvident impetuous parent was outside their comprehension, as was Una's reply.

"I don't suppose he knew that term had started."

"Well, he has so much to think of, it's no wonder he had forgotten," said Mrs. Carrington.

But if he had forgotten, wasn't thinking of us, what made him suddenly decide to have us out? That was the puzzle Una would not put into words.

"Why did you tear up that letter?" Mrs. Carrington asked again.

"I thought it might hurt him." For once Una did not use her usual subterfuge. "You see, I . . . can't judge what's happening." It was coming out in jerks. "He . . . he might need me. Edward—my father—and I are special. We always have been, even when he married . . . Louise." Mrs. Carrington sensed that Una hated to speak of her step-mother. "I was little then but—and I expect it sounds strange—even then he relied on me."

"Yet he sent you away to please this Louise." Mrs. Carrington forbore to say it—she had fathomed something of the disaster of Sir Edward's brief marriage to Hal's mother.

"Other men have wives," Una went on."They play golf, or shoot or fish; Edward does nothing but work—unless I'm there. At least I make him go for a walk sometimes, and we read."

"How long is it," Mrs. Carrington asked, "since you were with your father?"

"Almost a year," said Una. "We went out to him in Washington at Easter. He did make a flying visit to London about half-term but we just had lunch with him. He hadn't time for more."

"You have grown up a good deal in this year."

"I?" Una obviously meant, "What have I to do with it?" but, "Don't expect things to be exactly the same," said Mrs. Carrington.

"They always will be with Edward and me." Una had drawn herself up. Then, "He plays with Hal," she said more naturally. "They have fun. I'm not fun." She said it as she would have said, "I am plain," but Mrs. Carrington knew that Una had her own brand of fun, her own de-lights, and she was not plain. There was something of a water nymph about her—perhaps it was the whiteness of her skin—but Una was at the lanky stage and it would take a connoisseur to prefer her to Hal. Hal, with her small plumpness, would never be lanky and Mrs. Carrington thought with a pang of Hal's dimples, the bloom of her skin, the long curls.

"Curls are a disease of the hair," Una teased her sister.

"Then it's a pretty disease," Hal retorted, which was true. Most Gwithiam eyes were, to Una, an uninteresting grey-green "like mine and Edward's"; she did not realize how they could blaze true green with anger—or joy, thought Mrs. Carrington; she could guess that not much

joy had come the way of Sir Edward and Una—interest,
yes, but not joy. Hal's eyes were blue, the same wide-open
kitten blue that, in Louise, had briefly captivated—
"Trapped," said Great Aunt Frederica—their father. Una
was sure that Hal was the most adorable creature on earth
but, "Hal can't follow Edward," she said now; she did not
know how else to put it. "Would you read what he says?"
and she pushed an air letter, forwarded from Great Aunt
Freddie, across the desk to Mrs. Carrington.

   ... *someone to read with and talk to again ... We will
go for some of our prowls, shall we?* "He and I," explained
Una, "love walking about the little streets of a city." *Miss
Lamont and Hal can have their music. We will read or
play chess.* "We both love chess," said Una. "You see? ..."

   "I see," said Mrs. Carrington.

   "So ..." Una gave one of her small fatalistic shrugs. "I
tore up my letter."

   "That was kind, Una." Mrs. Carrington did not probe.
"You are probably right. A high position can be lonely."

   "But," and Una became an ordinary thwarted child.
"For me, just now!"

   "There are good schools in Delhi."

   "But not Cerne."

   "Una, you must not be a schoolgirl snob."

   "They are still not Cerne."

   "I grant you that—but I had forgotten; you will have
individual teaching—a governess."

   "At my age!"

   "It would have been better to have called her a com-
panion-tutor," Mrs. Carrington agreed. "But you must
have had people looking after you before."

   "Nannies or ayahs when we were young," said Una in
contempt. "While we were in Geneva we had a cook-
housekeeper, and Persians in Teheran, but now we look
after ourselves. You shouldn't make people level, then put
them down," and her deepest worry came out. "There's
something in this not ... straight."

   "Not straight?"

   "Yes. Not like Edward. Usually he asks us, consults—

after all we have been through a good deal with him. It's as if he had suddenly put us into . . . a different category —children."

"Well, you are officially children," Mrs. Carrington felt she had to point that out, and "There must be a reason."

"Yes, but what? Why doesn't he tell us?" and Una spoke as Mrs. Carrington had never imagined she would speak. "I don't want to go. I don't. I want to stay here at Cerne. Mrs. Carrington, if *you* wrote to him . . ."

"I have written," said Mrs. Carrington.

Dear Sir Edward,
   A parent's decision about his daughter's education is, of course, his own . . .

"Here we go," groaned Edward but, as he read on, his face grew more grave, frighteningly grave to Miss Lamont, sitting beside him. Miss Carrington had tried to be both tactful and restrained. *For Halcyon,* Crackers had winced as she wrote the name, *for Halcyon it does not matter so much; if your governess is as musical as it would seem from your letter, and so fluent in French, and insists on good reading, Hal will probably do as well in Delhi as here; she is, to say the least, not academic. Una is different. It may sound absurd to say of a fifteen-year-old that she hasn't much time, but Una has set her mind on going to University and every month counts. We believe that, given a chance . . .*

"Given a chance!" The words seemed to shock Edward. He walked up and down the drawing-room with the letter in his hand.

"I should have thought simply in being your daughter she had every chance." Miss Lamont's voice was melodiously low and soothing, even if it did have an inflection of singsong. "Perhaps this Mrs. Carrington has grown stereotyped? Perhaps a little fuddy-duddy?"

Edward had a sudden vision of Mrs. Carrington, groomed, alert, and by several years his junior, but deliberately shut it out. "Yes, that's what they all are—stereotyped," he agreed.

"And they must not make your Una the same."
"No, by God!" said Edward.

"That Miss will stay here as mem-sahib," Ganesh predicted to Ravi; doing the evening watering, with the smell of wet earth rising from the flower beds, they could look in at the lighted drawing-room where Edward and Miss Lamont were sitting. Ganesh had seen many employees of the high official families, European, English, American, Indian, and he, like Din Mahomed, the butler, whom everyone called Dino, Dino's two assistants, Aziz and Karim, and Ram Chand, house bearer-valet, and the guests' valet, Jetha, even Mitchu, the sweeper, had been swift to assess Miss Lamont. They had all known Eurasian half-caste nannies, but those had worn uniform and stayed in the nurseries, not, with head held high and fashionable clothes, sat talking and drinking martinis with Sir Edward, nor given orders in house and garden, "While the Sahib, *our* Sahib stays in an hotel."

"Why can't they stay together?" asked guileless Ravi.
"It will only be until the children come, but she is not a pukka Miss-sahib," said Ganesh, 'pukka' meaning proper, his eyes shadowed as if he were truthfully troubled. "These babas have no mother," he said as if he were trying to explain it to himself.

"Then, naturally, there must be a woman to look after them."

"But she is not pukka," Ganesh said again. As if it mattered, thought Ravi.

Edward was still reading Mrs. Carrington's letter: *You say you have found a governess-tutor, but can one woman, however brilliant, give a girl of Una's potentialities all she needs? It is the specialist teaching that worries me, rather than the all-round subjects . . .*

"Isn't it a pity," asked Miss Lamont, "to let a girl specialize so young?"

"Specialist teaching isn't necessarily specializing." Edward did not mean to sound so dry but when worried he

was always curt. "It seems Una is something of a mathematician."

"You mean arithmetic? Algebra?" But Edward was not
listening. Without finishing it, he had discarded Mrs. Carrington's letter and, opening a second, gave a deeper groan.

"What is it?" asked Miss Lamont.

"My Aunt Frederica," said Edward.

Eddie, are you mad? Great Aunt Frederica was neither
tactful nor restrained. *It is mad to take Una and Hal out
to India! At their age! At this time, when term has started
and you will soon be in the hot weather!* Aunt Freddie's
exclamation and interrogation marks seemed to fly off the
page and hit Edward. *And what in the world do you pro-
pose to do with them—especially Hal? You can't keep
girls of school age incarcerated nowadays and Hal is her
mother's daughter. I won't rub that in,* wrote Aunt Freddie
and proceeded to rub it in. *You ought to know what it
means. You know she can twist you round her little finger
as Louise always could. It is asking for trouble!* Then,
suddenly: *No, I am wrong. The real concern is not for
Hal but Una. Think, Eddie, think! When Kate died you
sent Una to Kate's mother. When you married Louise you
took her back again. That didn't last long. Hal was born
and Louise turned against Una. Poor mite, she was sent
back to Lady Osborne. Lady Osborne died, you took Una
home—if home it was. Louise left you—which was a
mercy—and Una saw Hal, whom she loved and protected,
batted back and forth across the Atlantic!—*Edward saw
a little girl hurled across oceans— *and though Una was a
child she was old enough to be aware of the long legal
battle you fought, quite rightly, to keep Hal.* Edward
remembered once hearing Una say, "Children shouldn't be
posted around like parcels," but he did not think it had
disturbed Hal. "It's nice to have your father and mother
both fighting to have you. It makes you feel wonderfully
important," Hal had said.

Then all those changes, Aunt Freddie's letter went on.
*School in Geneva, Teheran, Bangkok, dozens of changes
of places, names, friends! Now, at last when you had given*

in to my pleadings and sent the girls to a proper school—
only English schools were proper to Aunt Frederica—*and
Una is settled at Cerne, absorbed and at ease, and Hal, to
put it bluntly, is safe, you uproot them again and decide
in this thunderbolt way to take them to India! ! !* Think,
Eddie, think.

*As for the governess, I must say flatly, that I should
feel a good deal happier if I had chosen her myself.*

Edward had read it aloud to Miss Lamont; those under-
linings, question and exclamation marks seemed to call for
reading aloud, but he had also read out some of Mrs. Carrington's. "They seem to think it serious for Una. Do
you?"

"I begin to feel sorry for Hal," said Miss Lamont.

"You needn't be. It is usually Hal who takes the lime-
light. Una somehow gets left out—except by me, of course
—but now all of them at home seem united." He was not
to know how that casual but certain 'at home' made Alix
Lamont feel shut out, a hybrid outsider, and "Your Aunt
Frederica is hardly polite about me, is she?" Miss Lamont
could not help saying.

"She doesn't know you," but Edward said it absently.
"Could this really spoil Una's chances?" he asked.

"That's for you to decide," and Miss Lamont bowed her
head. Her fingers pleated the folds of her dress as she sat
still and silent: Alix Lamont knew well how potent that
stillness and submission could be and, sure enough, "What
they forget," said Edward, "is that I am a man, not a
machine."

"Hallo!" said Edward a few minutes later. "Here's another letter—from Una herself." He turned the envelope
over and saw the postmark. "It's at least a fortnight old."

"Indian posts!" exclaimed Alix.

"It was written before Una knew," he said, then
chuckled as he read it out:

Care Pater,
    Supplex tibi scribo impensa vivendi crescet; pecunia ergo,

*quam mihi liberaliter das, mihi non satis est. Alterum tantum
peto, sine quo pauper ero.*

Audi, Pater, et inclina aurem tuam.

"I'm afraid you'll have to translate for me," said Alix.

Edward thought for a minute, then: "It's schoolgirl
Latin, of course—Well, Una hadn't learnt any Latin until
she went to Cerne. 'Dear Father, I write to you as a sup-
pliant. The cost of living rises, therefore the money you
generously give me is not enough. I ask for twice as much,
without which I shall be a pauper. Listen, Father, and consider.' In other words," said Edward, "give me more
pocket money." He laughed again. "It's just a joke. I
wrote to her in German; she knows I know she doesn't like
German and is bad at it."

"Bad! Good enough to read a letter."

"She has retaliated, that's all," and, "Little monkey!"
said Edward and chuckled again.

"Mumma, I'm frightened."

"Frightened? You?" The bulk of Miss Lamont's mother
looked up from the long cane chair where she was lying;
her eyes, completely trustful and all that was left of the
daughter's beauty in the ruins of her face, grew wide. "But
Ally, you are never afraid."

"Mumma, he writes to her in German, she answers him
in Latin."

"My God!" said Mrs. Lamont.

Seldom these days did her poised elegant daughter come
to see her so late in the evening, but as soon as Edward
had left to go to his dinner Alix had taken out his smaller
car.

It was a Diplomat, the government-approved Indian-
made car and the despair of Chinaberry, as the United
Nations Tamil chauffeur was nicknamed because of his
almost blue-black skin. "No good. Often going wrong. Six
weeks for repair and spare parts," Chinaberry had told
Edward in disgust. He had tended the U.N.'s Cadillac for
six years now with love and it was discrediting, to China-

berry, that a cheap Indian car—"Not cheap, abominably expensive," said Edward—should be seen in his, Chinaberry's, garage. "This is United Nations Number One house," he would have said, "and my new Sahib is Director of United Nations Environment and Research for Asia, the whole of Asia," he boasted, "Secretary for the Conference as well," but, "The Government discourages imported cars," Edward told Chinaberry.

"Cadillac was imported."

"Long, long ago," and with the courtesy Edward always used, "even toward servants," said Alix—"Particularly towards servants," Edward would have corrected her—he explained to Chinaberry: "As a foreigner and a newcomer I must be carefull to fall in with your Government's wishes." Chinaberry thought nothing of his Government's wishes and was certain Edward could have bought another Cadillac, "or at least a Buick."

"If I were an Indian I should have to pay over a hundred percent tax," Edward explained.

"But you are not an Indian," Chinaberry could not fathom Edward's wish to share.

"I can drive the Diplomat if Chinaberry won't," Alix had said.

"Not in Delhi. With all these bicycles and scooter-taxis in such teeming streets, it's so easy to have an accident. You might find yourself in a riot if you touched a child or, worse, a cow. Remember, a cow is holy," said Edward, "and there are too many children."

She looked at him uncertainly; she still did not know quite how to take him. Then, "Too many children, unfortunately," he added and sighed. "No," he went on, "this is a city where a woman ought not to drive."

"Hundreds do—because they have to," Alix could have added; instead she coaxed: "It will only be in New Delhi, to the parade ground or the Gymkhana Club. The girls will want to get about and I shall take great care," but now she drove into the Old City, through the Lahore Gate, threading the narrow labyrinth of streets behind the Chandni Chowk, Old Delhi's 'moonlight square' and biggest commercial street. One of Ganesh's mem-sahibs would have driven more courteously but Alix dodged bullock carts and tongas, using the strident hooter, brushed too closely by three-wheeled scooter-taxis, bicycle rickshaws, dazed cows, coolies with loads or barrows, pedlars, *pai-dogs*; she shouted at children, made white-dressed Indian gentlemen leap for the gutters, and, putting her bright head out of the window, exchanged invective with Sikh taxi drivers—only Alix's stream of words was faster. "Child of a swine!" shouted Alix, *"Ullu-ka-pattha*—son of an owl." "Have you slept with your mother?" she demanded. Edward would have been astonished.

She had stopped the car in a space where bullocks and ponies were tethered round a post among cohorts of bicycles and scooter-taxis—Alix called them phutphuts; some 'first class,' grander than others, more roomy, were painted scarlet and hung with tassels like a children's toy. Alix had locked the car and chosen an older urchin among twenty jostling smaller ones to guard it, then picked her way down an unlovely gulley where old car parts were sold. "They will take the hubcaps off your car and sell them to you again while you are bargaining," she could have told Edward. The line of booths was hung with rusty bicycle chains, spanners, old headlamps and heaped with battered car seats, trays of springs, nuts, bolts; worn tires were piled in the road and the air was filled with the stench of hot oil, burning rubber, and the clang of iron being beaten out.

Above the lane and overhanging it were houses. Edward, once exploring the Old City, had wondered who had built them, at the turn of the century perhaps, tall, gracious, with scrolled iron balconies. Some of the balconies were covered in with fine grilles to screen the women; the pediments were carved or ornamented in plaster, but now the house fronts were hung with boards: Malik Amrit Lal Patney, advocate.' 'Goodwill Electric Company.' 'Perfume, Incense, Chewing Tobacco.' 'Happiness Coffee and Tea House,' but most of the houses were hotels with ambitious names: the Regal Hotel: the Savoy: Métropole: Grand-

Mahal: and squeezed between two large ones, its board hung even more crooked, the Paradise Hotel.

In the welter of cookshops, stalls, vegetable sellers' baskets, tea barrows, barrows for sherbet, and sugar cane, for ices—'Mango Duet,' 'Strawberry Delight'—and a dozen goats with their kids lying contentedly in the dust, it was difficult to find the entrance to any hotel, but Alix was accustomed and quickly threaded her way to the Paradise, stepped over the open drain that ran below the shops, tightening her telltale nostrils as she smelled the gutter cess, and went up the steepest and narrowest flight of the whole of the block.

"Mumma, you will never get up or down those stairs," she had said when Mrs. Lamont first chose it.

"Why should I want to, m'n?" said Mrs. Lamont. "My God, when do I go out?" Careful not to let the walls touch her dress or her white bag, Alix, this evening, had gone swiftly up the first flight and come out on the landing that was the centre of the Paradise Hotel. Here was the rickety office—much like a ticket office in a station—with a communal water-filter and refrigerator, while a few old steamer chairs, their cane blackened by twenty years or more of use, stood against the walls. In one a fat man lay asleep, his trousers unbuttoned over his pale stomach, his bare feet up on the boards of the chair, nutshells and betel stains on the floor around it.

In the peculiar sleaziness of a third-class Indian hotel, rooms led off the landing and their tattered green doorcurtains showed glimpses of, in one, a dormitory where bunks were let by the night; behind another was a humbly respectable living-room with beds, a line of clothes slung along a rope, a table, a cooking stove. In another, Alix could see young Westerners, European or American, in gaudy dirty Indian clothes, their feet bare as they sat or lay on the floor; a couple were twined together; one young man was asleep, his fair hair stirred by the breeze from a creaking electric ceiling fan. There was a sound of women scolding or quarrelling, of children crying; babies crawled in the corridor, children were everywhere while, in one doorway, an old woman, a grandmother perhaps, her legs and feet swollen with elephantiasis, shrilled and scolded at them. Radios sounded from landings far upstairs, raucously mingling with the street noises from below, and from the surrounding rooftops came the perpetual sound of crows.

The fat man opened one eye. "Going to see Mummy?" he asked. "That's nice!" Alix had not answered him, but had swept past disdainfully, and his eyes, wistful and brown, had followed her as she went along the corridor to a door hung with a curtain that was not stained or torn but new; it led to the hotel's best room, overlooking not the booths of car-parts gulley but a fruit market and a lane of shops. Alix lifted the curtain and went through.

"You!" It had been a cry of delighted surprise. "You! Ally!"

"*Don't* call me Ally."

A crone of an old woman was crouched at Mrs. Lamont's feet, pressing them with her hands, as her mistress, wearing a bright flowered wrapper, lay in the long chair made soft with cushions. In Mrs. Lamont, Alix's curves had turned to a mound of soft flesh; she was almost as swollen as the elephantiasis grandmother, but her eyes were as large as Alix's, the same deep brown, but without their watchful glitter; Mrs. Lamont's eyes, though, saw a long way and for a while she let the only noise in the room be the sound of the palm-leaf fan she was lazily using and the chink of the old woman's, Terala's, bangles that slid up and down on her arms as she worked. Terala's bangles were twisted wire, two iron studs made her earrings, and her white cotton sari was limp and grey. She herself was thin and light as a withered leaf. She did not dare to look at Alix but, "Ally, where are your manners?" said Mrs. Lamont. "You should wish Terala, m'n? and you haven't wished me."

"Mumma, I haven't time . . ." but Alix bent and kissed her mother—again the telltale nostrils drew in. Mrs. Lamont's face was powdered thickly as a clown's and, "Why do you use that filthy powder? Its scent is horrible."

"It is called Flowers of Heaven," said Mrs. Lamont undisturbed. "It only costs six paise."

"Phaugh!" but Mrs. Lamont liked everything strong and highly coloured, everything that smelled and tasted. Her room was crammed 'with life' Alix had to admit. It was a hotchpotch of good and poor: the rugs might be soiled but they were genuine Agra—Alix could remember them from her childhood homes in Pondicherry and Calcutta. There was sandalwood and brass; the bed had a red quilt and was heaped with dirty silk cushions like the long chair. There were Kashmir embroideries, Persian copper-fretted lamps, carved tables and brackets; on a shelf was a statue of the Virgin Mary, carved long ago in Gôa, but beside it a bazaar mirror was painted with staring roses. The doors were open to the balcony "and all the street noises and smells!"

In most of these hotels the ground floors were given over to restaurants and cookshops, their smells even more pungent than the lane and pervaded by the smell of frying in mustard oil; there were lesser smells of curry and spices, decaying vegetables, orange peel, of cess, and every hotel had at its steps that centre of gossip, the pan seller's stall, his betel leaves spread on blocks of ice, his pastes in doll-sized brass bowls among cigarettes and newspapers. Terala haunted the pan seller—she would not look at Alix now because she knew her teeth were stained red with areca nut —and Mrs. Lamont was forever sending her to the cookshop to buy *samosa, kabab,* or *kulfi,* the Indian version of ice cream, to keep 'just in case.' "But you *shouldn't* keep food," Alix often expostulated. Now she found that the meat safe on the window sill was clustered black with flies feasting on a cloth Terala had hung there and, "Mumma, can't you tell Terala to wash out that filthy cloth?" In the Paradise Hotel her "filthy" lapsed into "filthee" and she had almost screamed it. But, "What do a few flies matter?" Mrs. Lamont was quite comfortable. "Where there is food, there will be flies, and if they kill me, I am old." At that moment, a pair of cockroaches, alarmed by Alix, scuttered into the bathroom. "Ugh!" Alix shuddered. "Where is the phenyl? I brought you a bottle of Jeyes Fluid only last week. Where *is* it?" At the shrillness of her voice the palm-leaf fan paused, was still, then, "Ally, come here to me," said Mrs. Lamont and, after a moment, Alix turned, dropped to the wicker stool beside her mother, and buried her head in that capacious lap.

"She wrote it with a dictionary," declared Mrs. Lamont.

"Mumma, she's at Cerne. That's a famous school. They *teach* them there. That's why it's so expensive."

"The more expensive the school, the less they learn. Your father always said it. I'm sure she did it with a dictionary."

"Mumma, send Terala outside."

"But, Girlie, she doesn't understand a word we say."

"She will watch, gossip," and Alix jerked her head towards the door. Terala, standing, was almost as bent as when she crouched; she salaamed and, emaciated, crept towards the door; it was again like the passage of a leaf.

"Mumma, do you know what A and O Levels are?"

"Roads," said Mrs. Lamont promptly. "A is for important roads, O are less important."

"They are school examinations," said Alix.

"That is Junior and Senior Cambridge," Mrs. Lamont was certain. "And didn't you pass your Senior Cambridge with *honours?*"

"This is something . . . more modern and much higher."

"What could be higher than honours?" Like a big downy pelican Mrs. Lamont plucked soft feathers of reassurance from her own breast though she was bleeding with apprehension. "Come Ally, take heart. If she has German, you have French."

"Pondicherry French," said Alix bitterly and her head went down.

"Pondicherry! What nonsense, I ask you? Mère Génévieve was a Parisian from Paris and she said your accent was perfect, perfect! And see how fluent you are."

"Una may be fluent too. They have lived in Geneva and Persia."

"In Persia they speak Persian." To Mrs. Lamont that was fact, "and you went to France and England."

"I didn't go to England, Mumma. I only said I did."

"You nearly went. England is only across the channel— you have only to look at the map. My God, even with the nuns' help how we scraped and saved to keep you at the Conservatoire."

"And I threw it all away. Fool that I was."

"And wasn't that natural?" cried Mrs. Lamont. "You so high spirited, so lovely? And there was no reason, no reason at all for the nuns to withdraw their grant. I stopped praying for them im-me-diately."

"Anyhow, I wouldn't have gone back to teach in their old school," but Alix was still brooding. "I only had one year. . . ."

"And look what you did with that year. Look what you know!"

"Very very little," said this new frightened Alix. "You should meet Sir Edward."

"And didn't he choose you?" demanded Mrs. Lamont. "Wasn't it he who came after you, not you after him?"

"In—a way."

"So accomplished, so stylish," Mrs. Lamont went on. "One has only to see you to know how stylish you are. 'What a fine lady,' Mr. Lobo said that."

"Mr. Lobo!"

"Mr. Lobo is a man of taste." Mrs. Lamont was as dignified as Alix was withering. "He may be run down but that is what he is, a man of taste." Her voice, like Alix's, was rich and comforting, but its singsong was un- ashamed, as was her love and pride as she looked down at the beautifully dressed head in her lap and her hand, that had a permanent tremor, stroked its red sheen. "No, no," said Mrs. Lamont. "You are never afraid. My beauty. My queen," crooned Mrs. Lamont.

Alix raised her head and looked beyond her mother to the hotel's whitewashed wall; a small Indian votive lamp, a *deeva*, burnt in front of the statue; well, Hindu and Catholics are alike in many, many ways, thought Alix; the smell of the warm sweet oil was somehow comforting.

"And haven't you your music? Look how you can play. Look at the prizes for pianoforte you have won."

"Prizes!" but Alix sounded more convinced.

"And your voice! 'That is a glorious voice,' Soeur Marietta said that often to me. 'It isn't fair,' she said, 'that one girl be given so much.' Ally, you can swim, you can ride—your dear father saw to that. You dance, drive a car. None of these things could I do. Show me another teacher," demanded Mrs. Lamont, "who can do half as much. I see a brilliant future." Mrs. Lamont had become a soothsayer. "But not too brilliant for my girl. Come, Ally. Afraid? Of what? Two little schoolgirls, m'n?"

That is what they looked, coming down the gangway from the plane into the Delhi morning. Una and Hal were pale from the long flight, their skirts and blouses crumpled from being slept in, and they were wearing their green school cloaks. "Do we have to take those ghastly uniforms?" Hal had almost wept but, "No waste," Edward had written to Great Aunt Freddie. "At least we can't wear our berets and blazers," said Hal. "That wouldn't be allowed." Long afterwards Edward was to find Cerne's crest, worn embroidered on the blazer pocket, among Una's private things.

Una and Hal were used to packing at short notice and travelling unquestioningly by land, sea, or air; even at Cerne, until last holidays when Edward had left them at Gwithiam with Great Aunt Freddie—"And not come himself even though it was Christmas," said Hal—he had sent for them no matter where he was.

"You ought to have stamps on you," their housemistress had said. "We never know where you have come from."

"Well, I suppose these high officials have to be a kind of gypsy," Mrs. Carrington had said once to Mr. Rattray.

"Gypsies' children," said Mr. Rattray, "have disadvantages—if they want to be educated."

"Yes," said Mrs. Carrington and sighed.

A year ago she had sent for Una. "They tell me you could do quite well in mathematics, Una, given the chance." It was odd how often, with Una, Mrs. Carrington found herself using those three words.

"But I'm so far behind," said Una. No one was more conscious than she of what she called her 'gaps.' "I have been to so many different schools."

"You are behind," Mrs. Carrington had agreed, "but Mr. Rattray has offered to give you some special coaching himself."

Mr. Rattray was the senior mathematics master and Mrs. Carrington might well have expected Una to be dazzled but, "That will be very pleasant," was all that she said.

"Your father has agreed."

"It seems the shrimp has brains," Edward had teased Una in Washington. "Of course you get them from me."

"You are not a mathematician." Una had said it so flatly that Edward had not known whether to be nettled or amused.

"I really think he was nettled," Mrs. Carrington said afterwards.

"Most men," said Mr. Rattray, "would be proud to have a daughter with a brain as uncommon as that."

"He is," said Mrs. Carrington. "I know he is. It's a puzzle. In spite of his brilliance, Sir Edward, I should have said, was thoughtful. . . ."

"He isn't thinking now."

"Or not letting himself think. Well, I suppose he couldn't have reached the height he has without being a little ruthless." Mrs. Carrington sighed again.

"You will have to work hard," she had told Una in that interview.

"I will try," and Mrs. Carrington had guessed that behind those ordinary quiet words Una had vowed herself to Mr. Rattray and mathematics. I thought I had three years. Fool that I was, thought Una.

The plane was flying now over the Alps and through the small window Una could look down at the cruel peaks coldly white and blue in the moonlight. She had seen them in this way before, by moonlight and daylight, she thought. The shape of the plane made a small lonely shadow among them.

Hal, beside her, was curled comfortably in sleep; Hal had a knack of adapting herself no matter where she went. "Put her in a Siberian prison camp," Edward had said, "and she would soon be friends with every guard and prisoner and settle quite contently," but Una was not a Hal. What would Edward do, she wondered, if she, Una, had to be dragged kicking and screaming from the plane? Say I had hysterics and probably send for a doctor; she knew the wry answer.

At noon they would land. "Once you have felt the Indian dust, you will never be free of it," Edward often said that and, even in this unwilling journey, Una, from that long ago babyhood, felt the faint stirrings of nostalgia, of remembrance, but she pushed them down in her mind. "There is nothing there for me. I won't like it," said Una in the night. "I won't like anything or anyone in India ever again."

Edward was there to meet us, Hal wrote in her diary, *but at a special entrance, not with ordinary people. We were whisked through before anyone else by a police officer. There was a clerk from the office to see our luggage through the customs, a car and a chauffeur; the car had the blue, white-crossed U.N. flag flying. We never had anything like this before. How I love to be important.* Hal's diary had been given her for Christmas; it was of the kind that had brass clasps and locked, but she had already lost the key; that did not matter because the diary was as open as Hal; anyone could read it, and "It isn't we who are important," Una was to point out. "It's Edward."

"Dads!" In her excitement, Hal had shrilled out their baby name for him and all heads turned to stare. "They were staring already," said Hal at Una's sharp pinch and, when they reached Edward, she threw her arms round his neck and hugged and kissed him. "You looked so silly and what would Indians think?" Una said afterwards. "That I was glad to see him," said Hal but Mrs. Carrington had told Una that she had seen Indian children, after a long absence from their father, bend down and touch his feet with their folded hands, taking his dust. "I should have looked a good deal sillier doing that," said Hal and, "Una! Don't be so prim," but Una had had to take refuge in primness.

In spite of his importance, Edward, standing on the asphalt outside Hal's 'special entrance,' had looked small and lonely. Perhaps I never really looked at you before, thought Una on the gangway. I didn't know you were so slight, and you are a little stooped from working too long at your desk, I am sure. At this distance, Edward might have been anybody—or nobody—yet Una knew that at a snap of his fingers the big police officer standing beside him, all the policemen, probably the whole airport, would spring to attention. *When Sir Edward Gwithiam wants a thing done, it is done, willy-nilly,* a profile in a newspaper had said. *He has tremendous drive.* . . . and yet Una felt such a pang of pity for him that all her animosity faded. His hair was ruffled, as he always ruffles it under a strain, thought Una; then another thought came—Why should she and Hal be a strain? And there was reserve in the way, when Hal's exuberance had worn off, that Una said "Hello. Hello, Edward."

"Don't I get a kiss?" As soon as he held her, Una felt his tenderness, his concern, and her own came up to meet it. Dear wonderful Edward! And—I'm glad I tore up that letter. I'm glad, yes, glad I came.

If Edward were slight, Una was slighter and, "What have they been doing to you?" asked Edward. "They couldn't have given you enough to eat."

"They did, Edward, truly."

"You're nothing but a sheaf of bones. Never mind, Miss Lamont will fatten you up."

Wary glances from both girls. "Where is she?"

Alix had not come to the airport. "Better not force myself on them," she had told Edward. "They may resent having a governess, you know."

"Resent?" He was defensive.

"Yes. Remember their ages."

"Little girls."

"Not little, young—and old to have a governess. I will wait for you here."

The music seemed to roll through the rooms and down the steps of the house to meet them; someone, somewhere, was playing the *Appassionata* with strong capable hands that made the melodies throb and sing, not at all the way it was played at Cerne.

"Who is it?"

"Miss Lamont."

"She can play like that?"

"Indeed she can—and do many other things too—as I told Mrs. Carrington." Edward's voice was crisp; evidently he had not liked Crackers' letter.

Una had been so filled with herself and Edward that she had given scarcely a thought to this governess, Miss Lamont; nor had Hal. When they had wondered about her at all, they had visualized someone not young, not old, like their house mistress, plainly dressed and pleasant—"Edward is sure to have chosen someone pleasant," Hal had consoled Una.

"But what shall we do with her when we and Edward want to be together?" asked Una.

And we went into the drawing-room, wrote Hal in the diary, *and met Miss Lamont. Wow!*

The music stopped at once and Miss Lamont rose; she did not come to meet them, but waited for them to come to her as she stood by the piano.

It was a grand piano and, when have we ever had one, thought Una? This was a monster; she was to discover it was a concert grand, but it did not make Miss Lamont seem small; she was large, larger and taller than Edward, and the first feeling she gave Una was of power. Una was to see that first sight of Miss Lamont again and again in her mind—One of your hands was resting on the polished wood, your nails were polished too . . . I think you take great care of your hands, but they are big, the fingers wide at the top; no wonder you played so forcefully. You choose your clothes carefully too. Miss Lamont's dress was pleated into soft folds—I guessed it was Indian cotton. It was not the sort of dress you can buy and I knew you had had it made, and chosen it because its deep yellow colour set off your hair and eyes.

The hair was dark red which was startling in contrast with a slight dusky tinge in the rose and ivory of the skin, but, "Quite common Eursian colouring," Lady Srinevesan, Edward's experienced Indian friend was to tell Una. "Some Kashmiris have it too, but their eyes are usually pale, almost aquamarine—brown eyes with red hair are uncommon. The Lamont's, I must say, are superb." Indeed, in that first vision, Una found herself almost dazzled by the glow and colour of Miss Lamont. You made us, at least me—and Edward—look like creatures kept under a stone. Then Una saw that the brown eyes, for all their grandeur, had a watchful glitter and, You are not quite as much at ease as you seem, thought Una.

"So these are the girls." The voice was lilting, dominant, as Miss Lamont put out her hands to Hal, who took them as if she were mesmerized. "Halcyon! Why, you are *perfectly* named!" Una saw Hal blush—a phenomenon she had not seen before—then, "And Una! Let me look at you too. Edward, she is just like you!"

"Edward!" If Una had had hairs on the back of her neck they would have risen. "Why should she call him Edward?" she was to demand. "Probably they were friends before we came," said Hal. "She isn't an ordinary governess."

Releasing Hal, Miss Lamont had stretched out her hand to draw Una near, but Una had not consented to be drawn.

"You were horribly stand-offish," Hal told her. Una had shaken the hand, politely but briefly, and let it drop. For perhaps half a second Miss Lamont was disconcerted, but only half a second, then, "I expect you are hungry and tired," she said. "Put down your cloaks and have a drink of lemonade; Christopher, our cook, makes it fresh every day." "*Our* cook?" Una wanted to query but, "Edward, you must be dying for a drink," Miss Lamont went on; a white-dressed manservant was already busy at a tray of bottles, glasses, and chinking ice. "Luncheon will be ready as soon as we are," and Miss Lamont pulled chairs forward, brought a small table for Edward. "The girls can see their rooms afterwards." Does she arrange everything? thought Una.

"Have the babas come?" Ravi asked Ganesh.

Ganesh laughed. He had met them and Edward at the steps with celebration buttonholes of violets tightly twisted with maidenhair. "Babas!"

"Why do you laugh?"

"Look." Ravi took one glance through the long drawing-room windows and retreated behind the jasmine hedge to the lower garden.

"Sit at the foot of the table, Una, opposite your father. That's your place now." Miss Lamont was smoothly tactful. "You see, you are his official hostess," at which Una gave her a horrified glance.

Lunch began with slices of golden fruit that Una dimly remembered as papaya. Servants, led by an elderly butler whom Edward had introduced to her as Dino, offered hot food in silver dishes. Miss Lamont led the conversation with the same deft tactfulness, asking about their journey, England's January cold; Hal chattered and Una, almost against her will, was drawn in; she had seldom heard Edward talk as much.

Outside, sun flooded over the vivid scented garden and Edward was right—Una was back in India, or India in Una; she remembered the garden bird calls and crow-caws;

saw a swoop of green wings—a flight of parakeets. There
was the subdued sound of voices speaking the, to Hal,
mysterious language, but of which a few words came back
to Una. Even the smell in the room of polish from the
stone floors, the scent of sweet peas in the bowl on the
table, of papaya, the prawn curry and poppadums ordered,
Una guessed, especially for them. Her babyhood might
have been back—only, of course, I didn't have curry. . . .
"There was something called pish-pash," she said aloud.

Miss Lamont nodded. "They give it to children in India.
Fancy your remembering that."

"I remember it too," said Edward with distaste. "A baby
brew of chicken with rice. I used to have to eat it or you
wouldn't, you little wretch! You do not know," he said to
Miss Lamont, "the trouble I had bringing up these girls."

It was all affection and a gaiety Una had not seen in
Edward before; was it this that made her feel that something was, if not wrong—what she had described to Crackers as "not straight"?

To both girls, the Shiraz Road house was astounding. In
the hall, there was a fountain—a fountain in the house—
splashing under a bougainvillaea plant big as a young tree.
Una had taken in too the size of the drawing-room with its
long windows opening on vistas of garden; the room was
so big it stretched out of sight—there was an alcove round
its corner—and it seemed filled with flowers, those narcissi
and vases of roses. It had Persian carpets—she had
counted three of them in the drawing-room, and here, in
the diningroom was another; she looked down at its
border of leopards bounding away from hounds and horse-
men in a tapestry of turquoise, tawny browns, and pinks
and, "It's a hunting carpet," Edward told her. "I bought it
in Agra. I think I am going to collect carpets."

Edward collecting things? And, "Wouldn't Teheran
have been the place?" asked Una.

"I suppose so," said Edward, "but—funny," and he
looked puzzled, "I didn't want to collect them then."

"India is such an unhappy troubled country," Una had
said to Mrs. Carrington.

"It can't all be unhappy."

"Then it ought to be. How can people eat and drink and work when there's all that hunger and misery and disease?"

"You will find they can because they have to. Your father does. He leads a busy social life, entertains as, in his position, he must."

"Edward is frugal." Una had been up in arms at once but, "frugal" she thought now and, "Isn't this rather a sumptuous house for us?" she asked.

"Well, United Nations took it over from an American oil company. Their official houses are inclined to be lush," said Edward.

"It may be lush but I like it," said Hal and Miss Lamont gave her an approving nod. "So you should. It is beautiful."

"Alix chose new covers and curtains for us," said Edward.

Alix! Una's hairs rose again. How dare she choose things for us, and her eyes, as Una's eyes could, grew bright and green. "Did it always have a concert grand?" she asked deliberately.

Edward did not answer, his hand went to his hair but, "We need a piano—for Hal," said Miss Lamont.

"We"? "Hal is used to any old school piano," said Una.

"I hope we can do better than that." Again Una saw the watchfulness in Miss Lamont's eyes and how swift she was to smile sweetly at Hal, reassuringly at Edward in a glance across the table—a private glance, thought Una, who immediately became more captious. "Three servants to wait on four people!" she said when Dino and his underlings had left the room.

That touched a tender spot in Edward. When he had come to Shiraz Road he had tried to reduce the staff and failed. "Few households in Delhi keep to the old standards," he had told Dino. "We too must reduce," but, "Three table servants right," Dino had insisted. "Sahib will see. Here much much entertaining," and when Edward had answered that there should not be "much much entertaining" in such poverty-stricken times, Dino's adroit, "Yes, peoples very poor. Aziz has been here eleven years, Sahib, Karim seven. Where they get other work and they having families?" It was the same with Ram Chand and his assistant, Monbad. "Two men needed for the rooms, Sahib. Many many peoples staying. Come and go, many many." It was the same in the kitchen, though Christopher, the Gôanese cook, had now to manage with one cook's mate, not two; the same with the sweepers and the garden and, "Yes, we have a galaxy," said Edward now and sighed.

"You can afford it." Miss Lamont meant to soothe.

"That's not the point."

"I think the house should be worthy of you."

"A Chinaberry point of view," said Edward. He had no idea, of course, how that remark cut; Miss Lamont bent her head over her plate and a hot stain spread up her neck to her face; Una saw it but, oddly enough, not with satisfaction. As if the sun had gone in over the garden, the affection and gaiety had stopped—spoilt by me, thought Una. Hal gave her a vicious kick under the table; I deserve it, thought Una. Edward had put down the knife and fork and was looking grieved, then Miss Lamont lifted her head and Una saw that it was Edward not she, who had made the dint in Miss Lamont's composure.

"I suggest hot baths and bed," she said, getting up from the table. "Come along. I will show you your rooms."

They were in an L of the house where a wing was built out into the garden, the sitting-room; with tables, a bookcase was at the end. "This, or the veranda, will be our schoolroom." Miss Lamont's own room had another veranda and, in between right under her eye, thought Una, were two small bedrooms for her and Hal. As they were shown there was a certain tenseness. Miss Lamont had obviously been busy here as well. "You needn't be cross, Edward," she had said. "There was hardly any expense. I did it myself with Monbad and a *durzee* and found the things in the bazaar." She did not tell him that there had been trouble over the durzee. He was not the expensive haughty tailor who sometimes came to the house to make shirts or dresses, curtains or loose covers, but a humble little man she had brought from the Old City, an old man with silver-rimmed spectacles, his needles and pins stuck in his small embroidered hat that itself was like a thimble. He had cut the muslin for the dressing-table skirts too short, and the upbraiding Alix had given him shattered Shiraz Road.

"Is that how mems talk?" Ravi, who had never met one, asked Ganesh. This sounded more like the vituperation of a sweeper woman. "Owl! Pig! Son of a pig!" "And he a Moslem, remember," said Ganesh. To a Moslem, pig was doubly unclean and, "Certainly she is not a pukka Miss-sahib," said Ganesh. The finished rooms, though, looked peaceful enough—each, Alix thought, a dream of a young girl's room, pink for Hal, and, "Somehow I thought pale green suited Una. Are they all right?" Alix had asked Edward who had nonplussed her by being silent. "Are they— are they—not all right?"

"You must be prepared for Hal to plaster hers with photographs of pop stars," he said and made the worst of male comments: "It might have been better to have let them do the rooms themselves."

"But why, Edward? So unwelcoming."

He had not answered "Una—and all that muslin!" Instead, "They ought to have bookcases," he said.

"They have." Alix showed him two white painted wicker bookshelf brackets hung on the walls, and Edward had laughed. "Una grows books like grass. She would bring that down in ten minutes," and then, seeing Alix's distressed face, he had said, "All I can say is, if they don't like their rooms, they are ungrateful little girls."

They were not—at least not on the surface; good manners took over, of which, "Heaven be blest for them," Great Aunt Frederica often said. "At least they avert immediate collision." Hal's "How dainty!" would have been wholehearted if she had not been certain of what Una was thinking, but, "You must have taken a great deal of trouble —thank you," said Una.

For Hal there was a mandolin. "Can you teach me to play it, Miss Lamont? Oh, can you?"

"I can," and Hal took it at once into her room and, sitting on her bed, began to strum.

Standing on a small table by Una's window a set of chessmen was arranged on an inlaid board. The pieces were of sandalwood and ivory. "Ivory!" whispered Una, going down on her knees beside them. The sandalwood had the faint old Indian smell she remembered—Though I haven't smelt it all these years. There was no mistaking her pleasure. "Edward, they are exquisite!"

"Moghul," said Edward, this new extravagant Edward, but when extravagance is after one's own heart it ceases to matter, and Una, with awe, touched the little ivory white queen who held a bunch of delicately carved roses; the queens were in palanquins while each king rode in a carved howdah on a state elephant, the rooks were mounted on war elephants, the bishops on camels; the knights had prancing horses, while the pawns were kneeling bowmen. "Moghul!" said Una in ecstasy. Alix heard the difference in the tone and abruptly left the room; neither Edward nor Una saw her go.

"That's what I brought you out for," said Edward. "To play chess with me."

"Of course." Then Una looked up at him, her face back in its pale hardness. "Does Miss Lamont play chess?"

"So that's the trouble! You silly little skinny-ma-link," and Edward swept her up in his arms and kissed her.

"A monkey-man. Somewhere near me, in the garden perhaps, there is a monkey-man." It was strange that Una had so immediately recognized the sound that woke her. I could only have been about three years old when I last heard it, she thought, but it was unmistakable; the rattling of lead pellets fastened to strings round a small waisted hand drum. The monkey-men always rattled them with one hand while the other led a pair of dressed-up monkeys. There must be a monkey-man here now. Una swung her feet to the floor.

"We couldn't sleep," she and Hal had protested to Edward when he had ordered them to bed that afternoon. "We couldn't possibly," and in a few minutes had been fast asleep. "Well, you were tired and in a new element," Miss Lamont was to say. While Una had been asleep, someone had come in and unpacked her cases; her brush and comb were on the flounced dressing-table, her travelling clock by the bed, her slippers put ready. When she opened the wardrobe her dresses were hanging there; linen, blouses, jerseys neatly folded on shelves. Had a servant done it, or was it Miss Lamont? The same someone had switched on the electric fire. It was kind but, to Una, an intrusion; she did not like anyone to handle her intimate things just as, at school, she had disliked having them identified by name tapes, even initials. "I never met anyone so private," Hal used to say in exasperation. Hal had no private things; with her, everything was open, to be shared. "But then Hal is much nicer than I am," said Una.

In their big bathroom—Miss Lamont had her own—Una washed and towelled her face and hands, then brushed out her hair and put on a dress, because surely it would soon be time for supper or dinner—she did not know yet which they had in Shiraz Road.

The dusk had a chill, the Indian winter chill and she took a cardigan before she stepped out on the veranda.

She had dreaded finding Miss Lamont there, reading perhaps, watchful, but the veranda was empty as was the garden in the evening light. Then, over the rattle of the drum, farther away now—it must be at the back of the house, thought Una—she heard the piano. Miss Lamont was safely in the drawing-room.

Rays from the setting sun were slanting low over the garden, giving its colours a last brightness, but in shadows and corners already the light was growing dim and she remembered how brief twilight was in India. From the rapid transit through space and time, Una felt exhilarated, out of herself; at Cerne now it would be midday; she would have been among the other girls in the classroom, not wandering alone in the dusk of this tropical garden.

She stepped soundlessly along the path that surrounded the big house; in pots along the gravel were carnations that brushed her bare legs; she could smell their clove scent as she went round the L and paused at the back of the house to look into the drawing-room. Through its smaller back windows she could see the french doors open to the light beyond; a lamp by the piano cast a wide pool of brighter electric light that shone down on Miss Lamont and her hands on the keys; she had changed and was wearing something mulberry coloured; its fabric held gleams of gold. She knows how to dress, thought Una.

She herself seemed to have gone back in time, hiding from grown-ups and with a governess. Even the drum sound belonged. "Una, baba, come and watch the funny monkeys." Una remembered how they somersaulted in their patchwork clothes, walked on their hands, held one out for paise and how, given a slice of orange, they seized and pouched it, first picking out the pips with minute black fingers.

Across the grass from where she stood and behind a screen of poinsettias, a rough nasal voice was chanting or singing; there were catcalls and bursts of laughter, and soon Una was looking through the bushes to a row of garages with, above them, what must be servants' rooms; some were lighted—she could see clothes hung below the ceilings on a string, pots of marigolds, a mirror. Her nostrils caught whiffs again familiar; the smell of a hookah—hubble-bubble—and of biris, the pungent native cigarettes, and on the concrete forecourt lit by the outside garage lights, she saw a small crowd, all the house servants and, perhaps, some of their friends. The butler Dino, and two men—the other table servants? Una hardly recognized them without their turbans—were smoking the hookah; others, among whom she identified the old bearer, Ram Chand, smoked biris, but all of them were watching a space where a pair of monkeys capered as their master, in dirty white clothes and a dark red turban, sang, jerked their strings, commanded, or rattled his drum. If Una had shut her eyes she could have been back again, squatting on her heels as she still could, brought by Jetti, her Nepali ayah, to watch the monkeys.

Were they funny? No more now than when she was three did Una know what story the man was chanting, the monkeys acting; she was too far away to see them well but she heard guffaws, the men's excited laughter. Perhaps I ought not to be here, thought Una, and yet she stayed.

Then a car drew up, its door slammed and Edward strode into the courtyard. The drumming and chanting ceased abruptly; the hookah was left, biris stubbed out, turbans hastily reached for. "Turn that man out at once!" Edward spoke in English and Una could tell he was angry. "I will not have such things in the compound. Ram Chand, Dino, you ought to be ashamed of yourselves."

If he finds me here he will be angrier still, thought Una and disappeared like a wraith but, as she came back into the garden, she found she was trembling, and still hearing the drum, the guffaws, Edward's angry voice. "Well, people like obscene sights, you know they do," she told herself, "but with monkeys, poor pitiful monkeys! I'm glad I couldn't see it, but I hate all humans, thought Una.

Then, in the gathering dusk, she saw a light at the far end of the garden. It was coming from behind another screen of flowers, a tall hedge so fragrant that its white flowers flooded the air with scent. Una stole closer to look. Behind the screen was a thatched hut, low to the ground with a courtyard of sunbaked earth; it had a standpipe with a tap and a small bush in a pot. Mats were hung over the entrance but two were rolled up showing a lighted room and she knew there was one servant who was not watching the monkeys.

Yet was he a servant? The young man was sitting cross-legged on a mat at a floor desk on which he was writing—or not writing. He seemed to write a word, then gaze into space, his eyes looking directly at Una, though she was sure he had not seen her or her pale dress among the flowers. She saw his lips move and caught a murmur; he was trying over something to himself. Close by him a small brazier burned red; every now and then he stretched out his hands to warm them over the coals.

His lamp, unlike Miss Lamont's, did not make a pool of light; it was only a wick in an earthenware saucer of oil, the saucer shaped like a leaf, a lamp shape Una had seen in museums. But he ought to have a better light to write by, she thought.

Hem had said the same thing, and sharply. "This is ridiculous, Ravi *bhai,* when you have electricity. You will ruin your eyes."

"I like the soft light," and Ravi grew cross. "You don't understand. To write poetry, surroundings must be poetical. You are a dolt."

"And you will go blind."

The light was flattering; it threw a circle on the page on which Una could see characters; he was writing in one of the Indian languages and, from the narrow lines, it seemed to be a poem; his hand, holding what she thought was a wooden pen—Ravi would have told her it was an old-style reed pen: "Why not a quill or an ink brush?" Hem had teased—was lit to amber brownness and made a shadow on the page; the light caught his chin and the side of his young face, absorbed and utterly at peace. Against the amber colouring of his neck, the shawl he wore wrapped round his shoulders looked shiningly white and Una noticed he had a flower, a rosebud behind one ear.

> "*There is a lady, sweet and kind*
> *Ne'er was a one so pleased my mind . . .*"

"Come Hal, let us hear from you," Miss Lamont had said after dinner, then coloured, annoyed with herself. Try as she would, every now and again one of these little Eurasian colloquialisms slipped from her—she lived in dread of catching her mother's perpetual 'm'n?' "Why not? You are Eurasian," Una and Hal would have said.

In the big drawing-room, firelight flickered over the pale colours of sofas, chairs, and curtains—I had forgotten we had fires in India, thought Una. There was a smell of wood ash, of sweet peas again from Ganesh's bowls and vases, and the familiar smell of Edward's cigar.

Una had seldom seen his face as tranquil as, with her beside him, he leaned back in his chair smoking, watching and listening.

"Hal can sing, Edward—really sing!" Miss Lamont had exclaimed. Hal sang as naturally as a bird. Signor Brazzi, the visiting singing-master at Cerne, had had the wisdom to do little more than guard her voice "and teach her to breathe," he had said and, "She should learn languages seriously." But Hal had no intention of learning anything seriously. She simply sang.

". . . a lady sweet and kind." That, Una knew, was how Miss Lamont already appeared to her young sister.

> "I did but see her passing by
> Yet will I love her till I die."

but Miss Lamont was not "passing by." She was unmistakably here.

"Now you sing," Hal said to her, and the fuller voice, rich after Hal's treble, soared into the room as Hal, leaning on the piano, gazed at this dazzling new love.

> "Le ciel est, par-dessus le toit,
> Si bleu, si calme!
> Un arbre, par-dessus le toit
> Berce sa palme. . . ."

That poem should be sung calmly, detached as the night, thought critical Una. She makes it sound like honey, but Edward was rapt. "This is how I met her," he whispered to Una. "She was engaged to play and sing at a party in Calcutta."

"But—she's not a professional?"

"No, but she had to make every penny she could, poor girl."

"Every rupee . . . every thousand rupees?" Una had not

meant it to sound so insulting, but the effect was instantaneous.

"If you cannot appreciate . . . and cannot behave . . . I suggest you remove yourself and go to bed." Edward was at his cutting coldest; Una had seen many people shrivel under that—but for Edward to speak to her in this way, even if she had provoked him, was . . . incredible—Una was almost too stunned to think—and for an outsider, a Miss Lamont!—but as she stared at him with disbelieving eyes, it became a curt command. "Go to bed."

It was an hour before he came to her, an hour of turmoil for Una, but at least he came. "I'm sorry," said Edward. "All this work makes me on edge." He stroked her forehead, straightened her pillow. "Go to sleep, my silly, and stop thinking," and stayed with her.

Edward had thought she was asleep when she opened her eyes and, "Who is it who lives in the hut at the end of the garden?" she asked.

"Is there a hut?"

"Yes. Who lives there?" and Edward had to say, "I'm afraid I don't know."

TWO

"I have to go to Japan today," Edward announced at breakfast next morning.

"Today!"

"Yes, unfortunately."

"But we have barely unpacked," said Una. "Never mind. I have always wanted to see Japan, especially Kyoto."

"You? What is this to do with you?"

"But you said . . ." Una stared at him. "You wrote we should travel with you."

"When I'm on leave, not working. Cheer up," said Edward briskly. "I shall only be gone two or three days." He got up. "You have Miss Lamont. You can spend the time getting to know one another."

"Thank you," said Una.

"That's nice and gracious," Hal scolded her when Edward had gone. "Think how Alix must have felt."

They were to call her Alix; Una decided immediately it should be Alix/Miss Lamont. It was difficult, though, to keep to that; Alix knew so well how to disarm.

At first light the morning after Edward went, Monbad, the young house bearer, came along the veranda with a tray of tea, toast, and bananas. "Toast and bananas *now!*" Una said.

"You will see, you will need them and breakfast too." Alix/Miss Lamont had come into the room. "We are going riding. Hurry up and dress." She herself was in jodhpurs and an orange silk shirt—"and jodhpur boots," Hal whispered enviously. They only had walking shoes.

"You can ride?" Una had not meant it to sound rude, but Alix's colour rose and, as she drove them, she said, "I have ridden since I was four. My father taught me. He was in the cavalry, the Lancers."

In spite of herself Una was impressed. "The Lancers used to have gorgeous uniforms," she said.

"The President's Bodyguard do still; gold-braided turbans wound round a golden *kulla*—that's the peaked cap; they wear scarlet tunics, white breeches, Napoleon boots with golden spurs. Each man must be at least six feet tall and, when they ride in state, they have snow-white sheepskins under their saddles. They are on duty when, for instance, the President holds an investiture. Probably Edward will take you to one, then you will see them standing down the room with their lances and pennants. Before Independence they used to stand guard like that in the ballroom at Viceregal balls."

"Did you go to Viceregal balls?"

"Heavens! I was too young, only a little girl. My mother would have gone," said Alix, perhaps a little too quickly, "except that we lived in Pondicherry. Pondicherry was French, not British, so we only had Government House."

"Did your mother go to Government House?"

"Naturally," but, that's a lie, thought Una. "You will see the troopers," Alix had turned the conversation. "We shall be riding at the Bodyguard's parade ground."

"But are we allowed to?"

"Certain people have permission—diplomatic families, members of the Polo Club."

Diplomats they were used to, but polo . . . "Una, can

you believe it?" asked Hal. "At this time, at Cerne, we should have been doing P.T. before breakfast!"

The early morning was chill enough to be exhilarating; sunlight, though pale, seemed to spin round the car as they drove; every garden showed "showers of flowers," and gave glimpses of lawns and roses; creepers flowered over walls and gates and house pillars—And this is still January! thought Una, marvelling. Each roundabout had flower borders. "Delhi is called the city of fountains and flowers," said Alix.

"Parts of Delhi," Una might have said. The roads were as busy and crowded as ant passages, with workers on their way to offices, shops, hotels, hundreds of brown legs, thin for the most part, walking or pedalling bicycles or rick-shaws, or driving phut-phut taxis. The street cleaners sent dust up with their twig brooms, and little piles of leaves smoked on the sidewalk, giving off a clean acrid smell. Alix turned off the road and bumped along a side track with white notice-boards lettered 'private' and where, beyond clumps of trees, the green space of the parade ground opened; sure enough there were the troopers, wheeling and circling.

"But where are the sheepskins? The scarlet and gold?" They had to laugh at Hal's disappointed face. "Silly, you don't think they *work* in full dress," said Una. The uniforms were a drab grey-green. "But the turbans are still splendid," she said; they were, dark red, long-ended; "And see how these men ride," said Alix. The parade was over and they were "schooling young horses," she explained. "But come, let's look at ours," and she added, "I can't tell you how disappointed Edward is not to be here at this moment."

"What moment?"

"When you are introduced to your horses."

"Our . . . what?" And, "You mean . . . we have horses?"

"Look."

The three were waiting under an acacia tree which dap-pled their coats with shade and light as the grooms held them, ready to snatch off the checked cotton horse-cloths

—lettered 'G,' Una noticed. Alix stopped the car, Una and Hal tumbled out, and the horses turned their heads, cocking their ears; one of them whinnied a welcome as Alix went near. "This is Una's." The mare was a pale dun, her coat rippled with sable, darker colour in her mane, tail, and slender legs. "She is called Mouse," said Alix. "She's a little mettlesome, but Edward thought you could manage her; and this is Snowball, for Hal." A showy white pony with something of a palfrey in his thick-setness, wide-neck, flowing mane and tail.

For once Hal was speechless and Una so silent that Alix asked, "Don't you like them?"

"*Like* them!" said Hal.

"Of course we like them. It's just," said Una dizzily, "that . . . it's such a surprise."

"But you have ridden before."

"At school and in the holidays in Persia, but the horses did not belong to us. We never dreamed of having our own."

"Not at Gwithiam?" There was awe in the way Alix said that name.

"We're not—we weren't—that kind of people."

There was a third horse, a big handsome chestnut, and, "Is that yours?" Una asked Alix.

"That's Edward's Maxim."

"Edward's! He has a *horse?*"

"Why not?"

Why not? It was suddenly going too far. Una and Hal collapsed into giggles. "Edward, and a horse!"

"Why shouldn't he have a horse?" Alix demanded. "Why not, if he wants one."

"Edward wanting a horse!" They were overcome with laughter.

Again that colour stained Alix's neck and cheeks. "You are very impertinent girls." She had been prepared for hostility, had understood Una's resentment, but she had not visualized laughter. "Your father, like the rest of us, needs some recreation."

"But a *horse*." They leant against one another, weak with laughter.

"He plays no game, takes no exercise," argued Alix.

"He has never taken exercise." Una was wiping her eyes. "He just gets himself thin with work."

"But he must want it—need it."

"You don't know Edward as we know Edward. . . ." sang Una and, "What would he do with a horse," Hal asked rudely, "when he is in Japan?"

"Siam," sang Una.

"Assam."

"Funagity-pan." Then Una, catching sight of Alix's face, tried to say, "I'm sorry, Alix. I know you meant to be kind but it's true, you don't know Edward."

A burst of fresh giggles, but Alix had taken the measure of them. "I see it hasn't struck you," she said with silky smoothness, "that Edward might have come to like something different?"

The laughter stopped; Una's face was set again. After a moment Hal said, "Oh well, are you going to ride Maxim now, Alix?"

"Edward is generous enough to let me ride Maxim when he is away."

Beside the mare and pony, the chestnut looked enormous. "Well, he's seventeen hands," but Alix swung up on him easily. "We'll walk them on the edge of the parade ground until you see how they go." See how they go—not "How you can ride." Again that tactfulness that made Una feel so contrary, but, You have just had a brush with her and came off worst, she told herself. Better keep quiet; besides, riding Mouse was an irresistible happiness. The little mare was obedient to every pressure of Una's leg, the least touch of the rein. "You have good hands," said Alix.

From the parade ground, bridle paths led away to open land; Una could see the red-earth rides shaded by feathery-leaved trees. A posse of children cantered down one of them, the riding master behind. "Pony Club," said Alix and, "That's how we had to ride at Cerne," Una told her. "And we rode hired hacks," said Hal, "and in Geneva. In

Teheran we hired ponies too, but they were only little country ones."

Una looked down at Mouse with almost disbelieving pride. "Edward must have grown suddenly rich."

Alix was casting an anxious eye at Snowball, restive under Hal's too eager hands. "Don't pull at the reins, Hal. You'll only make him worse." Other riders passed them; families who looked at them with curiosity; two Indian women: officers: then a young officer on a dapple-grey mare. After a moment he rode back, then turned and came up to them, saluting Alix with his whip. "Isn't it Alix? Alix Lamont?"

"Good morning, Captain Singh." She would have ridden on but he reined in beside them; his eyes, that were gay, friendly—and bold, thought Una instinctively—had taken in her, Mouse, Hal, Snowball, and Maxim. "New post?" he asked Alix/Miss Lamont. "New people?" There was a touch of impertinence, of banter.

"Sir Edward Gwithiam has engaged me as companion . . ." Una and Hal were relieved Alix had not used the word governess. "Companion to his daughters."

"Sir Edward Gwithiam. Whew! You *have* come up in the world."

"Vikram!" Her voice was sharp, but he was unrepentant. "I myself have come down," he said, "as I well know, but am I not reputable enough to be introduced?"

"You're not reputable at all," but Alix was only half severe. "Girls, this is Captain Vikram Singh of the President's Bodyguard. Una and Halcyon Gwithiam."

"How do you do," but it was impossible for Una to be prim; set off by the grey's sidling and fidgetting, Mouse had begun to curvet too. Snowball followed, then bucked, almost unseating Hal, and the grey reared. "I had better take myself off," said Captain Singh, "and knock some of the devil out of this animal. Then, if I may, I'll come back and ride with you."

"*Arre! Shaitan!*" Alix shouted at Snowball. Una was to learn that Alix often lapsed into Hindi expletives when she was annoyed; now she caught Snowball's rein and brought him up beside Maxim. "Stop pulling, Hal; and Una, you should use your whip when Mouse fidgets like that."

"Thank goodness I didn't come off," said Hal. "Imagine if I had been bucked off in front of Captain Singh!"

"You don't have to bother about Vikram," said Alix, "and girls, please don't encourage him." Alix was unable to keep emotion out of her voice so that it sounded like a plea more than advice and, Why? thought Una. Why?

"He says he has come down in the world. What did he mean?" asked Hal.

"His father is Pratap Singh, His Highness Pratap Rajendranath Singh, Maharaja of Paralampur."

"I thought there were no Highnesses now, no Maharajas," said Una.

"No. Poor Paralampur. I wonder what he will do. They say he has been stripped of his purse as well. . . . Here is Vikram back," said Alix. "That grey isn't all that steady; Hal, you had better get off and hold Maxim for me. I will take Snowball round for a few minutes."

The Captain came and stood with them while, Una still on Mouse and Hal holding Maxim watched Alix schooling the pony, giving him a sharp cut with her whip when he tried his rebellious bucking. Captain Singh did not speak to the girls, only gave them an absent-minded smile, but they both stole glances at him. "I suppose he would have inherited?" Una asked Alix afterwards.

"Yes, he was the Raj Kumar." The fact that the young prince was stripped of his title, his palaces, land, and money, made him more romantic in their eyes—"Though it's quite right," said socialist Una. Vikram, too, seemed remarkably cheerful. He was lithe and slim as a girl, but obviously strong from the way he managed his horse; his skin was as ivory as Alix's and he wore a small, fine, almost pencilled moustache—"A dear little moustache," Hal whispered to Una. "Why does he wear a topee?" Una was to ask. "I thought no one had them now."

"Indian cavalry officers do, and the players wear them for polo."

"Did you notice his jodhpurs?" Hal sighed. Great Aunt

Frederica had been mean about theirs. "Surely in the land of jodhpurs," she had said, "if you need them, they can be made for you there?"

"They should be made for us here, in London," but they had to accept the ready-made ones Great Aunt Freddie grudgingly conceded. The Captain's seemed moulded to his slim legs, even his army shirt was graceful and his topee was wound with silk in the Bodyguard's crimson colours. But he isn't as good-looking as our young gardener, thought Una.

The day before, just before Edward left, she had asked again about the young man in the hut. "Who is it who lives down there at the end of the garden behind those flowers?"

"Probably one of the malis, the gardeners," said Alix.

"He's the second mali," Edward had said. "I asked Chinaberry."

"Why does he live alone, not in the servants' quarters?" asked Una.

"He's a Brahmin," said Edward. "They don't mingle."

"I thought Brahmins were priests, holy people."

"They are, but nowadays they have to be other things as well, politicians, lawyers, bankers, teachers."

"And gardeners."

"And gardeners, but they still keep their distance. Ganesh, our head gardener, has his own house in the bazaar. He has done well from the Americans and from the United Nations, has Ganesh. One day I will take you and Hal to visit his wife, if she will accept us."

"Why shouldn't she?"

"We are untouchables, you know."

"Edward! What nonsense you tell the child."

"It isn't nonsense. I want them to understand, Alix, get close to these people," but Edward had not known the second mali's name.

When Alix came back to the group under the trees, Snowball was quiet. "He just wants to see if you are firm with him," she told Hal.

"Let her keep between you and me," said Captain Singh as Alix and Hal remounted.

"You're not coming with us?"

"For a little," and, for the first time, he addressed Una. "If you have no objection, Miss Gwithiam."

"I?" Una was startled. "Oh no—I mean, of course not."

"Don't let Snowball dawdle or try any tricks." Alix was obviously not best pleased and, for once, spoke sharply to Hal. "Use your whip and your legs." Una rode apart—like a Brahmin, she thought, and smiled—but when they had ridden twice round, trotted, tried a slow canter, Alix asked, "Girls, would you mind if I let Maxim out? He needs a good gallop."

Sitting their horses, Vikram, Una, and Hal watched the flying orange-shirted figure scarcely moving in the saddle as the big horse thundered over the ground. "I had forgotten," said Vikram, "how stunning she is." His watching eyes were thoughtful—and determined? Una thought. "What a thousand shames," he went on, "she should have had to spend all those years with that fat slob Sethji."

"Seth . . . ?" Una had not caught the name.

"Sethji. Chaman Lal Sethji. Sethji means 'rich man,' and he is certainly that, but Miss Lamont did not get any riding with him, whatever else they say she did!" He laughed and, He doesn't realize how young we are, thought Una.

"Why is he a slob?" asked Hal. "What did he do to Alix?"

"Hal, you're not to ask questions." Una repressed her, then asked one herself. "Did you know Miss Lamont well?" she asked.

"In Calcutta and Delhi, everyone knows everyone." He seemed to have become aware he was talking to two young girls and, He is trying to pass it off, thought Una. "You mean 'everyone who is anyone' in your world," she said and, for the first time, Captain Singh looked at her; perhaps he found her eyes shrewd because, with obviously more truth, he said, "Let us say I know *of* Miss Lamont."

Alix came trotting back to them, her cheeks glowing

and, "If anyone ought to have a horse, it's she," said Una.

"Indeed yes. You should ask your father." Vikram slipped off the grey and went forward to help Alix dismount, but Una saw how skilfully she eluded his hand and, as if she had felt a warning, Una said, "Hal, you had better not ask Edward about the man Captain Singh called the fat slob."

Hal, though, had hardly taken in the name Chaman Lal Sethji. As the Captain and Alix/Miss Lamont came up leading their horses she asked, "Do you play polo, Captain Singh?"

"Couldn't you call me Vikram?"

Hal dropped her lashes under his look—he has realized how pretty she is, thought Una—but it was no more than a fleeting glance; his eyes went straight back to Alix/Miss Lamont. As for Hal, it was clear she had never seen anyone in the least like this young prince before and, "Do you . . . Vikram?" she murmured.

"As a matter of fact I am playing this afternoon. Miss Lamont, why don't you bring Miss Gwithiam and her sister?"

"Una and Hal," murmured Hal.

"No thank you, Vikram." Alix was crisp. "Come girls, we must go home now. Good morning, Captain Singh." But Vikram did not go.

"Miss Una, I appeal to you."

"Una is not interested in polo," said Alix.

"But I am." A spice of devilment had seized Una. "I watched polo in Teheran and would love to see it again. Thank you, Vikram."

On the way home Alix was ominously silent until: "You did that," she said to Una, "because I asked you not to."

"Not at all," said Una with a coolness she had not known she possessed. "I did it because we wanted to go. We're not babies, Miss Lamont. If you don't want us to do things you must give us a reason."

That seemed to drive Alix into a corner. "I can't give you a reason."

"Then you can't expect us to agree, can you?"

" 'Agree' is hardly the word to use between a governess and children."

Una shrugged.

"Oh, don't let's spoil things," begged Hal, but already a kind of patball had begun between Una and Alix/Miss Lamont. No, patball is too direct, thought Una; it was more like two people playing at shuttlecock—and the feathers of a shuttlecock are sharp-edged.

Alix, it seemed, kept house for Edward and, after breakfast, "I must see Christopher," she said. "Christopher and Dino and Ran Chand, give out stores, ask about flowers. Come and watch if you like. Dino, Ram, and Christopher have been butler, bearer, and cook at Shiraz Road for years," Alix told Una and Hal. "They know far more about this house than I do," and she deferred to them, merely asking what they wanted from the store cupboards she unlocked.

"Do you keep store cupboards *locked?*" Una was shocked.

"Always in India," said Alix. "Your servants would not respect you else. This big one holds the U.N.'s stores for official entertaining. Sometimes there are business luncheons or dinners, mostly stag ones, then we shall have to keep out of the way. This small cupboard is private for Edward, his drinks and cigars and so on." Alix praised the vegetables, eggs, butter, meat, and fish Christopher had bought fresh that morning; they were presented, invitingly arranged in a basket, for her to inspect. She praised last night's dinner too, complimented Dino on the table, smelled Ganesh's roses. Why then, Una wondered, was there such stoniness in Dino's, Ram's, and Ganesh's faces, such a surly look on Christopher's?

Alix ignored it. "Servants don't matter," she said. Their mouths may be shut in front of us, was Una's silent rejoinder, but they have eyes to see, ears to hear, and minds of their own—as have I, thought Una.

All the same, Alix's presence in the house made it

different from any she and Hal had known before. You sing about the house, thought Una, sing quite softly, I know, but the song has a lilt. You are a big woman but your step is quick and light, your hands deft and capable, and your hair is so bright that, in the sun, it seems to be haloed. No wonder Edward likes to have you here—but Una snatched that thought back. Miss Lamont is here for us, not Edward—but was she?

She watched Alix go through his ties, picking some out to be dry-cleaned, heard her scolding the washerman for a broken button on one of his shirts, then she sewed on another. "We didn't think of touching his clothes," said Hal in wonder.

"Well, it hardly came into your province, did it?" asked Alix. Does it into yours? Una wanted to retort but, instead, "Edward likes to look after himself," she said.

Alix calmly went on sewing. Then, "Don't you think someone as burdened as Edward needs these little things done for him?" she asked. She looked up and must have caught the displeasure—or was it jealousy?—in Una's eyes because, "Remember he doesn't know I do this."

But he knows he is better looked after, more comfortable than he has ever been in his life. Una did not say it aloud but it was the unpalatable truth.

They were to explore the Old City and, "Which shall it be?" Alix asked them. "The Red Fort or the shops in the Chandni Chowk?"

"The Chandni Chowk," said Hal, while Una said, "The Red Fort."

"Una is the eldest," Alix decided. "She shall have first choice," and, She's placating me, thought Una. She doesn't find me so easy, thought Una with pride. "Now you are here," said Alix with the same placation, "we must read some Indian history."

"Mrs. Carrington gave me a book on Indian history as a parting present," said Una. She did not mean it snubbingly, but it sounded like a snub. "Then I am probably superfluous," said Alix.

"Alas, no water runs in the channels now," said the student guide in the Red Fort. "The fountains do not play."

"The Moghul emperors all made water gardens," said Una. "Babur, the first emperor, even made the melon beds along the Jumna River." She was standing with Alix, Hal, and the Paralampurs on one of the lawns of the Red Fort, looking at the shapes of fountains, domes, and pillars against the blue Indian sky.

"Here the Peacock Throne was kept . . . this roof used to be silver . . . look at this inlay in the marble." Una would have loved to linger, listening to the guide. One pavilion ceiling had inlays of morning-glory flowers in lapis lazuli: a panel had carnations in cornelian. Everywhere were carvings; the soft sandstone had even been cut into delicate trellis screens. She could almost smell the sandalwood, the attar of roses, and the sweat of bowmen, the stronger smell of horses, elephants, camels. Birds flew in and out of the buildings; some were ordinary birds but there were parakeets, as there were in the Shiraz Road garden, darting in their brilliance—and there ought to be peacocks, thought Una. Doves were cooing "as they must have done three centuries ago." Una scarcely knew she had spoken aloud, but "Miss Una doesn't need a guide," teased Vikram.

"I shall send you passes," he had said of the invitation to polo. "My sister, Sushila, will be there—she will like to meet you both. I will call her this morning."

"He has Americanisms as well as English," said Una when he had gone.

"I don't suppose he knows which is which," said Alix. "How could he? He hasn't been out of India." She said it as if this gave her a secret satisfaction.

"Not to school?" asked Una. "I thought the young rajas went to Eton or Harrow."

"Vikram went to Ajmer, the College of Princes."

"College of Princes!" Hal's eyes were starry but, remembering Edward and his passion for accuracy, Alix had to say, "They call it the Mayo College now."

"The Mayo College! Poor little prince!" said Una, but

Vikram did not look at all poor, either at polo—"He had at least four ponies," Hal was to tell Edward—nor when, in spite of Alix's frown, he invited himself and Sushila back to Shiraz Road for tea. "I didn't think you would be so easily impressed," Alix reproached Una.

Sushila had come to them at the polo match and sat with them on the tiered benches. She was, Alix said, like her father, the Maharaja of Paralampur, thickset and heavy, with heavy spectacles. "I should have been the boy, Vik the girl," she said. "He is so very pretty," but Una found the little princess touching, far more likable than her brother. They both spoke English without a trace of accent; true Indian, though, were Sushila's nails with their brownish underskin, and she wore a small ruby stud in one nostril. Una forbore to mention it but Hal asked at once, "Did it hurt to put that ring in your nose?"

"I was three months old," said Sushila, "so I don't remember it," and Vikram taunted, "You haven't even had your ears pierced, you backward girls!"

"English girls of the upper classes do not have their ears pierced or wear earrings." Alix was lofty but, "Nonsense," said Una at once. "We shall have ours done tomorrow. Alix, will you take us to a jeweller's?"

"I will take you both," said Vikram, and soon, "The Paralampurs seem to be with us every day," Alix complained.

"We like them," said Hal.

"Especially Vikram?" suggested Una. "Of course." All the same Una wished she could have come to the Red Fort with Edward, or alone.

"This is the emperor's winter bath which took for each bath eight hundred pounds of wood to heat. The queen's bath—see, the floor is inlaid with tiny fountains that jetted rose water."

"What are those niches for?"

"Soap, I expect," said Alix.

"Indeed, no, madam. Flowers were put there by day, mica lamps by night, so that the water flowed over colour. . . ."

To Alix, Vikram, Sushila, and philistine Hal, the Fort, for all its fame, was a place of old, dilapidated buildings, and it was true the water channels and fountains were dry, the marble cracked, gold leaf peeling, paths littered with sweet papers and orange peel, pavilion floors stained red with betel chewers' spittle. "And those emperors and queens and people are all dead," said Hal, and yawned.

"I like them better dead, particularly the lovers," but Una did not say it aloud; to her, if they were dead, their stories were safe: The Emperor Jahangir and his queen, Nur Jahan—Light of the World: Shah Jahan and his steadfast love for Mumtaz Mahal—one doesn't think of an emperor being in love, thought Una, especially with other queens and hundreds of concubines in his harem—and Una thought of the queens in her chess set, the carved veils and roses in their hands; they too seemed steadfast.

"Una's in one of her trances," teased Hal.

"She is *ent*ranced." The guide was delighted with his own cleverness, but Vikram laughed, Sushila and Hal giggled, and when, next day, Alix, hoping to please Una, said, "I thought we should all drive out with Chinaberry and see the Qutb Minar," "I don't want to come," said Una.

"But Una, it's fascinating."

"Have you seen it?"

"N-no, but it's an architectural marvel, a tower of victory and there's an iron pillar there; they say it might have been made for King Chandragupta in the fourth century." Evidently Alix had been reading the guidebooks.

"No thank you," said Una. "You go with Hal. She'll bear it if Vikram's there. I will stay here in the garden."

A pause, then: "I'm sorry, Una, but you will have to come."

"Why?"

"I can't leave you here alone."

"Alone? There are at least a dozen servants here."

"That's partly why."

"For heaven's sake!" said Una.

"This is India. Other reasons apart, you are not accus-

tomed to it; you don't even speak Hindustani; besides, I
promised Edward," and, "Una, Una," pleaded Alix, "don't
be cross with me. I only do what I am told. You can argue
it out with Edward when he gets back. Meanwhile . . ."

"Meanwhile?"

"Don't spoil Hal's time, our time. If you don't want to
go to the Qutb Minar, let's all go to the zoo and see the
white tigers."

"*White* tigers?" Hal, who had come in, caught the word.

"Yes, these are animals you won't see anywhere else."

"You will," said Una. "They have them in the Bristol
Zoo in England," but as she said it she felt ashamed. It
was hard, she acknowledged, that someone as beautiful
and accommodating as Alix should have to pander to an
ungracious schoolgirl.

"You're so horrid," said Hal, "you are lucky *anyone*
should care about you," and Una agreed.

Una had not expected flowers in a zoo but, inside the
gate was a great bank of verbena at least a hundred yards
long; the zoo was set below Delhi's Purana Kila, the older
fort, and the gentle tints of its ancient stones set off the
flowers, bougainvillaea and thousands of roses. In the long
pools were swans, cranes, and the coral-legged flamingoes,
their feathers tinged with pink. "This is the most beautiful
zoo I have ever seen," Una had to say.

The tigers were ivory rather than white, ivory to cream;
the stripes were sable, the ruffs white, white paws, the eyes
jade green, cold and cruel. The original pair were Raja and
Rani and there were some two-year-olds, a yearling and
cubs, but the cages were pitifully cramped, the bambooed
enclosures too small; Hal and Sushila laughed at the cubs'
antics; Una was wrenched with pity.

"But you like them?" Alix was anxious.

"They are fabulous—like India; fabulosity itself!"

"There isn't such a word," Lady Srinevesan was to say.
"But, Lady Srinevesan, there is," said Una. "I looked it up
in the dictionary."

"You and your dictionaries!" was Edward's comment

when he heard. "Here is a girl," he told an American delegate staying with them at Shiraz Road, "who would like
the whole Oxford Dictionary, all thirteen volumes of it,
for her birthday."

"Yes, I would," said Una.

Lady Srinevesan had telephoned. "I want to give a little
luncheon for Sir Edward's girls."

"I won't go," said Una.

"But you must." Alix was shocked. "She's a minister's
wife."

"I don't care. I don't like her."

"You don't know her," but Una had seen Lady Srinevesan—"and heard her,"—at the Gymkhana Club.

Vikram's mother, Mrs. Singh or Mrs. Paralampur—"Or
is she still called Maharani?"—had asked Alix to bring
Una and Hal there to play tennis with Sushila and some
friends.

"I thought clubs in India were British Raj," said Una.

"Then Indians are more Raj than the British," said Alix.
"The Gymkhana is a great meeting-place on Sunday mornings." They had been asked for Sunday morning. "People
go there to have coffee or drinks, play tennis, or listen to
the band. In summer they swim and there is a stall where
one can buy fresh vegetables and flowers."

"Can you?"

"I am not a member," said Alix with edge in her voice
and, "Edward isn't a Club person either," Una had said
quickly.

Their group among the many on the lawn, sitting at
tables under sun umbrellas, had attracted attention. "Those
must be the Gwithiam girls—there, with the Paralampurs.
You know, Sir Edward Gwithiam. I had heard he was
bringing them out." Several women smiled graciously but
presently Una had become aware that two, sitting at a
table close by, were not smiling; one, middle-aged—an
American, Una guessed—solid in her linen dress, had a
skin unbecomingly freckled, but her eyes were brown—
and honest, thought Una instinctively. She was looking at

them with an even more particular interest than the other and, I have seen her before somewhere, thought Una, but where—and when? The other was a fine small Indian, alert, perhaps a little mischievous and wearing a superb silver-grey sari that matched the grey of her hair. They were looking, not at Una, but at Alix. Sushila, Hal, and the other girls were chattering; perhaps Una had seemed left out because, "Come," the kind old Maharaja had said to her, "Let me show you our Club." He heaved himself out of his chair; Una followed, but at every table, it seemed, the Maharaja had to pause, and she found herself standing behind the two ladies; they were talking in low voices, but as she strained her ears, she could hear.

"That younger girl, how old is she?" the silvery Indian lady had said. There had been a tinge of disapproval as she looked at Hal.

"Let me think," said the other. Yes, her voice was American. "Louise was some time ago but the child can't be more than twelve."

"Only twelve! Well, some little girls are coquettes at six. I don't envy the governess. I should have thought Edward would have brought a governess out from England."

Edward! Then she must be a friend, thought Una.

"I am surprised he did not consult me. Who is this woman?"

"She calls herself Miss Lamont. She was with Chaman Lal Sethji—you know, the Marwari millionaire."

"That shouldn't condemn her," but the American's voice was troubled.

"No, that shouldn't." The inflection on the 'that' had given a meaning that was unmistakable.

"She looks quiet enough to me."

Throughout the morning Alix had been self-effacing; she was dressed in dark blue which did not become her— "You *are* playing your cards carefully," Vikram had bantered her when he joined them—but, "Quiet?" the silvery lady had laughed. "With those eyes, and that fairy-tale hair? Watch young Paralampur."

"Vik, won't you come and play with us?" Hal had beseeched, standing ready with her racket. "Won't you play?" coaxed Hal, but, "I'm too lazy," Vikram had said. "Go and play with Shila and Bunny and Jo"—to Una's and Hal's puzzlement, these Indian girls had English nicknames—"I will stay here and plague Miss Lamont in your place." It isn't Alix's fault that Vikram is chasing her, thought Una. And Edward *chose* her. What right have they to speak of her like that?

Back at the table, "Who are those ladies?" she had asked.

Alix looked across the terrace. "They are friends of your father's. One is Mrs. Porter, from the American Embassy. The other is Lady Srinevesan."

"Are they nice?"

"Two old busybodies," said Alix.

They did not look busybodies, even in her indignation Una had seen that.

THREE

Edward's three or four days in Japan had stretched to a fortnight. "Didn't you miss me?" he was to ask them. "We hadn't time," would have been the truthful answer or, for Una, rather, "I was out of time." She felt she might have been in India for an aeon. "Well, the Hindi words for 'yesterday' and 'tomorrow' are the same," Alix had told her, "and the 'day before yesterday' and the 'day after tomorrow.'" Time seemed to have disappeared.

The girls had had their ears pierced in a jeweller's where, for an hour or more, they watched mothers, grandmothers, aunts, cousins choosing jewellery for a young bride. "March is the month for weddings," Alix told them. "They will spend a crore of rupees."

"What is a crore?" asked Hal.

"Ten million rupees."

"Ten million!" Una and Hal's small gold earrings were too everyday to think of by comparison but, "I don't know what Edward will say." Alix was uneasy.

"It's too late to say anything." Hal tilted her head to see

their effect in the looking-glass. "Besides, I don't think
he'll care when he sees how much we are enjoying ourselves."

"Is Una?" Alix asked slyly. Una did not answer but she
had to admit there were compensations in being in Delhi;
the sun and the flowers: the carefree feeling of light
clothes: being driven in the big Cadillac by Chinaberry—
"In Teheran we went in buses": to have servants attending
to the least lift of her finger: Mouse and the spacious
house: her Moghul chess set: prince and princess friends.
She and Hal helped Alix desultorily in the house; there
was no mention of lessons. They read what they chose;
Hal played the piano or her new mandolin and sang with
Alix. They went sightseeing—no protest from Una now—
visited the Paralampurs, sometimes watched polo at Vikram's invitation.

Every evening, too, they went to the Bodyguard lines
where the horses were stabled, "to see all is well," said
Alix, watching each syce's grooming with critical eyes,
approving food and giving the horses tidbits of apple or
sugar. Vikram sometimes appeared there too. "Had to
look at a nag," he would say—he used oddly dated words
—or, "See a pony for a friend."

"Don't encourage Vikram," Alix asked it again.

"It's just Vikram I want to encourage," said Hal.

Una had found out the young gardener's name, asking
not directly but craftily. "What is the name of the
sweeper?" she had asked Dino.

"Him Mitchu."

"And the cook's mate?"

"Him Paul."

"And the man who washes the dishes?"

"The *masalchi?* Him from Kashmir; he called Subhan."

"And the second mali?"

"Him Ravi."

"Ravi." She tried it on her tongue and liked it. She
asked Sushila what it meant. "Ravi means the sun," said
Sushila. Sun. That suited his golden colour.

Beyond the garden pavilion and set in the wall of the lower garden of Shiraz Road, there was an old summer house, almost buried in a tangle of Japanese honeysuckle and climbing roses that curtained it from the house and upper garden. Una had found it and adopted it. She liked to sit there hidden, reading at the rough wooden sun-dried table and, often, she looked into the humble lower garden with its seed house, flower patches, bamboo turrets of sweet peas, its rows of lettuce and tomato plants. There was the colony of seeding chrysanthemum Ganesh was carefully nursing in pots, and a medley of hoses, sprinklers, bundles of bamboos; it was chiefly in the lower garden that Ravi worked.

You wear a red rag bound round your head to keep the sweat out of your eyes. Una had become crafty too at watching him. If you think no one sees you, you will take off your shirt; your loincloth is always tightly wrapped round your thighs. Ravi wore, as Edward had said, the Brahmin sacred threefold thread. Now and again, thought Una, Ganesh sends you to the house to do the house flowers. I can guess you don't like that; you stay proud and silent as you squat on your heels surrounded by bowls and vases—and you don't arrange the flowers at all well. I can guess you despise us, thought Una.

Every evening at dusk you come out of your hut and set a light under your courtyard bush. Why, wondered Una, do you do that?

Hem had asked the same question. "You used to call these superstitions. You cried out against family customs, yet here in Shiraz Road, you light your deeva for this silly little tulsi tree that you call sacred."

"Old habit," said Ravi, yet with Ravi it was more than habit; it was an affinity that went far beyond ritual, that was in his poetry and gave it depth and life. "I do not know, consciously, why I light my deeva, make my early morning prayer and ablutions, but if I did not? . . ." Even he, a poet, could not put it into words but something would be missing, "Something cosmic, other world, bigger world," said Ravi.

"If you don't know why you do it, is it sense?" asked Hem.

"It is not sense. Perhaps it is percipience, beyond sense. You don't believe it."

"No," said Hem but added, "I wish I did."

When Una saw the tiny light she knew it meant Ravi had gone into his hut and she slipped down among the shadows in the garden to look through the screen of flowers, to watch him at his desk.

"Of course you must go," said Alix of Lady Srinevesan's party. "Her husband, Sir Mahadeva is a *minister*."

To Una there was something touching in the way Alix added, "She can see you meet the right people," and, when she left them at the Srinevesan house, "I wish you were coming too," said Una.

"And how is it, Ally, with that so disagreeable girl?" Alix had driven straight to the Paradise Hotel. "Come to see Mummy?" Mr. Lobo, as usual on the landing, had asked his usual question, his eyes happy. "That's nice." Alix did not answer but swept on to her mother's room.

"My God, Ally, I thought I was never to see you again."

"So did I."

"Did you bring any . . .?"

"Sssh Mumma!" and Alix said in Hindi, "Terala, go down to the cookshop; I could do with some real food, and I'm thirsty. Have you any coconut milk?" She took notes out of her purse and gave them to Terala.

"But have you brought any, m'n? Have you?" Mrs. Lamont was a slavering child.

"Of course, but tell Terala to hurry. I haven't too much time; it takes so long to get here with such traffic, but it's good to have even two hours off." Alix kicked off her shoes and sat down with a contented sigh. "My God! I wasn't born to be a nursemaid," but when the booty Alix had brought had been made over and Terala had brought the hot savoury food, there was the usual controversy.

"Mummy, where is your cutlery?" asked Alix.

"Cutlery? Cutlery?" Mrs. Lamont looked vaguely round. "You mean knives and forks and spoons? I don't know . . . somewhere . . . but you can eat with your fingers, Ally. It's so much more easy."

"Where are your standards?" Alix flashed. "Oh Mumma! How often and often have I *told* you."

"I have my standards." Mrs. Lamont also had dignity, but Alix was not listening.

"Mumma! Why won't you go to that nice home I found for you in Almora? It is run by the Sisters. Think," said Alix coaxing, "it is called the House of Rest."

"I don't like rest," said Mrs. Lamont.

"But you do. My God, don't you sit here all day long? You could have your own things, your own room and you know how you love the nuns."

"But not to live with," Mrs. Lamont would have said. She had fathomed weeks ago that Alix would rather she were not in Delhi at this time—fathomed? It was transparent, but Mrs. Lamont kept that unpleasant thought out of her mind and "Ally needs her Mumma," she would have said. "A girl must want to see her mother, surely, and how, shut away in Almora, could she, Mrs. Lamont, have kept tab—an avid tab—on Alix's doings so as to regale them, splendidly enhanced, to the other inmates of the Paradise Hotel? Mrs. Lamont liked the ragamuffin young Westerners from overseas who wandered in and out and were amused by Mrs. Lamont as she was amused by them. She gossiped with the Indian women, gave sweets and nuts to the children, and was paid state visits by Mr. Lobo. She liked the hotel's comings and goings, its noise and that of the bazaar; above all, she liked the smells, human, animal, and of food. Food!

"See, Girlie," she said. "Terala has brought enough for two—your favourite korma curry, meat pulao, chapattis, and green mango pickle. So much better you will feel when you have eaten. We can eat Indian fashion or Western. Why? Because we belong to both. I think that's nice." 'Nice' was a word she shared with Mr. Lobo but "Nice!" Alix said it with disdain yet, already, with long accustomed skill, she was mixing the food with her fingers, scooping a little up, then, with a flick of her wrist, bringing it to her mouth. When she had licked the last crumb from her fingers she could not help belching contentedly.

"But you haven't told me," said Mrs. Lamont. "How are you and she getting along?"

Alix surveyed her still sticky fingers and smiled. "I think I can say that soon she will be eating out of my hand."

"You ought to have come, Alix," said tactless Hal. "There was a wonderful buffet—chicken tandoori and curries and puries, and you should have seen some of the saris." "But if we had worn what you wanted us to wear we should have been overdressed," Una could have told her. Alix could not get used to the faded jeans and old jerseys Una and Hal liked or to what Edward called Hal's 'raggle-taggle dress,' a long one of limp cotton that she cherished.

"Your daughters, *your* daughters, should surely have English clothes?" Alix had said to Edward—she had nearly said 'shop clothes.' Until she went to Paris, Alix had never had a shop-bought dress and few enough even then—but, *They are coming to a poor and starving country,* Edward had written to Great Aunt Freddie. *I am here to organize, among other things, relief. Their clothes must be inexpensive,* but Alix had been allowed to send a list, and for the Srinevesan party her idea of what was due to a Gwithiam would have been touching if it had not been so inflated. "Those dresses are meant for the evening," Una had said. "It will be a big and fashionable luncheon party," Alix protested, but Una was thankful she had not listened as she saw Lady Srinevesan take in with approval their plain linens. Una had had a fight too with Hal over beads and bangles; as it was, the gold earrings made Hal look oddly adult; in imitation of Alix she used polish on her nails, and scent. "Just let Edward smell you, that's all," threatened Una. She knew at this luncheon that they would be on parade. "Well, I don't mind," said Hal.

"Well, I do."

Lady Srinevesan had certainly asked questions, all of them acute. "It was a sudden decision of your father's to bring you out?"

"I think it was a sudden appointment": "Not all that sudden." As the wife of a minister, Lady Srinevesan knew all about appointments.

"You have a home in England?"

"Yes, I suppose the house is Edward's," said Una, "but our Great Aunt Frederica lives in it. It is at Gwithiam, in Cornwall."

"Of course. You are Gwithiams of Gwithiam. I was forgetting." As skilfully as if she were picking a winkle out of its shell, Lady Srinevesan was winkling Una.

"That sounds grand but it isn't," Una said hastily. "Gwithiam is only a village—it's spoilt now with caravans and chalets—and our house isn't really big. Edward—we—sometimes spend our holidays there, particularly since we went to Cerne."

"But did you not mind leaving your school?"

"Heavens no!" Hal's answer was so fervent that everybody laughed.

"You like this new governess?"

"Yes, thank you." That was guarded.

"I understand she was at the Paris Conservatoire for a short while." There was an unkind emphasis on 'short.' "But you are not musical?"

"No," and Una was moved to say, "Alix was at the Sorbonne as well."

"That ought to be all right." Once again the emphasis that made a question of the 'ought.' Una felt herself prickle, but a young woman, as plump as she was delectable and whom everyone called Bulbul, came to Una's help. "The Sorbonne! My goodness! You girls nowadays are far too clever!"

"I'm not," said Una quickly.

"No?" Lady Srinevesan's eyebrows lifted. "Yet Edward told me you were hoping for Oxford."

"Not now," and that particular unhappiness came back. Lady Srinevesan must have sensed it because she said gently, "Your father tells me you share my love of poetry, Una. Will you come to some of my poetry evenings?"

"Amina Srinevesan runs quite a salon," Bulbul told Una, "but she doesn't ask dunces like me. She must be interested in you—and I am too. My name is Bulbul, Bulbul Misra. My husband is called Som. When you are tired of the Paralampurs, come and see us."

Tired of the Paralampurs! Then does everyone, thought Una, know what we do?

The Paralampurs were largely her own fault; she could have curbed Hal but her own new wilfulness made Una insist on accepting every invitation that the Maharani, pushed by Vikram, Una was sure, sent or telephoned.

It was not only the unspoken desire to flout Alix; both she and Hal were fascinated by Paralampur House; it was huge, as seemingly Western as Shiraz Road, but women's courts led off the public rooms and there were myriad other shut-away rooms, empty of everything but carpets and pillows. The whole house was sinking into decay but Una found something touching in the ugly Victorian furniture and in the remains of old extravaganzas—there was a dining-room with furniture made entirely of crystal, the chair backs strung with crystal beads like a chandelier, but broken, dim, and dusty; on one landing were life-size wax figures of dancing girls playing instruments, "like in Madame Tussaud's," said Hal marvelling. "My grandfather was fond of those," Sushila told them. "They don't work now." There was an enormous empty aviary, lines of stables, empty too except for Vikram's child pony which Sushila rode. "Vik rides the army horses," Sushila explained.

An elephant stable was bare: "Oh, I wish there had been an elephant," said Hal, but the howdah lay tilted against a wall, its gilt tarnished, the curtains rotting. Carriages were rotting too, the leather of a victoria's hood was cracked, a brougham had lost its wheels. "I used to play in them with the servants' children," said Sushila. "Mama won't let me now."

When we play tennis, Hal wrote in her diary of Paralampur House, *there are boys to pick up the balls; they
wear blue shorts and shirts with a crest on the pocket; the
servants have crests on their turbans too.*

"Well, most of their families have been with us for generations," said Sushila. Their uniforms were frayed and
not over-clean.

The Maharani often lamented, "You see what we have
come to. . . . Who could have dreamed . . ." but Una had
a growing affection for silent and courteous Paralampur
himself. He was, she thought, like the zoo's great white
tigers; there was the same heavy nobility, the wide forehead, the look of bewilderment as if, like the tiger, he did
not know quite what had overtaken him; but Mr. Paralampur, as Una felt she ought to call him—though Maharaja
suited him much better—was, she thought, the opposite of
the tiger; he had been, as it were, in a zoo, and was now
forced into the jungle of the world.

Mrs. Porter, the American lady of the Gymkhana Club,
was at the luncheon and when, after the buffet, the guests
strolled out into the garden, Una found herself alone with
her. "I wanted a quiet word with you," said Mrs. Porter.
"You have grown so like your mother—my dear Kate."

"Most people think I am like my father, but did you
know my mother?"

Mrs. Porter nodded. "Kate and I were at school together. I knew you as a mere baby." Her eyes seemed
troubled as they dwelt on Una. "My dear, are you happy
here in Delhi?"

"I am—in waves." Una could not explain more than
that but Mrs. Porter put a hand on Una's shoulder. "If
there should be anything too difficult, Una, please come
to me."

Why should there be anything too difficult? Yet, once
again, Una was struck by the honesty of ugly Mrs. Porter's
eyes. "Your mother gave me her confidence," said Mrs.
Porter, then, with a pat, let Una go.

She was not the only one who asked Una about Delhi and it was then that she brought out the word 'fabulosity.' "There is such a word, and I do think India is fabulous."

"My dear child!" said Lady Srinevesan; again those expressive eyebrows lifted. "India may have been fabulous once; it certainly isn't now. For one thing we haven't the money. Oh yes, a few of the rajas and rogues like Chaman Lal Sethji have it salted away in gold somewhere, but for most of us it is taken away in taxes. If I were not a minister's wife, I should count myself lucky to be able to have a house bearer and share a sweeper as Bulbul has to—she does all her own cooking," and Una thought unhappily of the galaxy of servants at Shiraz Road.

"My husband, of course, has official cars which I can use," Lady Srinevesan went on, "but when he retires we shan't be able to afford a driver. Ostentation is frowned on now."

"It would be—out of keeping?" Una had flushed at the word 'ostentation.'

"Indeed yes." Then Lady Srinevesan added, "When your father first came out he decided to live in one of the flats over the offices. He said your big house, 40 Shiraz Road, was to become the United Nations guest house. He told my husband he liked the new simplicity. I wonder," said Lady Srinevesan, "who made him change his mind." Una was quick to hear 'who' instead of 'what.'

No one, thought Una, could know Alix who had not heard her bargaining in the bazaar. Alix had taken them to the Westernized shops. Indian crafts were gathered together there in the politeness of fixed prices, guarantees. She had taken them to the Tibetan booths where flat-faced women in wide-sleeved robes and striped aprons, plaits wound round their heads, sold curios—"Highly pseudo," said Alix. They had explored the copper shops round the Jama Masjid, Delhi's great mosque, and penetrated to the horse copers' caravanserai where Alix seemed equally at home. They went to the ivory marts where the craftsmen worked in a courtyard, each in his own niche, not needing models or sketches. "Each knows in his mind," said the shopkeeper, "what he wants to carve."

Hal was particularly fascinated by the small ivory carved balls that had other balls carved inside them, yet were all in one piece. "How do they carve the inner ones?" she marvelled. The work was exquisite, but the price was far beyond her. Alix had been surprised by the smallness of their pocket money. "Is that all Edward gives you?"

"It's usually enough," said Una at once.

"In your Latin letter you teased him for more."

"You read *that!*"

"He read it to me," which, for Una, was worse, but Alix had gone swiftly on to say, "Never mind, Hal, I know a little shop where perhaps you could get a ball with four inner balls for fifty rupees."

"Fifty rupees." The shopkeeper pretended to faint. "Miss-sahib, I tell you: because you are new customer, because little Miss-baba comes from England, I give this ball, *give* it to you, for ninety-five."

"Come girls, we'll go to the Ivory Palace."

"I give what it cost me—no profit—I take ninety."

Alix rose; the shopkeeper flung himself between her and the door. "At least, take a little lemonade, a Coca-Cola. Mohan, Mohan," he called to his ragged boy assistant. "Bring Coca-Cola. Sit down! Sit down!" he begged.

"No, we waste your time," said Alix. "The Miss-baba has no more than forty rupees."

"Forty! You said fifty!" This time the cry was so shrill it seemed to pierce the roof. "Miss-sahib, I swear by my father and mother . . ." He broke into Hindi, Alix matched it and the real battle was on: imprecations, abuse, appeal, stony indifference on Alix's part; drama on the shopkeeper's. Twice he put the ball back on the shelf. Twice Alix got up to go. "Mohan, Mohan, bring Coca-Cola."

Hal was distressed but, "Don't you see, they are enjoying it?" whispered Una.

"Indeed yes." Sushila, who had come with them, was an experienced shopper.

"The shopkeeper too?" whispered Hal.

"Of course." Sushila's eyes were sparkling behind her spectacles.

A crowd had gathered. Even Chinaberry, who had escorted them, was smiling and when, swearing and tearful, the shopkeeper reached down the ball at fifty-five rupees, if Indians ever applauded, Chinaberry would have clapped.

"Too much loss! Too much loss!" the shopkeeper moaned as he dusted the little ball. "My children will starve." He packed it in bright pink tissue paper and gave it to Hal who hardly liked to take it but, "Take. Take," he urged, "and see, this is my card." He gave Una an ivory peacock holding cocktail sticks as a tail.

"But . . . I don't want it."

"Not for buying," he said. "As souvenir," and, "Come again," said the shopkeeper. "Come tomorrow."

"You see," said Una to Hal.

Alix was breathing as hard as the shopkeeper; both their eyes were bright, both were mysteriously happy. "I had to go to another five rupees, Hal," said Alix, "but I will make that up to you, and I think you have a bargain."

"Alix, that was splendid," said Una.

"I don't know how you did it," said Hal, cherishing her ivory carved ball and, "You are a better bargainer than my old ayah," said Sushila. They did not understand why Alix's colour rose and why her voice was curt as she said, "Come along, back to the car."

Chinaberry had opened the door for them when a man came pushing through the crowd that had increased round them. He was not an Indian, but near white, thought Una; fat, unkempt, a black stubble on his jowl, a bald spot in his greasy black hair. His coat and trousers, once white, were crumpled and unbuttoned, and a fat paunch showed through a dirty mauve singlet. He was an unlovely object but Una saw his eyes, the colour of prunes, she thought, soft and alight with admiration and joy. "Miss Ally," he called. "Miss Ally."

Alix looked at him and, "Get in the car," she told the girls.

"But, Miss Ally, I am Lobo. Mr. Lobo, friend of

Mummy." He had almost reached them. "Bring your young ladies in for a glass of sherbet. Ice-cream soda I have got or Coca-Cola." The eyes were pleading. "It will give me such happiness, Miss Ally."

"Take your hand off the door." Alix got in and slammed it. "*Chelo*—go on," she said to Chinaberry.

"Miss Ally." A pitiful knocking on the window. "You know Lobo. Ice-cream soda."

"*Jaldi chelo*," and Chinaberry drove away.

"Who was he?" asked Una.

"Some drunken tramp."

"But he knew your name. He called out 'Miss Ally,'" said Una.

"That . . . that was a form of Moslem greeting. '*Mis-Ali.'*"

"Alix!" Una, unnerved, began to laugh. She laughed so much she had to wipe away tears. Hal and Sushila joined in and they were overcome with giggles. "A Moslem greeting! Oh, Alix!"

"Mumma, you will please tell Lobo he is not to speak to me again—ever—anywhere."

"*Mr.* Lobo not to speak! Ally!"

"Don't call me Ally! My God! On top of everything else, do I have to put up with that?" Alix was walking up and down, her handkerchief twisted into a ball. "It is you, Mumma, that causes all this, living in this shamble place where you have to meet such dregs."

"No one is dregs," Mrs. Lamont was calm. "I am Ally's whipping-goat," she often told people and now, "You are speaking of my friend," she said with unperturbed dignity.

"Friend! A dirty, drunken, greasy swine."

"Ally!" Now Mrs. Lamont was stern. "You are not to speak of him like that. It is yourself you demean, not him. A little drunk he may be at times . . ."

"A little!" Alix snorted.

"But he is—courtly—and courtly to you."

"He made me make a fool of myself."

"Well?" Mrs. Lamont was so accustomed to being a fool that she saw nothing derogatory in that. "Sometimes it happens, m'n? Even to you! Don't make an enemy, I advise you. They can take revenge."

"Pooh! What could Lobo do? How dared he come near us?" flared Alix again.

"Ally! Ally! Be careful. I think you are on the urge . . ."

"*Verge,* not urge, Mumma." It was almost a scream as if Alix could bear no more and, "Come here," commanded Mrs. Lamont. "Come here to Mumma."

A ramrod back was turned, the handkerchief was compressed to the size of a walnut now, and Mrs. Lamont knew tears were running down Alix's face. "Girlie, come here," and Alix, as usual, came.

"Aie, that temper!" Mrs. Lamont sighed as she rocked Alix against her breast. "One of these days you will do more than you mean, but never mind now." Then, "Ally," she whispered. "I suppose you didn't bring . . ."

"My God, Mumma! I dropped the girls at Paralampur House and haven't even been back to Shiraz Road."

"Not to mind. Not to mind," said Mrs. Lamont. "Next time . . ." She paused and looked over Alix's head to the image above the small lamp. "Ally," she said after a while, "I am thinking Mr. Lobo is right. You should bring those girls here."

"Are you mad?" Alix drew sharply away.

"No. I am right." Mrs. Lamont nodded her head. "You should tell them—of me and of us. Tell them all."

"You don't understand." Alix's voice was biting. "They laugh at me."

"Laugh? Well?" Mrs. Lamont was bewildered. "Laugh? But isn't that nice?"

"That girl," Ravi told Hem, "is spying on me."

"What nonsense talk is this? Why should she spy?"

"She is a girl—do girls not like me?"

"Hardly a daughter of Sir Gwithiam," said Hem dryly, but Una seemed drawn to walk, hidden in the darkness, down the lower garden and watch this strange young gardener/poet going about his work—and minding his own business, thought Una longingly. "Ravi is far too selfish to do anything else," Hem would have warned her but, as yet, Una had not met Hem; two or three times she had seen another young man in the hut but had always shrunk hastily away.

"I wonder who made him change his mind," Lady Srinevesan had said of Edward, and Una remembered Mrs. Porter's troubled look as she had said ". . . If anything is too difficult . . ." Una felt she was being caught in a web of insinuation she did not understand; and, 'Mis-Ali' a Moslem greeting. That had been funny, but it was a lie. Yes, Alix/Miss Lamont told lies. Why? thought Una— and Edward ought to know. The thought of Edward calmed her; he must soon be back, then I can talk to him, she thought, and pressed closer against the flower hedge to let herself be drowned in scent; but she saw Hem and vanished.

"I tell you she does," said Ravi.

"Does like you? Or does spy?"

"If she spies she must like me. I shall have to leave," said Ravi.

"That would be madness. Ravi, what could be more ideal for you than this?" and Hem went on to entreat: "Think. No one will dream of looking for you here."

"Right under their noses!" Ravi had to laugh. "But all that has blown over long ago," he said.

"Has it? I must remind you again: Injit and Prasad are still in jail" and, "*You* have not been chained." Hem said it with sudden fierceness. "You have never had the warders steal your food when you were desperate with hunger . . ." Hem choked, then became his usual controlled self. "Ravi bhai—you cannot be sure. In any case, a little girl cannot harm you. Stay here and write your poems. It is unique oppor-tun-ity," he urged in English which he did not speak nearly as well as Ravi.

"Hem, you are always so pompous."

"And you are always silly. Think what Doctor Professor Asutosh said of you when you took the English prize."

"Babbletosh Asutosh!"

"The mantle of Tagore." Though Hem, too, half mocked, he was impressed. "For an astute boy Hem Sharma is strangely simple over this young Ravi," Doctor Asutosh, Vice-Chancellor of their College had said, and, "The mantle of Tagore," breathed Hem.

"Bullshit," said Ravi yet, in this garden, the words were not offensive because they fell into their right place; bullshit was manure, welcome for flower and vegetable beds, and Ravi ceased to be annoyed. "Anyway, I should prefer Kalidasa's mantle."

"Not really?" Hem was sarcastic. "Who was Kalidasa?" Una was to ask and Ravi to answer, "Our equivalent of your Shakespeare, only better," but now he was haughty and told Hem, "I don't want anyone's mantle. I shall make my own."

"Then it will be pyjama-kurta in the brightest possible colours," said Hem and Ravi laughed and clapped him on the shoulder.

In the evenings at Shiraz Road, when they were alone, Alix and Hal played and sang while Una listened, or Alix read aloud in French. "Edward would be pleased to know we were studying something," said Alix. She read *Lettres de mon Moulin*, "A bit easy for Una, but I think right for Hal."

"Una thinks I ought to have *Les Malheurs de Sophie*," said Hal who had not forgiven Una about the bungles.

Alix read French simply without the elaborations of her singing and piano playing; she did not swell her voice, nor use her hands; probably nothing had overlaid the stern standards of the martinet Parisian nun of whom she had told Una—Alix's Mrs. Carrington, guessed Una—and the passion of the old teacher in that classroom of Alsace, the flag and the children, the patriotism came alive, even for Hal. "And now, something for Una," Alix said one evening as she closed the book. "Una must read."

"I learn more by listening to you," said Una. "Alix, read that Charles d'Orleans poem about the spring."

> *"Le temps a laissié son manteau,"*

read Alix,

> *"De vent, de froidure et de pluye,*
> *Et s'est vestu de brouderie*
> *De soleil luyant, cler et beau."*

The cadences brought into the Delhi drawing-room all the freshness of France in spring and Una sat entranced. If only we could keep to things, she thought, things, not people; those words have lived for almost six centuries, while people come and go, and if only we could be big. . . . Then, "Leave off thinking," said Una to Una. "Give yourself up. Listen," and, "Alix, read it again," she begged aloud.

> *"Rivlere, fontaine et ruisseau*
> *Portent, en livree jolie,*
> *Gouttes d'argent et d'orfaverie,*
> *Chascun s'abille de nouveau: . . ."*

and, *"Le temps a laissié son manteau,"* finished Edward's voice in the doorway.

He had not warned them, nor ordered Chinaberry to meet him but, arriving on a late flight, had quietly taken a taxi from the airport. As he waited in the doorway until the poem was finished, no scene could have been more after his own heart: Alix reading, with Hal hanging adoringly over the back of her chair, Una close beside her, all three in complete accord. Then, at his voice, "Edward!" The girls almost tumbled over their feet to meet him; the book fell forgotten. "Edward! But why didn't you let us know? Why didn't you tell us?"

"I wanted to take you by surprise."

"Or see how we were doing?" What Alix really meant was, "See how I was doing," and Una paused. Alix's eyes were bright with temper. Why?

"Edward, you must have some dinner," but this offer was brushed aside. "I had it on the flight." He and Alix were looking over Una and Hal's heads at one another and, "Come along, Hal," said Una, her voice tight. "Edward's tired. You and I had better go to bed."

Alix waited till they had gone then let it break. "You trusted me." He had not heard her voice as high. Then, as if panic had struck her, she stopped and, "You trusted me with them," said Alix. "Edward, I should like to give that trust back to you as the complete and shining thing it was."

"What *are* you talking about?" asked Edward.

"Never mind," and she was back in her accusation. "You said this was to surprise us. Wasn't it rather to catch us unawares so that you could see how things were with Hal and Una—particularly Una?"

"Alix! I never dreamed . . ."

"And what did you see? What did you see?" she taunted.

"You," said Edward.

Alix had been beautiful, her head bent over the book, light falling over his favourite mulberry, gold-shot dress; she looked more beautiful now. "Upbraiding me," said Edward and, "Hasn't it gone well?" he challenged her.

"Very well."

"Haven't they both been happy? Interested? They look new girls."

"You do trust me then?"

"The only thought I had," said Edward, "was that I couldn't kiss you there and then. When is this going to end?" he groaned.

"We must be patient."

"Patient! When you are so close . . . when I must look at you and only look. Be so near and not touch you. Oh Alix! Alix!"

"We didn't ask Edward about a horse for Alix." Hal, in her pyjamas, had come into Una's room.

"We can't ask him now." Una was terse.

"Why not?"

"He's tired." She could not be more explicit than that.

"He didn't look a bit tired. He looked excited. Come on."

"Hal, come back. Come back," but Hal had gone. Una had to go after her.

The servants were in their own quarters so that Hal had not stopped to put on her dressing-gown and slippers, nor had Una, and, in pyjamas and bare feet, they made no sound on the veranda. "I expect she's telling him all about us," Hal whispered. "Hope to goodness she's tactful about Vikram," but there was no sound of voices from the drawing-room. They looked in at the open doorway and stopped.

Hal gave a gasp. Una clapped a hand over Hal's mouth and silently as two white shadows they raced down the veranda to Una's room. "I don't think we were meant to see that," quavered Hal.

FOUR

"I didn't know they ever lived in," said Hal.

"Who?"

"Love women."

She and Una had separated the night before without another word and Una still felt she could not speak. At breakfast Hal had looked from Edward to Alix, Alix to Edward until Edward had asked, "What is the matter, Hal? Haven't you seen us before?" at which Hal went scarlet, Una white. "If they had had any sense they would have guessed we had seen them," Hal said afterwards, but Edward was too jovial to notice, while about Alix there was a quiet arrogance; it showed in the way she spoke to Dino, told Hal to sit up. "You are too old to fidget." Now Una was changing for dinner and Hal had come into her room.

"And I thought it might be Vikram," said Una bitterly.

"It probably is," said Hal, "as well. Men need women. Sushila and I were talking about it the other day; her father has dozens."

"Hal! You don't *know* . . ."

"Sushila should. Una, you're so innocent!" Hal was bouncing up and down on the bed. "All the same, I think we should keep Alix. At least she is interesting and fun. Suppose she had been some prissy old governess. Why, we might have found a Crackers!"

"Don't!" Una cried out as if Hal had said something unbearable. For her it had been a tragic day.

As she had guessed, on Edward's coming back, the schoolroom table had been made ready on the veranda. "It will be pleasant to work out here," said Alix, and it had certainly begun pleasantly. Una had been glad to feel her books, her work tools, under her hands again; then, "Where are your exercise books from Cerne?" asked Alix.

"We didn't do exercises exactly—not in the senior school. We made notes and did our studies on file papers like these."

"Oh!" Alix had looked swiftly through them and as swiftly closed them. "Very impressive, Una," she said, "but we shall have to do things my way." Una was silent and, "No two teachers are alike, are they?" Alix had asked. Una had not answered but her hands under the table had been pressed tightly together.

"Were you praying?" asked Hal.

"It wasn't much use if I was."

Today we did dictée. In her diary, Hal noted down everything Alix ordained. *We did arithmetic revision.*

"But that's Hal book," Una had said when Alix gave her the exercise.

"Una, I find you conceited."

"Well, you shouldn't be so cocky," Hal told her afterwards. "You made plenty of mistakes in your dictée."

"Because she went too fast. She wanted me to make mistakes." Una had to write them out ten times. "Like a baby," she said, writhing. As the week went on, her dismay deepened.

Alix read us Appreciation of Mozart. Una guessed it was from one of her old papers at the Conservatoire. "Well—if it was?" *We did Indian history from the book Crackers gave Una, dreadfully boring, but then we went*

*into the kitchen to Christopher who taught us to make
prawn koftas. Yum! Yum! We did English Essay and
World Literature.*

There had almost been open trouble over the world
literature. "I have a beautiful book," Alix had said. "It
opens with the first books in the world, scratchings on
rocks, or clay tablets, then on papyrus, up to the present
day."

"Does it include the Indian epics?" Una was interested.

"It may include them but it is more important to read
what the world has written. I collected this outline in magazine numbers," Alix said proudly.

"Magazine?" Crackers' "Don't be a schoolgirl snob,"
echoed in Una's ears. But . . . but . . . she thought.

"What is the matter, Una?"

"For literature one needs *books.*"

"Isn't this a book?"

"Of course it is," said Hal. "The pictures are splendid."

"Thank you, Hal."

Hal, nowadays, was no help to Una; from that moment
on the veranda, when she had seen them, for Hal, Edward
and Alix had a rosy aureole of romance. "Alix really is
lovely," she said to Una. "Have you seen her with her hair
down?"

"I expect I will," said Una wearily.

We went riding, chronicled Hal. *Snowball bucked me
off but Alix did not mind. Alix took us to polo. Alix is
teaching me Funiculi Funicula on the mandolin. Alix . . .
Alix . . .*

The lessons suited Hal exactly, especially the singing
and cooking with Christopher. "He says I'm a natural
cook."

"A natural greedy," but Una hardly had the heart to
tease and she knew Hal was not listening.

"My koftas turned out perfectly this time," she said.
"When I marry Vikram he *will* be surprised."

"Don't be silly. You won't marry Vikram or he you,"
but things Hal said had a way of coming true and Una
would not be surprised.

We did dictée. Dictée seemed to be Alix's refuge. *Today we looked at photographs of books written on papyrus and of The Book of the Dead.* . . .

"It sounds interesting," said Lady Srinevesan after one of her cross-examinations of Una.

"It is, but . . ." and Una was inspired to say, "It's all sugar biscuits and I need bones. Bones!" said Una desperately.

"Her French isn't sugar."

"Damn her French." Lady Srinevesan was caught unawares by Una's passion, but, "There is nothing," Mrs. Carrington could have told her, "more likely to be furious than a young thing frustrated." "If it wasn't for Alix's French," Una yearned to say, "Edward wouldn't have been taken in"——or would he?

We did needlework, wrote faithful Hal. "I'm not asking you to make buttonholes or do darning," said Alix.

"They would at least be useful," muttered Una. Alix had bought embroidery frames and found tapestry designs. "The chair seat is for Una to make and Hal, this little stool cover is for you."—Alix spread out the silks. "Well?"

"I like the colours," said Una, "but . . ."

"I don't want any 'buts.' " Alix was crisp. "Put the canvas in your frames and start." "I'm afraid Una objects," she told Edward that night.

"Nonsense. Girls ought to learn to sew."

"It isn't sewing," said Una. "Edward, do I have to do it?"

"You will do as Alix tells you."

"But Dads . . ." That private name was only used in moments of real appeal. "This is fancy work and there are so many serious subjects I ought to be doing in the time."

"But are you the best judge?" He came and sat beside her and gently put back her hair.

"Mrs. Carrington said it." Una was dogged.

"Mrs. Carrington has one person's point of view. There are others." He kept his patience. "Una, I do know how hard it is to change methods and schools . . ."

"You don't. You didn't have to. You went straight on.

Dads, at Cerne . . ." She knew she was estranging him again; he had seen Alix's gesture of despair when she heard the name Cerne and, "At Cerne it seems they have made you into an ambitious little prig," he said.

Tears pricked Una's eyes but she held them back. "If you can be ambitious, why can't I?" but, before she could speak, "I am not going to have this, Una. Understand?" said Edward. "Understand?"

Una was beginning to understand—only too well.

Today we did Appreciation of Bach—I don't appreciate him, wrote Hal. *Una had dictée. I found the same dictée in an old book of Alix's labelled Sainte Marie High School for Girls, Pondicherry. She has been using her old books for us.*

Alix had not been pleased. "You two ought to have been detectives," she said.

"You left them in the table drawer," Una pointed out. "Besides, they hardly apply to us."

"Why not?" Alix's colour had come up; her voice had risen too.

Una did not answer.

"Why not? Una, I want to know."

"They are old-fashioned—and limited, if you want to know." Una said it deliberately.

"Limited?"

"Yes. If we had stayed at Cerne," Una went on, "I should have sat my Additional Mathematics at the end of this year. Here, in two weeks, we haven't done one hour, not one hour of maths."

"Indeed we have," said Alix. "Haven't we been revising your arithmetic? . . ."

"Decimals, fractions, percentages. I did those when I was nine. I need *mathematics,* Alix, Pure and Applied."

"Pure and Applied . . ." Alix's voice rose higher and, below the veranda, a dark head with a red cloth tied round it looked up from the flower bed.

"Pure and Applied Mathematics and Latin as well as your French. There are examinations, Alix."

"Examinations are not the be-all and end of everything."

"No, but they may be the beginning. I want to go to University. . . ."

"Want, always want," said Alix. "What *you* want, Una, regardless of anyone else. Couldn't you think of Edward? Of Hal? Of me?"

"Don't you want things—all of you? Of course you do." Una still spoke quietly, but her eyes were dangerously green. "Anything else is cant."

"Una, you had better stop. Stop now," Hal whispered urgently.

"I can't stop," but Una found that, oddly, she was out of breath.

Ravi waited with interest. There was something in the way this foreign little creature stood up to the Mem that found a fellowship in him—he had not forgotten Alix's ferocity with the durzee over the trouble with the muslim and, "That girl is brave," he told Hem afterwards.

Then Alix spoke, not with the force she had used on the durzee, but as if Una were an animal that might bite. "Una, I—I sympathize . . . and I will see what I can do, if you will settle for a little interlude of . . . less ambition."

"Una, please," begged Hal.

Una did not know where she found the necessary hardness but, "I haven't time for interludes," she said. "Mrs. Carrington would tell you . . ."

Then Alix lost her temper. "Mrs. Carrington! Mrs. Carrington! My God, your Mrs. Carrington! It was she who taught you to behave in this arrogant way. May I remind you that Mrs. Carrington isn't here and I am," and recklessness possessed Alix. "You want to do mathematics. Very well. You shall do them and do them and do them. Give me the books you were using at Cerne."

"I was using this Elementary Mechanics."

"What," Alix's look seemed to say, "can mechanics have to do with mathematics?"

"We had reached this page," Una showed her.

Alix turned the pages, trying to control her fingers. "Take this down."

"That's too far on."

"Take it down."

"May I take it from the book?"

"No. I shall dictate it," and Alix began: *"An inclined plane is such that the line of greatest slope makes an angle of thirty with the horizontal. Given that the acceleration due to gravity is ten m/s vertically downwards . . ."*

Ravi's head was up from the border. "That girl does quite senior mathematics," he told Hem. He was caught unawares with surprise and this time Una saw him. He can't understand English, of course, but he knows there is trouble, thought Una.

"A ball is thrown . . ." went on Alix with more directions and finished, *"find the time when the ball meets the plane again and the range of the ball up the plane."* She shut the book and said, "You can work through that on your own."

"On my *own?*" Now the dismay was on Una's side. "I haven't done inclined planes before. I need to be taught."

"Take it out to the pavilion and try." It was obvious Alix wanted Una out of her sight. "Try. Then, if you can't . . ."

"If I can't, you can't show me, can you? Can you?" Una demanded. Alix did not answer, her fingers were openly trembling as she pretended to arrange her pencils. "Teach!" said Una scornfully and threw the book over the veranda rails. "You couldn't teach a junior. I don't believe you have ever taught. You have never studied projectiles or even calculus, have you?"

"N-no," said Alix.

"You may have been at the Conservatoire," said Una, "but I don't believe you ever set foot in the Sorbonne. This is a . . . governess sham!" She did not know where she found that word, but Alix paled—from fear? or fresh anger?

"Go to your room."

"I should prefer it."

"You will stay there until I tell you to come out."

To be treated like a child suited Una. The more Alix did

that, the more she played into Una's hands—but presently Hal came tiptoeing in.

"Una—Alix cried."

"I'm glad."

"She has tried so hard," pleaded Hal. "Una, she is nice."

"Is she?"

"Everything is so happy and easy."

"Is it?"

"Yes. Why can't you be? Why do you always have to be so prickly and difficult? Why?"

"Because I am honest, that's why. I wish I were not, but I am."

"Is that why you called it a sham?"

Una nodded with her back to Hal. Her throat felt too choked to speak.

Hal was perplexed. "Edward and Alix are lovers, but that's not really our concern."

"Isn't it?"

"Una, do stop answering questions with questions."

"But isn't it? Don't you see," Una choked. "She said I wanted things. *Edward* wanted Alix living here with him, but he couldn't have her, not while he is God Almighty, God damn blasted Director of United Nations Environmental Research for Asia." Una mocked the titles that had filled her, as much as Great Aunt Freddie, with pride, "and Secretary of the Conference and Sir Edward Gwithiam, K.C.B. . . ."

"Why couldn't he?"

"Because of Lady Srinevesan and Mrs. Porter and Bulbul and—yes, the Paralampurs; because of Delhi, because of the world. There was only one way to make it respectable," Una almost spat out the word, "and that was to bring us out from Cerne and say Alix is our governess. He is so in love he couldn't wait. He didn't think of us."

"Sushila say he'll get tired of her," Hal offered. Hal, of course, had told Sushila at once. "She says they always do."

"I don't think Edward will," said Una hopelessly.

"He got tired of Louise," said Hal.

"No, she got tired of him. Edward is . . . faithful." Una said it even more hopelessly.

"Will he marry her?" Sushila had asked.

That had startled Una. "Would Vikram?"

"Vik!" It had been Sushila's turn to be startled. "Of course not. Besides, Vik will soon be betrothed. Papa is arranging it. Our family is traditional but English people are so different."

"I thought Edward was." Una had said it in a whisper, and now, "He wrote that he was lonely." Her voice was so thick with tears that the words came unsteadily. "He said he needed me to talk to—needed us. Now I think he would like us to go to bed at eight so he could be alone with her. He said he and I would play chess." She looked down at the chess set she had loved so much standing untouched on its board: the kings in their howdahs on the elephants: the palanquined queens holding their bunches of roses: the bishops on camels: the knights' horses: the bowmen. "I suppose it was meant as a consolation prize. Booby prize!" said Una. "He hasn't played chess with me once!" and she swept the pieces on to the floor.

"Wake up. Please, please wake up."

Una was heavily asleep after the dragging miserable day. Hal had brought lunch to her on a tray, taken it untouched away. At four o'clock Alix had come in. "You are playing tennis at the Club with Bulbul Misra. Get dressed; and Una, this afternoon Edward makes his long speech to the Ministers; there will have been a great deal of argument and he will be tired and strained. He is not to be worried. Do you hear?"

Una had said, "I hear," but that evening when she had changed for dinner, Ram Chand's "May I in-coming?" sounded at the door of her room. "Tsst!" He had found the chess set on the floor and was picking up the pieces; those that were unbroken, he put back on the squares, the ones that were shattered or splintered he wrapped in his soft duster. "I take and get mended."

"Throw them away," said Una. "I don't want them."

"No, Missy, no," and the old bearer had said, "Our hearts much sorry for you, Miss-baba," and Una had seen why Alix had not let the servants come near her. It seemed there was a rising tide amongst them against Alix. Why did they dislike her? And why should they like me, wondered Una? She could have understood it if it had been Hal. Already Hal knew of all their families, their home villages; she was knitting a jersey for the sweeper's, Mitchu's, little boy, and had bestowed her new pink cardigan on Ram Chand's granddaughter who was getting married; English woollens were prized, but Ram had made Hal get Edward's permission before he would accept it. Una had done nothing, said almost nothing. Like her? Why did they not dislike her too? Yet Monbad had followed Ram bearing something on a silver salver; the salver was a sign of honour—Monbad, nearer their age and less punctilious than Ram, usually handed things to the girls. "The mali found this in the garden. It is Miss-baba's book."

Una nearly said of it too, "Throw it away. I can't use it," but their sympathy, chiefly unspoken, made her feel less forlorn and she had taken the book and had not, as she had meant to do when she reached the privacy of bed, cried; instead, almost too tired to care, she went straight to sleep. Now someone was shaking her, speaking through the clouds of sleep. "Una, wake up. Una. Una." Struggling with sleep Una opened her eyes; kneeling by her bed was Alix, Alix in a kimona, the famous hair down and streaming over it. Una could catch the fragrance of her skin, see her white face. "Is anything—the matter?" Una asked stupidly.

"Una, you're not awake. Wake up. I had to come to you."

"Why?"

"To beg you."

"Beg?" Una was still stupid.

"Beg you not to tell." Alix was weeping now, her hands clutching Una. "I know it was wrong. It's true—I cannot teach you, but I didn't know how high the standard was, even that there was such a standard. How could I know? You are quite right—I didn't go to the Sorbonne, but the nuns sent me to the Conservatoire with the idea I should come back and teach for them, but it all went a little to my head and I . . . left after a year. I have always been counted so clever and I thought I could get away with this but I didn't know what clever meant until I met Edward and you."

At that Una wriggled uncomfortably under the bed-clothes. "I'm not clever," she muttered, "just ordinary." She was awake and clear now.

"You are brilliant—you and Edward. If you tell him, he will send me away."

"Not while he's like this," but Una did not say it, only, drearily, "He won't."

"He will. I am—only new," and, for a moment, Una almost took Alix into her arms to comfort her—almost, not quite. "You have had his love from the day you were born," Alix was saying. "It's—rooted. You are secure. You don't have to build your life on lies."

"I wouldn't, not if I were a sweeper's child," but Una did not say that either.

"You don't know what it's like to be poor, to grow up in squalor."

"Not squalor," objected Una. "It couldn't have been squalor."

"You can't imagine, can you, what the poor parts of an Indian city are like to live in? Not just to look at, but to live in; or what it is to be a nobody and have to fight for every chance you get? Be shut out, swallow people's insults —and their charity." Una knew how Alix's nostrils widened when she was angry. "I know I sometimes used . . . doubtful means, but I had only my wits and, Una, I have an old mother to keep who is helpless. It has been bitter, sometimes disgusting." There was a ring of truth in that and Una raised herself on her elbow to look at Alix. "You mean Mr. Chaman Lal Sethji?" she asked.

"Who told you about him?" Alix flared. "That vulture Srinevesan!"

"It wasn't Lady Srinevesan. I—heard," and Alix bowed her head.

"I suppose everybody knows. Yes—Sethji." She shuddered. "But now . . . when I met Edward, I couldn't believe my luck. I thought we were all happy. I tried . . ."

"I know you did."

"Then why break it?" asked Alix. "Oh, Una, if you will have a little patience, I will talk Edward round, be able to explain. We can get you professors or, perhaps, I can persuade him to let you go to the American International School. We can make some pretext but let me do it in my own time—in my own way. Una, promise—I beseech you. Promise you won't tell."

Una had had enough. "I won't tell," she said, lay down and turned her back.

"Mrs. Porter, may I ask you something?"

The weather had turned unexpectedly warm and they were at the American Embassy pool. "The first swim of the season," Alix had said. "Soon all the pools will be open." Mrs. Porter had invited them and, "I have asked Wilbur and Terry, our Ambassador's twin boys, to meet you. They are just your age," Mrs. Porter told Hal. "Older," said Una but Hal looked coldly at the two freckled thirteen-year-olds, with their tow-coloured heads, shy grins, at their jeans and sweat shirts printed with names "of baseball teams, I suppose," and crinkled her nose. She played Ping-Pong with them but treated the boys loftily and hardly spoke at tea when they devoured doughnuts, ice cream, and glasses of milk. Wilbur after Vikram Singh! Hal's nose had been eloquent, but now she was swimming and diving happily with them. Una was not bathing; as usual, when any trouble came, her menses came too, "out of period," as Matron at Cerne would say, and this afternoon Una was looking pallidly plain and hollow-eyed in a way that seemed to touch Mrs. Porter's capacious heart and she was so kind that Una could gather herself to say, "May I ask you something?"

"Of course you may, my dear."

"Please tell me what it is you know about Miss Lamont."

"What it is," not "what you know." Mrs. Porter's plump freckled fingers drummed on the table and the sun sent flashes from the jewels in her rings—she had unexpectedly magnificent rings. "Una, I don't want to upset the applecart."

"It is upset."

Then Mrs. Porter asked, "How old are you?"

"Fifteen"—and today far far older than that, Una wanted to add.

"Then you should be old enough." Mrs. Porter looked across the pool; everyone was out of earshot and, "She isn't Miss Lamont," said Mrs. Porter. "She is a Mrs. Tanson. They say her husband was a coffee planter who fell in love with her out here—she must have been most beautiful—and followed her to Paris where they married. Perhaps she was dazzled—he, too, was good-looking. He brought her back to India, but it didn't turn out well, and he disappeared. Of course, she has a perfect right to use her maiden name, and she must have had a hard time, poor girl." Mrs. Porter spoke as if trying to keep a fair balance in what she said. "I believe her father was a Canadian sergeant in the Veterinary Corps; at one time he was attached to the Remount Depot in Calcutta, where the army horses come in from Australia to be broken and tamed. The mother is Eurasian from Pondicherry."

"Not French?" asked Una.

"Well, Indian-French," said Mrs. Porter. "The girl—Miss Lamont—went to school there to a convent where Amina Srinevesan often gave away the prizes. Amina comes from Southern India too."

"I see," said Una.

"Una, those sort of things don't matter nowadays."

"Lady Srinevesan thinks they do. She treats Alix as she wouldn't treat a servant."

"Indians are more suspicious of mixed blood than we are—but with Amina Srinevesan it wouldn't be that."

"What is it then? Mrs. Porter, what did Alix do when she was with Mr. Chaman Lal Sethji?"

"I believe she was companion to his wife."

"Was she his mistress?"

Una had expected Mrs. Porter to be strait-laced but Mrs. Porter only said, "They say she was—Delhi gossip, which often isn't true. What is true is that Sethji dismissed her very suddenly."

"Why?"

"Nobody knows but it seems there was—a lack of probity."

"Probity." It was a grave word and Mrs. Porter was grave.

"I feel it in her, Una, so does Amina Srinevesan; so, I think, do you. That is why I do not like you, Kate's daughter, and Hal of course, being in her charge."

"She isn't in charge." Una would dearly have liked to say that, but could not deny it.

"Mr. Sethji may be sharp in business, but he is an honourable man. I don't believe he would have done anything unfair; but in any case," said Mrs. Porter, "to pretend you are what you are not, to know what you do not, is lack of probity. Your father has given Miss Lamont his trust, and that's why I am uneasy. You and Hal are young; no one knows what you may do next, not even yourselves."

"We?" Una was startled. She had not thought they were talking about her and Hal. "What could we do?"

"You don't know," said Mrs. Porter. "That's why, in a strange country like this, Eddie needs someone completely trustworthy."

Alix, brought up in what Bulbul Misra called "old India," had a siesta every afternoon. Hal, as usual, followed her idol. "After all, we are out early."

"I wish, Una, that you would rest too," said Alix.

"I can't sleep in the day." Besides, Una liked what she called 'the empty time.' The servants, off-duty, went to their quarters and were probably asleep as were Alix and

Hal; even the birds were silent, even the lizards still, the whole garden drowsed in the warmth and sun, but Una was not drowsy; she was too harrowed with despair.

"You can't really want to do those ghastly-sounding sums," said Hal.

"They're not ghastly when you understand them."

"But can you?" Hal asked it doubtfully. It did not seem to her that anybody could.

"I could if they were explained to me. I have to. They're —they're my language," said Una.

"Then?"

"Then nothing. I expect I'm done for," and Una tried to shrug.

Long ago, when she was three or four, she had been given a little doll—by Mrs. Porter, she thought suddenly. Why, I do remember her! It was in Calcutta; it was really the figure of a doll, so small it had fitted into a matchbox but, cast in metal, it was weighted so that if it were knocked over, at once, or slowly, depending on the hardness of the knock, it stood upright again. "A ninepin doll," Edward had told her.

"Ninepin?"

"Made to be knocked over."

"And stand up again."

Una had made it a private little garden in sand; she remembered the feel of the hot sand as she stuck flowers into it, scarlet and yellow flowers, *gōl mohur,* she remembered the gōl mohur trees with their brilliant sprays would be out soon here in Delhi. She had made a pool from a river shell; the Shiraz Road fountain tinkled into the pool in the pavilion; it seemed to Una much the same as her shell and as secret, but why should she think of it now? The doll had been lost, probably in one of their innumerable packings, but it was as if it sent her a message.

She did not believe for one moment in the professors Alix had talked of, nor that she would go to the International School. At my age, the pupils would be going back to their own countries to take examinations. She was, too, tied by her promise not to tell Edward, but, "Don't just lie down," said Una to Una. "There must be other ways. If you write to Crackers, she might find a correspondence course—there must be such things. Meanwhile, you try by yourself." And, the next afternoon, she found her *Elementary Mechanics* that Ram Chand had carefully put in the bookcase. Someone had cleaned it—she was sure the book had fallen into the wet flower bed—probably the someone was Monbad—but then she saw it had a marker; neither she nor Alix had put one there; it was marking page 71, not a usual marker, but a feather, a tip feather from a peacock's train, lucently blue and green, with the iridescent eye in a feathered fringe that scintillated with colour as it caught the light.

Who had put it there? Someone who cares, thought Una. For the first time since the scene with Alix she felt warmed—and titillated; she picked up the book, a pad, and her pencils and went out to the summer house.

At first the green and shade seemed cool, inviting, and, sitting down to the rough table, she began to work: *"If the slope of the plane is 30 degrees to the horizontal and the force of gravity vertically downwards,"* she murmured aloud, *"then the component of the acceleration perpendicular to the plane in the upward direction will be — 10 cos 30° m/s$_2$."* She wrote, *The cos of 30° is $\sqrt{3/2}$ so that will make the acceleration —$\sqrt{5/3}$.*

In the same way the acceleration along the plane would be—10 cos 60° or—5 m/s^2 since the cos of 60 is ½ . . .

She looked it over and could see no fault in it. "But how do I do the next part?" She knew the formula $V = u + at$. "But how do I apply it to this?" she asked hopelessly. "How can I find 't' if I don't know 'V'? The acceleration will be negative but that doesn't get me far." It was closer under the creepers than she had imagined and there was sweat on her forehead. "$V = u - gt$. But where do I go from there?" She had looked up the answer and knew that the time of flight should be $2/\sqrt{3}$ seconds, "But how do I get this? How?"

The sun glare from the garden hurt her eyes; the scent of the honysuckle made her dizzy, but she kept doggedly on, writing the equation out again and the value for 't' of $V = u - 2g\sqrt{3}$, but still it seemed to make no sense, and she sat staring at it. It was hopeless. I can't, thought Una, I can't. I'm beaten.

She heard a rustle, as if creepers had been pushed aside, then, behind her, a warmth; there was another soft movement, as of muslin clothes—indeed a muslin sleeve brushed her cheek—and a new smell mingled with the honeysuckle scent, freshly washed skin, a slightly onion-scented breath, and something she was to learn was coconut hair oil. Then a hand came over her shoulder; it was a brown hand on a strong wrist that wore an amulet, a darkened silver seal on a red cord, and on to Una's scrubbed and tormented page it laid another feather with another iridescent eye. "Just to tell you," said a voice in English, "that I am I. Then, please do not be frigtened."

Una was not frightened, not even startled; in the dreamy, scented warmth, the voice simply seemed natural and it seemed natural too when she looked up and whispered, "Ravi!"

"You know my name?"

"I asked Dino. I . . . I have been watching you."

"I know you have, Miss Spy. Very well, I watched you back."

"You write poems," she said. "That's why you put the feather as a marker. I should have guessed at once."

"And what did you think of my feather?"

"In England we should say a peacock feather brought bad luck." How strange, thought Una, that she should be able to say to this particular young man exactly what she thought.

"Here not at all," said Ravi. "On the reverse, the peacock is sacred, very emblem of India; and I hope the book was properly cleaned." His pronunciation was a little stilted—"pro-per-lee." "The earth was wet and you threw the book hard. Hard! *Ari bap!*" He laughed again and stopped. "That Miss Lamont is no good for you, I think."

"I knew you were listening but didn't think you would understand English."

"No, Ravi the chota mali shouldn't understand or speak English. Perhaps I am Master Spy." Una thought she had never seen such white and even teeth.

She seemed small and pale sitting there below him who was so large, brown, golden-brown and merry; that was the word that suited him as he stood laughing down at her. I was right, thought Una. He is far more attractive than Vikram Singh, by far the most attractive person I have ever seen.

He moved round and sat on the summer house's other wooden chair—the honeysuckle and creepers hid them both from the upper garden. "I suppose I should ask you, Miss-baba, may I sit down?"

"Don't be silly," and Una found herself laughing; there was something in Ravi that stirred happy, easy laughter— and I said I should never laugh again, thought Una.

"I have spoken English since little," Ravi was saying, "and I was reading it at St. Thomas's College. Had I stayed at College I should have taken a first, probably with honours." He said it curiously without conceit, with the assurance of a young cock-bird.

"And you didn't stay?"

"No." There was a momentary shadow. "I—I was persuaded into a—a Group the authorities do not like," then he cheered. "And had I taken a first, immediately everybody would have wanted me to do something . . . my father would have wanted I come home and manage our estate; my mother that I should become doctor; my uncle would have wanted me in government service, diplomatic. My Group wanted me in politics. But, you see, I did not want any of those things. I wanted writing poems."

"Are they good poems?" Una had been to one of Lady Srinevesan's evenings where she had stayed mute, watching and listening; she had not, of course, been able to judge the poems in Indian languages, though she had liked their rhythms; but had secretly thought most of those in

English worse than poor and, "Are your's good?" she asked warily.

"Very good." He was serious. "Better now than I could have believed. I wanted peace in which to write them and it is peaceful in your father's garden," said Ravi. "Until someone throws a book into a flower bed."

"I am sorry," but Una could not feel sorry.

"No, no. You were brave," and Ravi said, "That Lamont! But why do you not tell your father?"

"I promised I wouldn't."

"Even at your expense?"

"Even at my expense." This seemed so strange a philosophy to Ravi that for a moment he did not talk. Then, "Unfortunately," he said, "I have chiefly forgotten my mathematics but I am arranging for you. I have a mathematical friend, Hem, Hemango Sharma. He is at present in Medical School, but he is most good at mathematics. He took them at St. Thomas's. Hem shall come here and teach you."

"But . . . how?"

"At the back of my hut is a loose—do you call it a paling?—in the fence. No one can see, but it is my entrance and exit—and Hem's. He comes through it to visit with me. Hem will bicycle here one, two times a week in these afternoons when no one is about and slip in here with me."

"You will be seen."

"Hem and I have the art of disappearing." Again there was that shade in Ravi's voice, "and I shall stand guard while he instructs you."

"But . . . suppose he doesn't want to."

"What I want, Hem wants." Ravi was certain. "He will come."

"I certainly will not," said Hem.

"Hem, you said yourself she is only a little girl."

"She cannot be all that little if she is doing calculus," and, "Ravi, don't! Don't . . ." pleaded Hem.

FIVE

"If you consider," explained Hem, "the component of velocity perpendicular to the plane, there will be an instant when the ball is still, when v equals 0."

"Of course," said Una. "Of course."

What, asked Hem, had made him give in to Ravi and come? Pity? "She is so badly treated," Ravi had said, but how could a poor medical student pity Miss Una Gwithiam? "No, it was purely the mathematics," said Hem.

"It was curiosity," said Ravi and it was true that Hem could not helping being curious about this girl who had so improbably made friends with her father's gardener, "Because she doesn't know you are anything else," said Hem.

"She senses it. Yes, she is very much taken with me," said Ravi, preening, but for the moment it was Hem who had Una's whole attention.

"Look at the equation," he told her. "When the ball is still, v equals 0, so if you use the equation $V = u - gt$ and put $V = 0$ the initial speed in this upward direction is 10 cos 60° and you have $0 = 5 - 5\sqrt{3}\ t$ which gives t $= \sqrt{1/3}$ seconds as the time taken to reach the highest point."

It was as clear an exposition as any of Mr. Rattray's and, "Yes," said Una. "Yes."

"Then the downward journey will take the same length of time, so that the total flight time is $\sqrt{\frac{2}{3}}$ seconds, which is the answer you want. Do you understand?"

"Yes," said Una again but more firmly. She was beginning to feel the satisfaction, the little surge of power and mastery that she had felt at Cerne under Mr. Rattray. "I think I understand."

"Now that you know how long the flight is," Hem went on, "you can easily find the distance, on range, along the slope . . . by considering the equation of motion along the line of greatest slope. $v = u - g \cos. 60°t$. . . . Miss Gwithiam, you are not listening, I think."

"I am. I am," said Una hastily.

"Let me look," said Ravi and Hem had to watch the two heads as they came together over the book, Ravi's hair black and glossy, Una's almost green-brown in the creeper-filtered light of the summer house.

Then Una looked up at Ravi, her eyes alight with mischief. "You are not properly dressed," she told him.

"I am not?" Ravi pretended to be indignant.

"No, you haven't a flower behind your ear."

When Una came to think of it, she had never had a friend of her own before. There were people she had liked, of course, but then Edward always moved on. Inevitably they would one day move on from Delhi, but she shut that out of her mind. True she had been quite a long time at Cerne but the girls there, and Mrs. Carrington and Mr. Rattray, had to be shared. No one shared Ravi, for some reason she discounted Hem—"Well, I am always discounted," Hem would have said—and too, Una now had a secret which was a satisfying little tit for tat to Edward and Alix.

At the slightest sound from the house, a footfall on the veranda or path, Ravi slid behind the creepers to the flower beds and all anyone saw was the chota mali at his work weeding, while Miss-baba Una, apart and alone, was bent over her books in the summer house.

"Alix," she had said. "I think I have worked that problem out. Let's see if I have the answer right," and watched while Alix guilelessly produced the answers book.

"Quite right." Alix was relieved. "I must say, Una, it does you credit."

"Perhaps I can go on by myself—for a little." How strange that anyone so adept at deceiving should be so easily deceived. "But Alix doesn't know enough to suspect," Una told Ravi.

"How is it, Ally, with that disagreeable girl, m'n?" Mrs. Lamont asked again.

"I think I have the measure of her," said Alix. "If I give her time for study and respect her precious dignity."

"Heavens! Your patience."

"Yes, I think I have won. At least now and then I can take my eye off her," said Alix.

Two mortars are placed side by side and fired simultaneously with the same speed and same bearing. . . . One shell is fired at 70 degrees to the vertical, the other at 70 degrees to the horizontal. Prove that they both land in the same place and compare the heights to which they rise.

"Now try and work it through," Ravi told Una.

"I shall not come again," Hem had said to Ravi after the first time.

"But you must."

They had been back in Ravi's hut and Hem had been in what Ravi called 'an unreasonable temper.' "I do not like this and it is no good."

"It is every good," said Ravi. "Hem, please. Please!" and, in the end, they had compromised. Hem would teach Ravi, Ravi could teach Una. "But how much mathematics?" asked Hem.

Prove that they both rise in the same place and compare the heights.

Ravi tapped his pencil against a trail of honeysuckle and a shower of minute ants fell on the paper. "When I was a little boy," said Ravi, "I used to eat ants because someone told me they would make me wise."

"And did they?" asked Una.

"Hem says not."

"Tell me about when you were a little boy."

"I was only child. They did not let me go away from home, so I suppose I was alone, but we had a gardener," he said, looking at the garden, "an old man not unlike your Ganesh. I used to follow him everywhere he went. I remember one day he bought me a toy watering-can with his own money and he must have had most little. I used to water his feet—nice grateful child. His feet were dark and cracked and horny. He was my best friend; perhaps it was he who made me like gardens and gave me the idea of this."

"Go on," said Una.

"Our garden, though, is not at all like yours. Apart from the vegetable patch it is straggling, dusty; no one bothers about English or special flowers; we have only a few hibiscus, oleanders, cosmos, marigolds, and there are cows tethered on the grass."

"Cows?"

"To most Indian people cows are much more important than flowers."

"Tell about your house."

"It isn't like the houses you see nowadays; it is made of old Punjabi bricks which are smaller than ordinary ones and have good colours. The roof has colours too of old tiles. There are verandas all around; you would not approve of them, every day their rails are hung with bedding —we *air* our bedding." Ravi was lofty. "The front veranda is for my father; his day bed is there, spread with a durrie and sheet and a heavy white *takia* to support him."

"A pillow?"

"No—big, round and long."

"A bolster."

"We say takia. My father sits there in the evenings looking out over his lands. The land is flat; he can see for miles and all that he sees is his. In his father's time it was more, much, much more, but at his death divided out among his three sons—that is our law—but my father's land will not be divided as I am only son."

"Then it will all be yours."

"Yes, and more—one uncle has no children—but I do not want it. Most people want to live in a little patch," said Ravi. "I want to live in the world."

"But this—it's the family estate."

"There should not be estates. Our fields are let out to peasants; you do not know how small those fields are—they have low clay walls built round them and are irrigated by hand from a well where the water is scooped out by a ladle on the end of a pole and let, one ladle after another, through the fields. Men and women work in the fields all day, go back to their huts at night. I should rather have a hut than my home, so I shall give the house away—maybe make it a hospital, give the peasants their fields. Keep only one or two for me. I remember," said Ravi, "when my father bought a new camel. She turned out bad-tempered but we lend her out for ploughing."

"Plough with a camel?"

"Certainly. She gives trouble but her driver loves her. I loved her too and used to ride on her. I bought her a necklace of blue and white beads and called her Rowena. My mother was reading me your Walter Scott's book, *Ivanhoe*. I might keep Rowena," said Ravi. "We grow mustard and wheat but if I kept all the land, co-operatively of course, I should grow roses professionally."

"But do they grow them here commercially?"

"For export, best roses in the world. Ask your father to take you to the rose farms; it is the only industry I like. Yes, perhaps I shall do that . . ." but Una was seeing a low house in a chequerboard of bright green and yellow fields, the shining water falling from the scoop as it was pulled up and down on its ropes; she saw a shaggy camel looming against the sky, high above a small brown boy hand in hand with an old man. "Our gardener did not hold my hand." Ravi had an uncanny way of reading her thoughts. "He held me with his thumb and finger round the wrist, as most Indians prefer."

"Go on."

"No. Hem will be cross with us. Back to your mortars, Miss," but, how odd! The mathematics for which Una had fought with such bitterness did not seem in the least important now.

"Una, where have you been?" They had stayed too late; Ganesh was old and slept long in the afternoon but on this day he was back and, calling for Ravi, had almost caught them and, "Where have you been, Una?" asked Alix again.

"Working in the summer house. Where else?"

Lessons at Shiraz Road had gone on though, but tacit arrangement between Alix and Una, in an attenuated form; Una worked at her dictées and French reading, her Indian history, enjoyed cooking with Christopher, but the needlework had been put away and only Hal listened to the *Outline of Literature*. "Una, are you sure you are getting on with those problems?" asked Alix.

Now Una had pulled a spray of honeysuckle and she, too, had jauntily put the flower behind her ear. "You don't look like Una," said Hal, staring at her. "What's happened to you."

"Nothing."

"Something," said Hal's look, though she was too loyal to say it. Perhaps Alix sensed that too, because she said, "I don't like this, Una. We get up earlier now it's warmer. You ought to rest too."

"None of the other girls here do."

"They are used to the climate."

"And I'm not used to sleeping in the afternoon. I told you, I can't do it, Alix. Truly, I can't." Una sounded alarmed and Hal cocked a suspicious ear. "I'm used to working then."

"Why not work on the veranda?"

"The summer house is shady."

"I suppose it's all right."

"Good heavens! It's not forty yards from the house," and, "We go out so much," said Una with a blandness new to her, "that I need the time."

It seemed that in Delhi even schoolgirls had their social round and Una and Hal had, "Willy-nilly," said Una, been caught up in it: riding, watching polo, swimming, going to concerts, charity fêtes. "You are Edward's *daughters*," said Alix, and Edward, to Una's surprise, abetted this. He even enrolled them for flower-arranging classes.

"Flower-arranging? Us?"

"*Ikebana*," said Edward.

"But we are not Japanese."

"It is the craze in Delhi this winter," said Alix as if that explained it.

"And Mrs. Mehta is running them," said Edward, "which is why I want you to go. Mehta is an influential man."

Is this Edward talk? thought Una mystified. When had Edward been influenced by influence? Every now and then, though, he seemed to surface, breathe his own air. "What has happened to us?" Una had asked him after one of the big dinner parties at Shiraz Road. "We used not to be so grand."

"No." For a moment he had looked puzzled. "I'm a quiet sort of bloke really." Edward did not use a slang word until it was so out of date it had come to be ordinary speech. "I don't know quite what has happened," and he ruffled up his hair as if Una had suddenly disturbed him— succeeded in disturbing him—but it did not last and, too, he was curiously unnoticing—"about us," said Hal. He had not noticed the rings in her and Una's ears, Hal's jewellery or her nail polish, though he did complain about the scent: "This isn't a hairdresser's shop." "But he never noticed when I didn't wash it off," said Hal and she too asked, "What has happened to him?"

Hal was in demand to play and sing, sometimes alone, often with Alix and, Alix is spoiling Hal's music, thought Una, worried. Hal sang sentimental songs, "*Parlez-moi d'amour*," or "Lucia." "She wasn't allowed to sing those at school," Una objected. "Signor Brazzi said she showed real promise," and, "Hal, don't sing those songs," Una begged.

"Why not?"

"They're full of tricks and you are getting a tremor, just like Alix."

"Good. That's what I want to be—just like Alix," but Mrs. Mehta, patron of the flower-arranging classes, had asked Hal to sing at one of her concerts, and did not ask her again.

"Don't you see?" said Una.

"What I see," said furious Hal, "is that with Lady Srinevesan and Mrs. Mehta you are getting to be an unbearable snob. What do you want me to do?"

"Sing," said Una, but Hal would not listen.

If Edward were going out, as he often did in the evenings, Hal telephoned Sushila, "To ask us to Paralampur House," said Una, and protested, "It's hinting."

"It isn't. It's asking," said Hal and explained, "Vik might be there."

"But isn't this all a bit old for Hal?" Una had said to Alix.

"Sushila isn't much older."

"Sushila is fourteen. Hal is only twelve."

"Everyone thinks I'm older than I am."

"But you're not," said Una and told Alix, "At Cerne she was a junior. She went to bed at nine o'clock."

"Prig! Prig!" Hal was more furious still and she asked again, "What do you want me to do? Play with dolls?"

Sometimes at Paralampur House the girls danced on the veranda to Vikram's record player. The only new thing in the house, thought Una. In schoolgirl tradition the girls danced with one another but if Vikram came in he would sometimes dance with Hal. "Come along, pussy," he would say.

Don't you see—to him you're just a little girl, but Una did not say it; she could not bear to put out the happiness

in her sister's eyes. It's Alix he's after, but she did not say
that either. Did not have to say it, thought Una.

As the darling son of the house, it never occurred to
Vikram to do other than he wanted and he soon dropped
Hal and went to coax Alix. "Come and dance."

"I am not here to dance."

The Maharani always asked Alix with Una and Hal.
"Well, the Paralampurs don't have to put up barriers,"
said Alix with disdain for Lady Srinevesan. "Aristocrats
don't," yet Una fathomed Alix would rather not have gone.

"Come and dance."

"I have told you—no." But there came a night when
moonlight flooded the old compound, turning the dusty
roughness of its lawns to silver, making shadows under the
trees. Vikram had come from a dinner at the Mess; he was
wearing the Bodyguard's dress uniform, white with scarlet
pipings, the silver shoulder chains and gold badges catching the light.

"Alix, come and dance."

Somewhere in the servants' quarters, a drum was beating and, from a bush below the veranda, a scent filled the
night, the same scent as from the flowers in Ravi's hedge,
and, "You can't want to spend your days—I mean nights
—talking to children and old people," Vikram had said.

"The Maharani Sahib is not old," Alix answered
steadily, "and Una and Hal happen to be in my charge."

"You could forget them for ten minutes."

"Vikram, go away," but he came round to where he
could see Alix's face.

"What if I won't?"

"I shall tell Sir Edward you are pestering me."

"And if I tell Sir Edward there was a time when you
were pleased to be so pestered?"

"Vikram, go away."

His voice changed to seriousness. Una could only just
catch it. "What if I can't?"

"Vikram, *please*."

Music from the gramophone mingled with the drum; the

veranda was filled with the pale skirts, dark heads of the dancing little girls.

"What if I can't?"

"Please go away."

I believed words then, thought Una afterwards. I though Alix was distressed. . . . Threading her way through the dancers she went and stood by Alix. "Shall we go home?" To her surprise Alix turned on her. "Must you cling to me like a limpet? Go and dance with the others."

"Yes, run along," said Vikram.

Run along! Una retreated, her cheeks as red as if they had been slapped. When she looked back along the veranda, Alix and Vikram had gone.

"So it is Vikram—or, rather, Vikram too!"

Som Misra, Bulbul's husband, said he had known Alix in Calcutta—"Chillie hot!" Som had said. "He may have known her," Mrs. Porter corrected when Una, turning Som's words over and over in her mind, was driven to ask Mrs. Porter if this were true. "Young men like to boast. But Miss Lamont is far too—wise," Una guessed Mrs. Porter had been going to say 'clever,' "to become notorious, but, Una dear, why are you asking? Has anything happened?"

"Nothing at all." Una, at once, was closed as an oyster. "Only . . ." she opened a crack, "why doesn't Edward know all this?"

"I guess your father doesn't listen to gossip."

"It's a pity he doesn't." Una could imagine Lady Srinevesan saying that.

That night Una had followed Alix to her bedroom and perched on the end of the bed, watching while Alix took down her hair; as she started to brush the dark red silkiness, it seemed what Lady Srinevesan had called it, 'fairytale' hair, part of the whole tale in which she, Una, was so strongly caught up. "It must be difficult to be so desirable," said Una.

She was thinking aloud and had not meant it as a challenge, but the brushing stopped and Alix looked at her in the mirror.

"You think you know something, don't you, Una?"

"Yes, I think I do."

"As it happens, you don't. While we were at the Para-lampurs this evening, I had a message from my mother saying she was ill and I had to go to her."

"Your mother is here in Delhi! Here!"

"Yes."

For a moment Una was as astounded as Alix meant her to be. "Where?"

"She is in a—a Home."

"And you have never taken us to see her. Why not?"

"She likes to be quiet. Besides, there are some things," said Alix, "I prefer to keep to myself."

Quite a number of things, thought Una. She was back to Vikram and, I don't believe you, thought Una. When you came in with Vikram tonight, you did not seem at all like someone who had been with an ill old woman; you looked . . . you looked as you did that morning when you had given Maxim that splendid gallop.

"Before you go," said Alix in the mirror, "and I should like you to go, I think you should beg my pardon."

Una got off the bed.

"Una, beg my pardon."

"I can't," said Una—and was gone.

"I have brought two new problems for Miss Una," said Hem. "Come, I will show you how to work them."

"She hasn't done the last two yet," said Ravi.

"Tell me about the inside of your house," Una had asked him.

"The rooms are low," said Ravi, "dark and cool, too cool in winter; our servants have to light braziers. The floors are covered with durries, cotton-made carpets, and the rooms would seem bare to you: little furniture—low stools with woven string seats and painted legs, cushions, those takias, a low table, a desk like mine, and, in the bedrooms, light beds and chests where we keep our clothes. There are two courtyards: the inner one was built for the women; my mother still uses it; my father likes her to be private."

"Private—a mother?"

"You don't know a Brahmin household. We each keep a little distance from the other. You and your father and sister and the Lamont, sit round the table for family dinner, but we eat separately, no matter how many people in the house; children apart; my mother now and again with the other women; my father invariably alone, usually any time will do. Everywhere you go in our house," said Ravi, "you see someone coming or going carrying a tray, a silver tray with bowls, the food strictly orthodox."

"No meat, of course," said Una.

"Meat! Our dogs have to be fed out of the house not to contaminate it. My mother always says she can tell the smell of a meat-eater; no meat, nor fish, nor eggs, not even onions."

"Why not onions?"

"They make one coarse, interfere with meditation. My father, you see, has endless taboos. Taboo! taboo! taboo! No, I can never go home," said Ravi. "I have become intolerably coarse; it is contact with Hem to whom these things are superstition, but," and Ravi was serious, "seeing Hem's work has made me boil for my mother. She wanted so much to be doctor. She went to school in England and to College. Now she spends her days counting *degs* of *dal* and corn and vegetables, in drying chillies, making *papars*."

"Those thin big biscuits that are spiced?"

"Yes, and making mango pickle and waiting on my father. What a waste!"

"Is it a waste?" asked Una. "She must have taught you English."

"Yes. Of course I had a tutor but I gave him nothing but trouble. It was she I obeyed."

"I think she started your poems," said Una. "So it wasn't a waste." She looked down at the rough table and the pads and pencils, Hem's carefully worked, neglected problems, the closed *Elementary Mechanics,* and, "Ravi, will you read me your poems?" she asked.

"If you will come to my hut tonight."

"Tonight?" For a moment Una was startled and then saw he was not thinking of her but of the poems.

"This is not right," he said, meaning the summer house. "It is too lazy. For mathematics you can combat that— they are clear, precise. . . ."

"If we did them," said Una, with a moment's guilt.

"We will do them," said Ravi, but went straight on, "For poems you must be wide awake to listen, feel. Come tonight."

"But . . . would it be safe?"

"Why not? Your night watchman smokes and dozes. Twenty thieves could break in and he would not hear or see. Your little Hal will be asleep. As for your lady and gentlemen—I understand they are occupied with one another or often there are guests and they stay late talking. The Lamont seems usually to be there."

Una's face hardened. "I will come."

SIX

"Lady Srinevesan, do you know a poet called Ravi Bhatta-charya?" and Una dared to ask, "Or does Mrs. Mehta?"

The flower-arranging classes had brought an unexpected bonus for Una. Mrs. Mehta held them in her own house—"One of her houses," said Alix. "The classes are not for herself, of course not—the Mehtas must be millionaires; they have money all over the world. They are for her especial charity." All ladies prominent in Delhi's social life were patrons of especial charities. "Tuesday is my leper day," said Bulbul. "I take tea and sweetmeats and cigarettes to the Leper Settlement." Lady Srinevesan's charities were legion.

Bulbul, Alix, and most of the Indian ladies were deft at *ikebana*. "One white camellia with maidenhair fern in a pottery vase," crooned Bulbul, or "Lotus roots and two red roses with grass sprays in a basket." Narcissi with pebbles in a hollow log was Alix's best success. Mrs. Mehta had admitted Alix. "Well, Parsees are more open-minded than other Indians," said Alix. "They have travelled more and are widely cultured."

"She couldn't be more cultured than Lady Srinevesan," Una was loyal, but had to admit that Mrs. Mehta, slim, big-featured with a gold pince-nez, wearing her sari on her right shoulder in Parsee fashion, was in a class apart. Lady Srinevesan obviously thought so. "It's a privilege for you to meet her." "Amina Srinevesan has told me about you," Mrs. Mehta had said, but she refrained from asking Una any questions about Edward or Alix. "She is interested in things, not gossip," said Una thankfully and now, "A poet called Ravi Bhattacharya?" she asked.

She had waited, that night, until eleven o'clock, then rolled up her quilt and arranged it in her bed in a sleeping shape; for the face she used a conch shell she had bought in the bazaar and for hair spread a soft brown-greenish scarf; in the shadowed room, anyone looking in expecting to see Una "would see her," she told Ravi.

Hal was asleep. There had been business guests staying at Shiraz Road, but their rooms were in darkness as was Alix's room and the drawing-room; only in Edward's was there a light, though a glimmer came from the watchman's lantern where he sat against a pillar. Stealthily, Una had slipped off the veranda onto the grass, pale under the waxing moon; it had been wet to her bare feet and the pavilion floor was cool as she had stepped through its arches. Then she had gone boldly out across the lower lawn to the hedge of flowers, Queen of the Night—Raat-Ki-Rani—Ravi had told her their Hindu name. "The darker the night, the more scented it becomes." Una had not thought she would ever go beyond that scented hedge but now she was in the courtyard at the hut door. "Ravi," she whispered. "Ravi."

He was ready for her. Una wondered what he had been doing all this time. "There is always the empty quiet before you come," he was to say. Now, "I had better pull the *chiks* down," he said and had untied the rolled-up matting that hid doorway and window; closed, the little room was intimate. A mat was spread and on the table were saucers of nuts and sweets, saffron-coloured balls of sugar and grain flour. When Una had tasted them, she sat like a child on the matting, hands clasped in her lap, eyes fixed on Ravi as he began to read.

"This poem is a poem of water. Water in light, but not moonlight, sun. Water reflects all life." He was gracefully fanciful. "In sun, colours are more true; water lilies are not pink or the colour of cream, they are white and red. . . ."

"Water lilies are often pink and cream." Una felt obliged to point that out but, "Hush, or how shall I read?" said Ravi.

It was warm in the hut room; the small light enclosed them in a circle, Ravi and her; of the night outside, Una could see nothing, only catch the scent from the Raat-Ki-Rani. There is no one else in the whole world but Ravi and me, thought Una. Ravi, me, and his poem—if only it had been another poem.

He finished and Una was silent—had to be silent. "You don't like it?" and, though it cost her a pang, Una had to say "No."

She thought she would be expelled from the hut, but, to her surprise, Ravi was exuberant. "Now I really respect you. That poem," he said, "goes no deeper than my skin."

"It sounded beautiful," said Una, "but . . ."

"Meaningless."

"And . . . not true," said Una.

Ravi nodded and from the desk shelf took a book of a kind that was new to Una, a thin book, its page unlined, bound in a red cotton cover; quilted with white stitching, it was tied round with a soft white string. A secret book, thought Una, the most secret I have ever seen; more secret than Hal's diary even if that were locked. It appealed to her secretive self. "You see even the book is Indian," said Ravi. "So many of my friends, other Indian poets, are busy, very busy; they are writers of poems of Dylan Thomas, e. e. cummings, all your poets. I am not busy. I look and listen, taste and smell. I feel. That takes a long time but these poems are of nobody but myself. I have not shown them to anyone, not even Hem." He meant particularly not to Hem. "They are Indian; yet, folk poems of the city and village—and true!" Ravi spoke with sudden fierceness. "What I call truthful writing. Those others are not true. Listen . . ." but Una was suddenly bold enough to interrupt.

"Let me read them," she said and held out her hand for the book.

Ravi had not read well; as soon as he started the poem, he had dropped into the singsong drone in which, she was sure, he had been taught to read poetry. The water poem had not only been a disappointment: "It made me squirm," said Una afterwards, but those in the red quilted book she knew, with certainty, would be different and, "Please let me read them," she said.

"But . . . will you know them so quickly?"

"I shall know them." He glanced at her, was reassured, and handed her the book. "I wrote them in Hindi and in English," he said. "I hope they are plain."

They were plain and spoke of plain, intrinsic, and indigenous Indian things, as much as if they were made of India's fine cotton, pure wool, real silk; her wood, strong as teak or resilient as bamboo—there was much of bamboo in these poems: "Strong as a man, yielding as a woman, simple as a child," Una had heard Edward say of the bamboo, "and in the country it costs nothing," Ravi added when she quoted this—useful bamboos but resilient, answering with a rustle of sharp-pointed leaves to the least breath of wind, making shadows that danced in sun or moonlight. "And the shoots are delicious to chew," said Ravi. In these poems were Indian sounds to which Una was growing accustomed: the creaking of bullock cart wheels beside motor horns and the light hiss of bicycle tires; the chinking of bangle against bangle; the chants coolies used as they strained at their loads: the plod and pattering of hooves, big and little, buffaloes or goats, in the dust: the cheap tinkle of a temple bell, or the minute

silvery clash of a pair of rare cymbals: a baby's wail: the
callousness of a monkey-man's drum, but always, distinct
and unexpected, a flute—Krishna's flute? thought Una.
Krishna, the handsome young bold god who enticed the
milkmaids.

There was the taste of Indian food: the *luddu* Ravi had
provided for her just now, of other sweets tinged with the
taste of rosewater, of warm fruit and coconut milk: of
curries.

There was the smell of sweat and hot dust, of dung
smoke from fires or, acrid, from burnt leaves: of Ravi's
own hair oil and the heavy night-flowers.

As Una read, she saw flat-topped houses, huddled as in
the city or lonely in the plain: she saw thatched huts, clay-
walled: palm trees and flowering trees: a sky of paper
kites: meadows of the yellow mustard Alix and Ravi both
talked of: pools and rivers that reflected the sky. A boy
set paper boats in a stream to join the mile-wide rivers—so
many Indian toys were made of paper. A corpse lay, lonely
and small, on the bank while the mourners picnicked
round it, lighting their own small family fire before they
set the pyre alight.

Who saw the hoopoe fly? asked Ravi in one of these
poems; there were hoopoes, black and white and crested
in Delhi; there were also hawks and vultures, those birds
like rocs, waiting as they circled patiently above a dying
cow or paidog, *or the corpse of a Parsee,* wrote Ravi.
There were parakeets, peacocks.

There was the touch of hands: young men walking with
their hands linked: a dancer's hands painted with henna:
the old gardener's hand leading the child Ravi with a
thumb and finger round his wrist. There was the feel of a
girl's wet hair, of the wet clinging cloth of her sari as she
came from bathing. There was pain, of bellies swollen by
starvation: the rack of fever: of bleeding from sores, human and animal: the shriek of pain when a bird seller put
out a bird's eyes to make it sing more beautifully.

As Una read in her clear, schoolgirl voice, Ravi sat

motionless except that once, when at the end of a poem
she paused and turned the page, he lifted his hand and,
with the back of it, rubbed his eyes as if disbelieving; then
he let the hand drop helplessly as she began again. Una
did not notice; she was immersed in the poems. She read
the last one and, in the silence that followed, looked up.
Ravi's face was wet with tears.

"Ravi! Did you mind my reading as much as that?"

"Mind!" Ravi dashed the tears from his eyes. "I am
'*ullu*'—an owl. Silly ullu! But I didn't know they would
sound like that."

"Nor did I." Her voice was husky.

"But . . . do you like them? Like them?" he demanded.

Una had no words to say what she felt; her joy and, yes,
pride, were choking her. Years ago—it was not six months
but it felt like years to Una—she had turned in a Latin
translation for Mrs. Carrington and, "It is seldom," Crackers had said, "seldom that I can say I am completely
satisfied, but I am satisfied now; Una, I congratulate you."

From Crackers that had been supreme praise and Una
reproduced those schoolmistress phrases now. "It is seldom," she said, "that one is completely satisfied, but I am
satisfied now. I congratulate you, Ravi."

He was radiant. "Read them again, I command you. No
one else," he informed the room, "no one but Una is ever
to read my poems. But wait," he told her. "I must give you
a drink, some fruits before you go on. This is more hard
work than maths."

He brought her milk in a tumbler of brass, a slice of
papaya. She read his poems through again, then they began to talk them over. When Una reached her room it was
past two o'clock.

"Ravi Bhattacharya? There are so many Ravis," said
Lady Srinevesan.

"Only one," Una wanted to contradict her but, "I
remember a Ravi," said Mrs. Mehta. "So do you, Amina.
Yes, Ravi Bhattacharya. He was a St. Thomas's College

boy, one of the few worthwhile ones." For Mrs. Mehta to say that was worth having, thought Una. Mrs. Mehta had opened vistas far beyond Lady Srinevesan's amateur poetry evenings. Poets, musicians, artists from over the world came to stay with the Mehtas and, "Sophia is particularly kind to the young," said Lady Srinevesan. Una herself had found that; though she was a failure at the flower-arranging, Mrs. Mehta had singled her out, taken her to concerts, lent her books.

"Perhaps she thinks I'm a charity," said Una, but secretly she was pleased. Mrs. Mehta—*the* Mrs. Mehta—thinks me worthwhile; so does Lady Srinevesan—and not because I am Edward's daughter—they don't take much notice of Hal. Mrs. Porter seems to like me. Bulbul does too. That perhaps was oddest of all. I should have thought Bulbul would have liked Hal, but it was Una Bulbul invited, and Una had made friends with Bulbul's husband Som, "And Som is not easy to please," said Bulbul.

"Ravi, do you think I am very plain?" Una had asked him.

"Plain?" He did not know what she meant and, "Not pretty," said Una.

"You are not pretty," he said certainly, "but you have such a white skin—most white people are not white, they are yellow, yellow-pink. You are white. I like that—and your funny eyes."

"Una is much happier," Hal told Edward.

"Has she been unhappy?"

"Didn't you know *that?*" asked Hal.

"How did you come across this Ravi Bhattacharya?" Lady Srinevesan asked Una now.

"I . . . read some of his poems."

"I didn't know they had been published." The bright birdlike eyes were alert and, Be careful, thought Una; she said aloud, "They were not published. I found them in a St. Thomas's College book," which was not wholly untruthful; Ravi made his notes in his old college exercise books.

"He wrote a poem that I remember," said Mrs. Mehta. "It was about a river. I liked it so much I asked him to write it down and I learnt it.

"Here in the river is life,
life in the river and pearl
life in the wings of the bird, in the boat that is painted with eyes,
in the porpoises, joyously turning, wet and blue in the sun,
and the river is Ganges water with a ritual life of its own . . ."

"Yes," said Una and, almost unconsciously, went on until:

"the finality of the pearl, the gentleness of the flowers,
are evenly swept away; the boat of itself floats down
till the nets are lifted and gone and the fangs of the night
come again,
and the little influence of daylight is lost along the plain,"

she finished it.

"You know it as well as that?"

Una blushed. "I . . . I learn easily by heart."

"You say poetry well," was Mrs. Mehta's only comment, but Una knew Lady Srinevesan was studying her.

"I remember him now," and Lady Srinevesan said, "Ravi Bhattacharya ought to have tried for the Tagore Prize."

"What is that?"

"Sophia, as usual, started it."

"Many a young musician's first concert is given with Mehta money," Edward had told Una. "Many a young poet supported while he is writing his book." Ravi wouldn't take money, thought Una proudly, he works, but she wanted to test out her swan and If, thought Una, if . . .

"The Tagore Prize is awarded every year in memory of Rabindranath Tagore," said Mrs. Mehta, "by the Institute of Fine Arts of which Amina is President."

"It was once for Bengal only," said Mrs. Mehta. "Now I am glad to say it is for all India. It carries a grant of five thousand rupees—and publication, of course—so it is our most important poetry award."

"I couldn't have won the Tagore Prize," said Ravi when Una, excited, talked to him.

"Why not?"

"Because I . . ." then Ravi stopped. "I didn't go in for it."

"Why didn't you? Mrs. Mehta said . . ."

"I don't want prizes," said Ravi. "Not five thousand rupees, nor fifty thousand. I have enough with fifty."

"But you want to be published."

"I shall be in time." No one, thought Una with gratification, could call Ravi expedient, or even adaptable over poetry—with his poems he was like a rock. "Don't be meddlesome," said Ravi and teased, "That's the Westerner."

"Indians want to get on too."

"Only when they are Westernized, like Hem. You can't leave anything alone. 'Get busy, Ravi,' 'Get a typewriter, see how fast you can click,' 'Get stamps, forms, envelopes.'" He was not altogether teasing. "You will get me a secretary next."

"I will be your secretary," said Una.

"Then I shall run away from you, you and your Mehta. Oh, don't be so serious, Una, laugh. . . ." and Una laughed. She could not help it. If anyone, these days, had looked at Una they might have seen a smile that lurked at the corners of her mouth where it had been "So serious and prim," said Hal; but no one looked at Una. They were too busy looking at Hal.

As soon as they heard Edward come up the steps from the car Una knew something was wrong; he did not bid his usual courteous good night to Chinaberry or say any word to Ram Chand waiting to take his briefcase; instead he came into the drawing-room and demanded, "Where is Hal?"

"On the telephone as usual. Why, Edward?" Alix was concerned. His forehead was furrowed with worry, the back of his hair on end. "Read this," said Edward. "Just read it." 'This' was a thick-papered typewritten letter in a long envelope with American airmail stamps.

"What is it?"

"All I worked and fought for, five years of it, to be undone in a few weeks!" Edward was walking up and down. "Una, you had better go away."

"If it concerns Hal, I had better stay. What is it, Edward?" Una had gone to him, taken his arm, but he shook her off.

"A letter from Louise's lawyers. Some busybody," said Edward in wrath, "some infernal busybody gossip-monger has written Louise a cock-and-bull story about Hal leading a rackety life here in Delhi, going to dances, going to clubs and races and having an infatuation with a young raja."

"Vikram," said Una, "but it couldn't be Vikram. Besides, he isn't a raja."

"Of course he isn't."

"And this isn't true." Alix, bewildered, had finished the letter. "It simply isn't true."

"It may not be, but it's enough." Edward was bitter. "As Hal is only twelve it makes succulent reading and gives Louise just the handle she wants. They are questioning my custody." For the first time he turned on Alix. "I trusted you," said Edward, "yet you let Hal have this—this friendship with young Paralampur."

Alix seemed unable to speak and Una came to her rescue. "It was all our friendships and you knew about it, Edward. You knew we went to the Paralampurs." Her calmness seemed to calm him, but why was Alix so cowed? She sat, apparently stricken dumb and raising piteous eyes to Edward. Tell him, Una was urging silently. Tell him it's you Vik is after and put him out of his misery —or would that be worse misery? And then Una knew why Alix was afraid: I might tell him, thought Una. Shall

I? It was a titillating thought but she only repeated "You knew about the Paralampurs."

"I didn't know this . . . this!"

"You couldn't, because it doesn't exist. Vikram likes Hal; she amuses him."

"But she's a little schoolgirl." Alix, with a grateful glance at Una, had recovered her speech. "Hardly of interest to a young man about town like Vikram Singh. Besides, he has far too much respect for you and your position—and his—to abuse it. Una is right. There's no harm in it. This letter is a distortion." But Edward was too shaken to be soothed.

"Have they ever been alone?"

"Only when they were dancing or riding and even then you or I or someone were not far away. For the rest, Una, Sushila, and her friends were always with Hal. The Maharani, or I, or their hostesses were always there. What are you suggesting, Edward?" Alix had risen and now was almost as angry as he. "Do you mean I haven't taken care of Hal?"

"Of course you have." She had given Edward pause. "I apologize, Alix."

"If it would help you to know," Alix was still angry, "the fact is that this silly boy, Vikram, has—notions—about me."

"*You!*" Edward swung round. "How dare he?"

"I told you, he is a silly boy; an empty-headed charmer."

Cheat! thought Una. You cheat—sacrificing Vikram without a word when you and he . . . Cheat! Una knew she had only to say that and, in his shaken state, Edward would probably believe her. "I am disgusted with you, Alix," Una wanted to fling at her. Then why don't I speak? Because . . . I have seen, thought Una, seen deep into you. You are not in love with Edward. How could you be? But you and Vikram are two alike. . . . She could still see the Vikram of that moonlit night in his white and scarlet and gold. How can I blame you, Alix? thought Una and held her peace.

"But who could have written this?" Edward was still holding the letter.

"Mrs. Porter? She is American."

"Gussie wouldn't embroider; besides, she doesn't know Louise. No, it's some highly coloured interfering mischief-maker. Who?" He was walking up and down again. "Who wrote it?"

"I did," said Hal, stepping into the room.

"*You!*"

"Yes. I thought Louise ought to know," said Hal. "She *is* my mother."

"So you wrote this . . . this balderdash?"

"It isn't balderdash. That lawyer person is quite right. I am in love with Vik, head over heels."

"But why make him a raja? Say you are going to dances and races?"

"I thought it would make it more interesting for Louise."

"Interesting! Good God."

"Vik should have been a raja," argued Hal. "We did go to Sushila's fancy dress party; we do dance on the veranda and polo is very like racing."

"God almighty!" said Edward. Una had to laugh but, for the first time in all these weeks, thought Una, he really looked at Hal and, "Since when have you been wearing all those gewgaws?" he demanded. "Go and take them off—at once, do you hear?—and that stuff on your nails. Why the hell, Alix, have you been letting her go about bedizened like this?"

Alix palpably did not think Hal was bedizened. "It's only a few bangles, Edward. Girls grow up more quickly now—besides, it's only in the house. I don't let her go out in them."

Una opened her mouth—and thought it wiser to shut it again.

"Go and take them off," said Edward to Hal, "and wash your face. Wait. Has Vikram Singh ever . . . er . . . kissed you?"

"No," said Hal. "But he will. Unless you're so horribly

mean you won't give me a dowry I shall marry Vikram. Sushila thinks you can probably talk the Maharaja Sahib round."

"Oh, can I? May I remind you that you are only twelve years old?"

"Sushila says plenty of girls are betrothed at twelve. . . . I should have thought you would be glad to get a daughter settled." Hal was near to tears. "Sushila says it's quite a business."

"Miss Sushila seems to be running our affairs. Well, you can tell her," said Edward, "that, as soon as I can arrange things, you are going back to England where Aunt Frederica will find you another and stricter school."

Hal stared at him, burst into sobs, and ran to Alix.

"It's no use crying," said Edward who, as they all knew, could not bear to see Hal in tears. "No use, do you hear?" He was still walking up and down when Ram appeared. "Telephone. Captain Singh, Sahib."

"I'll go," said Hal, the tears miraculously dried.

"No," thundered Edward, but Hal had broken from Alix and gone.

Edward flung up his arms in despair. Then he, too, had to laugh. "But seriously," he said and stopped laughing. "This is serious. Louise lives to make trouble."

"Edward," said Alix. "I have been thinking and I believe you needn't be quite so extreme. Sushila goes back to school at the end of this month. It isn't a 'school for princesses,' as Hal likes to think; Paralampur cannot afford even the girls school at Gwalior and Sushila goes to the Convent in Darjeeling—a humdrum but good convent school. Why not send Hal there for the summer? If you return her to England, it might make these lawyers imagine there is something in this, whereas if she goes with Sushila it will seem natural and you can tell them it is all school-girl romanticism, that you are friends with all the Paralampurs, dispossessed rajas who lead a quiet family life in Delhi, and you send your daughters to the same convent boarding-school. That ought to silence any lawyer."

"It would solve it," said Edward slowly.

"Then have a word with Paralampur himself. I understand arrangements are going on now for Vikram's marriage; it should be easy to agree that he shouldn't visit Darjeeling or the little girls."

"Cara, you think of everything!"

Cara! Edward always seemed embarrassed at using English endearments; he had never called Una or Hal as much as 'dear,' but Una's heart sank as she remembered how he used to call Louise 'bambolina'—little doll. No one could call Alix 'little doll,' but cara . . . He had, too, put his hand on Alix's shoulder—even with Una in the room. "It seems no harm has been done."

"What could have been done?" Alix's eyes were wide, theatrical. "I swear to you, Edward, it would be impossible for either of the girls to be alone with a young man for half an hour without my knowing it."

Una had to look down at her hands to hide her smile.

"Miss Gwithiam," Hem said in the hut, "you ought not to be here."

"Won't you call me Una?" but Hem ignored that.

"Afternoon in the summer house was different. If your father knew about this! Altogether, this is not a suitable friendship for you, nor for Ravi."

"On the contrary, it helps us both."

"Yes, I think you help me," Ravi had admitted. Was it because, except for his mother, he had never had an audience before? Una came to the hut every night, even when they had been late at a concert or cinema or to the Paralampurs and, "You are the most still person I know," Ravi had said.

Una patiently read aloud, stopping when commanded and sitting without moving or speaking while Ravi turned words over in his mind, or tried to find one. She knew better now than to suggest and sat, an image of stillness, her hands folded on her knee, her eyes looking at the desk, the floor, the roof, the courtyard, anywhere but at Ravi—

even a look was an intrusion when he was at work. "The most still person," he said, "and yet you give me power," but, "It must not be," said Hem.

Ravi had slipped out to buy milk and food—the bazaar shops, it seemed, did not close day or night, and Una and Hem were confronting one another.

"Do you always lay down the rule for Ravi?" Una, putting back her hair, looked Hem full in the face so that he noticed her eyes, foreign in their green clearness —so much younger than her voice, thought Hem, and he was less stiff as he said, "No friendship is suitable if it has to be hidden."

"What does Hem do?" Una asked Ravi when he came in.

"I told you—he is in Medical School."

"But isn't he rather old for that?"

"He is very old—two years my senior at College—he is also more than clever. He took a first."

"Please to stop speaking about me if I were mere flies on the wall," said Hem.

"Hemango Sharma is our Principal's, Doctor Babblebosh's, blue-eyed boy," said Ravi.

"How can an Indian be a blue-eyed boy. Dolt!" and Hem and Ravi started to wrestle. Una was surprised to see how strong Hem was but she had to stop them. "Hush! You will have our watchman here."

"Where does Hem live?" she asked Ravi when Hem had gone.

"He lives in an annexe at some house in South Extension. That's a suburb of New Delhi."

"Haven't you ever been there?"

"No. He gave me a key; he wanted me to go there and take showers. Hem is all hygiene, hygiene, hygiene, but I like my lota pouring in the sun—and I don't like the new suburbs. Besides, why should I go and see Hem when he comes so often to me? And why are you asking all these questions? What is Hem to you?" asked Ravi.

"Only that it seems to me," said Una, "that Hem cares a great deal more for you than you for him."

To Ravi this was entirely natural, but, "You are Ravi's best friend?" Una had asked Hem.

"There is nothing best about me."

"I think there is." She said that only to dismiss Hem but, as soon as she had spoken, Una had found that it was true. She liked this dark unbending boy who had none of Ravi's ease and charm, but she knew that Hem would not have made friends with her unless with Edward's approval; would not have masqueraded as a gardener.

"Well, Ravi is Ravi, Hem is Hem," he said when Una spoke of this. "Besides, I am no use at pretending—I haven't the wit. Either I am a gardener or I am not." And you are as honest as the day, thought Una, which was inconvenient when she was in love with secret, scent-filled night.

"Una," said Mrs. Porter, "I feel I should write to your Great Aunt Frederica."

"Aunt Freddie?"

"Yes, I seem to remember she had considerable influence with your father."

"Write to Aunt Freddie—about what?" Una almost said it, but Mrs. Porter forestalled her. "There is a great deal of talk going on. I feel I must write to her about Miss Lamont. It seems Edward is sending Hal away to school; perhaps your Great Aunt could prevail on him to send you back to Cerne."

"Back to Cerne!" Una said it in uttermost dismay.

"I thought that, above all, was what you wanted."

"Long, long ago," but it was not long, not much over a month. "Please, please, don't write," Una wanted to cry. She tried to compose herself and, "I don't think we need worry Aunt Freddie," she said. "With what you have told me, and all I understand now, I think I can manage Miss Lamont."

"My dear, a girl of fifteen is no match for a woman of thirty-five."

"Alix is only thirty."

"I think she is more. Una, be careful," but, "I don't think she heard me," Mrs. Porter told Lady Srinevesan. "She seemed to be sleepwalking."

A ring appeared on Alix's hand. "What is it?" asked Hal. "A topaz?"

"Yes," said Alix.

"Did Edward give it to you?"

"Yes," but, "Haven't you noticed I am wearing it on my right hand?" said Alix.

All the same, there was a new air about her; Alix's eyes were not as watchful now; they seemed confident and, Something has happened, thought Una, something definite? Nor did she believe the ring was a topaz. For two days she hesitated—"I think I didn't want to know," she told Ravi. Then she asked Edward, "You gave Alix that ring?"

"As a matter of fact I did." Over any other question Una would have been amused to see Edward look like a small boy as he used to when scolded by Great Aunt Freddie. "Alix has been very good to us—and I was unjust to her, over Hal."

"It's an uncommonly beautiful ring, Edward. What is it?"

"It's a brown diamond."

"I didn't know there was such a thing. A brown . . ." Words failed Una and Edward looked still more sheepish. "But it must be very, very rare?" she said when she could speak.

"As a matter of fact, quite rare. I did rather gasp when she chose it."

"*She* chose it?" I might have known. Una thought silently, Where is he being taken? What is he allowing to happen to him? Aloud she said, "It must have cost thousands of pounds."

"Not as much as you would think." Edward was hedging. "Alix happens to have a friend who deals in precious stones."

"Has she a friend who deals in concert grand pianos?"

But he had lost his temporary sheepishness and looked so happy that Una could not say it. "I think it looks like Alix," and, challenged perhaps by her silence, he said, "I should like you to know I was proud to put it on her finger."

Then it is serious, probably definite. Something like panic filled Una; she felt sweat on her neck and behind her ears, but she pressed her hands tightly together and nerved herself to say, "I suppose you know that before—us"—she could not bring herself to say 'you'—"Alix lived with Chaman Lal Sethji."

Edward's slap across her cheek tingled and made her eyes smart with tears.

"How dare you repeat gossip," said Edward. "Cruel gossip. Alix has always had to earn her living."

"Since Mr. Tanson ran away." Una held bravely to her point.

"So they have regaled you with that tidbit too, have they? Alix married Tanson as a young, young girl, almost a child. He abandoned her and she hadn't the means to trace him."

"Until you helped her."

"I am lucky enough to have some money and influence. As for Chaman Lal Sethji, he is a young Marwari and up-to-date; he wanted to bring his wife out of purdah and Alix went as companion *to his wife*," said Edward with disdainful emphasis. "Being Alix, she became much more."

"That's what they say." Una was steady in spite of the smart in her cheeks, eyes, and heart.

"She persuaded him to let his daughters go to college—something few Marwari girls have done—and made it possible for his wife to have some share in his social life."

"Why did she leave?" But Edward was too angry to go on.

"Never let me hear such talk again. Of all people I abominate," he said in fury, "it is insinuators."

"I didn't insinuate," said Una. "I said it."

What is happening to Edward, Una thought? Then,

What is happening to me? Edward was quite right to slap me. I said that about Chaman Lal Sethji in malice. "*You* malicious!" She seemed to hear Mrs. Carrington's voice, meet her eyes; they haunted her all the next day. "If you have hurt anyone, acted uncharitably," Crackers had once said, "you will not be comfortable until you have done something to atone. Take the first opportunity to do, for that person, something kind," and, next evening, "Edward, couldn't you get a horse for Alix?" Una asked. He knew without telling she was trying to make amends and smoothed her hair. "She rides so well," said Una.

"It would be much better than a ring," said Hal. "She could ride Snowball when I'm gone, when you have got rid of me"—Hal was mournful—"but she's too big for him and so is Una."

"And it is hard on her being left when we two go off riding together," said Una.

"You want Alix to come too?" Edward was pleased and Una had to say, "Of course."

She was startled by his next words. "As a matter of fact I bought Mouse for Alix."

"Mouse?"

"Yes, but we couldn't find a suitable horse for you and Alix insisted you should have Mouse. She said we could easily find or borrow a mount for her."

"So Alix gave me Mouse," said Una slowly.

"In effect, yes. Typical of her," said Edward. "Completely selfless."

"Is she?" Una burned to say it with Lady Srinevesan's inflection. All the antagonism was back. Alix wouldn't be selfless for nothing—or am I being horrible? Horrible or not, Una's pride and joy in the little mare was gone, as it had gone from her chess set. That was back on its board; Ram had mended it, or had had it mended, so finely that no one knew it had been broken, except Una, Hal, and himself, but Una was certain she would never touch it again—"And never ride Mouse," she vowed.

Ram Chand brought them a card: *Mrs. Jacques Lamont*

with, crossed out on the corner, an address: *Flat 2, Seaview, Rue Suffren, La Ville Blanche, Pondicherry*. The card was old and not clean—it looked dirtier by contrast with Ram's polished silver salver. "Mrs. Lamont? Who can that be?" asked Hal and Una said, "I think it must be Alix's mother."

It was Hal's last afternoon. Though she had protested, stormed, sulked, wept, Edward had stayed adamant and, with Sushila and the rest of the school party, she was travelling to Darjeeling tomorrow. She had been mollified a little by being given a farewell dinner to which the Paralampurs were to come that night, including Vikram, "under my eye," said Edward. At four o'clock Alix had said, "Girls, do you think you could manage if I went out for an hour?"

"Why not?" asked Una.

"I had hoped Mrs. Porter would ask you to go swimming. I rang Lady Srinevesan but she is at a meeting." Alix had had a fright over Hal and was uneasy at leaving them. "But there's something I have—neglected. It's been such a rush getting Hal ready."

"Another ghastly uniform." Hal's gloom came back.

"I have to go or I wouldn't leave you."

It isn't to Vikram, thought Una. You haven't changed or put on scent; in fact your hair is untidy and you have your big white bag, the one you take for shopping. Perhaps this time it's genuine.

"Promise me you won't go out. Stay together in the garden or here in the drawing-room. Hal can practise, Una can work at the writing-table, and . . ." And don't tell Edward, Una finished silently for her.

Alix had scarcely gone when a bicycle rickshaw turned, or tried to turn, in at the gate. It was stopped by the gatemen.

"Alix's *mother?*"

"She say she not go away until she sees Miss-babas." Ram was disapproving.

"Of course she musn't go away. Ask her to come in at

once," Una commanded and she and Hal ran down the steps to meet her.

The rickshaw-man's thin legs had to pedal like flywheels to bring the rickshaw along, its load was so gargantuan. Mrs. Lamont seemed a mountain of fat, made fatter by her cushions. Alix had had made for her mother dresses like her own, plain of silk or cotton in suitably quiet colours but, "I don't like quiet," and, "I don't like plain," Mrs. Lamont had said. "I like loud," and her dress was a remnant of Pondicherry days, "when I went to the races," but, "She must have a dressing-up box," whispered Hal, which happened to be the truth. Mrs. Lamont's dress was of white lace over violet silk and with it she wore a feather boa. "It was *my* mumma's." "Oh, I wish I had that," said Hal. The silk straw of the hat was a little crushed—it, too, had lain in the dressing-up box—it was trimmed with black velvet and had a mammoth crimson rose. The hair was frizzed in an imitation of Alix's auburn—once it must have been the same glorious colour, but the dye had turned it to rusty orange; the face, too, was rouged and powdered into a travesty of Alix—and Alix could be like this when she is old, thought Una.

Mrs. Lamont carried a card-case, a handbag—its white had yellowed—and a red parasol with which she prodded the ricksaw-man. "*Agē! Chelo, chelo! . . .*" As the bicycle stopped at the foot of the steps, waves of Flowers of Heaven engulfed Una and Hal.

"Well, here I am at last," cried Mrs. Lamont. "My God! This is a wonderful place you have here. A palace, m'n? No wonder they would not let me in."

"We are so sorry," said Una. "They didn't know who you were."

"No matter now. No matter." Mrs. Lamont waved the insult aside. "The gatemen tell me my Ally is out." Her eyes lit up. "Come, girls. Let's make hay until she comes back. Take my things." Hal took the card-case and bag while, using the parasol as a stick and with Una's help to heave herself up, Mrs. Lamont struggled from her cushions as the rickshaw-man bent himself double to try and get his breath. "You must show me your house, your rooms that Ally told me she got ready. Ally's room too, and all your dresses, m'n? I want to see everything. My God! Why am I so fat? Ally tells me it is my own fault—I eat too many sweet things, but what is life if you don't eat? Pull, girls, pull."

One on each side, they brought her into the drawing-room where she collapsed on a sofa. "On all of the sofa," Hal said afterwards.

"You must be Una," said Mrs. Lamont. "Ally said you were disagreeable. You don't look disagreeable at all. Come, give me a kiss. And Halcyon . . . why, you are lovely"—it came out unmistakably as luv-el-ee. "My God!" said Mrs. Lamont, looking round. "This is as big as Government House in Pondicherry. What lucky girls you are, m'n?"

"I will order some tea," said Una.

"Tea," declared Mrs. Lamont, "is bad for me. It gives me much indigestion and swelling—you never saw such swelling. Girls, I will take a little Scotch."

Whisky? At four in the afternoon? They were surprised.

"Scotch whisky," but, "Is no whisky," said Dino when he was summoned.

"No whisky?"

"No whisky, Missy-sahib."

Una looked at his obstinate face. "There is plenty. Bring whisky and soda—at once." It was Edward's voice but, as Dino turned to obey, Una added, "Dino, she is old."

If Una had known it, she could have made no stronger appeal; Indian reverence for the old is innate and, for all their disapproval of Alix, the servants saw nothing wrong in Hal sitting on the floor rubbing Mrs. Lamont's feet when she had kicked off the high-heeled satin shoes in which she had tottered up the steps. "Press them a little for me, darling. They swell like boils in my shoes. I should have brought my old Terala, but that lazy owl of a rickshaw-wallah said he wouldn't pull her as well. Besides, Ally would have been shamed. If Terala is so shabby, shouldn't Ally have bought her a new sari when I asked her, m'n?

Ten rupees it would have cost but, my God, it might have been a hundred." Una brought a small table to hold the glass Dino had brought—a single whisky in a tumbler. "No, no soda," said Mrs. Lamont and, "Haven't you a decanter? I didn't think Sir Eddie would measure pegs."

"Bring the decanter, Dino."

"Better no more, Miss-baba."

"Bring the decanter." Grumbling, Dino submitted. Una went to the pantry to fetch cakes, poured a second drink— "The Little Flower will bless you, darling." Una doubted if the Little Flower would, the whisky disappeared so fast. Three times she picked up bag, handkerchief, card-case. "Give me back my card. Now I have found my way to you, why should I not call on other of Ally's high friends, m'n? Why should I be hidden away, I ask you? Ally is a good daughter but, yes, she hides me away. It hurts me very, very much," and Mrs. Lamont wept a little, dabbing at her eyes with the handkerchief which seemed to have been steeped in scent. "Can you believe it, I shouldn't have known your address, or met you dear girls, if Ally had not dropped a letter that Mr. Lobo found."

"Mr. Lobo!" said Una.

"Yes, he is my very good friend, but Ally uses him as if he were a pig. A pig! And so he brought this letter to me. 'Ally does not want me to go there,' I told him, 'and I, Hortense Marie Lamont, do not go where there is not welcome for me.' Girls, am I welcome, m'n?"

"Of course you are," said Hal and Una said, "Why not?"

"Why not, indeed? That is what Mr. Lobo told me. 'Besides,' he said, 'you should go. You should certainly go. You are her mother, and should see what this Sir Eddie is up to. If you make Miss Ally angry . . .'"

"Miss Ally," and Una remembered Alix's 'Moslem form of greeting.'

"'If you make her angry,' Mr. Lobo said, 'all the better.' He said that, but Ally cannot help herself. God help her with that God-awful temper."

"Has she a God-awful temper?" Hal had seen only a

tinge of it in that lesson morning on the veranda. "And Una was the worst," Hal remembered.

"Well, let her be angry." Mrs. Lamont held out her glass. "One little drink more and you shall show me over your place and I will tell you tales about Ally, m'n?" Her eyes were snapping with delight—and the alcohol, thought Una. She had not dreamed Mrs. Lamont could drink so much; the decanter was half empty. "Try and put my shoes on for me, sweetheart," she told Hal, "and we shall go."

Hal was struggling with the swollen feet when there was the sound of a car stopping in the porch, a door slammed, angry steps; then Alix was in the drawing-room and they had a glimpse of the God-awful temper.

"*What* are you doing here?" she towered over her mother.

"I came to see you, Ally." It was a whimper.

"And I had gone to see you. Get up—get up at once. How dare you come when I expressly told you not to. Dressed up like a clown," scolded Alix. "Disgracing yourself and me. It was Lobo set you on to this, that disgusting pig."

"Alix, don't, don't," pleaded Hal, but Alix shook her off.

"She wants to see the house," said Una. "At least, now she is here, Alix, let her see what she wants."

"You keep out of this, both of you." Alix hoisted her mother from the sofa and propelled her to the steps.

"My shoes."

"Never mind your shoes. You can go barefoot."

They saw the old puckered face where tears were making runnels through the powder; the hat, with its nodding rose, was on one side, the boa trailing, as, between silent watching servants, Alix thrust Mrs. Lamont in front of her down the steps and into the Diplomat. Una gathered up the parasol and card-case, Hal followed with bag and shoes. Alix snatched them and threw them into the back seat. "*We* didn't want you to go," said Una loudly to Mrs. Lamont, and Hal, dodging Alix, leaned through the open car door and kissed her.

There was silence between Una and Hal after Mrs. La-

mont and Alix had gone. Hal looked as dazed as if a
balloon had exploded in her face—and it was a balloon,
thought Una. At last, "Did you know Alix could be like
that?" Hal asked.

"Yes, I knew," said Una.

"Poor, poor old lady," Hal covered her eyes with her
hands as if to shut out Mrs. Lamont's face; then she took
her hands down. "I'm glad I'm going away to school. I
don't think I want to stay here any more. Una, why don't
you ask to go back to Cerne?"

It was Mrs. Porter over again and Una said, "I couldn't
possibly go back."

"Then let's talk to Edward and perhaps he will send
Alix away."

"That isn't likely. Besides . . ." and Una contemplated
what it would mean if Alix were sent away. It wouldn't
suit me at all, thought Una. It would be the end of our
freedom, mine and Ravi's. "One must be fair," she said
aloud. "Alix has had a hard time and, remember, she is in
love."

"I'm in love with Vikram but I wouldn't treat Louise
like that—and Vik wouldn't let me."

Neither would Ravi, thought Una. "Nor would Edward," she said, "if he knew. . . ."

"But why doesn't he know? Why doesn't she tell him?"
Deceit always made Hal desperate. "Why? Why? Why?"

"It's difficult for you to understand," and, you are only
twelve, thought Una. You haven't had time to be stained,
she thought with a pang of guilt. She could not say that to
Hal and so used Alix's words: "You have nothing to hide."

"If I had I wouldn't hide it." Hal was fierce and, I'm not
fit to stay in the same room as Hal, thought Una.

"Alix is a juggernaut, a cruel hypocrite juggernaut. Lend
me your handkerchief, Una. I'm going to cry."

"Then Vikram will see you with red eyes and a swollen
nose."

"If Vik is going to marry me, he had better see me as
ugly as possible," and again Una felt respect for her young

sister. She put her arms round Hal and hugged her. Hal broke down. "I loved Alix. I worshipped her."

"I know you did."

"She's a beastly bitch," said Hal, drying her eyes.

"Not altogether." Una was judicious.

"Why does she have to be so mysterious?"

"Because she is afraid"—but Una did not say that; instead, to divert Hal, she began to invent, as only Una could, tales of Alix, Mrs. Lamont, and poor fat Mr. Lobo; how they were part of a circus in which Alix did *haute école,* Mrs. Lamont was the elephant, Mr. Lobo the clown; how Alix was a siren from the sea off Pondicherry, half woman, half mermaid—"That's why she sings so well." She had been spawned by a white whale—"Half brown, you mean," said Hal—who was always followed by a faithful seal which smiled, with no idea how hideous he was. When Alix came back she found them in fits of giggles.

"What are you laughing at?"

"You," and Hal spluttered, "Oh Alix! You told Una your mother was a quiet old lady who live in a Home."

"She could well be in a Home!" That was Una as again they collapsed. The giggles were deadly to Alix. She began to breathe quickly.

"Don't be offended," said Una, wiping her eyes.

"We liked her," said Hal. "She asked us to tiffin and said she would give us a proper prawn curry. What is tiffin?"

"My mother is—not quite right in her mind." Alix was immensely dignified. "Sadly, she is a little mental which is why she dresses up and talks . . . also why I have kept her away."

"Oh Alix! Don't put on so much lace." Una did not care how rude she was. "She isn't mental and we're not fools. We can see what your mother is and why shouldn't she be? Hal is right. We liked her."

"She is much nicer than you." Hal too, did not care now what she said.

"You will have a good tale to tell Edward, won't you?" Alix was white, her nostrils dilated.

"We're not tattlers," said Hal but, "Ask us not to tell him," Una taunted. "Go on. Ask us." Then, suddenly, she did not want to be cruel but serious. "There is someone who ought to tell him," she said gravely to Alix. "You— for your own good," and the stately Alix crumbled and started to cry—as if all the fright had come back, thought Una, watching. She had a strange instinct to go to Alix and steady her; to say, "Hush, hush. It will be all right, if you will trust us and tell the truth." A strange thing to say to my enemy, thought Una.

SEVEN

"Will they send you too away to the hills?" asked Ravi.

Hal had gone. She and Sushila had been handed over at the airport to a large capable escorting nun of whom "Even Aunt Freddie would have approved," said Edward.

"Will they send you away too?"

"I don't think so," said Una. "They still need an excuse for Alix living here. No, I'm still gooseberry."

"Gooseberry? What is gooseberry?"

"Having to be there when you are not wanted," said Una.

"Wouldn't you like to go to Bulbul this evening?" said Edward.

"Mrs. Mehta has asked you to the Music Festival. You should go," Alix urged.

"Lady Srinevesan rang."

"They can't get rid of me enough," said Una. For instance, they had fallen in easily with her not riding Mouse.

"My back aches."

"Then perhaps you had better not ride." To Una it had become a point of honour but they scarcely noticed.

"I thought you loved Mouse," Edward did say on the fourth day. At that tears rose but, "I do, but my back aches," she managed to say.

Alix was sharper. "You are doing this to make me unhappy."

Una opened her eyes wide in pretended innocence. "But it should make you very happy. Haven't you a lovely little horse to ride?"

"You are an abominable girl."

Una shrugged. Her shrug was one of her best weapons. It always nonplussed Edward, silenced Hal; it had even disconcerted Mrs. Carrington, and, pleasingly, it infuriated Alix.

Una drove out with them to the parade ground and walked while they rode. She treasured these solitary early mornings; nobody spoke to her, though now and again she had to step back out of a horse's way as she wandered in the fresh coolness under tasselled trees that dappled the paths with their shadows. Sometimes she climbed up to the ruined monument on the Knoll; it was used now as an art school and the students' attempts at sculpture were set up among the bushes; and she watched the President's carriage horses, groomed to satin, trotting heavily round their open school. She saw a mongoose: hares: often peacocks with their hens: and heard partridges, the cock calling "Pateela, Pateela." At this time Ravi was busy with the morning watering, or swishing the lawns with those long bamboo canes or gathering flowers for the house before they wilted in the sun, but Una could say his poems, murmuring them as she walked.

"Good-bye our afternoons," Ravi had said when Hal went. She had been a useful decoy, taking most of Alix's attention and it had become difficult "and dangerous," said Hem, for Una to slip away in the day. "But we must keep our nights," said Una. "The poems are so important." Ravi was to try for the Tagore Prize. Una had persuaded him and Hem reluctantly agreed. "I suppose you are safe by now." Ravi said, "It would be imbecile not to." "But I wish," Hem said, worried, "you would tell Sir Edward of this work." Hem knew that almost every night Una and Ravi worked at the poems, Una in her guise of stillness and patience. "I wish you would tell."

"We shall," said Ravi. "Listen, I shall tell you how it will be. It will be in the hall called Vigyan Bhawan, when everyone is gathered there to hear the poets who have been chosen finalists for the Tagore Prize. We, the ten poets who will read, will be on the rostrum. Una and Sir Edward—you must prevail on him to come, Una—will be in front seats, of course. Then, when I am called, I shall announce"—and Ravi became dramatic—" 'I, Ravi Bhattacharya, write in Hindi and English both. I will read the Hindi but, since I am not well versed in pronouncing English, I call on my friend, Miss Una Gwithiam, to be so kind as to come and read with me'—and you, to your father's amazement, the amazement of everyone in the hall, will rise and ascend the platform. We shall sit as we are sitting now and read my poems turn and turn about, and your father will see without explanation."

"He *will* be astonished," said Una.

"Indeed! and more! When I win the prize, he will be filled with admiration and we shall cast ourselves at his feet."

"Not in the Vigyan Bhawan."

"It would be best. He can hardly refuse forgiveness when so many are there. Besides, he will be so proud that you, his daughter, know me."

"Ullu," said Hem.

"And remember, it is not for long," said Ravi. "Only till the end of April—already we are in March. The poems for the Tagore have to be in by the fifteenth April which is Baisakhi—our New Year," said Ravi, "when everything new will begin, including my fame."

"You have to write the poems first," Hem reminded him.

"Almost they are written."

"And they have to get among the chosen ten."

"They will."

"Then still they have to win."

"They will."

"Una, you at least should have some sense."

"I think it is sense to believe in the poems," said Una, "and to believe in Ravi." The words were said in Una's sensible clear schoolgirl voice, but Hem, looking at her eyes, saw the worship in them. Abruptly he got up. "Good night."

"This isn't your writing."

Una, coming into her room, stopped abruptly. Alix was at her desk turning over her notebooks. "It isn't your writing." Alix's eyes were wide with alarm. "It isn't, is it?"

"No."

"Why?"

"Because it's somebody else's," said Una.

"My God! What have you been doing?" Alix was aghast.

"And what are you doing, looking in my private books?"

"It's my business to look."

"Then why didn't you look before?" It was a good taunt. "That is what Edward will ask, isn't it? It really has been simple of you, Alix, to believe all this time that I could have worked those problems by myself—*all this time,*" said Una with an emphasis Alix could not miss. Alix sprang up, pushing back the desk chair so violently she overturned it.

"I'm going to shake you like the little rat you are."

"I shouldn't," said Una, though it took all her courage to stand still. Alix, she thought, is physically frightening. "Ram Chand and Monbad are just outside," she said. "I have only to call them." That had its effect; Alix picked up the chair and put it in its place though her fingers were shaking as Una remembered they had trembled that day on the veranda. She is trying to control herself, thought Una and, "Wouldn't it be better if we made a pact?" she asked.

"A pact?"

"Yes."

"What sort of pact could be made between us two?"

"That I won't monitor you, if you don't monitor me."

"What do you mean—'monitor'?"

"Split on one another." Una was brief.

"You are asking the impossible. I am your governess."

"Ostensibly. Do you think I don't know about you and Edward, Mrs. Tanson?"

At that Alix's head came up. "I am no longer Mrs. Tanson. I am sorry to disappoint your spite, but my divorce is through. I am waiting for the decree to be made absolute."

"And Edward has already given you a ring," but Alix did not answer that. "Una, I appealed to you once," she said. "I appeal to you again." She looked down at the book. "You must tell me what you have been doing."

"As you can see, mathematics."

"With whom? I must know."

"You can't know because I am not going to tell you." Then Una relented—"Or was it that I saw Alix was too frightened to accept the pact," she told Ravi, "and right to be frightened. If Edward had made that fuss over Hal she knew he would be worse over me," but, "Don't worry," said Una to Alix. "Presently, when it is time, I shall tell Edward all about this. You see, it is to be a surprise for him."

"A surprise for Edward!" The relief was so palpable Una almost laughed. Then Alix drew back. "You're not lying to me?"

"*I* don't tell lies,"—"Only withhold truth," Una should have added and the next moment, "Are you *sure* Edward would approve?" asked Alix.

"I know Edward," but Una felt a rap of conscience—or sense? Would, or could, Edward approve of the sham figure in her bed? Of her being, usually alone, with a young man in his room until the early hours of the morning? "It's only while we make the surprise," she said.

"We?" Alix pounced.

"I'm with someone," and, before Alix could speak, "If it eases your mind," said Una, "the—the person is a friend of Lady Srinevesan's and Mrs. Mehta's."

"Ah! You met there." Again the wave of relief. "I wondered how you could possibly . . ." Una did not contradict her.

"This is bad news." Hem was worried. "What if Madam Alix questions Lady Srinevesan?" said Hem.

"She can't without exposing herself. Alix has the wit to see that."

"She has plenty of wits," said Ravi.

"Up to a point," said Hem. "After that she is stupid, stupid enough to use force. Una, I find myself wishing you were afraid of Miss Lamont."

"She is strong," Una admitted.

"Yes, she could put Sir Edward in her pocket," Ravi laughed.

"Which is where he is," said Hem, "and that is not a laughing matter. It disturbs me."

"It needn't," said Una. "She wouldn't dare do anything to me."

"It still disturbs me. Ravi . . . Una. Tell Sir Edward now."

"I can't tell," said Una. "I gave my promise and she and I have made a pact. Don't worry, I can manage Alix," but, as she said it, Una remembered Mrs. Porter's "My dear, a girl of fifteen is no match for a woman of thirty-five."

"Edward, do you think I could go to the American International School? Go now?"

Una had cornered him in his dressing-room before dinner. "The International School?" Edward bent to the looking-glass to tie the bow of his tie. "It would hardly be worthwhile. On the first of May they close for the hot-weather vacation; besides, they only prepare you for college there, not at all the same as A levels or your work at Cerne."

"So you think I have been doing the same work as at Cerne?" Una was glad her face was out of the range of the looking-glass so that Edward could not see the scorn with which she asked that silent question. "The British School then?" She asked that aloud.

"But why, Una? I thought you and Alix had come to terms."

"We have." But . . . there was something Alix had said in their encounter. "While we are talking, Una, there is one thing—nothing to do with any pact—but a thing you are doing, deliberately—and I have had enough of it. You will start riding Mouse."

"My back still aches," said Una.

Alix had laughed.

"If you are—friends now, why?" Edward was asking.

"Without Hal, we are together too much. Please, Edward."

"It wouldn't be worthwhile," he said again. "Besides, I have—plans. The Conference is due to have a month's recess and I thought I would take you away."

"Take me away! Not *now!*" In her dismay Una said it, but Edward was too intent to hear.

"Yes. I mean to show you something of India before the weather gets too hot."

"Do you mean Alix and you and me—or you and me?" Una had to say it though, "Jealous?" Edward would probably say but, as if he were the old Edward of percipience, he went on, "I mean just the two of us, you and I. I thought we would go south then up to Darjeeling and visit Hal, catch a glimpse of the snows—if we are lucky, Everest—and you can't leave India without seeing Fatephur Sikri and Agra and the Taj. Wouldn't that be worth waiting for?" asked Edward.

"What will you do with Alix?"

"Oh, Alix will be all right," and Edward hummed as he picked up the white lawn handkerchief Ram had carefully folded for him.

"You sound happy," said Una.

"I am." Edward paused. "Do you know, Una, I don't think I have been happier in my life."

It was still cool enough to have breakfast in the pavilion. "This is one of the garden's enchanted spots," said Edward. It certainly was enchanting; bougainvillaea filtered light over the table and the sun reflections from the pool made patterns with flower shadows on the pillars. The fountain splashed in the pool where goldfish spread their fins; the garden smelled of roses and stocks, "though those are almost over," said Edward.

Next to him Alix poured coffee, the gold-brown stone on her finger caught a flash of the sun—Una was sure he would have liked to kiss that finger only she, Una, was opposite him. This difficult daughter, he was probably thinking—then she forgot him and Alix; her eyes were fixed dreamily on the lower garden and, in her mind, she was saying over a line from the poem she and Ravi had been working on last night. Her lips must have moved because Edward smiled at her across the table. "Una is saying her *japa*."

"What—is a japa?" She was jerked into awareness.

"A mystical phrase or holy word that is given you by your guru—your teacher."

My guru, thought Una and smiled. What a handsome young guru.

"No one else must know your japa," said Edward. "You say it over and over again until you are detached, almost in a state of trance."

"Am I in a trance? Perhaps I am."

"It releases your spirit. Have you a japa?" asked Edward.

"You said no one else must know." Edward laughed and, "That turned the tables on you," said Alix.

Peace. Laughter. Sun. Love. There were not many moments like this and Edward shut his eyes.

"Sir Edward, may I speak with you, please?"

Edward opened his eyes. "Mr. Sen!"

The Indian clerk, piloted by Aziz, had come to the garden pavilion. "I am interrupting, but . . ."

"Not at all." Edward was courteous as ever. "Alix. Una. This is Mr. Sen, who is in charge of our United Nations Stores—in fact, acts as our quartermaster. He does all our buying and distributing. I expect he has come to make his monthly check. Sit down and have a cup of coffee, Sen."

"No, thank you, sir. It is just . . . I should like to speak with you."

"Well, speak." Edward was jovial.

"Priv-ate-ly. It is a private matter." Mr. Sen was not jovial. "Please to come, sir. It is better private."

Private or no, in half an hour it was all over the compound—even Una knew. "Twelve, thirteen bottles of whisky missing from the stores," whispered Ram Chand. "Dino is to go."

"Dino! It can't be true."

"Is not true." Ram was more than sad, he was smouldering. "Baba"—he called Una that only when he was deeply moved. "It is not true."

"Here, Scotch whisky costs a hundred and fifty rupees a bottle, more than eleven pounds of your money," said Mr. Sen. Edward had been through a bad half-hour. "Din Mahomed has been here more than twenty years," said Mr. Sen, "and, in all that time, there has not been half a kilo of sugar or one cigar for which he has not accounted."

Dino stood in front of them. A small man, his brown face seemed to have turned ashen grey; the fierce upturned moustaches, of which he was so proud, worked as he swallowed; his eyes, brown and trusting as a dog's, were fixed on Edward. Dino had always trusted; now he was afraid.

"Have you ever taken whisky?" Edward asked it straight.

"Never, Sahib."

"Have you ever lent your keys to anyone? To Aziz? Karim? Christopher?" It would have been easy for Dino to say that he had, but the answer came back, "Never, Sahib."

"Then who else, Dino, but you could have taken it?"

Dino was silent though the moustaches worked, the forehead and his eyes seemed to swell, and Mr. Sen, sweating with embarrassment as he spoke, said, "Please ask yourself, Sir Edward, who it is you have brought newly into this house and to whom you have given your keys."

Edward stared and a stain of anger came into his face. "You mean Miss Lamont. Dino, ask the Miss-sahib to come here at once.

"Alix, a dozen or more bottles of whisky are missing from the service stores. Do you know anything about them?"

"I? What could I know?" asked Alix. "I give out your stores from your own cupboard. Dino has a list and, in front of me, takes what is needed from the other cupboard and I enter the things in the ledger."

"The cupboards are never left unlocked?"

"Not by me," said Alix. "But . . . and I have to confess this, Edward, two bottles have been missing from yours." Dino gave a gasp; his skin grew greyer.

"Why didn't you tell me?"

"I thought I might have miscounted. One must be scrupulously fair, but I have been watching." She looked from Edward to Mr. Sen, from him to Dino.

"No bottles are missing from the stores of the Sahib," said Dino.

"And a dozen and one from U.N. cupboard are gone." Mr. Sen's voice was high.

"Am I supposed to have taken them?" Alix asked. "Really, Mr. Sen! What would I do with thirteen bottles of Scotch?"

"Exactly," said Edward but Mr. Sen was steady.

"Dino has been here twenty years, Miss Lamont."

"With every opportunity for thieving. If you enquire, Mr. Sen," Alix chose her words deliberately, "I think you will find Din Mahomed Mansur is a strangely rich man. I am sorry," said Alix. "But this is a conspiracy and I refuse to be your stool pigeon."

Fortunately, for everyone it was a busy day; a Scandinavian delegation had arrived for consultation on the Conference and Edward was "drowned in work," as he complained that evening. His nerves had been rasped by

Dino in the morning, even more at the office; "I work in a continual din; radios blaring in the street, children, scolding women, hawkers, car horns, even cats; it all comes up even to the third floor; add telephones, quarrels, arguments, endless comings and goings—and now there is all this extra entertaining." As soon as he came in Edward had to dress and go to a reception at the President's Mansion, then dinner at the High Commissioner's. "I shall come straight home after dinner," he told Alix, but even then three of the Swedish delegates were staying in the house and needed to be entertained.

Una had spent the day out of the way with Bulbul. "I cannot understand what you, a clever, serious girl, can see in Bulbul," Lady Srinevesan said often, but Bulbul was a relief from the effort and tenseness of Shiraz Road, especially now when Una was missing Hal. The house felt empty and, today, ominously quiet, perhaps because Alix was not singing as she worked. "I think everyone needs, now and then, to be silly," Una could have said and, too, she found Bulbul reassuring. She might be frivolous, empty-headed, but there was a binding love between her and her young husband, and Som was serious and responsible enough to please even Lady Srinevesan.

Alix had taken Una to the Misra house and, as she drove the Diplomat out of the porch, Una had seen Chinaberry spit on the ground behind them. She was suddenly nervous. "Alix, what will you do all today?"

"Plenty," said Alix. "I must go and see my mother and don't forget Edward has this huge dinner tomorrow: at least sixty men and Aziz is not used to taking command. I have to go to Connaught Place to pick up the petit fours and sweets that Christopher wants: go to the Cottage Industries and order extra flowers. Borrow long tablecloths and chafing dishes for the buffet, count the cutlery and crockery we hire, make sure it is clean."

"You will be alone in the house."

"Why not?"

Una did not answer but suggested, "Why not see your mother, do the shopping, and come back and have lunch with Bulbul?" It was on the tip of Una's tongue to say, "Bulbul doesn't mind you," but she bit it back. "Come to Bulbul's."

Alix patted her knee. "Una, I can't believe it but are you trying to protect me?"

"Chinaberry spat," said Una.

Alix was unmoved. "The servants hate me—naturally."

"Why?"

"Because I get in the way of their graft—am wise to them." Then Alix turned her attention from the wheel for a second and looked into Una face. "It isn't my fault, you know," said Alix, "that Dino has had to go."

In that moment of inattention a phut-phut taxi had hurtled onto the roundabout across their road and Alix had to brake so sharply that she almost sent Una through the windscreen.

"*Ankh nahin hai?*" screamed Alix through the window. "Haven't you any eyes? *Suar ka bacha!* Child of a pig!" The taxi driver screamed back but Una had heard something else; the jerk had sent Alix's bag across the back seat, the white bag she used for shopping and surely a large one for the elegant Alix? It flew across the seat as if it were heavy, two shapes were still rolling inside its soft leather and Una heard an unmistakable chink. She knelt up in her seat, stretched back, and felt through the white calfskin.

"What are you doing?" Alix, driving on, let the car swerve dangerously. "What are you doing with my bag?"

"Looking." Una slid back into her seat and, as they pulled up at Bulbul's, "I have looked," said Una.

She stayed with Bulbul until the last possible minute; they went to the Ashoka Hotel to swim, ate the lunch that Bulbul cooked as casually as she did everything else, lay on her bed listening to gramophone records, talking and laughing. Som came in and Una had to say reluctantly, "I must go home." "Stay to dinner—you can help me cook," said Bulbul and Som agreed, "Yes, stay. Telephone Shiraz Road and tell them. We will go for a walk after dinner in the Lodi Gardens, then drop you home." Una thankfully stayed, but Alix must have heard Som's car because she came out of the drawing-room to catch Una on her way to her room.

"Did you have a good time?"

"Yes, thank you."

"I am waiting for Edward. He will be tired."

"Yes. I had better go to bed."

"By the way," Alix tried to speak casually. "I shall tell Edward the whole truth—when it suits me."

"So shall I," said Una, but, "Miss-baba, please, will you come?" said Ram Chand, and Una found a deputation waiting in her room. Aziz, already wearing Dino's official kulla of dark blue and gold, his long blue turban, had been busy with dinner for the Swedish guests, giving his orders to Karim and a new young table-servant, but here were grouped the older servants, Ram Chand and Monbad, Christopher, Ganesh, the sweeper, Mitchu. "Miss-baba," said Ram as their spokesman. "We want that you go to the Sahib and speak for Dino."

"Because you can speak," said Monbad.

"Because I think you know," added Ram.

"Scotch whisky sell in the bazaar at a hundred and fifty rupees one bottle." Christopher, the Goanese, shook with anger. "But Dino, he never take as much as one peg. She take," said Christopher.

"But how do you know?" Una hedged.

"Baba, we were here when the old lady came." Ram Chand spoke like an authoritative grandfather. "Miss Lamont not steal for selling; she take to her mother in that hotel. Chinaberry know that hotel."

"Then why don't you make this deputation, all of you, to the Sahib?"

"Sahib not wish to believe us," said Christopher and Ram Chand said, "You, Miss-baba, must tell."

It was not only the servants. That night, when Edward had come in and, after half an hour's talk, Una had heard him and the guests go to their rooms and, peeping through her door curtains, knew that Alix had gone to Edward, she slipped down to the hut and found Hem with Ravi. They, too, were waiting for her and Hem spoke with a sternness equal to that of Ram Chand. "But how can I tell Edward?" asked Una. "I gave Alix my word."

"Oh, you English!" said Hem. "You will break a faithful old servant but not a schoolgirl promise!"

"Dino has gone. . . ."

"And I suppose you will tell us Sir Edward was generous not to call the police," sneered Ravi.

"He is generous. He doesn't dream. . . ." Una was torn almost to tears. "Oh, don't let such ugliness into our hut."

"It is in our hut," and Una, though she would have liked to hide her eyes, saw Dino's face when he had met her on his way from the storeroom; saw the servants—and the trustful way they looked at me, thought Una and, "What am I to do? What am I to do?" she whispered.

"Be coward? That will improve things very much." It was the first time Ravi had taunted her but he was justifiably angry.

Hem came to her; for once, he laid his hand on her shoulder and, he understands the misery and fear, thought Una. "We are sorry, Una, but, in his present state, there is only one person whom Sir Edward might believe, and that is you."

Una looked up into his face, so plain and dark compared to Ravi's, yet it gave her courage. "No. There are two persons," she said.

"Who else?" asked Ravi. "Who?"

"Alix," and Una said, though she quailed, "Somehow, tomorrow, I must make Alix tell."

"You may be a clever little person," said Alix, "but don't forget we made a pact."

It was not a good time to beard Alix; the day had been full of troubles, a whirlwind of them, and Una had to admit she saw clearly why Edward needed an Alix, admit too that for this role Alix was superb.

In a household of, mainly, hostile servants—and those on her side were weak-kneed—Alix brought order out of chaos. Sixty or so men of all nations were coming for dinner and there was no Dino in whose accustomed hands everything could be left. Aziz lost his arrogance and wept, saying he could not possibly manage; the new young table-servant, pale with apprehension, wanted to leave; worst of all, Christopher, though he had extra cooks, turned surly. It was no wonder: one of the ministers had accepted and now his secretary brought a list of the dishes he preferred to eat. "I think that's rude," said Una, but to Alix it was perfectly acceptable. There were to be two long buffets, vegetarian and nonvegetarian; the most orthodox Hindus would accept the invitation but not eat—nor would Ravi's family, thought Una—but there were still many for whom dishes must not have the least taint of meat, not even cheese or eggs, not even spices. There would be Moslem guests for whom nothing must be made with alcohol or wine, "or pig," sighed Alix, "which cuts out bacon. The same for Jews and for them, too, no shellfish, and their meat must be kosher."

"Then how?" marvelled Una.

"Oh, there will be something for everyone," said Alix, "and they will pick and choose their way." Christopher's chicken curry with curd was famous, his prawn koftas and fish cooked in coconut milk, but there had to be western food as well.

"I didn't know people gave parties like this—in private houses—except places like Buckingham Palace," said Una.

"You must have seen them in Teheran and Geneva," but Una shook her head.

"In Teheran we were too young, and Edward was only a counsellor; in Geneva when he was lent to the United Nations we lived quietly."

"Well, don't you think it's exciting?"

"I think it's dreadful."

"*Dreadful?* This?"

"Yes, a party like this in a country where people are so poor they can't exist. If Edward were in his right mind, he would think so too."

"Edward is very much in his right mind. You will see,"

said Alix. "He will go from strength to strength, but he needs help—background help."

Una saw that clearly. When Christopher's hollandaise sauce curdled, he threw the saucepan at Paul, his mate. Alix went in, anointed and bandaged Paul who was burnt —"only slightly, thank heaven"—diverted Christopher by praising his elaborate spun-sugar toffee baskets, to be filled with ice cream, and made the hollandaise herself, smooth and delicate enough to satisfy even Christopher. "Hollandaise *is* temperamental," she said, salving his pride.

Through the Paralampurs she borrowed waiters from the Gymkhana Club, helped Aziz and Karim set out the tables with damask cloths, plates piled ready, rows of polished spirit-lamp chafing-dishes that would be lit under the bubbling dishes, while Una, with the new young 'third' inspected glasses, counted out cutlery, filled salt cellars and pepper pots. The veranda was made into a bar under Ram Chand, Monbad, and two borrowed barmen and, everywhere, Ganesh set bowls of flowers, white roses, and smilax for the buffet tables, more roses for the drawing-room while Ravi silently rebanked the steps with pot after pot of fresh carnations. Though Una passed him and he passed Una, he did not give her a glance and she felt his condemnation.

A lorry brought ice, another chairs. Alix went twice to the confectioners in Connaught Place and to the Gymkhana Club, but by four o'clock it was all in train, even the kitchen was working quietly, "And don't forget," Alix told Christopher, "I shall be here in the background if you need me. The dinner is for the sahibs." That was a clever remark; they were not working for Alix but for the honour of the house. They don't like her but they must honour her, thought Una.

It was not, though, done without toll. Una should have been warned by the glistening of Alix's skin, the way she walked too quickly, the control in her voice, and the frown getting deeper between her eyebrows. She had already been wrought up yesterday and, "Alix is getting into a mood," Hal would have said. "Grown people have moods," Hal said. "When I'm grown up, I shan't!" which, Una thought, was probably true. Hal would have concentrated on the party and danced her way through it, but Una could not wait. Perhaps it was the contemptuous thump with which Ravi had set down the pots of carnations and, when Alix went to wash, Una followed her. "I must speak to you, Alix."

"Now?"

"Yes."

"You can't wait until tomorrow?"

"No, I can't." Una was trembling. "Nor can anybody." The servants could have, easily, but Una was thinking of Ravi's taunt, "Be coward." "Nor can anybody."

"What anybodies?"

"Everyone in this house but Edward."

"Edward!" Alix's eyes seemed to widen, then narrow. "Una, keep out of this."

"I can't, because I know now what they know. You know too."

It was then that Alix had said, "You may be a clever little person, but we have made a pact. I thought English schoolgirls were honourable."

"I'm not going to break our pact. You are."

They both saw the door curtain move. "You see," cried Alix. "We're in a nest of eavesdropping and spies." She wrenched the curtain aside, but no one was there—yet it might have been Ram: Monbad: Mitchu: and, "We can't talk here," said Alix. "For God's sake, let's get out of this house. Wait." Una heard her go to the telephone in the hall but could not follow the rapid Hindi. Then Alix came back. "The horses haven't been exercised today. With all this tamasha I forgot them. It won't hurt now to leave the house for an hour. We're going to ride."

"But . . ."

"There is no other way we can be by ourselves; you started this, Una, so you will finish it. Put on your jodhpurs and shoes."

Una's nerves gave way. "I don't want to come."

"You are coming," and, "Go and get dressed exactly as I said." It was almost a scream.

Alix drove the small Diplomat to the parade ground as if it were a racing car and skidded to a stop in a cloud of dust. "Get out."

Maxim and Mouse, with their syces, were waiting in the shade of the trees as they had waited that long-ago morning. Long ago? Only five weeks, thought Una. Has all this happened in five weeks? Gulab, Mouse's groom, led the little mare out with a smile. "Miss-baba ride Mouse again? Good. Very good."

Una was tempted to tell Alix, "I'll ride Mouse if you will stay here on the parade ground," where other horses were being cantered, trotted, and schooled, where the Pony Club children, so innocent and resolute, were having a lesson in the school, but Alix, on Maxim, was already turning towards the rides under the trees. "Come along."

"I won't ride," said Una.

"Walk then. Bring Mouse," and, savagely, thought Una, Alix commanded Gulab to let the reins go. "Ullu! Owl! Fool! Give them to the Miss-baba."

Gulab hesitated. "Miss-baba perhaps like first in the school," and, mistaking Una's whiteness, "Mouse good pony, Baba. No give trouble. Good Mouse."

Una was able to answer his troubled expression with a smile. "I'm not afraid, Gulab," but, as she walked Mouse along the ride after Alix, her knees felt weak. All at once she knew, too, what she had been missing; she longed to mount the brilliant little mare she had loved so much, and chase after Alix, perhaps race her. A good canter might exorcise us both, she thought, get rid of this evil. It was, too, the sensible thing to do; she might even run away from Alix—Mouse, nimble and small, could turn and twist so that the mare was quicker than Maxim, but some ram-rod stiffness in Una would not let her give in, and, her head high, she walked and led Mouse.

They came to a place behind the ruined tower art school, and the sculptures set up in the grass. Here the trees were thicker so that, more hidden from the rides, there was an open space of red earth patched with dried-up grass. Alix dismounted, led Maxim to a tree and came to Una. "Well? What is this ultimatum?"

Facing one another, Una saw desperation in Alix; her face was still the colour of ivory, but old ivory, yellowed from its cream glow; her hair lay in dark rings on her forehead; she was riding bareheaded though Edward had forbidden any riding without hard hats. Sweat glistened on her neck. "Well?"

"It's just that . . . Alix, you must confess." It was jerked out.

"Confess? To a priest? Or to Edward?" Alix was mocking.

"To Edward." Una made herself be steady.

"And what do I have to confess?"

"First . . . about the whisky . . . for your mother."

"Ah! At least you do me justice that it was for her, not to sell in the bazaar." For a moment Alix broke. "Una, you have seen her and know she has to have it. How else can I get it? Indian whisky's so bad and you know the price of Scotch. Edward gives me everything but he only pays me a little."

"Ask him for more."

"Ask Edward *for money*. That shows," said Alix, "how little you understand how things are between him and me."

"That's beside the point. The point is you must tell him."

"I have told you I will—but in my own time. I must wait."

"Dino can't wait." The words were inexorable but Una still felt that pity. "I do understand, but tell him, Alix; tell everything from the beginning, about your troubles and your mother and Mr. Lobo. Tell him why Chaman Lal Sethji sent you away. The real reason."

"You have ferreted that out? Ferreted everything." At each name Alix had grown more taut and, it seemed, taller.

She was breathing hard but Una was so much in earnest she had forgotten all caution.

"Tell him how it was you took the whisky—and why. Tell him even about the maths. Edward is a loving person. You can trust him, Alix. Tell."

"What if I won't?"

"There isn't a won't. You must."

"Must is a word you can't use to me," said Alix, "but I can use it to you. You must remember you are only a little schoolgirl who should keep her nose out of other people's business. I am here to teach you and I am going to teach you a lesson—in obedience. We shall begin with quite a little thing. Get on Mouse."

"I have told you—I won't."

"Get on Mouse." Alix was advancing, her thonged whip in her hand.

"Alix! You wouldn't hit me?" Una could not believe it. She backed close against Mouse.

"If you don't get on Mouse, I shall whip you."

"Don't be absurd." Sheer disbelief gave Una courage and she said disdainfully, "You can't whip someone of fifteen."

"I can whip an impertinent child. Get on Mouse."

No answer.

"Very well then," said Alix. "Stand away from that pony," but Una did not move.

"Una, I warn you once more; get on Mouse. If you don't I shall hit you."

"Hit me then," said Una and turned her back.

The plaited lash of the whip whistled in the air and fell across her shoulders. It cut and stung but Una shrugged.

The shrug was enough—or too much; the lash fell again with all Alix's strength behind it as Mouse snorted and plunged and pulled.

"You are insolent," Alix panted. "Insolent from the first moment when I held out my hand to you. I held out my hand but you wouldn't take it. You worked against me, ferreted, gossiped, and I tell you why—because you are jealous. You don't want Edward to be happy, let him have love. So . . ." For the third time the whip whistled as the lash came down, but Mouse plunged so heavily that she pulled Una over onto the grass and Alix caught herself up with a sob. Then, her voice shaking, she said, "Now will you get on Mouse?"

"I—can't," said Una on the ground.

There was the sound of hooves and someone came cantering through the trees. It was Mrs. Porter; stocky and heavy, her khaki breeches and shirt did not become her, but her seat was firm, her hands skilled as she guided her mare towards them but, under an old-fashioned felt hat, she looked flushed and anxious. "I found your syces . . . agitated." There was a pause before the word: "I'm afraid I don't speak Hindi and could only understand 'Miss-baba.' Has there been an accident, Miss Lamont?" Then she saw Una on the ground.

"Why, Una!" and she was off her mare and came leading it, looking from Alix's ravaged face to Una.

"Mouse got away," said Alix. "Una came off and was dragged. I just managed to catch them on Maxim." The way Alix shook was convincing.

"Is she badly hurt?"

"Winded—that's all." The words came in gasps from Una. "Not h-hurt."

"Hold Mary Jane." Mrs. Porter gave her mare to Alix and bent over Una. "There's blood on her shirt."

"Back's . . . a bit . . . scratched."

"I must get her to the car." Alix tied the mare beside Maxim.

"If we helped you up," Mrs. Porter's hands went over Una's legs and thighs, "I think there's nothing broken. If we helped you up, could you sit on your pony? We will lead you."

"Not . . . Mouse." Una shuddered.

"Get on Mary Jane then. She's dead quiet. Come—I will help you. Come. Slowly. Gently. That's a brave girl," Mrs. Porter coaxed.

In the dusk Edward came running down the steps to

meet the car. "He couldn't have heard already," said Alix mystified, but the agitation was not for Una. "Where have you been? For God's sake, Alix! Things are frantic. I telephoned but you were out. Out—and we have no Dino and you have the keys. Five of the Danish delegates have turned out to be women so I have had to ask as many of our Indian guests as I could get hold of to bring their wives." Then, as he saw Alix come round to Una's door to help her out, "What has happened?"

"Una's had a fall," which was truer than the explanation given to Mrs. Porter. A fall, yes, and a shameful fall.

"God! How badly is she hurt?"

"She's not hurt, just a bit stunned and scratched."

"I will carry her in."

"I—can—walk," said Una.

"She can, Edward." To him Alix was blessedly calm. "Here are the keys—let Aziz take out more stores: cigarettes and cigars: drink: chocolates. I will get Una to bed. She will be all right if she lies down."

"You are sure. She looks terribly white."

"If I'm not sure, I will get Doctor Gottlieb. How many more guests?"

"At least fifteen . . . How can we . . . ?"

"Don't worry. There is plenty of food, but it's nearly seven o'clock. You had better go and change. Tell Aziz and Christopher I will be with them in ten minutes. Come, Una."

"I can—go—by myself," said Una, "and I'm not stunned. I'm stiff, that's all." Painfully she negotiated the steps. "You had better go yourself and see to things," she told Alix but Alix followed her to her room.

"I must look at your back."

At that Una flamed. "If you dare to touch me I shall telephone Mrs. Porter. Go away. Leave me alone."

Edward was hovering in the hall. "Is she all right? Hell! Wouldn't it happen now!"

"She has had a fright—and I expect she will be stiff and sore in the morning. Now don't fuss," said Alix. "Everything is in hand. Chinaberry has gone for extra plates, cutlery, and glasses and I will see they are clean. Christopher is quite happy. Do as I told you—go and change."

"Alix." He caught her hand. "I want you to put on that white and gold dress. You will receive with me."

"But Edward . . ."

"Do as I say. I won't have you kept in the background any longer—and wear your ring."

"It . . . will be an open declaration."

"All the better," said Edward. "It's only a matter of weeks before everybody knows."

"Your Indian friends won't like it."

"Then they can go home," and Edward went to his room.

"Telephone, Sahib."

"Not now, Ram. I am dressing."

"Is Porter Mem-sahib, Sahib. I tell her Sahib is dressing, but she say is urgent. She must speak."

"Hell!" said Edward, and went to the telephone.

"Edward? Edward, I want you to come straight over here—now!"

"Now! My dear Gussie! In a few minutes I shall have something like seventy guests."

"I don't care if you have three hundred."

"Can't it keep till the morning?"

"No. I must see you. You must come."

"I can give you five minutes, Gussie, no more," said Edward in the Porter's embassy house.

"Then I'll be brief. You know Miss Lamont and Una were riding? So was I. When I drove up to the parade ground I found your syces—not in agitation, indignation, Edward."

"Well? I know Una had a fall. She said she was all right, but Alix—Miss Lamont—has put her to bed."

"But what did she do first?"

"What do you mean?"

"I don't know," said Mrs. Porter. "That is the trouble."

She was concerned and distressed. "Miss Lamont said Una came off and was dragged. If Una had been dragged, she would have been dusty, her clothes torn, her arms grazed. She was clean."

"What do you think happened then?"

"That is your duty to find out." Mrs. Porter put her hand on his. "Edward, wake up. Una was—cowering. There was blood coming through her shirt."

Edward put Mrs. Porter's hand away and rose, looking at her with distaste. "You are trying to insinuate that Alix —*Alix* did something to Una? Alix, who is so devoted? I know Delhi is noted for backbiting, for intrigue and gossip, but I never imagined this—and I may as well tell you, Gussie—you are speaking of my future wife."

"You are going to *marry* Miss Lamont?"

"As soon as her decree is made absolute."

"Miss Lamont—after Kate!" It was Mrs. Porter's outspoken honesty. "Forgive me, Edward, I shouldn't have said that."

"You certainly should not."

"I had forgotten there was Hal's mother," but there was still genuine sorrow in Mrs. Porter's voice as she made a plea. "In that case, let me have Una to look after until she can go back to Cerne."

"Thank you." Edward was icy. "But Una is perfectly well looked after where she is. Good night."

When it was dark, Una crept out.

She had not been able to face changing and now her shirt was stuck to her back; the welts were stiffening. Ram Chand had brought her a tray of food, but when he looked at her had clucked, taken it away, and come back with a glass of hot sugared milk. I suppose I am in a state of shock, thought Una. Why else was she shivering on this warm night?

"Baba, go to bed."

"Yes, Ram, I will," but Una had sat on in her chair, listening to the noise and voices until, with darkness, the guests left the garden and veranda and went indoors; then she put the familiar dummy in her bed and stole out. From her veranda she could see, through lighted windows and doors, a crowd of people, hear the chatter and laughter, and clatter of knives and forks on plates. She had a glimpse of Alix, regal in a white dress brocaded with gold—as if the gold were stars for Alix triumphant. Una caught her breath in a sob. She smelled cigar smoke; two men came towards her, pacing the lawn, talking as they smoked; she shrank back behind a pillar.

She had meant to go to the hut but found herself too shamed and sick at heart. When the men turned, pacing back, she made her painful way to the summer house, helping herself by the pillars of the pavilion and the fountain; its small sound seemed loud in the garden's quietness. She sank down on the wooden chair and dropped her head on her arms on the table; the movement hurt so much that she gave a cry.

It was only one cry but Ravi heard it. He had come out to set the deeva light by his tulsi bush. "I did not want to do it before with all those people in the garden." Arrested, straining to see in the dark, his eyes caught a pale shape in the summer house and, holding the deeva in his hand, shielding its flame with the other, he came swiftly across the lawn. "Una!"

"Ssh! There are guests, men, still in the garden."

"I thought you were at the party," Ravi whispered.

She shook her head, no longer able to speak. Ravi, holding the tiny light, looked from her face to the rigid lines of her body, her clenched hands—she had clenched them in an effort not to cry out again. He took in the fact that she was still in riding clothes, that her hair was tumbled, and her shirt . . . Ravi held the light closer, put out a finger and touched the shirt. "What are those marks?"

"I—think—they are blood."

"Did *she* do this?" Ravi was stunned as Una nodded. "Where's your father?"

"At—the party. They all are."

"Is he blind?"

"He didn't—think to look."

"Didn't think to look! She did this to you!"

"Because I faced her. I tried to make her tell, but I

couldn't do it, Ravi. I failed you all. I went to her room and she . . ." A sob was forced out.

"Took you out and beat you up—I knew you had gone riding—*beat* you. How?"

"With—her whip. It had a—a lash."

"And no one has been to you . . . seen to you." Ravi gritted his teeth.

"She tried. I wouldn't let her. Now, they are all at the party. Ravi, you must help me," but Ravi shrank.

"I might hurt you. I am not used . . ."

"Please." But, "Go back to your room," said Ravi. "I will fetch Hem. He will know what to do."

"Hé Bhagwan!" said Ravi when he saw Una's back. "My God!"

Hem had come bringing with him a small bag. "So you are a real big doctor," Ravi would have teased him at any other time. They were in Una's bathroom where she had bent over the basin while, with warm water and cotton wool, Hem had competently soaked away the blood-dried shirt and the welts were revealed in three angrily red and swelled stripes across Una's back. *"Hé Bhagwan!* We'll go to her room tonight, Hem and I, and thrash her!" Though the party was noisy they spoke in whispers but even in a whisper Ravi was savage. "Thrash her!"

"That *would* be wise," said Hem. "Put the police on your trail again and what good would it do Una?"

"Police? . . ." Even in her dizziness and pain, Una had heard.

"I have not told you but I have been in prison," Hem said quickly.

"You said 'your trail,' not 'my trail' to Ravi."

Hem did not answer, only said, "Hold tightly to the basin. I am putting on a spray. It will be cold and may sting."

It did. Una swayed so that Ravi had to hold her while Hem covered the stripes with gauze. "Now—see if you can find her nightclothes," he told Ravi.

"Clean pyjamas—in the chest," Una was able to gasp. Hem was washing her face and hands and neck.

Ravi brought only the pyjama top. "Never mind," said Hem and to Ravi, "Go outside." Then Hem undressed Una, taking off her shoes, drawing off the jodhpurs, her socks and underclothes; with careful gentleness he put her arms into the jacket, drew it round her and buttoned it with his skilled dark fingers, then, lifting her, carried her to bed. The dummy he dumped in the wardrobe. Then he gave her a pill and a drink of water. "You will be more comfortable now, I think."

"Hem." Una caught his hand. "I tried to do it—for poor Dino—but she was too strong, Hem. I tried to make her tell."

"She will tell," said Hem, "because she will have to."

"Hem, thank you for . . ." Una choked.

"No more now," said Hem. "I will come again tomorrow night and give it another dressing—if Ravi thinks it safe. You will be very stiff and sore but let us hope there is no infection. Try not to disturb the pads; do not go to bathe; also, keep out of the sun." Gently he unloosed her clasp. "Now go to sleep."

He found Ravi outside on the veranda, waiting in the shadows. "I think she will sleep now. I have given a sedative," then, as Ravi moved, "Don't go in, bhai. Let her sleep."

> *"Nini, baba, nini*
> *Makhan, roti, chini*
> *Khana, pina, hogaya*
> *Mera baba sogaya*
> *Nini, baba, nini."**

"Is that—one of your poems?" whispered Una.

"It is a lullaby, older than the hills. My ayah used to sing me to sleep with it every night."

"When you were a little boy?" Hem's pill was working and Una was growing sleepy. "When you were a little boy."

*Translation: Sleep, baby, sleep / Butter, bread and sugar. / Eating, drinking is over. / My baby will sleep. / Sleep, baby, sleep. 'Nini' is baby-talk for sleep, like *'fait dodo'* in French.

"Not even a boy; in my babyhood."

"Nini, baba, nini . . ." It was as soft as the hum of a spinning wheel, drowsy as the rhythmical pattings—only the patting was by a young man's hand which perhaps was why Una did not quite fall asleep. Ravi was almost tranced by his own song when suddenly he stopped, raised his head to listen.

Neither of them had noticed that the house had quietened, that the party must be over, the last guest gone. Two people—Alix and Edward by their voices—were coming down the veranda. Swift as a snake, Ravi slid under the bed and pressed himself against the wall. Una, suddenly wide awake, lay still, her eyes ostensibly closed, but watching the doorway under her lids.

"I told you so. She's asleep." Edward's voice was loud and slurred.

"We ought just to look . . ."

"N-nonsense. C-come, Cara." His arm drew Alix away. "Come to bed."

After they had gone Una broke into uncontrollable weeping.

There were no more nursery words. "Una—not to cry. Not to cry." Ravi was lying on the bed beside her, kissing her. The tears, salt and warm on his lips, moving him to a passion of pity. "Do not cry. They are not worth it, let them go."

"Ravi. Ravi."

"You are so little I'm afraid to touch you."

"Touch me. Come closer."

"But . . . if I hurt your back."

"Let it hurt. Oh Ravi! Come close."

When Una woke she was sure it was a dream, but, turning her head, she smelled a faint scent on her pillow, Ravi's coconut oil.

EIGHT

It was spring: the strange warm Indian spring when the imported English winter flowers had wilted and the tropical ones came into their own—hibiscus, oleander, poinsettia; a mauve creeper had flowered on the walls—Edward called it petrea—and the brilliant orange-fingered 'golden shower' bignonia spread far across the porch, while the bougainvillaea were like fountains; in every road, park, garden were flowering trees; the scarlet flowers of simul trees whose pods would swell and burst into cotton. "The flowers must be picked or the cotton blows everywhere," said Ravi: there were soft fuzzes on the rain trees: coral trees in bloom while the kadumbo was covered in honey-scented balls of yellow fluff. "You will see the kadumbo in paintings of Krishna playing his flute. I think," said Ravi, "he is playing his flute for us."

Ravi's desk was deserted; the poems, as with Una's mathematics, forgotten but, in the early hours, Una had to steal back from the hut to the house, often only just before dawn, and each time it was harder to go. Am I like the girls in the Keats poem, "creeping thin with lust"? If so, she did not care; and I'm not thin; indeed, she thought her whole body was altering. "Id-eal-ly, if you were Indian, your silly little breasts should be soft and swelling as the pods on the simul trees," Ravi teased her.

"They are getting bigger, I'm sure they are."

"Maybe, but you haven't elephant hips. Now elephants are really very graceful."

"And I'm not?"

"You! You are a stick-insect-trinakit." Then he grew serious. "If I love you too much, I shall kiss you away."

Hem, as he had promised, arrived for nightly dressings but after a week he ceased to come; the back was healing —And love with Ravi does not hurt me any more. Indeed, in these days Una had an easy laxness she had never felt before. Thoughts of Dino, thoughts of Alix, had receded into the background. There was nothing she could do about either. She had tried, tried with all she knew, and been defeated, but there was something restful in being defeated; unlike her little doll, Una was content to be knocked down. One day, she knew, she would have to get up again but for the present all she wanted was to lie out in the garden, in the shade, as Hem had advised, and let the warm quiet hours slip by.

"Una, the Maharani is on the telephone."

"Tell her I'm not well."

"Mrs. Mehta wants to know if you would like to go to the Kuchipudi Dance Drama."

"It's a lovely name, but no."

"Lady Srinevesan says she will call for you and take you to the Kabul Exhibition."

"No thank you."

Bulbul, when—out of curiosity, thought Una—she arrived uninvited to the house, asked "What has happened to you?"

"I had a fall."

"It wasn't on your head, was it?"

"No. Why?"

"You are different."

Everything was different. "Mrs. Porter hasn't rung. I was sure she would. Why hasn't she?" Alix was so timorous one might have thought it was she who had had the beating, not Una.

"Need we tell her today?" Alix had asked Edward that morning after the dinner. "Must it be today?"

"Do you want her to hear it from Bulbul Misra—or Lady Srinevesan, or Gussie Porter?"

"Then let me tell her."

"It's better from me," said Edward. "You can write to Hal but Una and I have always been close."

"I know." But, Alix had thought in terror, suppose . . . She felt her neck and hands cold while Edward beside her was debonair, cheerfully unaware. "Just plain happy and proud," he would have said, but perhaps he began to sense something because he had bent forward and taken her hands. "What are you afraid of, cara? Una is not easy, I know, but once you are part of the family she will give you her loyalty—and no one is more loyal than Una," but when Una had come hobbling along the veranda, Alix had had to put the coffee-pot down; her hand was visibly trembling. It trembled more when Una had let herself down into her chair with a grimace of pain. She was, as Hem had said she would be, so sore that when she moved the pain from the welts made her set her lips, not to cry out; and there was another soreness: Ravi had been carried away—I carried him away. I, insignificant Una, whom Vikram treats as a child, I can give Ravi joy, and she had bestowed such a radiant smile on Alix that Alix was transfixed.

"Una," said Edward. "We want to tell you ourselves before you hear it from anyone else—I expect it's all over Delhi even now. Alix and I are going to be married."

"Married!" Una had known it, of course, but now it had come she felt a curious shock—and dismay. "No, Edward, no," she wanted to cry. "Don't do it. Please, please don't. There isn't one person who loves you or even knows you —even Hal—who won't be sad, and there are things that, if you knew—you will have to know them—will be tragedy for you. I can tell you . . ." Then why don't I tell you? Sitting there, Una knew with certainty she had power to stop this, to save Edward. Then why not? Alix's eyes were fixed imploringly on her but it was not Alix that stopped her; as if she had been given new eyes, Una was seeing Alix as Edward saw her, not only as beauty but a cornucopia—the word seemed to suit Alix—of sweetness, warmth, comfort, things he had lacked perhaps all his life; strongest of all in him was desire and how can I, now, be the one to spoil that for Edward—after last night, thought Una? Perhaps, she thought, I'm the only person in Delhi who can understand this, and aloud she only said, "Could I have some coffee while you tell me about it?"

"Alix got her decree . . ."

"The day you gave her the ring," Una finished for Edward.

"You guessed. . . ."

"That wasn't difficult. We don't have many diamonds in our family, do we? Certainly not brown ones." Una said that for Alix; it meant, "Don't think I am won over. I'm not."

"The term of waiting has been shortened, owing to my circumstances," Edward went on. Then, almost pleadingly, he asked, "Couldn't you be a little happy for us?"

How can I? Don't you know *anything?* thought Una. Yesterday, it would have driven me to despair; now it hardly seems to concern me—or does it? A thought had struck her that made her start; the Tagore Prize, and she asked anxiously, "When will it be?"

"In about five weeks—the fourteenth of April is the first possible day. Next day is Baisakhi, the Hindu New Year, a new beginning. We will have a honeymoon later when I go back to Japan."

"That will suit me very well." Incautiously Una had said it aloud and, "What do you mean?" asked Edward.

"I mean you won't be needing me any more. I—I can go back to school," and, to head them off, Una said, "You see, I know quite well why I am here. It was inconvenient at the time but I bear no malice."

"Of all the chits!" exploded Edward, but for a moment Una beamed at him. "I hope you will be wonderfully happy." The beam faded. "Oh Edward, don't, don't . . ." she could have cried, but he had got up. "I must go to the office. Good-bye, you impertinence." He bent and kissed her, then kissed Alix, who rose. "I will see you to the car." She doesn't want to be alone with me, thought Una but, when Alix came back, Una was drinking coffee, calmly eating buttered toast. "I must say," said Alix, "that, as Edward says, you are loyal."

"To him, not to you," and Una said, "Alix, from now on you will do exactly as I wish."

"I can't do that."

"You would like me to show Edward my back? Tell him about those bottles?" and Alix was silent. "For one thing we shall give up the pretence of any schooling," said Una.

"Very well."

"You will take Mouse for yourself."

"Very well."

"And keep out of my way."

"Very well."

Una ordered Alix, "When you go to see your mother or if you ride,"—Alix now sometimes rode with Edward in the early mornings or, if he were too busy, exercised both horses in the evening—"you can drop me in the Lodi Gardens. The rides are dusty now. I should rather walk there."

From the first time she had walked in them, Una had loved the Lodi Gardens; to her they were the most beautiful of Delhi's flowering parks. She had been there with Edward, Alix, and Hal, now and again with Bulbul and Som—they liked to walk out after dinner. "I must have some air," said Som. Paths of paved stone wound under the trees, beside water channels that opened into a pool with a fountain; the breeze scattered spray from its tall plume far across the lawns.

Even birds seemed peaceful there, water birds quietly wading, parakeets and mynah birds quiet too, and the peacocks kept their trains folded, the feathers glinting green and bronze while their necks shone unbelievably blue as they pecked and scratched. It seemed a unique place for a friendly—or loving—stroll and, "You can fetch me on your way back," Una told Alix.

"But walk there alone?"

"Heavens! Haven't I been in the country nearly two months?" And Una was not alone. There were hidden walks and oases of bougainvillaea so dense "that no one could see us there, or hear if we talk quietly," said Ravi.

"You are running a risk if you want to keep this secret," said Hem.

"You can keep watch for us."

"Thank you, bloody no!" Hem was often disagreeable these days.

"A pity when we are so agreeable," said Ravi.

All the same, Hem kept watch for them. "Una . . . Ravi . . . The Misras' sweeper is walking their poodle," and Una, alone, would stroll past, though she did not lose sight of Ravi waiting among the trees. When it was safe, Hem would tactfully disappear while she walked with Ravi; and into Una's mind would come a picture of herself in class at Cerne, serious pale Una in Cerne's green jersey and pleated skirt, and here was this nymph, her thin dress blown against her bare legs by the breeze as she walked hand in hand with Ravi in his deep-blue kurta and fine white muslin salwar-pyjama. It seemed to make it more real that they should walk here in daylight. "One day we can walk as we please. No one need keep watch," said Una, yet she wondered if ever again she would know a spring like this—spring not only in the world, thought Una, spring in me.

There were some pale trees with delicate mauve and white blossom. "Kachnar," said Ravi, "but you must never plant one near a house or it will steal its soul." Una treasured the things Ravi told her about trees and flowers, though she knew he had learnt them from Ganesh or that old gardener of the Bhattacharyas'. "Never pick flowers in the evening. It is cruel to pick them then—they are going to sleep. I wish you were a flower," said Ravi. "I would be cruel and pick you and keep you all night."

"Oh Ravi! Ravi!"

Then, suddenly, one evening when she and Alix had just come in, Edward arrived home early. "The Conference is closed. We leave tomorrow," he said.

"What a tour!" said Lady Srinevesan. "You lucky, lucky child. I wonder how many Indian girls have ever been asked to go on a tour like that," but, "You must remember," said Una, "When you rank as a child, you are ordered, not asked."

Lady Srinevesan's eyebrows lifted. She made no comment but said afterwards, "I took a mental note of that."

"Imagine!" said Edward in the Kailasa temple at Ellora, "imagine those stone-cutters digging out this enormous cave from above on the hill, working their sculptures from top to bottom with those primitive chisels." The temple was wider than the Parthenon, half again as high, and even accustomed Edward was awed. Over the gateway, the architect had left an inscription: 'How did I do it?'

"You don't care in the least how he did it, do you?" said Edward and, though Una could feel his disappointment in her, she could not answer "I do."

"Ellora? Ajanta?" Una had asked it almost stupidly. "What are they?"

"You know quite well." Edward was impatient. "Temples, enormous temple caves, carved straight out of the rock, Buddhist in Ajanta but some at Ellora are Hindu or Jain. Then I thought we would fly down to Cochin," he had said. "It's a fascinating old port, and drive up to the Wild Life Sanctuary; the charm of the sanctuary there is that you go by water, not by car, and can glide close up to the animals. I shall have to pause in Madras for work but you shall see some dancing. We shall make a detour back through Delhi to reach Agra on the twenty-ninth because that is the night of the full moon. Then Fatephur Sikri. Then we'll stay at Varanasi—Benares—on our way to Darjeeling and Hal. Which will you find more important," Edward bantered, "Hal or the Himalayan snows?"

"But this will take a long time," Una had stammered. "Won't Alix . . . ?"

"Alix wants a little time for herself. It seems this Home her mother is in hasn't proved satisfactory."

"No." Una could imagine that.

"She wants to settle her in another and better one in Naini Tal. I can help her there—then I'm giving her a fortnight in Paris. She will need more clothes."

Una's lips twitched. *A poor and starving country. I am here to organize relief . . . clothes must be inexpensive.* "I hope you have given Alix plenty of money," said Una; Edward did not take in the satire.

The time in Delhi; those six short weeks, had passed in a flash; this month was endless. Ajanta: Ellora: Cochin: Periyar: Madras. They were simply steps in a pilgrimage of exile to Una. "Would you like to go home?" asked Edward in despair.

"No." Una could not help wincing as she said it; Ravi had given her a snub. "It's a good thing you are going," he had said, cheerfully matter of fact. "It will give me a chance to finish my poems. They have to be in on the twenty-fifth."

"Finish them without me?" As soon as she made that protest Una knew it was stupid. "*I* am the one who writes the poems," said Ravi.

She had comforted herself by sending postcards to Hem. *Hemango Sharma, All India Institute of Medical Sciences.* "Though really they were for Ravi," she was to tell him.

"I knew that, but you might have had the sense to send them in envelopes. I was thought to have a rich tourist woman infatuated with me."

"Oh!" That thought had not occurred to Una. "Did it send you up or down?" she asked.

"On the money side, up; in regard, down."

"Poor Hem!" but she did not sound contrite, merely amused.

So they came to Agra. "I wanted to be here for this

moon, Budh Purnima," said Edward. "It's said to be especially bright at this auspicious time, perhaps a promise moon. That would be fitting for me, I hope," and Una silently added, "For Ravi and me, too."

Edward would not let her visit the Taj Mahal until he was sure the moon had risen above the dome and, as Una came out on the entrance steps, it seemed to her as if the whole Taj soared into the sky. The cool lustre of minarets and dome seemed as high above the garden, where water channels glimmered and there were walks, lawns, cypress trees, as the Emperor and his queen had, in their lives, been above even the noblest of men and women. "Well, Taj means a crown," said Edward.

Youths and girls, Indian and Western, were gathered on the entrance steps, silently looking; even their transistors were hushed; it was only the middle-aged who talked, they and the storytellers above on the wide terrace, a man or a boy, standing in a ring of pilgram villagers or people from the bazaar and skilfully telling, "in couplets," said Edward, listening, "and wonderfully embroidered," the love story of Shah Jahan and Mumtaz Mahal, Pearl of the Palace, and how she had followed him in every battle he fought until she died bearing his fourteenth child, and how he had loved only her until death laid him beside her, under this marvel of beauty he had built for her. Inside, under the dome, visitors thronged reverently round two inlaid marble oblongs, guarded by fretted marble screens, but the real tombs were in a vault far below; no touch or footstep must profane the royal sleep and, "Edward," said Una suddenly, "I'm glad I came."

"And I'm glad to hear it," said Edward. "I was beginning to feel I was dragging you round in chains."

Standing on the terrace, they listened to the storytellers; they had had to take off their shoes and to their bare feet the marble was still hot from the day's sun, yet a breeze blew from the Jumna River. "There is always this breeze like a whisper in the Taj," said Edward, and then, from under the dome, came the sound of a flute, silver-toned, unearthly, enticing yet pure as all flutes are, perfectly

fitting the night. Edward and Una stood entranced together, as they had been long long ago, thought Una and,
in this moment, Edward did not mind that it was the cool
small hand of his daughter he held, not Alix's; nor Una
that it was Edward's, not Ravi's.

The sound stopped as if the flute had been snapped in
half. There were cries and angry shouts, a rumpus under
the dome, and then they saw two of the guards roughly
impelling a young man across the terrace; he still clutched
the flute, silver in the moonlight, but his long dark hair
was tousled over his face as he struggled, the muslin of his
white shirt torn, his feet stamped upon, as he was jostled
and hustled down the steps. "But why? Why?" cried Una.
"He was only playing. Edward, stop them! Why don't you
stop them?"

"I expect," said Edward, "they think he profaned the
tomb."

"But he didn't. It was beautiful. He meant it as a trib-
ute. I'm sure he did," and it was when the flute song
broke that everything broke, thought Una afterwards;
until then there had been no uglinesses. When they came
out of the Taj Mahal gatehouse Una heard a monkey-
man's drum.

Edward had stayed to talk to the entrance guards,
perhaps about the young musician, and she walked across
the courtyard to where, among a group of men, the rough
nasal voice was chanting or singing as a pair of monkeys
capered in the moonlight. There were the same guffaws
and shouts of laughter she had heard round the monkey-
man in Shiraz Road but this time, she was close enough
to see why. The little female, when she was jerked, obedi-
ently held up her tattered quilted skirt, but her eyes
were darting backwards and forwards looking for nuts or
fruits; only when the male approached her did she squeal
into life, trying to escape from her string, but the man
held her. The male monkey circled round her gibbering,
walking on the backs of his hands as front paws. The
laughter rose as he closed in. As Una stood unwillingly
mesmerized, there were cries of *"Shabash! Shabash!"* as

he sprang, *"Shabash!"* and, "Come away at *once!"* said
Edward behind her.

On the way back to the hotel, "Those monkeys seemed
to be acting a play," said Una; she tried to make her voice
normal which was not easy; she still seemed to hear the
monkey sobs. "What would it have been?"

"Something from the Ramayana, or the story of Radha
and Krishna."

"Krishna?" Krishna of the flute, the tender love play?
"Oh no!" cried Una. Now the flute seemed to be sobbing
too.

"They often take one of the great epics for this kind of
travesty." He spoke lightly but Una forced herself to ask,
"Edward, why did the female monkey squeal so when
. . . when the male took her?"

Edward's "Never mind," was short and Una hardly
knew what made her go on.

"I want to know. Should it have hurt so much?"

"Perhaps he was a big monkey."

"He was—and she was small. She screamed but he
went on. It was . . ." Una shuddered.

"The man probably gave the male monkey bhang or
some such drug to make him randy. Now, that's enough,"
said Edward.

It was enough. Una was sick.

"But why let it upset you so?" asked Edward when,
spent and white, she was in bed.

"They were . . . perjuring themselves." Una could
explain no more than that.

"Who?"

"The people and the monkeys."

Edward became matter of fact. "Monkeys can't perjure
themselves. They can't speak, you silly-billy."

"That's just why." Once more Una retched. "They were
helpless." They did not know what a show they were
making of themselves, helplessly twirled on the end of a
string, beaten and drugged into making their pitiful tricks

that started automatically at the signal of that nasal chant, the beating drum.

"The man ought to be prosecuted," said Edward.

Next morning Una was sick again.

"I think Agra must be the smelliest city in the world," she said as they drove through the streets.

"Wait until you smell Calcutta," said Edward. "There . . ." but, "Don't," said Una hastily. "Open the car door."

"I told you when you came," said Edward when the retching was over. "You mustn't be squeamish if you live in India."

"I know but I keep heaving," and, too, Agra was hot. Una felt curiously limp and when, on their last day, there was a city electricity cut that meant no air conditioning, no lifts, toiling up to the fourth floor, she felt as if her legs were paper, and when she reached her room her face was green-white, her hair soaked with sweat. Am I going to be ill? Yet, next morning, driving out at dawn to Fatephur Sikri, she was radiantly well.

They were so early that, in the deserted sandstone city, there were only workmen collecting tools and baskets. Una and Edward picnicked among the bougainvillaea, sitting on the steps of Jodh Bai's pavilioned palace. "She was Akbar's chief Hindu wife," said Edward, "daughter of the Raja of Amber who gave her to the Emperor as a truce. Akbar had a chief Moslem wife as well and a Christian one; he is said to have had five thousand women in his harem."

"Not as many as Krishna," said Una.

"But these were historically real, and not one of them," said Edward, "could give the Emperor a son until he came here to this hill where a saint called Salim was living as a hermit. Salim told Akbar he would have three sons and, sure enough, Queen Jodh Bai produced Prince Salim, later called Jahanghir, and soon there were two other little princes. Come, I will take you to the saint's mosque and tomb, if you have finished eating all the oranges."

"It's only oranges I want to eat," said Una. "Oranges and oranges."

In honour of the saint, Akbar had moved his capital to this beautiful small city he had built on the hill; it had kept an air of completeness though it was given over to tourists, workmen, "and peacocks," said Una; the peacocks were so tame they came near for pieces of bread and fruit, gazing at Una and Edward from bright eyes oblonged with white, "as if they were decorated," said Una. They walked proudly, lifting their feet, but when they scratched the dust for insects the feet became usefully mundane. There were still elephants lines, camel stables, and stables for more than a hundred horses—their sandstone tethering rings were still on the wall. Edward showed Una the Treasury: the Mint: the small palace of Birbal, Akbar's astrologer and favourite storyteller: the audience halls, a debating chamber "for men of every religion," and, for lighter moments, the parchesi pavement where the 'pieces' were dancing girls, and the open pavilion where Akbar took his exercise playing blindman's bluff with the court ladies. Una bought a postcard for Hal, and for Hem one of the tower the Emperor built for his especial elephant. In those days punishment was often being trampled to death by an elephant, but this elephant was so wise he could sense innocence and, "If he refused to trample, the victim was freed," said Edward, and "This is the pigeon post office. Akbar used to send his messages by pigeon post." What a perfect way to send a letter to Ravi!

The saint's, Salim's, tomb broke the harmony; its marble and tessellated mother-of-pearl seemed ostentatious against the plain sandstone of the city walls and courtyards, yet the tomb was hallowed. As Una and Edward crossed the courtyard, a young couple came out, she in an old-fashioned *burkha* whose lattice showed her eyes; Una saw she had been weeping and, on the four-poster bed that incongruously stood inside the tomb, there were fresh rose petals on the satin counterpane and rupee notes. "They have been to pray for a child," said the custodian. An old man sitting cross-legged on the floor in the corner whispered a rhythm of prayer. "Some rich family are paying him to sit here and pray all day."

"For a child?"

"Of course," said the custodian. "All who come to the tomb of Salim very much wanting a child."

Edward went out into the courtyard but Una hardly knew he had gone; rooted by the bed, a quiver was running through her as if she had been touched by the saint's finger. Slowly she emptied her purse of its notes onto the counterpane. She wished she had some rose leaves.

"Not sick again!" said Hal.

They were in the Rest House at Tiger Hill where they had ridden out from Darjeeling in the early hours to see— "If we are lucky enough," Edward had said—"the dawn flowering of the snows." They had been lucky; the far-off ranges had turned from an outline of white-streaked grey to a flush of pink, then to deep rose and gold that ran along the range. It had been a shock to Una to find how high her eyes had to look up in the sky to see the great peaks; Kanchenjungha towered, but Everest looked almost small because of the distance across the cloud-filled land. It had been an awesome moment but afterwards the smell of sausages being cooked in the Rest House for breakfast, worse, the smell of the pony-men's rancid butter tea had undone her; she had to fly to a bathroom that smelled too of dank whitewash and phenyl and begin her daily retching over a tin basin.

She and Edward had found Hal 'blooming,' as Edward wrote to Alix.

Yes, like a flower, prettier than ever and not changed too much. She loves the nuns and the nuns love her. The Paralampurs are coming up so she may, after all, see Vikram, but under impeccable circumstances.

Hal had been allowed to come out of school and stay the night with Edward and Una.

She can't do that with Paralampur; it is only allowed with parents,

but, for this short while, Una and Hal were back in their old camaraderie. Una was longing to talk to someone of her bubbling excitement and who as safe and loyal as Hal?

"Not sick again!"

"Naturally."

Back from Fatephur Sikri, Una, sitting cross-legged like the old Moslem in Salim's tomb, but on her bed, had tried to calculate: "If only I were tidy-minded, and marked my diary as some girls do," she reproached herself, "or kept a journal like Hal. I wasn't swimming the day the American pool opened and Mrs. Porter told me about Alix. Yes, I am a fortnight late," she calculated. "A fortnight is nothing. But you are unpredictable," she told herself, "you have always been—after Ravi you could expect your rhythms to be upset," and, "You are feeling so limp because you are on the verge of having a period," Una tried to tell Una, yet again had come that quiver and she had lifted her pyjama jacket, looked at her breasts and was sure they were bigger. I am altered all over, she thought. But—could this have happened so quickly? Yes, she had heard of girls—women, she corrected—who, after the very first time. . . . It could be, Una decided. Could . . . If only there were someone, anyone experienced I could ask; immediately she thought of Hem, but she would not see Hem for perhaps another ten days—in her impatience that seemed interminable. Then, in Darjeeling, every morning had come that daily retching. "What do you mean—'naturally'?" asked Hal.

"I am going to have a baby," Una said firmly.

"A b—!" Hal could say no more; for the first time in Hal's life, Una saw all colour drained away from her face; her kitten eyes were wide with terror, her mouth dropped open. Then, "You—can't—mean—it," whispered Hal.

"I do."

"It isn't possible."

"Why not? I am the same as other girls."

"But . . . you don't know anybody. No one has ever even looked at you."

"That's what you think. It may surprise you to know that while you were hero-worshipping Vikram Singh, I have had a lover."

"But . . . you *couldn't* have."

"I ought to know."

"Holy Smoke!" said Hal. She looked at her sister with, Una noticed, a new respect. "Who is it? Una, who? Who could it be?"

"Never you mind," said Una. "I'm not going to tell you now, but everything is . . . different."

It was. Different again. Quite, quite different, thought Una, from those days of dreaming in the garden. These snows, this little town of Darjeeling, often above the clouds, with its merry Tibetan-faced people, its ghosts of British India shown in the hundreds of red-roofed villas where the English in power had always spent the hot weather, the Mall, the Club, old Government House, all for Una, faded into insignificance beside the spell of this that had been placed inside her—Ravi's child.

"But—what are you going to do?" asked Hal.

"Wait. That's what all mothers have to do." She, Una, a mother!

"They will never let you," said Hal. "Golly! Wait till they find out!"

"They won't have to. I shall tell them by and by."

"But as soon as Edward and Alix are married, they will want you out of the way, probably send you back to Cerne. Holy smoke!" said Hal again. "This *will* be a surprise for Crackers."

At the mention of Mrs. Carrington, Una came out of her spell; she was a schoolgirl again (not yet sixteen) "And far too sensible, well-informed, and controlled to get into any sort of trouble," as Mrs. Carrington would have said. Then . . . trouble? This isn't trouble, objected Una. It's joy, and deliberately she pushed all thought of Mrs. Carrington away—Mrs. Carrington, Edward, Alix, Aunt Freddie, everyone; theirs was another world.

"You must be afraid," said Hal.

"Of course, but happy afraid."

"Will he—the man—help you?"

"I'm sure he will. I can't wait to tell him."

"But . . . are you sure? Oh Una, what will happen to you if he—your he—doesn't help? Where will you go? Who will take care of you?"

"Darling Hal. He will."

"I spent and spent," said Alix. "I had an orgy."

Alix had arrived back at Shiraz Road two days after Edward and Una, but Edward was submerged with work, getting things in order for the Conference reconvening. "Once I am ready, we should be able to have twenty-four hours peace." Una had been sent to stay with Lady Srinevesan and though Alix, newly chic and polished, had fetched her, the house was so alive with servants and preparations Una had no chance to go to Ravi.

"You had a good time?"

"Gorgeous."

"Did you manage to settle your mother?"

"Yes, thank God—with the nuns, in a lovely house in Naini Tal. Think Una, I shall be able to give her anything she wants."

"Including United Nations Scotch," but Una forbore to say it. What did it matter now? Edward had seen to it that Dino had found work, "in the Italian Embassy, promotion for him," and it all seemed best forgotten. Alix had brought Una a Guerlain scent spray; a month ago Una would have put the spray straight back on Alix's dressing-table; now she shrugged and let it stand on hers. It too did not matter. Nothing mattered until, late that night, she had been able to run down the dark garden to Ravi as if she had never been away.

In the house, Edward was probably enjoying his Alix— that was the term they used, "My lord pleasured me," but "Ought I to touch you now?" asked Ravi.

"Perhaps not," said Una. "I don't know." She and Ravi, stopped abruptly on the brink, looked at one another in dismay. Then, "Better not," said Ravi and turned away but he could not help being cross.

Ravi, though, had accepted the idea of the baby as he would have accepted the seed of a poem—it had come. "But I wish we really knew. I am almost sure," said Una, "but if we knew for certain . . ."

"If you can stay here alone for a while, I can get Hem."

"At this hour?"

"He won't mind. In any case, he will be studying. This is one more study. He will come."

"Dear Hem. He is like our brother," but when Hem came he was far from brotherly.

"How dare you come to me? I am only a student. Una can go to her own doctor."

"I couldn't." At the thought of Doctor Gottlieb, Una recoiled.

"Then Ravi can damn well find one."

"Hem, Hem," and now Ravi did call him brother. "Bhai, who else can I turn to? You have always helped me—always. Think how easy it is for you to have a test made at the Medical School. There it is an everyday affair. If we use another name, no one will question—while for us it is life and death," said dramatic Ravi. "You cannot be so ungenerous. If we don't know, how can I help Una?" At that Hem made a movement—whether to go or stay Una did not know—but Ravi had his arm round Hem's shoulder. "Look, Una, I will leave you with Hem. He will tell you what you have to do."

Next night Hem came back and flung the report slip on Ravi's desk. "You would think neither of you had ever heard of sensible things to do." Hem was in a towering rage.

"It is our first love," Ravi pleaded and, getting angry too, "Sensible!" said Ravi in disgust. "This is holy thing," and he quoted, *"The woman is the fire: her womb is the fuel: the invitation of the man is the smoke: the door is the flame: the entering is the ember: the pleasure the spark . . ."*

"Yes," whispered Una.

"In the fire," Ravi went on, *"the gods find the offering: from the offering springs the child.* That is the Upanishads," he said proudly.

"Maybe," said Hem. "It is also everyday, and the truth is that neither of you gave a thought to the consequences."

"We thought you would help—and be glad."

"Glad! Think of the trouble this will cause." Always that word 'trouble' . . . 'get into trouble.' It was as if a cold premonition had touched the baby.

"Why should there be any trouble?" asked Ravi. "It is only a little more than two weeks to the Prize-Giving. Then everyone will know openly of Una and me."

"And of this?"

"Why not?"

"So all can rejoice?"

"Why not?"

"Every reason. Really, you are impossibly silly," said Hem. "Ravi, think of your parents. To them this will be ab-ys-mal disgrace." In his agitation Hem split the syllables which seemed to make them more grave. "Disgrace with any girl, let alone an English one of whatever position. And you," Hem turned to Una, "Do you think Sir Edward will let his daughter have a child by an Indian —a servant?"

"Ravi is not a servant."

"He certainly is."

"How can Edward prevent it?"

"Think!" Hem was short and Una looked at him aghast. "Edward would never . . ."

"Wouldn't he? To him you are still a child." Hem's anger had gone; all at once he seemed afraid. "Ravi, Una, go in the morning to Sir Edward and tell him everything."

"Before Ravi's poems win?"

"Yes."

"No," said Ravi and walked up and down the hut, keeping away from Hem. "It would spoil everything."

"It . . . it would take away the . . . piquancy." Una felt she had found the right word.

"Isn't this more important?" Hem was still immovable.

"It can all be fitted in." Una sounded uncertain, then made up her mind. "We mustn't tell him."

"And how long before the Lamont will guess?" said Hem.

"Alix! I hadn't thought of her."

"Then you had better. She could guess now. You say you have morning sickness and soon, physically, you will alter. It may already be five weeks."

"But . . . they couldn't do anything." Una still clung to her spell.

"Wake up." Hem was rough.

"But how could they?"

"With a doctor, of course. Wake up," said Hem again. "You are living in the twentieth century. This could be terminated in a few minutes—for many girls in their lunch hour, but for you, I can guess it would be in a hush-hush nursing home."

"Don't." Una wanted to put her hands over her ears. "Don't! You are brutal, Hem. Brutal."

"If it is brutal to speak the truth, then I am brutal."

"Ravi! Ravi!"

Ravi came to her and put his arm round her. "No one," he told Hem grandly, "is going to touch my son."

"Then you had better protect him."

The grandeur faded. "How?"

"Take Una away—and quickly."

"Where?"

"That's your affair. I can only tell you," and Hem stood stiffly as if he were a soldier, though he spoke in medical terms, "there is conception: the test is positive and, even at this early stage . . ."

"It means 'Yes,' " said Una in ecstasy.

"It can be terminated, probably safely," said Hem, "up to twenty, perhaps twenty-six weeks. After that, I doubt if Sir Edward would risk it. So, if you want this child . . ."

"Of course we do."

"The next four months, about, is your dangerous time."

"Then . . . for four months we should have to hide." Ravi's dismay was evident.

"*She* would have to hide. You could take her somewhere and come back for the Tagore Prize. I think you needn't be afraid of coming back," Hem said contemptuously. "No one would connect a poet genius with one of that idiot gang."

Edward and Alix were to be married next day. "What will he get that he hasn't had before?" asked irreverent Ravi.

"To be fair, a wife. That's what he longs to make her, so . . ." Una shrugged. "They will only have one night away. Edward must be back on Friday for the opening of the Conference; it assembles on Saturday."

"Saturday is a holiday. It is Baisakhi."

"Not for them. They assemble, then resume their talks next week."

"So we shall have twenty-four hours," said Ravi.

"For what?" asked Hem.

"To do what you said. Take Una away, to a safe place."

"And you think they won't find you?"

"I think not." Ravi was as cocksure as Hem was contemptuous.

"Where are Edward and Alix going?" Vikram, who had suddenly appeared in the drawing-room at Shiraz Road, asked Una that.

"I think to the Rest House of the Bird Reserve at Sultanpur."

"But . . . it is the closed season on all the jheels—swamps—no shooting." Vikram was astonished.

"Edward likes to watch birds, not shoot them."

"Think of the Lamont spending her honeymoon looking at birds through binoculars! Sir Edward will probably have her up at dawn! Poor Alix! I should have thought she would have wanted the Princes' Suite in the Lake Palace at Udaipur, and flown there in the blowfly," which was the nickname of any big embassy's private plane.

There was something so bitter in Vikram's mocking that Una stared. He got up, went to a window, and stood with his back to her.

"Why have you come here?" asked Una.

"Foolishly—to have a last look. Talking of shooting . . ." the mockery broke, "I could shoot your father."

"Because he won?"

"He didn't win. It won—or rather, they won." She was surprised at his passion. "Tell me, Una—why is it so important for me to make little pure-bred Rajput Paralampurs?"

"It isn't."

"My father thinks so, but Una . . . I know Alix," said Vikram as if the words were pulled out of him. "I know her through and through. I know what she is, what she does, all the lies and disgraces. She needn't pretend with me but when Sir Edward finds out, as he must—then what?" demanded Vikram. "He is besotted with her but I . . . I love her."

Una had not thought she could hear Vikram speak so humbly and truthfully, serious truth. The slim shoulders moved as he kept his back to her; she knew he was in tears, And I thought he was just an arrogant playboy, thought Una.

"But if you love her, then why?" she asked.

"My father would stop my allowance. I should have to leave the regiment. You see, we're all in leading-strings."

Monkey-strings, thought Una, 'playing to the drum'— but I'm not, thought Una. Nor is Ravi.

"Besides," Vikram went on. "What bait nowadays can I hold out that would compare with his?"

"If she needs a bait," said Una, "she's not worth having."

"That's what I tell myself. It makes not the slightest difference." He turned. "There was one night, one special night . . ."

"I know," said Una. "I was there."

"Were you? I don't remember you. Next morning I bought her a ring." His hand shook as he brought a case out of his pocket and showed it to Una, a small, deep-coloured ruby in a plain circlet. "I bought it back from my father's treasury after they seized it. It was all I could afford. Anyway, before I could give it to her she had your father's diamond—*that* diamond!"

"I'm sorry," said Una.

"Once upon a time," said Vikram, and though he held his head high, she could see his wet cheeks, "I could have given her a ruby really the size of what they say, a pigeon's egg; pearls in ropes and emeralds bigger than you have ever seen. . . . Oh well!" He put the case back in his pocket. "It will make a nose ring for my orthodox Paralampur wife."

"How do I know you will be faithful?" Una had teased Ravi.

"How should I not be?"

"Your Krishna had sixteen thousand wives."

"Principal ones only eight. You will be the only one. In any case," said Ravi, "I could not afford more."

"You cannot afford one," said Hem but Ravi and Una would not acknowledge that.

"When the danger time is past, Una will come back and we shall declare ourselves. Meanwhile I shall have won the Tagore. Sir Edward will have double reason to agree."

"Agree to what?"

"That we should marry."

"Idiot boy. Englishmen don't let their daughters marry at fifteen."

"Not if she is with baby?"

"Besides," said Una, "I count myself as Indian now."

"Your father does not."

"I don't want to be English any more."

"But you are."

"Ravi has an uncle in Kulu who has promised him some land," said Una. "Ravi says it is fertile there and we shall grow fruit." Una saw a cloud of cherry blossom below shining Himalayas. "We shall build ourselves a home there, a little hut like this."

"And how will you furnish this lover-nest?" asked Hem.

"We won't. I tell you we shall be Indian: some rugs or

mats: cushions: takia—much what Ravi has now. We shall eat off *thalis* and *katooris*."

"No, we shall be more simple than that," said Ravi. "We shall eat off banana leaves."

"Bananas don't grow in Kulu."

Una ignored that. "Christopher is teaching me to cook Indian food. We shall have hens, a cow, be peasants."

"You are not peasants."

"N-no. I shall have to learn to type. Type Ravi's poems."

"You can't eat poems. On what will you live?"

"On Ravi's prize money." They were astonished that Hem should ask. "You see you can eat poems," said Una, "and Ravi will write others. When I am twenty-one I shall have money from my mother."

"Six years is a long time to go hungry."

"You are very disagreeable," said Ravi.

"And you are a pair of cuckoos in air."

"Not if you will help us," Una begged.

"Help yourselves," said Hem, and left them.

"Why is Hem so cross?" asked Una.

"He is afraid for you. Afraid of what your father and that whore might do to you—and afraid of handing you over to careless me. I am careless, Una," Ravi was serious for once. "You will always have to be the sensible one."

Una did not feel sensible. "Perhaps if Hem had helped us, we might not have been so childish," she was to say. It was childish, but then there is always a childish excitement in running away.

NINE

"Watermelon. Watermelon. Cool juice of watermelon."
The clanking train wheels below Una seemed to be saying
that—had said it all through the night. Brought in by
camel from the riverbeds, palest green and coral red
dripping with juice. Una's mouth was parched, every bone
in her body ached; her eyelids felt brittle and dry and her
temples throbbed. It is fun to do things with Ravi—that
had been her gospel. "Fun—until it becomes fact," Hem
had said.

To begin with, it had been fun. "After the wedding
lunch I am to go to Bulbul's," she had told Ravi when
they made their plans. "They won't need me any more."

"To be Miss Gooseberry?"

"Yes. I am to spend the night with Bulbul."

"Have you told her?"

"Not yet."

"Oh! You will pretend to go to Bulbul's."

"Don't forget. Chinaberry will take me."

"He will be winked—if you do as I tell you. First thing

in the morning I shall take leave from Ganesh. 'I have to attend to my maternal uncle's funeral rites.' " Ravi put on a solemn expression. "As I am the eldest living male relative, Ganesh cannot refuse me. How much money have you?" Ravi asked Una.

"About two hundred rupees. Edward gave them to me for spending on our tour but I didn't buy anything."

"Little thrift! And I have some hundred and fifty saved. We are rich. We can go anywhere."

"But where are we going?"

"There is a train for Varanasi about six o'clock." Ravi's eyes sparkled. "It is the day before Baisakhi, so there will be many many pilgrims. We shall be pilgrims too. That will please my grandmother."

"Why please your grandmother?"

"Because it is to her we shall be going. I am very favourite."

"But—will she accept us?" To Una, grandmothers were even more likely to be shocked than parents. "If your father and mother . . ."

"My grandmother," said Ravi, "is in the third stage."

"What third stage?"

"Of life. We Hindus have, or could have, four stages in our lives. First, like me, as a student, when we go 'out into the forest' as we call it, learning to fend for ourselves—nowadays it is more the city jungle. Next we should be 'householders.' "

"You will have to be that now, in Kulu, with our baby—and I suppose I shall too, only I haven't really been a student yet. But at least," said Una, "I shan't have to darn your socks; one doesn't need socks in India."

"Kulu can be most cold—you will certainly darn my socks." Then Ravi said with reluctance, "I do not know that I am ready to be a householder."

"You will have to be. You have done it now," Hem would have said, but Una slipped her hand into Ravi's. "We shall simply be us. Tell me about your grandmother's third stage."

"The third stage is retirement—not in the way you

mean, but in our way, a shedding of the world. She has no concern in it. That's why," said Ravi, "she will not interfere with us."

As Ravi had planned, Una went in at Bulbul's gate— "We're not grand enough to have gatemen"—and hid behind the hedge until Chinaberry drove away; then, on tiptoe in case any of Bulbul's household stirred, came out of the gate and walked swiftly round the corner to Ravi; she would have run but that might have drawn attention. Ravi was waiting in a taxi driven by a turbanned Sikh. The driver had been smiling. "Does he guess?" asked Una, fearful.

"How could he?" But, all the same, Ravi stopped the taxi at a house in a quiet road. They pretended, as Una had done at Bulbul's, to step inside the garden then, holding Una's hand, Ravi led her stealthily past the rows of modest villa houses, their stucco shining yellow in the sun, windows shuttered against the heat, to one that had a small separate gate. "Hsst!" said Ravi as he cautiously opened it. Ravi, thought Una, would have made a splendid actor.

"Where are we?"

"This is Hem's annexe—where he lives."

"But Hem said he wouldn't help us."

"I haven't asked him but I have the key."

The annexe was a little building standing in a patch of sun-dried grass and separated from the house by a line of hibiscus bushes; the long stamens of the flowers in the circle of brilliant cup always looked to Una like tongues thrust out; let them be out, she thought and, defiantly, picked a flower; she brushed her cheek with it and it left a pollen stain. The annexe had its own front door. Ravi took out his key and opened it.

So this was where Hem lived—in this shuttered coolness grateful after the heat; as Una's eyes grew accustomed to the dim light she saw how neat and practical was the room; nothing could have been more different from Ravi's poetically shabby hut. There was an iron hospital bed with a red blanket—Hem had probably bought them as discards: a wardrobe of cheap wood was built in—no clothes on a string for Hem; he was, Una guessed, as private as she. There was a filing cabinet, a wooden chair and a desk with notebooks and papers exactly placed; a typewriter. In the cupboard of the kitchen beyond she could see a sink, a small gas stove, a shelf of enamel plates and mugs, a sauce-pan, "and he uses that often to boil up specimens," said Ravi, shuddering. A shelf had been put up for medical books and, on the filing cabinet, a microscope was carefully protected by a cellophane cover. "Doctor Babbletosh lent him that—and gave Hem the typewriter." These told of Hem as a doctor, but there was no clue of Hem himself, no picture or photograph or ornament: no sign of food such as Ravi's chillies and spices: no tulsi plant. "Doesn't Hem have anything of his own?" asked Una.

Ravi laughed. "He wouldn't know what to do with it. But I do—I do." Ravi picked Una up and laid her on the bed.

"Not here." Una struggled. "Not on Hem's bed."

"A new experience for it, I bet." Ravi's face came closer to hers. His hands were undoing her dress, but Una still resisted. "No, Ravi."

"You have to strip anyhow."

"No."

"Why?" asked Ravi.

"You said we wouldn't because of the baby."

"I have unsaid."

"And Hem—wouldn't like it."

"But I like it," and, as always, Ravi had his will. Ravi—ravishment. Is that where the word comes from? Of course not, thought Una, one is Hindi, the other from the French, but today Una was not ravished; she could not surrender herself—perhaps because it was Hem's bed.

Afterward they dyed her hair in the sink: "Your skin is brown enough from swimming and sunbathing, but your hair . . . you must wear a wig," Ravi had said.

"It's too hot for a wig."

"Then we must dye you."

Ravi painted her eyebrows and lashes with the same dye; it stung her eyes and the tears made the dye run. "All the better," said Ravi. "As my bride you have just been parted from your mother. Your eyes are red with weeping. Now go and dry your hair in the sun."

"But I'm naked."

"Put on your bodice and skirt."

"What shall I wear?" she had asked Ravi.

"Have you a sari?"

"I have the Rajasthani clothes Alix bought us for the Paralampur fancy dress."

"Rajasthani will be a little uncommon," Ravi had demurred, "but never mind. There will be pilgrims from all over. Go and get them," and, "Too clean," he had pronounced when she had brought the long full skirt, the bodice that stopped below her breasts, the *orrhni*—veil. "Give them to me and I will dirty them a little. You always wear *chappals*; they will do for your feet, but this jewellery looks too trick. Haven't you any bangles?"

"Hal has some silver ones."

"If they are not too good. It doesn't matter if they shine; being a bride your jewellery might be new, and I will be a good husband and get you some earrings and beads. You must have a bundle and I will get a tin trunk for myself." It was a yellow tin trunk, painted with roses; it made Una laugh.

Now, as she put on the skirt and bodice—they looked used and crumpled—she remembered them at the Paralampur dance, stiff in their new brightness. It had been a hurtful idea to dress her and Hal alike. Una could still see the folds of Hal's skirt swinging as she danced, the delicious plumpness under her bodice, the way her earrings and bangles had tinkled as she tossed her head and talked, excited because even the grown men, Vikram's friends, had wanted to dance with her. Una had hardly danced at all, but spent most of the evening talking to the old raja who had wept a little—because of the wine, perhaps—as he told her how the Singhs of Paralampur were descended from the sun—and now here was his staid little companion running away with the sun itself? She would not, though, let Ravi know she thought of him as this and, "You have ruined Hem's towel," she said severely.

"He will have another." Ravi threw it into a corner.

"At least wash out the sink. Ravi, what have you moved from it?"

"One of Hem's horrors." It was the body of a squirrel in a jar of spirit; with it, on a slab of marble, were a dissecting knife and a small array of tools. "Ugh!" said Ravi.

"It isn't 'ugh.' Hem has to understand. He must have been dissecting," but Ravi only said "Ugh!" again and pushed the slab aside.

"Come, let me plait your hair. It's dry enough. Look, I have bought you such a pretty *chotti*," and he showed Una the black thread cord ending with silk tassels for tying her plait, but Una was still contrite. "We have spoiled Hem's work, disturbed it."

They had disturbed more than that. When Hem came in that evening and opened the shutters onto his garden, he saw his disordered room.

"We must clear up," Una had said.

"We haven't time. It is getting towards the rush hour; we may have to wait an hour or more for a bus or to pick up a phut-phut."

"But it isn't fair to leave it . . ."

"Hem will understand."

Hem understood only too well. Una's small case stood on his desk where it had pushed aside his papers; it was not properly fastened, a strap of ribbon was hanging out and he opened the lid. The clothes Una had worn were carelessly stuffed inside; almost mechanically Hem took them out and folded them: a dress, a slip, a lacy pair of briefs, and a brassière, absurdly small, it seemed to Hem.

"But . . . I must have some underclothes," Una had said.

"You won't need any," and, when she blinked, "What do you think those women wear under their skirts?" teased Ravi.

"Can I have a handkerchief?"

"Poor people don't. You hold your nostrils delicately

with your finger and thumb and blow. You may bring a comb."

."And my purse?"

"Certainly not. I will get you a small waist-bag for tucking into your skirt—a *batwa*—it will hold a few rupee notes; the rest you will give to me."

It had been a wonderful feeling of lightness for Una to walk out of her bedroom in Shiraz Road leaving everything behind; it was more wonderful to feel her body bare under the skirt, and the bodice, her midriff open to the sun, the only weight Hal's bangles sliding up and down her arms and the earrings Ravi put in her ears. What a blessing we had them pierced, thought Una. The veil protected her head and neck, she could hide in its folds, and it was comfortable to have her hair plaited back; she scarcely felt the chappals on her feet. Ravi's trunk held some of his books and his poems—"I could not leave them behind"—and Una tied a toothbrush and comb in her bundle. "Could I have a cup? I don't like station ones."

"You mustn't fuss. At the station I will buy a surahi." Una had seen the long-necked pitchers, earthenware to keep the water cool. "You can drink from that."

"I should spill it."

"Wait. This will do." On the desk Hem had a small brass tumbler to hold his pens and pencils. Ravi emptied them out and they rolled across the desk, some onto the floor. "It is believable," said Ravi, "that you could carry a cup like that."

Their laughter seemed still to be in the room as Hem looked at the scattered pencils, his best pen on the floor. He saw the towel tossed in the corner, the black-stained sink while the jar with the squirrel and his dissection slab were pushed out of the way. It gave a feeling of rejection, almost of insult. Then Hem's gaze came to the disarranged bed, the dented pillow; on the floor under the bed lay Una's hibiscus flower.

Hem picked it up but his usually steady hand was shaking. He carried the flower to the window and found he was weeping.

"Don't pick your way like that." Ravi said it hardly moving his lips.

"The platform's filthy," Una whispered back.

"You are supposed to be accustomed. Don't notice the filth. Walk." Walk—on spat-out betel-chewers' stains, spat phlegm, banana skins, orange skins, peanut shells: goat dirt: runnels where people had urinated against the walls. Walk, avoiding circles where a family had camped and was cooking on a brazier, or where a mat or bedding had been laid down. Una was jostled by coolies in crimson tunics shouting to make a way as they carried baggage on their heads; by humbler passengers carrying bedrolls, baskets, tin trunks like Ravi's, or babies lolling on their hips or wicker crates of hens on their heads. She dodged tea sellers, Coca-Cola sellers, wheeled stalls of hot spicy food, fruit sellers, and edged round barrow stalls selling newspapers, toys, and, always, peacock-feather fans. The railway officials should have looked smart only that they left their brass buttons undone and the drill of their white uniform was dirty. "Here," said Ravi in Hindi, stopping at a carriage in which a bench was empty under a window where the corridor divided it from the cubicle compartment inside.

"It is a passageway," whispered Una. "Everyone will brush past us there."

"It's the only empty space." Second class would have been more comfortable but Ravi had said, "If we are missed, in third class we shall be ants among ants." Now Una saw how true that was: the cubicle was crowded to bursting and, "Quick!" said Ravi, hoisting her up the train's high step. He put the bundle and his trunk beside her to keep his place. "I will go and buy water and some food."

As the train pulled out and Una saw the shanty slums along the track, huts contrived of sacking, palm leaves, old sheets of corrugated iron, straw or woven thatch, some standing on wet ground with glimpses of reeking gullies, stagnant water tanks, in the same city as spacious Shiraz Road, she remembered that, the last time she had been on a train, on the way to Agra, she had felt shamed in her luxury with Edward in the air-conditioned coach, separated as carefully as if she were behind glass, as in fact she was. "Sensible people would be grateful to live in Shiraz Road, be able to travel in air conditioning," Hem had said when Una voiced her guilt.

"Not Ravi, nor I. We should rather be with the 'have-nots' than the 'haves.'"

"You say that on full bellies!" Hem had been angry and Una thought she saw a glimpse of what he must have been as a student, a passionate hothead. Was it Hem, she wondered, who had led Ravi into what she had fathomed as his mysterious 'trouble'? "What do you know of India?" asked Hem. "You have seen Delhi, beautiful exhilarating Delhi," and he mocked, "city of fountains and flowers."

"I have seen the Old City."

"As a curio. Suppose you had to live in one of those 'interesting' alleys where the houses vomit garbage and the gutters are choked with faeces."

"Don't," Una shrank.

"Don't! But they are. That's why Indian back streets are a hotbed of flies and disease. When you have no water to wash with, or you wash with too little, you pass on dysentery. How would you like that?"

"I wouldn't, but . . ." Una stumbled, "I love the Indian simplicity, and they don't grab."

Hem began to laugh. "My little Una! Don't you know we are the best in the world at 'grab' and also at graft? Don't you see that you fool Westerners, boys and girls, are trying to live as Indians are trying not to live?"

"Hem, don't be crosspatch," said Ravi who was bored but, "Where is the sense," Hem had stormed, "if you have been given brains and the luck to be trained to use them, why don't you try to do something that will truly help— serve like Una's father?"

"Like Edward?" Una had been dazed.

"Yes, he and his kind."

"In all this—panoply?"

"The panoply is not his." That, Una knew, was true,

"and it is a pinch in the ocean," said Hem. "It doesn't matter. What do you think they do with their brains and time and money?"

"Buy brown diamonds—you don't know everything," Una could have said but would not give Edward away. Instead, "this 'serving,' I suppose, is why you have started all over again in Medical School," she had asked.

"That is my business." Hem had been suddenly gruff.

"I still don't want to have what other people haven't."

"A lofty wish," Hem had mocked and before three hours had passed in the train it began to feel far too lofty.

It was partly the smell coming out of the carriage: of food: of biris: of bodies pressed too tightly together: dust, fumes from the engine—sitting close to the window Una caught those: of cess from the latrine at the end of the coach. "I couldn't go in there," she said when need arose.

"You must," said Ravi, "or to the women's latrine at the next station, but that will be as bad."

"There's only a place for your feet—no pan—I can't squat down."

"Other women do."

Una came back, pale, clammy. "Ravi, there's . . . no paper."

"What did you expect? There's a tap and your hands."

"Ouh!"

"Wait. I'll find you a piece of newspaper."

As the train had started to rock across the plain, twilight fell and melancholy had settled on Una—a sadness that was to come on her at twilight for years; 'cowdust time' Ravi had told her it was called in Bengal and here, too, in the north, cattle were being driven home to villages in the fields that lay along the track. The cattle raised humble clouds of dust; she could see the twinkling of lights among the trees, smoke going up from fires where the evening meal was cooking. Cattle, men, children were going home and Una, curled on the narrow wooden seat beside the window, knew she had no home; or, by choice, had Ravi. His hut in Shiraz Road was an expedient, as much as Edward's great house was for Edward. Will we, Ravi and I, ever have a home, Una had thought? It suddenly seemed unlikely and the hut in Kulu a dream; this train, hurtling and rocking them along, was taking them—where?

It was better at the stations when it slid into a babel and swarm of life. Leaning from her window, Una watched the people and the barrows pushing along the train; she wished she had a palm-leaf fan, but would not ask Ravi. He took her tumbler and brought her some tea; she had thought she could not drink it, but it was unexpectedly good and took the stale taste of Edward's wedding champagne out of her mouth. It was amazing, too, what a comfort to her was Hem's small brass tumbler; it lessened the feeling of forlornness, but why should she feel forlorn when she was with Ravi? Una sat up straight, smiled, but the loneliness, the sense of abandonment grew. She slid her fingers into Ravi's hand but he would not hold them; it was too bold for an Indian wife.

Una knew she was terribly tired, yet she could not sleep. It was partly the food that kept her awake: the *samosas* Ravi had bought in a cup of dried leaves sewn together were spicier, hotter than any she had tasted, the chappatis heavier, and the little pot of *rabbri*—milk and sugar simmered in pannikins to a thick cream—rich and sickly. "Couldn't you get any fruit?" she whispered longingly, but "Don't fuss," said Ravi.

If only, she thought, the other travellers would put out the lights; if, for one minute, they would stop talking, or stop the transistor that whined so loudly they had to shout and shrill over it. "You don't understand," Ravi whispered. "You are so spoiled. To them, to travel is like a party." Some of them were pilgrims—one couple, Ravi told her, had come from the delta of the Ganges, far away in Bengal. A pilgrimage, made perhaps once in a lifetime was for a holy day—and a holiday. "To them this train is a luxury. They might have had to walk," but, I am too thin to sit all night on a hard wooden bench; my bones stick out, thought Una, yet many were thinner than she. "You have been fed on butter and sugar," they would have said. "Overfed." She had not their zest for life; ants or not, they brimmed with it and in the compartment, the talk, chatter, laughter, repartee, eating, and smoking went on. Ravi, of course, was questioned and parried each fresh one with good humour, often bringing laughter, but it was most suitable that his small bride should be silent, shrouded in her veil, her face resolutely turned to the window. Perhaps they were disappointed she did not steal glances at them from under her veil so that they could guess at her prettiness, or plainness; did not make sly whisperings to Ravi to set them agog. "But the shy ones are often best," they would have said.

"We go to pay our respect on our wedding to my grand-mother," Ravi told them.

"An exemplary young people," said a portly Punjabi.

"Yes, when you think of young people nowadays," said a large lady and, as she fought her way out of the compartment to go to the latrine, she bent and spoke kindly to Una who could only shake her head. "Is she weeping?"

"She has left her mother." Ravi said it with such mock seriousness that Una had to giggle. The woman saw her shoulders shaking. "Tut, tut. Poor *batchi*—she *is* weeping." She gave Una a motherly pat and when she came back passed out some sweets. "Eat . . . eat." Una hid them in her bundle.

Watermelon . . . watermelon. Pale green coolness dripping juice; the green became a flock of parakeets that flew into Una's face, hard as the wooden toys sold on the platform barrows—her head had knocked against the window; for a moment she had slept. At last the compartment was hushed; the transistor turned off. Bundled and huddled on one another the travellers slept—a deep sleep of exhaustion. If only I could lie down, thought Una. I shall die if I don't lie down. She had pretended her back ached so that she need not ride Mouse; its ache was excruciating now. She thought of the second-class carriage Ravi had eschewed where at least they had padded seats. If only I could lie down.

In the early hours of the morning a family got out, leaving an empty bench. The other travellers did not stir but at once Ravi slipped in, lay down full length and was asleep. Ravi, without a thought of me! When I'm so tired. I sick with his child! Una could not believe it, but Hem would have laughed. "You will have to get used to the ways of the Indian male." At least, though, Una was able to curl down on her bench and relieve her aching back.

It seemed hours after sunrise when they came to a station for breakfast. Ravi brought her tea and sweets. She was hungry but, "Sweets! Sweets for breakfast!"

"That is our custom." He was in a huff. "To ask for toasts would be suspicious. Look, this is your favorite *luddu.* I bought it especially for you," but Una was starting to heave. "Take them away or I shall be sick."

"Sick! Sick! That's what you say all the time." Ravi was tired too. "I am sick of you." Then he softened. "What *do* you want?"

"Watermelon," but now Una saw it out on the stalls it was buzzing with flies. "Not watermelon. Oranges," and Ravi bought a few dried-up oranges. In a hand machine on the platform a boy was crushing sugar cane; Ravi took Hem's tumbler and brought it back filled. It was a peace offering and, though the juice was unbearably sweet—and full of dysentery germs, I expect, thought Una—she drank it.

As the morning went on the heat in the carriage grew burning. She could feel sweat running down her back from her hair. Would the dye run too? Then she saw that on the inside of her arms a rash of bright red spots had come out; she thought, by the tingling, they were on her neck too, down her back and under her hair. "Keep your arms in your veil," murmured Ravi. "The rash shows you are English. My God, are you going to be ill?"

"I think it's only prickly heat." In the famous seventeenth-century diary of William Hickey, one of his loves had died of prickly heat, but Una was learning the guiding principle of a good Indian wife, self-effacement, and, "It's nothing," she assured Ravi.

"We shan't go all the way to Varanasi," Ravi had said. "They may be checking all trains."

Una thought it unlikely. "Edward and Alix will only just be back from the Bird Sanctuary."

"You never know." Ravi was determinedly dramatic. "We shall leave the train at Sevapuri, slip into the crowd," and, just after noon, Una found herself standing with her bundle on a platform that seemed to be in the middle of nowhere, the surahi in her hand, while Ravi found the tickets. No one in the sleepy little station looked at them, or stopped them, and in a moment they were out on the road that wound away from the shambling town.

"Wait, I must get some more water."

"Is it drinking water?" Una was dubious but in many Indian towns, rich men, to gain merit, install shelters with filtered water, free for the public. There was one near the station. "*Seva puri*—seva means to take care. See, I am taking care of you," said Ravi.

"Isn't it, rather, the rich man?"

By the water shelter was a milestone. *Varanasi 22 kms.* "Shall we find a bus?" asked Una.

"They may be checking buses. It is safest that we walk."

"I can't walk 22 kilometres."

"It is only fifteen miles. Come."

"In the middle of the day, in *this* heat, an English girl and pregnant!" Hem would have exploded, but Ravi put the rose-painted trunk on his shoulder and blithely led the way to the dust track beside the road.

"Come along," Ravi had to order every half-hour.

"I can't."

"You must. Come *along*."

Una held her veil across her mouth and nostrils to keep out the dust that swirled every time a car, lorry, bus, or tonga passed, swerving off the hard surface of the road, or when Ravi caught up with a bullock cart; her eyelashes were stiff with dust and her eyes smarted and stung with it and tiredness. Her skirt was white up to her knees, her skin burned, but worst of all were her feet; they were not supple yet, hard-skinned as were most Indian women's, and the chappals had blistered them. Una was certain she had plodded for miles behind Ravi, watching a damp patch spread wide on the back of his kurta as the sweat ran down from his neck.

"How far have we come?"

"Perhaps ten kilometres."

"Only ten!"

"Come along."

"I can't," but this time Una managed not to say it.

They had paused in a village where Ravi, with sudden thoughtfulness, had taken Una's veil, his own chuddar—shoulder cloth—too, and run them under the village tap; the cool wetness was grateful but the veil soon dried; Ravi's chuddar, wound on his head, stayed wet far longer.

"Isn't there another village?"

"No. Come along."

The fields each side of the road had been harvested and bullocks or buffaloes were working, trampling the cut wheat with a heavy wooden beam that they drew in a slow circle; women with flat wicker scoops were sifting the grain into huge jars; as they sifted, the chaff rose in golden puffs. They would stay in the fields all day, sometimes singing, often chattering, though the heat shimmered from the stubble. At evening, when the jars were filled and the slow carts creaked home with them to the village, the women would gather up the straw and carry it in mountainous heaps on their heads—probably carry a baby too. They drew in their buttocks so that they walked erect and lightly. "You don't know how to walk," Ravi told Una.

If she stepped on to the asphalt it was so hot it scorched through her chappals and was sticky, and now they came to a stretch along the dust track where the mahowa trees had dropped their yellow flowers in heaps which were fermenting in the sun; they gave off a heavy sickly smell that made Una feel dizzy. "No wonder," said Ravi. "The villagers make them into wine; children come out and gather them in the early morning. You can eat the flowers too, fresh or cooked."

"Don't," said Una. She could not get the smell out of her nostrils. "How far now?"

"We have only done another kilometre. We haven't gone half-way," but Una was forced to gasp, "Couldn't we have a rest? Go on when it's cooler?"

"Arré! Sust!" which was hardly fair, but reluctantly Ravi led the way off the road to where, in a field, was a patch of shade from a mango tree. The field was empty except for a donkey, hobbled and thin, pulling hopefully at a few stalks left among the stubble; a hawk circling, circling in the glare of sky made Una's eyes ache still more as she watched it. "This is a horrible place," said Ravi.

"I know, but I can't go on yet." Una took the tormenting chappals off her feet.

"It will be your fault if they catch us," Ravi scolded.

"Why should they look for us here?"

"There may be police all along the road."

"Then they will catch us anyway."

Ravi spread his chuddar, dry now, on the ground, poured water from the surahi into Una's tumbler. "Not too much—it will make it harder to go on," drank himself and spread the remains of their food. Una shook her head.

"You must eat."

"I can't. It's those flowers."

"Can't, can't, can't," Ravi mocked again. "Una, how you fuss!"

"It isn't me. It's him." She patted her stomach and Ravi was repentant.

"I forget. I still can't believe it."

"You will believe it by and by," and for all the discomfort and the heat, the bone hardness of the ground, its dust, her prickly heat, blisters, headaches, and nausea, Una was content. She lay down on Ravi's chuddar, put her bundle under her head. The sound of the traffic, bus horns, wheels, the shouts and thwacks of the carters, the shuffling feet, grew dimmer. Una was asleep.

She was woken by a cry, discordant yet, she was sure, part of this Indian landscape turned by the sinking sun to a mist of pink-gold like the cinema clouds she had seen in Indian films of Krishna's heaven. Still drugged with sleep, she raised herself on an elbow to look and thought she was back in one of the parade ground rides or at Fatephur Sikri, because a peacock was standing not twenty yards away from her, a peacock with three hens. Her patch of shade was lost in the slanting rays that lit the stubble, haloed even the donkey and caught the blue lustre of the peacock's neck, the delicate crown of feathers on his head, his train spread in all its glory as he displayed it before his hens, fanning it backwards and forwards around him as he posed. The cry did not come again; instead, he began to dance. The train fanned, the legs strutted, trod for a moment and then came a paroxysm of quivering from his feet to the crown of feathers, sending a dazzle of colours into Una's eyes and the eyes of his hens. It was meant to dazzle; he gave a dart towards the chosen hen and returned to his quivering.

Ravi was still asleep; no one on the road had glanced or paused; it was only she, Una, who had been chosen—yes, chosen, thought Una—to see the peacock love-dance; she, Una, and the half-starved donkey who was watching as gravely as she. This was not imperial Fatephur Sikri; in this peasant field the air smelled of petrol and dust, not bougainvillaea and roses; there was a continual noise of traffic but cock and hen were oblivious of anything but their mating and, That is how it should be, thought Una. The peacock was like Ravi—or Ravi like the peacock— regal with his colours, crown, and train that was not a tail as people supposed, but made by the wing feathers, while she, Una, was the hen, drab with only a glint of colour— but a necessary hen; the chosen one was getting ready to crouch, the other two standing by like handmaidens; the peahen crouched low and Una had felt this abasement her- self, almost a worship of Ravi's act of love. Not that I should ever tell him so, thought Una. Of course not; it was private of privates—like the 'womb house' in some of those temples she had seen with Edward, the innermost sanctuary where, meeting the God it enshrines, the worshipper is born again.

"I can't appear before your grandmother like this."

"Of course you can. I tell you—she will not even see your clothes."

"She will smell them. Ravi, I'm reeking."

"Your fault for jumping into the puddle."

"I didn't jump. I fell."

"I told you not to lean against the door."

For the last eight kilometres, Ravi had flagged down a lorry and made a bargain with the driver. "You slept so long that, as it is, we shan't get to Varanasi till midnight."

"You slept longer." Una had not woken him until the peacock had had his way.

"I did not want to sleep at all. It was you who insisted."

"*You* slept on the train."

Una sat against the lorry door; she had been so tottering with exhaustion that it seemed to her the kindest vehicle she had ever met. No wonder its driver had decorated it with jewellery—the lorry wore a long black tassel, bound with beads that hung from the windscreen to the bonnet. Do lorries wear jewellery? Are jewels on lorries? "Am I delirious?" asked Una.

"Are you going to sleep *again! Kya wabalē jā-n*—pest of my life," scolded Ravi. "Don't you know you are a dead weight on my arm?"

"Then don't hold me."

"I have to hold you. The door isn't safe." It was not safe. When the lorry had stopped and Ravi took his arm away, Una had tumbled out into a puddle. Of what? She could not see, but she could smell cess on her clothes.

"We must stop and buy me a sari," but they were engulfed in people—men, women, and children. One moment Una was against a man's hot burliness, against his spotless muslin shirt; the next, against the nakedness of a holy man; the ashes with which he had smeared himself rubbed off on her. She knocked against women; some execrated her: some pushed her on with a pat and a smile.

Once she was against a baby and could feel its tiny help-lessness between her and its mother. "Careful, Ravi, or I might crush it."

"Don't talk English to me."

"But what *is* this?"

"A procession."

"For Baisakhi?"

"I don't know. There are always processions in Vara-nasi. Fortunately it is going the other way."

Una could see a banner, lettered and hung with mari-golds; something was being carried: a corpse? a bride-groom? a god? Around it, people were chanting, beating on miniature cymbals.

"Ravi."

"Hsst. A Hindu wife would not say my name."

An old man pushed a bicycle over Una's toes: strapped onto its handlebars were an iguana and a huge adjutant stork, both limp and dead. "Do they eat those?"

"For God's sake, stop asking questions." Una was banged, pushed, flung sideways, as Ravi pulled her through the crowd; a hand snatched at her bundle and clawed her as she tugged it back. Beggars followed a procession: a man, his leg withered, hopped with a stick: a malformed boy with a lolling head was dragged in a homemade cart, and a crone who whined seemed to fix her sightless eyes on Una, but *"Agē chelo!"* shouted Ravi. *"Jao. Hā t jao—* get away." He dragged Una into a wide alley; at the far end of its lane she could see a glint of silver—a river. The river Ganges, thought Una.

"Who were all those people?" Ravi had stopped for breath.

"I told you I don't know. A funeral perhaps."

"A *funeral?* They were singing, playing cymbals. I thought funerals were sad."

"Preconceived notion, but maybe it was a bridegroom procession—but probably pilgrims."

"Pilgrims! But I thought pilgrims were—reverent?"

"Can you not be reverent and enjoy yourself?" Ravi was still out of temper. "I told you—a holy day is a holiday."

Remembering the dead iguana, the filth from the puddle, the clawing at her bundle, Una shuddered and, "I thought you loved India," said Ravi.

"I do."

"Until your fastidious little nose is rubbed in her. I tell you, in the morning those same people will go at dawn to pray, to wash in the river ritually, immerse themselves, which is more than you will do, you hypocrite." How could Ravi, even in his fatigue and dirt, be so unkind? Una's prickly heat spots seemed to be in her throat and eyes now, only they were prickly tears. She turned from Ravi and ran.

"Where are you going?"

"Where you said I wouldn't go. To wash in the river."

"Una—come back. We are at my grandmother's . . ."

"In the river . . ."

"Una, don't be a fool."

Her voice floated back to him: "Bring me a clean sari."

"You can bathe in the house," but she was already at the river steps.

It was a private ghat lit by one small flickering light; its steps of worn stone led deep into the water. There was no one else there and, dropping her veil and chappals on the steps, Una stepped down them until she was breast high and took off her bodice to let coolness flow round her. She could feel the current eddying; it must be strong farther out; even here it lifted her skirt so that it spread in a circle on the water—which is probably filthy—and she thought of babies' dead bodies, ashes, and the bones Hindus called 'the flowers' and which the priests threw into the river, but nothing, at that moment, Una thought, was more filthy than she. Something sinuous caught round her waist making her gasp, but it was soft and light, only a soaked garland of marigolds. The current took it away as the river took everything—no wonder it was sacred. *Ganga mai*—Mother Ganges: mother of rivers everywhere—cleansing, purifying.

The fun and excitement, the tiredness, sickness, aching, hunger, and thirst were running from Una like the water and she had a longing to let herself slip away too, calmly into this calm. It would save so much trouble. Why did she suddenly think of that? "Let go . . . Let everything go." It was as if her own voice commanded her, but Ravi spoke from above on the ghat. "You look like a water-lily," said Ravi and indeed she glimmered white in the round leaf of her skirt.

"Come," and now Ravi's voice was soothing and kind. "I have been to the shops and brought you a clean sari. Come—my grandmother is waiting."

Grandmother . . . Ganga mai . . . what did it matter?

In the clean sari, her hair blown in the river breeze—she had undone the strange plait—and hand in hand with Ravi, Una walked back up the alleyway until they came to a door, narrow, studded with nails, and set in a high mud wall. Someone was watching for them because it opened and Ravi drew Una through. "Safe!" he said in exaltation. "We are safe!"

Just after two o'clock the next afternoon, starting on his way back to Delhi, Ravi, as he stepped jubilantly through that door, came face to face with Edward.

TEN

"Lady Gwithiam!"

Alix had come up the steps between the salaaming servants while Ganesh presented his celebration buttonholes: a red rose for Edward, white for Alix. "Salaam." "Salaam." They would not have done that for her yesterday. The hall was filled with amaryllis, white-belled lilies and, looking down the vista of the drawing-room, Alix could see vases of them mixed with tall white larkspur; there were bowls, too, of white roses so that the whole house looked bridal. "Ganesh always knows which side his bread is buttered," Ravi would have said, but Alix drew a long breath of satisfaction and triumph as, with her hand on Edward's arm, she turned, not towards the schoolroom wing down the veranda, but to what, in her mind, she called 'the master bedroom' where Monbad had already carried her cases.

The night in the guest house was over; she had sat patiently all evening with Edward watching the birds fly in from the Jumna River to the shallow lake—cranes, huge-winged, their long necks and legs stretched out: pelican:

duck: while an adjutant stork waded in the water near them, steadily fishing. There was the call of the cock partridge, Una had heard in the parade ground rides, "Pateela, pateela": the honking of geese, the sound of their wings as they took off from the water towards the fields where the wheat was being harvested. As the sun had sunk, the 'jheel' water turned silver-grey so that the white birds showed—"like pearls," said Edward.

Alix had made their dinner into "a feast for just us two," said Edward. She had brought his favourite champagne, Ruinart Reserve from Paris, "And I'm afraid we drank too much," said Alix.

"Never mind. Never mind anything," Edward said and, in the morning, he had taken her face in his hands and reverently, yes, reverently, kissed her forehead, eyelids, lips, and, for the first time, his love words were English. "Thank you, my darling and my glory."

I have won, thought Alix in the hall. The scent of the lilies was "A bit overpowering?" suggested Edward—but for her they were a waft of incense; she, the girl without a chance, half-caste—"Out-caste," she had said in bitter moments—condemned to be a housekeeper, governess, and what Chaman Lal Sethji had called her, thief and whore. That was yesterday, all the days before yesterday—today was Baisakhi, a new beginning, and she was Lady Gwithiam. Alix lifted her chin a little higher, her hand clasped Edward's arm more firmly. She had won.

It was then that they heard the voices: one, loud, jolly, unmistakable, that Alix knew only too well—a chill went through her as if the sun had suddenly gone in. "Lady-sahib's father and mother in the drawing-room." Ram Chand said it in happy malice.

"Father?" stammered Alix. "I haven't a father."

"It seems that you have now."

Two corpulent figures as oversize as the amaryllis lilies were coming from the drawing-room and, "Mumma!" cried Alix, "Mumma! Mr. Lobo!" and then—"Typical of Alix" as Edward said afterwards—"My God, Mumma, where did you get those clothes?"

Gone was the dressing-up box gown, the silk straw hat,

and boa that Hal had envied. Mrs. Lamont was a vision in purple and orange—"You see, I too can wear trouser suit" —but hers might have been made to fit the whale Una had invented. She wore white sandals, the ruby polish on her toenails flashed, as did the plastic shine of her gargantuan white handbag. Mr. Lobo was equally new and resplendent, but where his starched drill suit would not meet he had redeemed it by an indigo blue shirt-vest. From his fingers dangled a small white-wrapped parcel. Cakes or sweets, Alix was sure. He bowed profoundly to Edward and Alix but Mrs. Lamont advanced with outstretched arms. "Yes, here we are," she cried in ringing tones. "We have come to wish you. What a surprise, m'n? And you thinking I am in Naini Tal. Ha! Ha!" When Mrs. Lamont laughed it was truthfully like the shaking of a vast purple jelly—if jellies are ever bright purple. "A jolly jelly," whispered Edward to Alix who saw, with the same astonishment she had felt with Una and Hal, that Edward was not repelled but amused—and kind, as if he found her mother endearing. "My dear girl," he was to tell her, "do you think I hadn't guessed that somewhere in the background you had relatives like these? I wasn't born quite yesterday, and your mother is so natural," and Alix watched with a pang of envy as he allowed himself to be engulfed, pressed to the softness of Mrs. Lamont's bosom. Softness he could endure but strong scent and cheap face powder mixed with sweat was too much; Edward extricated himself as quickly as he could and emerged to shake hands with Mr. Lobo, while Mrs. Lamont embraced Alix.

"Come Ally, let me look at you. Ah! you have taken care of her, Sir Edward, and she really is Lady Gwithiam." Mrs. Lamont wiped tears, tears of joy, she explained, that were making the same runnels in her powder as those tears of shame shed the last time she was in Shiraz Road. "Lady Gwithiam—we read it in the papers. My daughter's wedding in the newspapers! They say it will be in the London *Times*. My little Ally—Lady Gwithiam. You could not be born as beautiful as you are for nothing, m'n?"

"Mumma, *please*."

"Look at her, Basil, look!" cried Mrs. Lamont to Mr.

Lobo. "He has always seen what I see, believed what I believed," she explained to Edward. "Ah, Sir Edward—no, I must call you Eddie—if you knew how this brave girl has plotted and planned and toiled for this."

"Mumma!" Alix was as shrill as her mother and, "Hush Alix," said Edward, his hand came under her elbow. "Forgive our surprise but you see, Mrs. Lamont, I thought you were happily settled in this Home at Naini Tal."

"I wasn't happy and it wasn't a home." Mrs. Lamont said it roundly. "Nor was I settled." She shook with mirth again, then she did not laugh. "Ally, my Ally thought she could put her mother in a Home, out of the way with the nuns." Mrs. Lamont had acquired dignity. "I think you, Eddie, would not have done that."

"No, I would not have done that," and Alix knew he had ceased to be amused.

"This gentleman, Mr. Lobo, I have known for a long time. Ally too, though she does not choose to allow him." Mrs. Lamont's voice trembled a little. "He it was who used his savings and came to Naini Tal and took me, but do not think it was to trouble you. No, we shall not trouble Lady Gwithiam." Mrs. Lamont's chin lifted exactly as Alix's lifted in moments of pride—or pain. "You are not the only ones to get married, m'n? This afternoon Father Gonsalves will marry Basil and me. We are going to live in McCluskiegung; that is an Eurasian settlement—this, of course, if you can lend us a little money to buy a bungalow. We invite you to our wedding—though you did not invite us to yours. In any case we have come by to wish you, and Basil has brought you some cakes." Mrs. Lamont's eyes were so brimming with tears that they looked like drenched pansies. "Do you not kiss me, Ally?"

"Kiss her at once," Edward hissed at Alix, propelled her forward and said aloud, "I will too, if I may."

"Ah Edward! Edward! Yes, Eddie I shall call you." Once again he was submerged and Mrs. Lamont was radiant. "We mustn't be cross, m'n? So many, many times I have forgiven Ally and what is one more? Come Basil. You must kiss the bride. Now why don't we," she demanded, "have a nice wedding drink?"

"A good idea," said Edward.

"Then perhaps you will give us tiffin and we shall all go on to the church."

"Mumma, Edward has important work he must do."

"Nonsense. They must stay for—tiffin." Edward was stern with Alix. "Go and see what Christopher can conjure up. Tell Aziz to bring drinks."

"That is my generous boy. Did I not tell you?" Mrs. Lamont asked of Mr. Lobo. "Largesse. Largesse. Did you see the ring he has given Alix. My God, what a ring! Eddie is noble and generous. Can I forget," she asked, "how ever since Ally has worked for you, week in, week out, you have sent me that whisky."

"Mumma! Be quiet. Edward does not like such things mentioned."

"I shall not mention, I shall tell. Ally said not to thank you. Your right hand was not to know what your left hand did. Ha! ha! but I know and now it need not be secret, m'n?"

"But—have I sent you whisky?" asked Edward.

"Who else? Each time Ally came to me she brought it— and none of your cheap Indian brands, the very best Scotch. Come—I must kiss you again."

"Scotch!" Round the edge of the purple hat brim Edward looked at Alix standing—pilloried, she could have said—in the doorway.

"I am a bad old woman, Eddie—I love my drink and you did not stint. My God, bottle after a bottle."

"Perhaps a dozen?" His eyes, grey-green like Una's, were cold.

"At least a dozen. More." Mrs. Lamont chortled. "God bless you, Eddie."

"You must excuse me, Mrs. Lamont." Edward disengaged himself. "Alix is right. I have some work to do. She will give you luncheon and I hope it is a good one. My felicitations—on your daughter." Alix heard the irony in his voice. "Good-bye." He took her mother's hand and kissed it, "and I hope you will be happy—you too, Lobo. I will see about the bungalow. Good-bye." He passed Alix without a word.

"Edward." She ran after him.

"I will see you this evening."

"But . . . you must have something to eat."

"I don't feel like eating."

"Edward." She put her hand on his arm. "Isn't there—anything you can say to me?"

His hand removed hers. "Only that I thank God Una wasn't there to hear." "She knows"—but Alix did not tell him that; at this moment, to Alix, Una was less important than a fly.

"Where is Una?"

"She must be still at Bulbul's. She will ring. Edward, try to understand," and, at Alix's anguished face, there was a shade of relenting.

"Perhaps—presently—I can bring myself . . ." He had to force the words out. "But to think you let a servant—let Dino . . ." His own face contorted. With an effort he said, "Give them some food—and money. That's chiefly what they came for. I will send Chinaberry back from the office with some cash. Then he can drive you to this —this ceremony and to catch the train to McCluskie-gung."

"I should rather drive them myself."

"You are not to drive while you are in this state." Then he does still care a little. Hope came into Alix's eyes, but went out as he said, "Do you think by now Chinaberry doesn't know?"

Alix's shamed head sank lower as Edward stopped, hesitated, and, as if he could not bear any more to be close to her, ran down the steps.

"You must have a bath and change, wash your hair. Wash away all traces of Mumma's abominable scent." Since Edward left her Alix had found it necessary to order herself like this. As soon as she had come in from the exhausting shameful afternoon she had flung drawing-room and dining-room windows and doors wide to let the smell drift out. "If you put on one of your new dresses—no, perhaps the mulberry one he loves—do your hair simply, be quiet, perhaps play to him . . ." surely, surely

Edward would forgive her, understand, see how circumstances had forced. . . . He must see, at least, I am a conscientious daughter, "even if, at times, a cruel one." That came like an unwelcome echo. "I only did it to spare him"—"snare him," came the echo. Alix went quickly into the bathroom.

She came out on their bedroom balcony to dry her hair in the sun, brushing its length over the rail then tossing the brightness back. Its fall, the glorious colour and sheen, reassured her. Alix never went to a hairdresser and had her own scent, subtle, "so unlike poor Mumma's." If Edward came in now how could he resist her? For the first time since they had heard Mrs. Lamont's voice, Alix smiled.

She became aware that there was an emptiness in the garden. It must be five o'clock. Through the open drawing-room door, she could see Aziz arranging the tea tray. This was garden-watering time and she called to Aziz in Hindi, "Where are the malis?"

"Ganesh doing fresh flowers for dining-table. Chota mali has gone to his village."

Alix almost vented her pent-up temper. "How was he granted leave when we were not here?"

"It was for his uncle's funeral rites. There was no son."

Alix, as well as Aziz, knew that was an incontestable reason. Then it struck her that the house was empty as well. Was Una not back?

She went along the veranda to Una's room and knocked, something she would not have done before—a governess has the right to go into her charge's room. Una's stepmother knocked.

"Lady-sahib?" Monbad was there, gone in to turn down the bed.

"Is the Miss-baba not back?"

"No, Lady-sahib."

"Has she telephoned?"

"No, Lady-sahib."

"She is late." Alix knew she would be thankful if Una were not there when Edward came back—how defend herself in front of all-knowing Una? She thought she might ring Bulbul and ask her to keep Una another night, yet a latent feeling of worry woke in Alix. She looked round the room; Monbad was putting out Una's night clothes and, She hasn't taken her dressing-gown and slippers, thought Alix, nor her hairbrush. She went into the bathroom. Una's sponge-bag was there, her bath powder, soap; only her toothbrush was missing. When Monbad had gone Alix opened the cupboard; she knew Una's dresses, her clothes. Surely, with Bulbul and Som she would have changed for the evening? Yet all her dresses were there. In the dressing-table drawer, Alix found Una's shoulder bag. She must have needed that—engagement diary: pencil: handkerchieves: the new ivory powder-case Hal had given her as a parting present: dark glasses: everything was there—except a comb. A toothbrush and a comb. Travelling light. That phrase filled Alix's mind. "Don't be silly," she told herself. "Una is forgetful," but even if she had forgotten her bag she would surely have sent round for it—she had been at Bulbul's all day—and then Alix saw one other thing was missing, the wallet that matched the bag. Una had taken a toothbrush, comb—and money.

For a moment worry flared into panic, then, "Nonsense. Nonsense," Alix said and went to the telephone. "Bulbul? It's Alix Gwithiam."

"Oh, hello." Bulbul's clear happy voice came down the line. "I saw it in the papers. Congratulations." Something like amusement in the way Bulbul spoke lit Alix's temper again. "Bulbul, why hasn't Una come back? You know how Edward worries if she's late—but you are both so damn casual."

"I am not damn casual as you call it." Bulbul had a temper too, "and how can Una be late when she isn't here."

"Then where is she?"

"Isn't that for you to answer? I haven't seen her or heard from her all this week."

"Not seen . . ." The panic was real now but Alix swiftly covered it. "Oh, of course! I'm sorry, Bulbul, but with all this . . . newness—I don't know whether I am on my head or my heels. Of course, Una is with Lady Srinevesan," but Bulbul was not mollified.

"Then Lady Gwithiam had better ring Lady Srineve-san," she said and put the receiver down.

As Alix turned from the telephone she saw something, small and blue, set down at the end of the veranda: as if mesmerized she walked towards it, then: "Monbad! Monbad!" she cried. "How did this get here?" It was Una's case.

In it were her clothes, tidily folded. *"Hé Bhagwan!"* said Monbad. "Then something *has* happened to the Miss-baba!"

Alix was waiting in the hall when Chinaberry drove Edward up. Edward came straight to her. "Alix, I was too harsh. The truth is you shattered me." He would have kissed her, but she held him off. "Tell Chinaberry not to go."

"Why, Alix!" Edward looked as tired and strained as if he had gone through a battle, "As I had," said Edward, but Alix was white to her lips and, "Chinaberry," the words were thick as if she could hardly speak as she asked in Hindi, "Where did you take Miss-baba Una after lunch yesterday?"

"To Misra Mem-sahib's, as she said."

"Alix . . ."

"Wait Edward. Chinaberry, did you see her go in?"

"At the gate. She said not to drive in—Misra Mem-sahib might be sleeping. She would not let me carry her case, but it was small. I saw her go in at the gate."

"And drove away?"

"To take you and the Sahib to Sultanpore. Those were my orders." Chinaberry was mystified. "Have I done wrong?"

"No, no. Go and get your food now, but don't put the car away. We may need it."

"Alix."

"Not here. In the drawing-room," and there, distraught, she faced him. "Edward, I shall have to shatter you still more. Una has gone."

"Gone? What do you mean—gone?"

"I don't know," whispered Alix. "But she has—disappeared."

"*Una?*"

"I hope . . . it is just that she has run away."

"Run away! You hope she has run away. Are you out of your senses?"

"I mean . . . hope it is nothing worse."

"How could it be anything worse? Why should it be?" and, "Run away. What preposterous absurdity! Why should she? We had just had that long and happy time together."

"Perhaps it was meant as—as a farewell."

"Don't be ridiculous."

"I wish it were ridiculous—and don't forget you went without me."

"You mean she is jealous?"

"I wish I thought it was just that."

He swung round. "I thought you and she had come to terms."

"I'm afraid they were terms you would not have approved."

"But . . . she was with Bulbul. I will ring Bulbul."

"I have. She hasn't seen or heard from Una for a week." Alix caught his arm. "Edward, be careful. There is more in this than we know, than even I know. Una hasn't taken any of her things—not even clothes."

He passed his hand over his face as if to shut out a bad dream. His hair was on end. "She wouldn't have run away. She must have been abducted."

"Then why did she pretend she had rung Bulbul and arranged to go there? And hoodwinked Chinaberry? It isn't," said Alix slowly, "because she hated and despised me—and she had reason as—as I shall have to tell you, Edward. I believe . . ." and Alix seemed to have a weight that bowed her down, ". . . Una has gone away with somebody. Come and look at her room," she said.

Edward had stood on the embroidered rug and watched as Alix showed him the cupboard, the dressing-table untouched; Una's dressing-gown and slippers: the books she had been reading. The tidiness was impeccable in the small white room. A letter from Hal was unopened on the desk, as were the notebooks. The ivory and sandalwood pieces were marshalled on the chess board and, "I didn't play one game with her," said Edward. Again his face had contorted. "Perhaps . . . perhaps I deserved this." Suddenly he bent: the sandalwood king, in his elephant's howdah, wore a little cocked hat. It was lettered "Edward" and sealed.

"Of course—so I couldn't open it," said Alix.

When you open this, Una had written in a minuscule hand, *I shall have gone. Please don't try and find me, first because you can't and secondly because I am not coming back—nor shall I want any of my things; as a matter of fact, I shall not be Una Gwithiam anymore. That sounds as if I were becoming a nun—far far from it. I am with someone who has made me happier than I have ever dreamed of being—so please tell Alix this has nothing to do with her.*

"Thank God," said Alix, "and thank God it is this— nothing more terrible—kidnapping perhaps . . ." She had not been able to go on.

For reasons of our own, Una had written, *we shall stay hidden for two or three months, which is why, now, I cannot tell you his name, only that he is Indian and you will like him.*

"Like him!"

When the right time comes you will know everything and I think you will be pleased.

"Pleased!" Edward almost choked.

Meanwhile I am happy and well and looked after, so please trust me. You have your new life. Let me have mine. Love. Una.

"Love—Una . . ." Edward could only repeat the phrases as if they were branded into him. Savagely, he crumpled the note, then seemed to crumple too.

"You swore to me," said Edward. "I swear. That's what you said." Anger had set in and he was icy with rage. "I can hear your voice now. 'I swear to you it would be impossible for either of the girls to be alone with a young man for half an hour without my knowing.' That's what you said."

"And what I believed." Alix's chin had come up. "You must remember, Edward, I spent the nights with you."

"Nights! What could she possibly have done at night, where gone? With watchmen, sepoys at the gate?"

"I don't know."

"Exactly. You don't know. I trusted you."

"And I once asked you to take back your trust. Do you remember?" Alix's eyes, as her mother's had been, were brimming, but in hers there was anger as well as grief. "I knew from the beginning Una was too much for me."

"Nonsense. Ridiculous, preposterous, absurd nonsense!" Edward was striding up and down the drawing-room. "Not Una! Hal, perhaps, but not Una. Besides, how could she, when we knew her every movement, every hour?"

"Did we?"

"Then we ought to have done." Alix's head sank lower. Then she raised it. "We will find her, Edward. We will find her, if we have to turn the whole of India upside down."

"Don't be silly. That would be like looking for one small ant in an ant heap the size of Everest!"

"Why, Edward!" Lady Srinevesan rose in surprise as Edward and Alix came into her drawing-room. "Lady Gwithiam!" If there were a shade of reserve in that they did not notice it and, "Thank God, you are alone," said Edward.

"Yes, Dev is at the Club. His eternal bridge." Lady Srinevesan's quick eyes had taken in their consternation. "What has happened?"

"Amina, may we ask you a few questions—alone?"

"Of course, but first, let me get you a drink or some coffee. No, not a word," as Edward would have waved that aside. "You both look like ghosts."

"Not coffee," said Alix. "They are expecting us back for

dinner. Edward has had nothing to eat all day"—this lacerating day—"but a drink would be good," and, when they came, she and Edward sipped them gratefully.

"Now?" Lady Srinevesan, wearing one of her favorite silver saris, sat down to listen. "There is no one to overhear. The servants have gone. What is this about?"

"About—Una," Edward could scarcely say her name.

"Edward," Alix had pleaded, "wouldn't it be better to do as she says? Trust her—leave her alone?"

"Alone! She's a child."

"I don't think Una has ever been a child. I'm afraid of —damage."

"Good God! What worse damage could there be?" asked Edward bitterly.

"I don't know but . . ." Alix had not been able to find words. Then, "I haven't been completely blind," she said. "I do know some of it. The trouble is, I believed Una. I didn't think she would lie."

"Who taught her to lie?"

"Both of us. Wasn't it a lie that brought her and Hal here in the first place?"

"Don't fence with me, Alix. This disaster . . ."

"It may not be disaster." Alix had regained her poise though her heart seemed to be fluttering in her throat and she was breathing as if in a physical battle. "Edward, just after Hal went, I discovered . . . I looked in Una's mathematics book. . . ."

And now, "Amina," said Edward to Lady Srinevesan, "Amina, do you, can you, recall Una's being especially friendly with some friend of yours, or of Sophia Mehta's? We guess a young man and a mathematician."

"A mathematician? That sounds more like one of Dev's friends, but they would hardly be young. Here the young are all artists, musicians, writers—of course, one of them may also do mathematics."

"But do you remember Una's especially talking to one of them?"

"The trouble with Una," said Lady Srinevesan, "was to make her talk at all. Usually at any affair or party she stayed in my shadow, or Sophia's—but why?"

Alix took up the story. "She told me that someone—she guessed it was a man—was helping her make a surprise for Edward. I guessed it was something to do with Indian literature, poetry—or history."

"Literature or history—then why the mathematics?"

"That same someone had been helping Una with hers," said Alix.

"Without your knowledge?" Lady Srinevesan's eyebrows were raised.

"For a time." Alix flushed painfully. "Then, of course, I found out, but she said it was a secret, part of this surprise for Edward, and told me the man was a friend of yours, at least someone you knew, you and Mrs. Mehta, so I thought she must have met him here."

Lady Srinevesan shook her head. "I am completely mystified. Poetry and mathematics seldom go together . . . music now, but Una isn't anything of a musician. You are afraid," she asked, "that Una is involved with this young man?"

"Deeply involved." Edward was too desperate to keep it back.

"She must have been with him over and over again." Alix said it hopelessly.

"Could it have been at Bulbul's?" but Lady Srinevesan answered her own question. "It couldn't. Bulbul isn't interested in that sort of thing. Una and Bulbul frivol, which I have *never* understood."

"She took refuge with Bulbul from me," but Alix did not say it.

"Think, please think," urged Edward. Lady Srinevesan still shook her head; then a remembrance made her wrinkle her forehead. "Wait . . . there is what may be a tiny, tiny clue. Una did ask me about someone—a young poet—who used to come here and read, though quite long before her time. She asked Sophia Mehta too. His name was Ravi Bhattacharya."

"Ravi Bhattacharya. We don't know anyone called that."

"Ravi was an outstanding young poet—outstandingly handsome too, but I remember being surprised she knew his poems because none of them had been published—so far as I know. She knew one of them so well that she could say it by heart and recited it in a dreamy sort of way. When Sophia commented, she blushed."

"*Una* blushed."

"Yes, I thought it untypical."

"And you are sure she didn't meet him here or at Sophia Mehta's?"

"Quite sure. He disappeared. It must be two years or more since we saw him. I was told he had gone underground, been concerned in some trouble with the Praja Swaraj—the People's Freedom Party—but, and how could I have forgotten *this*?" cried Lady Srinevesan, "I had meant to tell Una she would meet him. Ravi Bhattacharya has reappeared. In fact, he has applied for the Tagore Memorial Poetry Prize. I'm sure he'll be one of the finalists. The judging will be held at Vigyan Bhawan at the end of the month."

"Then he is probably here, in Delhi."

"He will be here on the thirtieth. All the finalists must read their poems, but he may be nothing to do with this. In fact, I don't see how he could. How could they have met?" asked Lady Srinevesan. "And remember, girls of Una's age often get a fixation on a poem."

Now it was Edward who shook his head. "Una isn't that sort of girl. Besides, if a poem particularly struck her she would have shown it to me."

"I can guess," Lady Srinevesan was cool, "that lately, there were several things Una did not show."

Red mounted again in Alix's cheeks. Desperately she defended herself. "It sounded so innocuous—a surprise for Edward."

"But there are surprises and surprises," said Lady Srinevesan.

"Ram Chand."

"Huzoor?"

"Ram, in this house you are our most trusted and confidential servant."

"That was Dino, Sahib." Ram was still unforgiving, but Edward was asking for mercy.

"You know that Una Miss-baba has disappeared?"

Ram did not say that everybody knew it. He inclined his head.

"Ram, have you ever seen, ever known, a young man, a Mr. Ravi Bhattacharya come to the house?"

"Ravi Bhattacharya?" Startled astonishment made Ram jerk from head to foot.

"Well? Speak man."

"There is a Ravi," said Ram. "But . . ."

"But?"

"He is of the house, Sahib."

"*Of* the house?"

"Yes, Sahib. Ravi Bhattacharya," said Ram Chand, "is Sahib's second gardener."

They searched Ravi's hut. "Wait till this gets about Delhi," Edward was grim.

"It mustn't get about Delhi. We shall find them," said Alix, "and it may not be this Ravi Bhattacharya." She could not believe it. "Under our very eyes—and with a servant."

"Ram," Edward had asked. "Did you, did any of you notice the Miss-baba as being—friendly with this young man?"

Ram drew himself up. "None of us would so forget ourselves as to do such a thing."

"But was he one of you?"

As soon as they searched the hut it was obvious he was not. There were the usual things of any servant's room: the string bed, mat, clay oven, pots, pans, platters and bowls, clothes on a string, but Edward's eyes went straight to the desk and, "Ah!" said Edward.

"Yes, Ravi could read and write," Ganesh, for whom Edward had sent, spoke in Hindi. "I do not know why he was gardener . . . I thought . . ."

"You thought?"

"To myself," said Ganesh with dignity, "I thought he

might be a college boy in trouble—but Ravi was older than that. He had many many books," but Edward had already lifted the desk lid. "Bowra! Day Lewis's *Poetic Image* . . . *Form and Style in Poetry*, W. P. Ker . . . Some garden boy!"

"Who is W. P. Ker?" Alix was past pretending now.

"One of our greatest professors of English—Oxford, Cardiff, London."

"Suppose they search your hut?" Una had asked Ravi.

"Why should they search my hut? No one has any reason to connect me with you," but Una was still uneasy.

"Shouldn't we hide the books?"

"And make Ganesh suspicious at once? Hardly I should have taken books to go and cremate my uncle," and, "Ravi is coming back," said Ganesh with certainty. It seemed as if Ravi were; there were fruit and stores in the *doolie*, clothes on the line and in the chest.

"But if he had taken Una he would not be coming back," said Alix.

"Tomorrow or the day after," said Ganesh. "He asked me to buy him curd and milk, light the deeva for his tulsi plant. If he had . . . left," Ganesh would not say 'gone,' "with the Miss-baba, why should he ask me to do that?"

"I don't know." Edward felt he was falling deeper and deeper into mystery. "You are sure the hut is exactly as it was?"

"As it was," said Ganesh.

"I have left nothing—nothing that could connect me with you," Ravi had told Una. His prize poems were with him in the small tin trunk. "All the copies?" asked Una. "Remember I copied some of them for you."

"Do you not think I am extremely careful?" but Hem could have warned Una that even Ravi's extreme carefulness was careless and, "Wait," cried Alix. As Edward took the books out, she had caught sight of one at the bottom of the desk. It was an exercise book; she pulled it out and took it to the lantern Ganesh held. "Poems," said Alix. "Poems or drafts of poems," and, "Edward, it must be this Ravi. Look. Oh Edward! some are copied in Una's hand."

They turned the exercise book over. The faded purple cover was stamped in gold, rubbed now and faint, but there was a crest, and a name. "St Thomas's College," read Alix.

"I remember him," said Professor Asutosh. "I think most people who met him would remember him. He had exceptional charm but Bhattacharya was an idealistic boy and easily carried away. He was difficult to deal with because he was so contradictory; he wanted to be popular, one of the college bloods, yet had fits of being solitary, idle and dreaming, cutting lectures, staying out after hours— he had plenty of money for bribery. When he was in these moods I thought he was most himself; that false swagger came from a feeling of inferiority."

"Was he inferior?"

"Indeed no. He was most gifted and his father owned land, a big house—in fact, a whole village near Ambala, but Bhattacharya was kept at home, privately tutored while most of our students have had years at the Doon School or the Mayo College at Ajmere. Consequently, he lacked experience—and discipline."

"A mother's boy?"

"More a father's. Sri Bhattacharya is elderly, a Brahmin of a sect extremely strict, and felt school might contaminate his son during the impressionable years. It was only when the family tutor confessed the boy was beyond him that he was sent to us—I believe at the mother's insistence; it was too late to instill discipline and I was not surprised when young Bhattacharya got into trouble."

"What trouble?"

"He joined the Praja Swaraj—I am sure, first of all, for idealistic reasons—a movement against the establishment —but, as these movements quickly do, it became violent and he had to drop out of college in his last term. A great pity; as I said, he had more than an ordinary gift. If this is true about your daughter . . ."

"It must be," said Edward. "We compared the writing in her mathematics book. It was this Ravi's."

"I still pray God it is not," Professor Asutosh was grave.

"If it is, comfort yourself that she may have better taste than we have. Even in his college days, Ravi Bhattacharya was an outstanding poet."

"Then why a gardener?"

"I suspect he had reasons for being hidden. In that connection," said the Professor, "there was something I could not understand. The boy had a friend, perhaps two years older, one of our senior students, a young man called Hemango Sharma. He befriended Bhattacharya—I think Hem took pity on him—Ravi was unmercifully ragged for his airs and graces when he first came, and he was not used to being ragged. I can guess, too, that Hem Sharma tried to persuade him away from the Party; its ways are not gentle and even after Hem took his degree he watched over the boy. Almost two years ago there was an incident at a factory near here where a group incited the workers to riot; a foreman came out, a respectable middle-aged man, simply—and I believe mildly—doing his duty. He was beaten, held, and acid thrown into his eyes. The group got away but one young man gave himself up and was arrested—Hem Sharma."

"Well?" Edward could not see what this was to do with Una.

"Please listen. Hem would never have done such an act—or been accessory to it. I knew that, but the Trial Court found him guilty and he was sent to prison. He refused a defence, could not be induced to name the others, though methods were used . . . but I made him appeal against his own sentence. Hem is too valuable a young man for our society to lose; the Appellate Court held his conviction baseless—the witnesses did not agree —and Hem was freed. Though he had taken a first here, he is, I am glad to say, qualifying as a doctor—I confess with my help."

"Well?" Edward still did not see.

"Only this; if you want to find Ravi Bhattacharya, I suggest you go to Hem Sharma."

"Ah!" Then, "Not to the father?"

"He would probably not receive you; besides, I doubt if Sri Bhattacharya has his son's confidence. When the boy dropped out of college, his father ordered him to come home at once, or never come."

"And this Ravi did not go?"

"I'm certain he did not go."

"Then where is he?"

"I have told you: ask Hem."

Hem had been in bed when Edward's car drove up; in bed but not asleep. He had not been able to sleep since Una had been in his room; lying on his side, staring into the darkness, Hem had to face that fact. He had left her case at Shiraz Road, slipping through their secret fence, depositing it on the veranda, slipping out again and cycling away, but he knew quite certainly that, sooner or later, Ravi would be traced to him, and Edward's knock was no surprise. Hem, in his lungi—sleeping cloth—answered the knock and found Edward on the step.

"May I come in?"

"No." Hem was definite. "I know why you have come and it is evident that Miss Una changed her clothes here in my room—Ravi Bhattacharya has a key—but I was at the Medical School for my studies. She changed here but, Sir Edward, I do not know where they have gone and I do not want to know."

"But you were party to this?" Hem's coolness made Edward's temper hotter.

"I was not party. I knew about their attachment, but my advice was to tell it to you. They would not take my advice."

"You mean this Ravi wouldn't. I suppose it was a bit of a feather in his cap to seduce a well-brought-up English girl."

"There are well-brought-up English girls in the bazaar. I think I could have persuaded Ravi, but not Miss Una."

"Not Una. But . . ." Edward was firm in his belief. "He has abducted her."

"Not at all. They decided to go together. She has come to love Ravi."

"*Come* to love him? Then this has been going on for some time?"

"Quite some time."

"And you didn't try to prevent it?"

"Wasn't that a task for you and Miss Lamont?" Hem asked. "Besides, Ravi is not a child."

"My daughter is. Far under age. You must have known that your friend—this . . . this gardener—was committing an offence."

"Ah, but to begin with it was innocent. Ravi first spoke to Una out of pity." Hem had forgotten the 'Miss.'

"Pity! My daughter?"

"It was because she was your daughter that she had cause to grieve. For one thing, Miss Lamont, as she was then, could not teach her."

"This is the first I have heard of it."

"It remains." Hem was imperturbable. "Forgive me for saying this, Sir Edward, but I do not think Miss Lamont is fully educated."

"She was at the Sorbonne."

"She was in Paris. I think Ravi is not the only one to masquerade."

"You said 'was innocent.' " Edward changed the subject abruptly. "Then you confirm, with Una and—Ravi—it is not innocent now?"

"If to fall in love and make love is un-innocent; I am of the opinion your Adam and Eve did it before the Fall."

"Good God, man," Edward cried. "Don't you see I am in agony?"

"I have seen Una in agony too."

"Then you won't help me?" said Edward.

"I can't help you. I repeat, I do not know where they have gone."

"And," said Edward, "he went in and closed the door."

Edward was in the inner sanctum of the police headquarters with the Inspector-General of Police, Colonel Manoharlal Jaiswal.

"Not the police," Alix had begged. "Don't call in the police, Edward. Please. Please." She was almost hysterical.

"Talking to Colonel Jaiswal is hardly calling in the police."

From Hem, Edward had driven back to the Srinevesans'

where the minister had come in. Sir Mahadeva Srinevesan had listened closely and was shocked. "It's not possible," he said. "It's . . . incredible!"

"Not nowadays," said Lady Srinevesan. "You don't know enough young people. Think what they know, hear, read, see."

"But with an English girl!"

"The standing of English girls—any Westerner—is not very high here in India," she reminded him. "Remember how some of them behave; but Una—that, I grant you, is difficult to believe."

"She thinks she is in love." Edward had to defend her.

"Besides," said Lady Srinevesan, "it has always been possible where there is a young man and woman. Why else," she asked, "used we to guard our daughters so rigidly?"

"I thought I had." That was what gave Edward the most acute pain. "I thought I had."

Sir Mahadeva telephoned the Inspector-General on a private line. "This must be kept completely hushed. It could break into a world-wide scandal, embarrass the Government, to say the least. Think of the headlines." Edward closed his eyes with a rush of sickness. "Would you deal with it personally?" asked Sir Mahadeva. "They must be found without a whisper."

"There are whispers already," Lady Srinevesan reminded him. "I can muzzle Bulbul but . . . Well, we must try."

"We must not *try*," Sir Mahadeva had said. "We must succeed," and he had put his arm round Edward's shoulders in a warm clasp to hearten him. "We shall succeed. You will see."

An officer came in and laid a slip of paper on the Inspector-General's desk. "Nothing seems known against the young man Bhattacharya, sir."

"I understood from Professor Asutosh he had joined the Praja Swaraj," said Edward.

"We have no proof but it seems this Hemango Sharma has a police record. He was sentenced to three years."

"He appealed and was acquitted." In fairness Edward had to say it.

"So it seems." The Inspector-General was studying the paper. "All the same, it will make it easier to take him and, shall we say, urge him to talk."

Just before dawn, two plain-clothes men came for Hem. Edward was on his way to the village near Ambala.

"Go by all means." Unlike Professor Asutosh, the Inspector-General approved. "You never know. You might pick up something."

"Can't I come?" Alix had pleaded.

"You would only make things worse."

"Because I am Eurasian." Alix was open about that now. It was two in the morning, and Alix's eyes had seemed sunken in ringed sockets, her hair was roughly tumbled; she had made Edward have sandwiches, drink coffee laced with brandy. "You have to wait while China-berry eats," she argued. "He can't drive all night on nothing," and she had packed a basket for them too and filled a flask with more hot coffee. Edward neither thanked her nor looked at her, simply drove away.

"Sri Bhattacharya? I must apologize for coming at this hour and in this state, but what would you have done in my place?"

"I should have washed," said Ravi's father.

Edward was not used to being snubbed. He and China-berry had found the village on the Sarsuti River, the strip of country called the Holy Land because it was the cradle of Hindu faith, the first home of the Aryans in India. At any other time, Edward would have been deeply interested, particularly now when, in the early morning mist that hung over the sacred river, villagers were going down to make their morning ritual, to bathe and pray, carrying their lotas through fields, harvested and pale with stubble. In a hamlet of mud-and-thatch houses, the car came to a wall built of ancient thin Punjabi brick, with a pair of closed wooden gates. They were not opened for the car;

Edward had to wait while the gateman took in his card and wait another half-hour: "Sri Bhattacharya is taking his bath," Chinaberry explained. "He is making his meditation," was the next message and when at last Edward was beckoned in, it was only as far as the veranda where he was offered a wooden chair on which he had had to sit at least twenty minutes longer, listening to the house noises, splashing, sweeping, a pounding—perhaps of grain —subdued voices. There was a day bed on the veranda, spread with a white sheet and set with a takia covered in spotless white cotton, and, when Sri Bhattacharya finally appeared, walking stiffly and acknowledging Edward only by a silent namaste, he took his place there, drawing up his legs and sitting upright against the bolster, the folds of the white *lohi* he wore over his shoulders falling round him.

Was it possible, thought Edward, that this little old thread of a man was father to the magnificent young gardener? Sri Bhattacharya's legs and arms were so thin that they looked brittle; his head was covered with short grey stubble except where one lock was left raggedly long in orthodox Hindu fashion. He had not shaved and his skin had a fig-purple tinge as if he were cold and he was toothless; probably, thought Edward, he disdains false teeth but nothing could have been more unattractive than that watery mouthing as his lips moved. Was he praying? But a spot of fresh sandalwood paste on his forehead showed that he had already made his prayer. Chewing perhaps? Or was it a querulous habit? Edward could well understand why Ravi did not want to go home.

Sri Bhattacharya looked far over Edward's face as if he preferred not to see him and spoke: "Why have you come?"

"About your son," said Edward and, in a few short sentences made his indictment. There was no interruption or exclamation, not a quiver in the other's face, only the little eyes continued to look far beyond Edward.

When he had finished, Sri Bhattacharya said, "I have no such son."

"Ravi Bhattacharya is your son." Edward said it steadily. "He has committed an offence against my daughter. If he brings her here . . ."

"She would be immediately returned to you. Such a girl would not be permitted in my house."

Angry colour rose in Edward's haggard cheeks. "If you have daughters. . ."

"I have no daughters. I had an only son." There was a spasm in the face but, at the slight on Una, Edward's temper broke.

"You understand, Sri Bhattacharya, that I have no alternative but the police. This could be a criminal charge. My daughter is not yet sixteen. Your house could be searched . . ."

"They may search it. He . . ." Sri Bhattacharya would not say 'Ravi,' nor 'my son.' "He has not been here for two years, and he will not come back. I have given orders. His mother may have kept a few small things. . . ." The folds of the lohi, too, were quivering now and Edward's temper gave way to compassion; here was a wound, perhaps worse than his own.

"Sri Bhattacharya," but the shorn grey hair was held higher.

"I can do nothing to help you. It is time for me to take my meal. Good morning, Sir Edward."

The village, thought Alix, is ten miles from Ambala; that makes it some hundred and twelve miles from here. Chinaberry may take time to find it and I expect the road will be bad. Edward will need to talk with the Bhattacharyas . . . and Alix calculated he could not be back in Delhi before the afternoon, but soon after eleven o'clock he telephoned. "Send Ram Chand down to the office with a change of clothes and my shaving things."

"Where are you going?"

"To Varanasi. The Embassy people have been more than kind and are lending me their private plane. The Inspector-General is coming with me."

"You have found out something?"

"Nothing." Edward was curt.

"Then why . . . ?"

"I have a possible clue—that is all."

When Edward had come out of the Bhattacharya house, or been dismissed from it, he had found a woman waiting by the car—a lady, he corrected himself. Though her sari was plain white red-bordered muslin and worn in the old-fashioned way on the right shoulder, her jewelry unobtrusive, only a thin gold chain, gold stud earrings, her head bare, her feet in village sandals, she was—unmistakably noble, thought Edward. "How do you do, Sir Edward. I am Ravi Bhattacharya's mother." Her husband's English had been stilted; hers was as smooth as Edward's own. Years younger than her husband, she was taller than Alix; Edward remembered what a splendid specimen was their son—she had his golden complexion—bright wheat the Indians called it—more, there came to Edward a feeling of immense capability as she spoke quickly. "At times one is forced to eavesdrop and I heard. Sir Edward, try to understand: no worse blow could have fallen on my husband. Though he seems unfeeling, our son is his heart—and was his hope. In our *gotra*—the table of our family—there are ten generations of Bhattacharyas in the direct line. I am the mischief," she said it in earnest. "I was educated in the Western way and brought new ideas, persuaded him over Ravi, and now, to him, Ravi is tainted."

"And my Una, even if she were old enough to be married, would be the final taint?"

"There would be no pure heritage," said Srimati Bhattacharya, "so, even if circumstances were different, to my husband such a union would be unthinkable."

"And to you?"

"It is the way the world is moving, barriers are breaking but she is so young and they have been—unprincipled."

"Unprincipled? Yes," said Edward. "Tell me, did a brother-in-law or your brother die yesterday or the day before that?"

"Indeed no."

"That was why your son asked for leave."

"That was certainly unprincipled—but what I came out to tell you," she said, "is that I think it possible they—

Ravi—might have gone to his grandmother, my mother who lives now in retirement in Varanasi. She would take them in without question. Here is the address."

Now that there was a ray of hope, Edward, paradoxically, had an instinct to draw back as if he heard an echo of Alix's word 'damage.' "Yet I have to find them." That beat steadily in his tired brain. "I have to. I must. It is the only sane thing to do," and, "If your son is there," he asked, "How should I deal with him?"

"You must intimidate him." She was fierce. "Ravi can be intimidated, especially if anything threatens his work, but what to do with him, you must decide."

"Most mothers would plead."

"How can I plead? There is your daughter. You are right to be outraged with us. What you choose to do with Ravi you must do."

Edward's eyelids were coated with dust, red with soreness and tiredness. Now they were suddenly wet.

"I cannot plead," said Srimati Bhattacharya. "I can only trust."

"Where are you going?" said Edward to Ravi in the alleyway.

"To report back for duty, sir," which was true.

"In Shiraz Road?"

"Where else?" Ravi was trying to bluster it out. "I have been on leave of absence to perform the obsequies of my uncle." He was talking as stiltedly as his own father and the bluster withered under the sternness of Edward's look.

"This is your grandmother's house?" Edward could see it was built on the bank above the river, a tall house faced with pink stucco, the rooms overlooking the alley close-shuttered. Through the narrow door he could glimpse a walled garden, smell jasmine. "Your grandmother, Srimati Roy?"

"She is not at home."

"I think she is. You will take my card to her."

"I am not your servant."

"You have just said you were."

"She does not receive strangers."

"She received one yesterday. Come boy. Be sensible," said Edward.

"You must not lose your temper," the Inspector-General had cautioned him.

"It won't be easy. I should like to strangle him," said Edward.

"Understandably, but you must think how you are placed—and the Bhattacharyas, too, are not without influence. The Minister begged me not to cause embarrassment. Be cool," and, with an effort, Edward only repeated, "Be sensible. You know I have come for Una."

"Una? What Una?" but, before Ravi could make another futile attempt: "This is Colonel Jaiswal," said Edward, "Inspector-General and Chief of Police."

"Inspector-General . . . Chief . . ." Ravi's gasp could have filled the alley. He had dreaded a policeman but now the power of Edward's position dawned on him—the Inspector-General himself—and, in panic, "It is Hem Sharma who has given us away," shouted Ravi.

"No dramatics, Bhattacharya." Colonel Jaiswal was brisk. "Neither I, nor my men, could get one word from Sharma. You gave yourselves away. Now take Sir Edward's card in to Srimati Roy. Then you will talk to me," but Ravi's nerve had snapped; he dodged back into the house and would have slammed and bolted the door but for the policeman's quickness in putting his boot in the gap; they heard Ravi run up a stone staircase and his frantic cry of "Naniji! Naniji! Naniji!"

ELEVEN

"You are sooner than I expected," said Srimati Roy.

"You expected us."

"Were not you bound to come—though it might have been later."

"Srimati Roy, is my daughter here?"

"She is here."

"You did not turn her away?"

"That would not have been kind."

"Your son-in-law would have called her a pollution."

"Pollution—a young girl? You must forgive my English; until last night I have not spoken it for twenty years. Please sit down. You must take some refreshment. Ravi, order them to bring salt *lussee*—that will be cooling—lussee and fruits. Ravi beta." The last was said warningly. Ravi was kneeling by the day bed on which Srimati Roy was sitting as her son-in-law had sat, cross-legged but infinitely more upright. The rest of the big room was bare except for a painted chest and the low stools on which Edward and the Inspector-General were sitting; by the sunlit water reflections on the walls, the room overhung the river. *"Ravi!"*

Unwillingly Ravi rose. "I will go with him," said Colonel Jaiswal.

"Yes, I suppose you will not let him out of your sight." She nodded in acceptance or approval—Edward did not know which—and in a few minutes they came back with a grey-bearded servant who brought the cool curd drink served in silver tumblers with a plate of orange segments, bowls of nuts, and fresh shredded coconut; it was, as Srimati Roy had said, refreshing; she did not eat, but sat talking about everyday things until her guests had finished, when the policeman beckoned Ravi away, leaving her and Edward alone.

Edward had expected more aloofness—"Srimati Roy is an extremely holy woman," Colonel Jaiswal had said. "She lives in strict asceticism and spends most of her days and nights in meditation; probably she repeats the name of God a thousand times a day"—but the only sign Edward saw was that it seemed all her personal pride had ceased. Remembering Sri Bhattacharya's snub, he had insisted that they should stop at some hotel to wash and change their shirts; now Edward saw he need not have bothered. Srimati Roy would not notice such things.

Like her daughter, she was a tall woman which accentuated her thinness; she was emaciated to gauntness. Edward was sure that did not concern her in the least. "What does it matter?" Srimati Roy would have said. Her sari, of white muslin, was limp, almost revealing her shrunken breasts and the veil had slipped from her hair which was cropped to a rough whiteness. She wore no jewellery but Edward could see ring marks in her nose and ears; once, he guessed, the jewellery was of quality, certainly gold; now there were only the empty holes, from choice, he knew. As with Srimati Bhattacharya, he had the feeling of immense capability but here was more: the eyes, made bigger in the gauntness of the face, looked steadily beyond him, not to ignore him as her son-in-law had but, while recognizing him and his errand, fitting him into some infinite pattern far beyond this room and its reflections, even beyond the sacred river. Edward's urgent importances seemed to dwindle into perspective because this was not a willed peace, a shutting away, but peace itself, steady, kind, unruffled.

A police officer in uniform had come for Srimati Roy's loved grandson: a stranger broken her seclusion on a grave charge yet she was not disconcerted; in fact, she smiled absently on Edward. "Yes, I was expecting you. In your position, naturally there would be great hue and cry—not great in public sensation, we hope, great in intelligence. How could you not find them out?"

"If I had not come, would you have sent for me?" asked Edward.

"I think not. Better, I think, to let things take their course."

"Even when a young, young girl has been abducted?" Edward was still obstinate. "Where is Una?"

"The little one is asleep. She is severely overtired and I think has some heatstroke and, I suspect, a little dysentery."

"Heatstroke—dysentery." Edward reared up.

"Yes." Srimati Roy remained tranquil. "It seems Ravi gave her crushed sugar-cane juice, bought at some station; it is seldom clean."

"You have called a doctor?"

"I have treated her," Srimati Roy said with dignity. "You can trust me. I should so have treated my own daughter."

"Which is more than your son-in-law would have done." The morning still rankled.

"Indira, my daughter, is there. Indira would have seen to it," and Srimati Roy said serenely, "The attacks have passed so could you not let Una sleep? Now you have found her, what is the hurry?"

That nettled Edward. "The hurry is that a scandal might blow up in Delhi."

"Or be blown up."

"Exactly. Also I have work to do that some people think important," which made Srimati Roy smile again, but gently.

"Speaking of scandal," she said, "you must, I think, give up the thought of abduction. You have a phrase in law,

Sir Edward, 'the innocent party'; party is good, we are all made of parts, unfortunately often contradictory." She sighed. "Here there is no innocent party. Either both my grandson and your daughter are innocent or both are guilty—if you call it that."

"What do you call it?"

"Normal." Her voice was singsong but as mellifluous as it was calm. "I am well aware that I am harbouring what is supposed to be a crime. You may have surrounded my house with police. If they search, what will they find? A young man and woman in love. Is that not normal?"

"The circumstances are not."

"Ah! The circumstances." She dismissed them as if, thought Edward, they were a flick.

"You see no objections?"

"Perhaps a hundred. They do not alter facts."

"The fact is, she is under age, and they have run away."

"From what did they run, Sir Edward? From fear of their families. Fear is an ugly thing and should not be in a family, but my son-in-law, Ravi's father, lives by 'littles,' as I think you, Sir Edward, do, though perhaps not consciously; divisions, separations: Indian—English: caste—class: old—young. You make such trouble for yourselves, such tamasha, brouhaha—that is a word I thought I had forgotten. Well," she sighed again. "With such ideas why did you not safeguard her?"

"I thought I had," and Edward was filled with desire to pour out to this woman of calm his sorry tale. But Hindus don't tell their sins, he thought. "They wash them away in the river."

He must have said it aloud because Srimati Roy spoke. "It is a coincidence you said that. As soon as she saw the river from our alleyway, your little daughter did not wait, she went in to bathe herself, before ever she came to the house. Ravi said she ran there. I asked her why: her answer was simple. She said, 'To wash away the dirt.' She said more than she knew. Aie! Why make dirt, Sir Edward?"

"Don't!" Edward's cry was sharp. "Srimati Roy, you are right. This is all my fault. These last twenty-four hours have opened my eyes—painfully." I have made Una suffer, thought Edward, perhaps all her life.

"What pity it all is! She would have made a good wife for Ravi, but there is one valid objection. He is still a student for all his age. Aie! Ravi raja! He is as irresponsible as one of your cuckoos."

"Your daughter told me to intimidate him."

She smiled. "Indira is still fierce."

"What would you have me do with him?" asked Edward.

"I am not concerned."

"He is your grandson."

"Still I am not concerned."

"Yet you call him Ravi beta, Ravi raja."

"Old habit," but he had touched her. "If possible, Sir Edward, and you can make it possible, let him compete in this festival and read his poems. If he appears—and this Lady Srinevesan they talk of will, I am sure, help you—all scandal, if there is scandal, will be hushed, especially if you are there. If Ravi wins, he will gain esteem, most importantly from his father, put an end to their grieving and Ravi could go home."

"Sri Bhattacharva says he will not have him back."

She smiled again. "He will," and she gave him the little nod of dismissal which in Indian society means the end of an interview.

Edward rose. "I will go and see how Jaiswal and Ravi are getting on."

"With the intimidation?" but she was still unruffled. "Do that. Then my servant will take you to your Una."

"Go away," said Una.

Edward had scarcely recognized her; it was not only that she was wearing a sari, that her skin seemed transparent by contrast with the black hair, dyed lashes and brows, that she had grown even thinner—she was 'changed,' thought Edward, as if his Una had gone and this changeling come in her place. He had found her asleep, lying on a sleeping mat laid on other reed mats to give softness; a small clean white pillow was under her head, the floor around her strewn with neem leaves which, Edward knew, are cooling and refreshing. Beside her was a brass tray with a covered jug and tumbler; khus-khus, woven grass mats, had been hung across the balcony to dim the room; they had been freshly sprayed with water and the river breeze blew through them; Edward could hear the lapping of the river far below. No one, he saw, could have had better care, yet she looked so small and white lying in the big room that, more strongly than ever, he felt the pang, the tug at his heart Una so often gave him. "Una," he had called with utmost gentleness, but she must have been tense; she started in her sleep, sat up alarmed and, when she recognized him, it was with horror. "Go away."

"Una, I have come to fetch you. Dear, I am not cross . . ."

"But I am. I am—furious. I said 'Please don't try to find us.' "

"I had to. Do you think I could let an Indian—or anyone—do this to you?"

"He didn't do it. We did it. Oh, Dads, go away."

"My dear, I can't."

"Why?" she demanded passionately. "Why can't you? I helped you to get what you wanted—Alix." She did not notice Edward's wince. "Then why won't you help me to have Ravi?"

"It isn't as simple as that."

"It could be."

"Dear, it's impossible."

"It can't be impossible. It has happened. We are married."

"You are not."

"As much married as you and Alix. More—we are first lovers."

"I know, and I know how it hurts, but it can't go on."

"Why? Why? Why?"

"For one thing you are too young."

"Not now."

"Too young," repeated Edward, "and you come from worlds apart."

"In our world there are only two of us—us two, together."

"No world can be like that, and his parents would never consent, nor wou'd I."

"We don't need parents."

"But you need their consent."

"Why?"

"Because without it you cannot stay together. That is the law. Una, be reasonable."

"Ravi is my reason."

"Ravi could be charged and sent to prison, perhaps for seven years."

"He is still my reason."

"You cannot see mine just now." Edward's voice was filled with pity. "One day you will."

"No." That rang out as she sprang up from her mat. "I will never see."

"Ravi has."

She was still. "What did you say?"

"Ravi has seen sense. He has agreed to be put under surveillance by Colonel Jaiswal, the Chief of Police, who has come here with me. If Ravi stays under that surveillance, he will be allowed to compete for this Tagore Prize. Then he is going home to his father and mother."

"I don't believe it."

"And he has promised not to see you again."

"Not see me again? Don't be ridiculous."

"Not ridiculous, but wise."

"Ravi would never consent to that."

"He has."

"I don't believe it. I shall never believe it."

"Not if I bring him here in front of you and you can hear him say it?"

"He wouldn't . . . if we were alone."

"You shall be alone."

"With you listening? He would know you were listening, you and your police, ready to pounce on him."

"No one will listen. Ravi will tell you himself."

"Ravi!" Una was ready to run to him but the way he

stood, as if unwillingly, and just inside the door, his face sullen, arrested her. "Ravi?" she whispered uncertainly.

"Why did you have to send for me?" said Ravi. "Couldn't you take it from him?"

"What—what have they done to you?" It was still a whisper.

"Una, you don't understand. If I don't do as they advise, this could send me to prison." Ravi's eyes were wide with fear.

"Then you must go to prison."

"For ten years!"

"Edward said seven. I will be waiting for you when you come out," but Ravi did not seem touched by this promise.

"What of my work?"

"Poets write good poems in prison. Think of Oscar Wilde."

"Wilde was not a good poet, besides, in ten years . . ."

"Seven."

"Even seven, we shall not be the same."

"I shall always be the same," but Ravi shook his head.

"You think so now."

"*Think!* I *know.* Oh Ravi, Ravi—what *have* they done to you?" and Una did run to him. "Ravi, hold me. Tell me this is a bad dream. Isn't it? Isn't it?" but Ravi did not hold her. He shuffled uneasily under her clinging.

"The fact is, Una, we have to give in. They are too strong for us."

"Not if we go now. It was silly to come to Naniji, to your grandmother, near anyone who knows you. This room has a back staircase—I saw it when I went to the bathroom; it goes down to the garden where there is a gate to the river. Before you could count twenty, we should be among the pilgrims; you can hear them bathing now. There are thousands of them. How could anyone ever find us?" She was pulling on her chappals. "I have a hundred-rupee note; I hid it in my bundle." She snatched the bundle up. "If we are quick . . ." She stopped. Ravi was still standing motionless by the door where he had come in. "You—are not coming?"

"I can't."

"You don't want to come?" Slowly she put down the bundle.

"Want—not want—that is not the question. The fact is . . ." When had Ravi spoken of facts? "The fact is I want to read my poems. I see now that is of paramount importance."

"Paramount?" She said it as if it were an outlandish word.

"Yes. You yourself have told me so a dozen of times."

"That was—then."

"It still holds, and haven't I," Ravi asked indignantly, "paid penalty enough?"

"Penalty?" Stupefied, all Una could do was repeat these high-sounding words.

"It will be difficult enough to read the poems well, to do myself justice with these police fellows over me—*and* I have to go home, eat humblest pie to my father. Don't make it any worse for me Una, I tell you, this is over."

"How can it be over when our baby . . ."

"Chup!" As Ravi used the peremptory Hindu word, he was across the room with his hand over her mouth. "Look Una"—it was Ravi who whispered now as he took his hand down—"As soon as you get home you must tell Miss Lamont—as soon as you are home. She will know what to do."

"Do?" Una was still stupefied.

"Yes. Don't tell me," said Ravi, "that the same hasn't happened to her."

"The *same?* To Alix?" Una spoke as if he had uttered blasphemy. "To *Alix?*"

"Yes. All such women have ways and Sir Edward need never know," but Una had turned her back, her face to the khus-khus; ever after, the smell of wet grass brought back this pain.

"You said 'No one is going to touch my son.' " It was barely a whisper, but it reached Ravi. "You said that."

"I was foolish. Colonel Jaiswal is kind—he and your father—and they have made me see I was foolish and bad."

"They made you see this as bad? And you let them! You

let them!" His silence answered Una, his hung head and suddenly, "Get out of my sight," screamed Una.

"My darling." Edward had come into the room, walking on tiptoe as if I were ill, thought Una. Perhaps I am. She had been driven to the bathroom as soon as Ravi went, doubled up with a diarrhoea that afterwards left her weak and cold. Now she had rolled up the khus-khus and Edward found her standing on the balcony looking down at the river in the blinding afternoon sun; Una's eyes seemed blinded too, her face stupefied with shock. "Come, my darling," Edward would have put his arm round her but she drew away. "Don't touch me." She was stiff, rigid. "No one must touch me, ever again."

"Very well, but I must take you home."

"I have something to ask you."

"Ask, my darling."

"Edward, please leave me here with Naniji, with Srimati Roy."

"Here? In Varanasi?"

"Please. I like it here—and she would have me. You have seen how I am looked after."

"Leave you here in a house that, in a way, belongs to the man who has wronged you!"

"It wasn't wrong—until you made it wrong; besides, I won't see—him—again." She would not say Ravi's name. "It's Srimati Roy's house—not his. Leave me here for the summer."

"Varanasi, in the hot weather!"

"Yes. If you would let me, Edward, I can bear this."

"Already you look a hollow-eyed little ghost."

"Only because of the journey. I find it—lovely—here."

Edward had to admit he did too: the big almost empty rooms; the water reflections; even the pilgrim clamour from the river banks did not disturb the pervading calm. He remembered his own desire to confide in Srimati Roy but, "We couldn't trouble her," he said.

"Nothing troubles her. That's why I want to stay. I shouldn't worry her, nor she me. You can give me a little money—a little would do. Please Edward, please understand." I cannot tell you the real reason, thought Una, but Edward, please.

"I do understand. She is a wise serene person, but you are not thinking."

"I am," and she said aloud, "You don't need me now. You have Alix."

Edward flushed. "I have had to learn—painful things about Alix."

"From whom?" Una said it with polite dullness; what did Alix matter now?

"Some—inadvertently. Some from Alix herself."

"Poor Alix!"

"Yes." Edward, too, leant over the balcony to look down at the river and said in a low voice, "You don't know how ashamed I am."

"Of her?"

"Of myself," and he said, "Yes, I can understand your reason for wanting to stay here."

You don't, said Una silently.

"But apart from the other impossibilities, Ravi may well be kept here until you are safely back in England."

"I am to go back to England?" It was as if Una had woken up.

"Certainly—after this escapade."

"It isn't an escapade," but—England. That might be possible—if no one guessed until it was too late. I could hide it and Crackers would help me. England . . .

"No more argument." Edward was suddenly as brisk as the Inspector-General. "Come and say good-bye to Srimati Roy and thank her. We shall go back to Delhi in the Embassy's plane, and you will fly to England tomorrow."

"It was then," said Una, "that the real ugliness began."

They did not go straight to the airport; instead, Una was smuggled in by a side door to Varanasi's largest hotel, built well away from the crowded river bank. There in a discreetly emptied salon, the hairdresser. "who won't talk," said Colonel Jaiswal, "we shall see to that," was to try and take the dye out of her hair. "Does he have to?" she asked in despair. "I have such a headache and, Edward, I have diarrhoea."

"You must try and control it. If you can't, you can be taken to the ladies room." Since leaving Srimati Roy's house, Edward had grown oddly callous. "How can I take you back to Delhi looking like this? If you won't think of yourself," said Edward, "you might think of me."

The hairdresser used a stripper. "But the hair is too fair," he said. "I must use a bleach too." He anointed and washed, anointed, rewashed: anointed—waited; the bleach had to take effect. "I think she may faint," he said.

"She mustn't," said Edward in alarm. He brought cold water and they washed her face. He soaked his handkerchief in eau-de-cologne and made her sniff it, then gave her brandy and soda; to Una it tasted horrible and, though it helped the bowel pains, made her head throb unbearably under the dryer. "Could I have some ice?" She meant ice cubes, but they brought her ice cream. "Ough!" said Una.

Colonel Jaiswal found clothes in the hotel shops, but not to his satisfaction. "They are all too exotic—made to attract tourists. However, this more simple tunic and skirt may do," but, "I can't wear a skirt," Una told Edward, "not to go up a plane gangway. I haven't any underclothes," and Edward exploded. "Had you lost all sense of decency?"

"Have you?" Una wanted to ask but was too heartsick and weary. Where was the humble gentle Edward of Srimati Roy's house? Was it because he was going back— to that Delhi life? thought Una shrinking—but it was obvious that the waiting at the hotel for these, what he deemed, necessary machinations was rasping his nerves and, "We have been here four hours. Four hours!"

"I am doing my best, sir," said the little hairdresser. "With such fine fair hair it is difficult not to damage . . ."

"Damage as much as you damn well like," Edward wanted to say it, but turned his wrath on Una. "All decency!"

"A sari is perfectly decent without underclothes."

"You will *not* wear a sari, have anything to do with

India, ever again." The hotel manager's wife produced a pair of briefs, but the skirt without a slip hung limply, the tunic was too big. "It is the smallest they make, but you look a sight," sighed Edward. The hair had come out fluffy which seemed strange on Una; her browned skin had a pallidly grey look; her lips were cracked, her feet were blistered. "Yes, you don't walk—you shamble," said Edward hopelessly. It was only a wraith of Una that they brought back to Shiraz Road.

She had made one last attempt at rebellion. "If I must go back to Delhi, can't I go to Mrs. Porter?"

"In the American enclave? That's the last thing," said Edward.

Back in the Shiraz Road house, Una tried not to see anything: the familiar beauty of the hall with its fountain and bougainvillaea: the drawing-room beyond: the glimpse of the veranda leading to her forsaken rooms: the garden that throbbed with memories of Ravi. Ram Chand had come to meet them; the other servants were discreetly withdrawn but Una knew there was not a pair of eyes in the house that had not seen her brought home captive and, in their minds, disgraced. At the airport Chinaberry had averted his face so as not to look at her.

"Well, by luck we have settled it," the Inspector-General was saying, "and by luck, hardly a soul is the wiser."

Then don't servants have souls? thought Una.

"I can never thank you enough." Edward was fervent. "But you must come in, have a drink and some dinner."

Was this an occasion for a drink? Colonel Jaiswal hesitated. "It is after ten o'clock," but Edward was already calling down the hall, "Alix."

Where is Alix, Una wondered?

"Alix."

No answer.

"Lady-sahib in her room, Sahib."

"Why doesn't she come?" Irritability flared again. "Is she ill?"

"Lady-sahib is packing." Ram disappeared in haste.

"*Packing?* What nonsense is this? Excuse me, Jaiswal."

As Ravi had said, the policeman was kind; obviously he

felt Una should not have been left in the hall like a piece of luggage. He called, "*Kaun hai?*—Is anyone there?" and Aziz seized the excuse to come. "Is there no woman to see to the Miss-baba? Put her to bed?" Aziz only shook his head.

"You should at least sit down." The Inspector-General came to Una and as she did not move, he said, "It must be painful, after such an—adventure, to come home."

"Home?" Una spoke as if she had never heard of it. What home, she seemed to ask? Then, suddenly, "There is a little hut at the end of the garden," she told him, "where . . . where . . ."

No Indian can bear to see a child cry. To Colonel Jaiswal Una was a child and the big policeman went to her and smoothed the tormented hair. "There, there, batchi. It will pass," but this was not a child and Una disengaged herself. "It will never pass."

"Lady-sahib is packing." It was true; a suitcase was open on the bed and Alix was filling it with feverish haste. Another stood ready on the floor. Alix, usually alert, had not heard the car nor Edward calling her.

"What absurdity is this?" Startled, she slammed down the lid and stood—at bay, thought Edward. "Where do you think you are going?"

"The only place I know. To Mumma in McCluskiegung. The jewels are in that box, Edward. I have only taken some money." Her face was ravaged so that it looked— old, thought Edward, which, strangely, gave it more beauty; the eyes were enormous, dilated—with terror? thought Edward, puzzled. "My dear," all his anger was gone. "Were you as frightened as that?" He came round the bed. "You needn't be. Una is here, safe and sound."

Alix made a noise like a hiccough. "S-sound?"

"Yes. She is with Jaiswal in the hall. We need you. She must go to bed. She is exhausted and we need a drink and food."

"Edward." Alix spoke with an effort. "You will want me to go."

"Never." He could feel her shaking as he held her. "No

matter what you have committed—or I have committed—we are husband and wife." He tightened his arm round her. "Come, cara."

"You call me cara now. . . ."

"I shall always call you that," but her lips were stiff under his kiss.

"Edward, I have to tell you . . ."

"Not now. Jaiswal is waiting, which isn't right after all he has done."

The Inspector-General could not have dinner. "Thank you but no, Lady Gwithiam. We had sandwiches at the hotel," and, as Edward saw him to the car, "Your wife seems stricken," he said. "I hope there is no more bad news."

"She has been alone, most of these two days. It is the strain."

"Well, we could all do with a night's sleep. Put the little girl to bed. We shall look after the boy. Sleep well." He put a hand on Edward's shoulder.

"Now," said Edward, back in the drawing-room. "I have to put a call though to Aunt Frederica. Then we can have some food and all go to bed."

"Wait." It was Alix who spoke. "Wait. Don't speak to your aunt yet. This evening I . . . I rang up Hal."

When Edward had telephoned that morning for Ram Chand to bring his clothes, Alix had entreated him, "Couldn't you change here? Wouldn't you come back just for half an hour?" and Edward had put the receiver down, leaving her smarting from the rebuff.

The day before had lacerated Alix; this one seemed interminable. She had done the few things required of her —given fresh orders for food—"though I have no idea if the Sahib will want dinner"—checked Christopher's accounts: spoken to Ganesh about flowers. "Ravi has not come back. Should I engage another chota mali?" Ganesh had asked.

"Perhaps you should." As the afternoon grew late, she remembered the horses. They will be bobbery for want of exercise, she thought and, leaving Chinaberry in case he were needed for the airport, had driven to the parade ground. She had met Vikram. "What! All alone?" He was his usual mocking self. "Where is Una?"

"Away with Edward on . . . on a short trip."

"Away? He has gone already!" He had been as impertinent as she had feared he would be and she rode hastily away. A tussle with Maxim had made her feel better, as had a gallop on Mouse, and she was grateful to be soaked with sweat—an excuse for another bath, which took more time.

"The Sahib has come? He has telephoned?" She had asked it as soon as she came in; again after her bath. The answer was the same: "No, Lady-sahib."

She had tried playing the piano, tried walking in the garden, reading the paper. If only there were something I could do. It was at nine o'clock that she had thought of Hal—perhaps because of meeting Vikram. Hal! She might know something. Una wrote to her almost every day.

"But, Lady Gwithiam, Halcyon is in bed," said Sister Anthony at the other end of the line.

"Then get her out of bed," but Alix had had to wait ten minutes before she heard Hal, her voice lively with curiosity.

"Una run away!" Hal sounded thrilled. "Oh Alix! Who with?"

"Why do you ask 'who'?"

A momentary silence. "Hal!"

"Well, she wouldn't run away alone, would she?" It had sounded lame and, "You know something about this." Alix was breathing sharply. "Hal, you must tell. Edward is out of his mind."

"You won't be cross with Una?"

"We are too worried to be cross. Hal, you *must* tell. What do you know?"

"I knew she had a lover."

"A lover?"

"Yes. He must have been that."

"How did you know?"

"She told me, when she and Edward were here. I think she had to tell somebody, but she wouldn't tell me who."

"I'll tell you." Alix was grim. "It was Ravi, the young gardener."

"The gardener? *Our* gardener? Oh no!" Hal's shocked incredulity came over the telephone. "I thought it must be someone like Vik, but . . . a servant! How could she? And how can she have his baby?" wailed Hal.

"Hal! *What* did you say? Hal!" but Hal had burst into tears.

"I rang up Hal," Alix said now, her eyes on Una. "Then, remembering what Doctor Asutosh had told us, I went to see Hem Sharma."

Hem had been released. "There was no evidence," Colonel Jaiswal had said. "Of course we are watching him," and Alix had found him in his room. "Mr. Sharma," said Alix, "please tell me . . . is what Hal—Una's sister—told me of Una, true? That she is . . . pregnant. It cannot be true."

"It is. A test was made, under another name, of course, at the Medical Centre."

"Made—by you."

"Through—my offices."

"And you didn't tell Sir Edward when he came to see you about Una?"

"Why should I be an informer?"

"Nor the police?"

"I had the police last night," said Hem, "and all this morning. You may know what they do to you, but no . . ." and Hem had said with the utmost insolence, "I am sure, with your expertise, you have managed to elude them—but to answer your question, I succeeded not to tell the police."

"You rang Hal," said Edward now. "You saw Hem Sharma . . . about what? Can't you speak, woman?" He was too far spent for courtesy. "What *is* all this about?"

"Una knows."

"Well, Una? Is this more torture?" he asked desperately.

"Tell Edward," said Alix and hid her face in her hands.

Una stood up. "I think Alix has found out that Ravi and I are having a baby. At least, it was Ravi and I. Now—I can guess it is only I."

"Poor little Una," said Alix. She had taken her hands down, but Edward made no movement, did not say a word.

"Shouldn't . . ." Una looked at him beseechingly, "shouldn't one be glad about a baby? I am."

He did not answer but looked at her—as if I were repellent, thought Una. All his tenderness was gone. Oh, why does he make it so ugly? She stood up and backed away from him.

At last, "How long?" asked Edward.

"Perhaps six, or seven, weeks. He will be born in December."

"He won't." Edward had been white before; now he was ashen. "Alix, go and ring up Doctor Gottlieb. We can trust him. Ask him to come straight away."

Alix had risen too. "Edward, a test has been made. It was positive. I will ring up Doctor Gottlieb but—for what?"

"You know very well for what. He will take Una to a nursing home tonight."

"No." For the first time Una shrieked. "No!" "Be quiet," said Edward roughly. "Alix, do as I say."

"I can't."

"*You* can't." Edward was dazed; it was the first time Alix had opposed him and Una saw that her hands were clenched, her back rigid as she braced herself. "What has this to do with you?" asked Edward witheringly.

"Everything. You told me just now we were husband and wife—then it is everything to do with me and, Edward, this is too cruel."

"*Cruel?*"

"Yes. You are so great, Edward," pleaded Alix; "but what is the use of being great if you are cruel?"

"I'm not great—but cruel. . . ." He seemed to have to say it again to make it believable. Srimati Roy's words were in his ears: "Aie! Why make dirt, Sir Edward?" and for a moment he seemed to hear the serene lapping of the river.

"But what are we to do?" he asked, bewildered. "What else can I do?"

"Wait."

"Then it may be too late."

"If it is . . . my mother would say," said Alix, "that to interfere with this is sin."

"Your *mother!*" The momentary softening had stopped abruptly and the contempt in his voice made Alix's temper flare.

"How dare you speak of Mumma like that? She knows things you don't, things I had forgotten."

"Only what you were taught."

"Taught and believed."

"Mumbo-jumbo." Edward almost shouted it but Alix was suddenly quiet and dignified as she said, "Mumbo-jumbo is what you hear from outside and do not believe. What you feel in you is true. My God, I ought to know."

"Oh Alix!" Una stole to her and Alix put an arm round her.

"It's difficult for you to understand, Edward," Alix went on, "because you have never been what they call bad!"

"Nonsense. Of course I have."

"You haven't. I know—and that is what makes you so harsh."

"Harsh? Cruel? What other epithets have you for me?" but Alix was steady.

"Not harsh with other people, but Una is you."

That touched him. "I thought she was," he said slowly, "but not now. Not for a long time—only I hadn't the wit to see it. I don't know whose fault that is." As Edward said it, he remembered his own admission to Srimati Roy, "I have made Una suffer." Yet it was the very sight of her suffering, so worn, tormented, and dishevelled that pushed him into harshness again as he turned on Alix: "Are you trying to tell me I should let a child, an unfortunate misguided child, bear a half-caste bastard?"

"You're not to call him that." It was another shriek from Una.

"That's what it would be—another little unwanted."

"He isn't unwanted. I want him. I want him."

"Don't scream at me."

"I will!" but Una lowered her tone in helpless misery. "Hem said you would do this."

"Hem was right."

"That's why we upset all our plans. We had meant to tell you everything, after the Tagore Prize, when Ravi had won it. We had it all planned . . . then we knew this . . . Hem advised us to hide, that's why we ran away, but I still didn't dream you would . . ."

"Then you ought to have dreamt." Edward caught himself up and spoke quietly. "You mustn't be hysterical, Una. This—is done every day—thousands of times a day, because it is sense. It won't even hurt you."

"Hurt me. Kill my baby and it won't hurt me!"

"Think straight. It isn't a baby yet—just an embryo."

"It's you who should think," Una hurled at him. "An embryo is a baby. I ought to know. He is in me. He is mine and you are not to touch him. Not to touch him."

"That's enough. I will ring Doctor Gottlieb myself."

"I think this must be the first time in my life," said Alix, "that I have acted against my own interest. It's a new feeling," but her smile was wan.

"What can he do to you?" asked Una.

"I suppose put me away." For all her capability, her seeming sophistication, Alix's attitude to her marriage with Edward was that of the simplest Indian wife.

"Listen—he is on the telephone." Una's very skin seemed to creep with fear but, "Colonel Jaiswal?" Edward was saying. "Forgive me for disturbing you, but could you have some of your men posted here tonight?"

"Has something further happened?"

"Nothing. Perhaps I am nervous but . . ."

"The men are posted. I thought it possible there might have been a bazaar leak to some of Bhattacharya's old friends, someone in the Praja Swaraj hear a distorted story and so come to take revenge. Have you any such suspicion?"

"Not of them but—there's no one I can trust."

"He means me," whispered Alix. "But at least he isn't telephoning Doctor Gottlieb."

"A guard outside my daughter's room—both doors."

"So I can't run away again," whispered Una.

"That wouldn't be wise. They would only catch you—but you have been so brave, be brave still. Soon he will be less angry—already he was wavered, poor Edward. Perhaps he may not insist. . . ."

"But how not?"

"I don't know," said Alix, "but wait. Go to your room now and I will bring you a hot drink. Edward's guards will at least let me do that. Then, in the morning . . ."

"In the morning Una will go into Gottlieb's nursing home." Edward had come back. "I am sorry if I am harsh and cruel but it is the only sense. We're all too tired and distressed to talk any more, so, Alix, you had better not see Una again. Come Una, I will take you to bed."

"I will take myself," but she stopped at the door. "Ravi was the peacock." It was a whisper, but it filled the drawing-room. "He was proud and innocent."

"Innocent!"

"Yes, innocent—until you made him perjure himself," and Edward knew he had heard her use, or misuse, that word before.

"We had made a beautiful holy thing," said Una, "until you touched it. You didn't want me to watch the monkeys. You didn't even like the servants watching them or to have them near the house, but you have made us, Ravi and me, into monkeys—helpless, public. You said the monkey-man ought to be prosecuted. I think so too. Goodnight, Mr. Monkey-man."

There was silence in the room after she had gone. Alix sat with bowed head as if she were ashamed—for me, thought Edward. He went to the piano and leaned against it, his eyes closed. 'Harsh,' 'cruel' . . . he could repel those, but 'monkey-man.' Una called me 'monkey-man'—and it fits, thought Edward; everything and everyone seemed shut out by the rattling of that evil little drum and, Hideous, thought Edward, I have been hideous.

Then a voice broke through to him. "Edward, come here." It might have been Mrs. Lamont's voice, it was so warm with compassion. "Edward, come here to me," said Alix, and Edward came.

Una stood in the little muslined bedroom she had so joyously discarded—was it only three days ago? It was not yet three days. Here she was back, but it was she, Una, who was discarded now. Ram had come in with a tray of milk and sandwiches—Ram, not Alix. Perhaps he had been moved with pity, because he said, "Eat, baba . . . or drink."

Eat . . . drink . . . go to bed . . . in the morning . . . The commands made no impression. Nothing will make an impression any more, thought Una. Then, at the bathroom door, she heard a muffled knock.

"Ssh! It's only Hem."

For a moment a wild hope had stirred in Una, but Ravi was probably in Varanasi; even if he were not, he would not come now . . . only Hem. Una opened the bathroom door. "Hem!"

"Ssh!" Hem whispered. "The place is bristling with boots and turbans."

"Then how did you get here?"

"They followed Miss Lamont—I beg pardon, Lady Gwithiam—and, of course me. We were both trailed, most thor-ough-ly. I must say in this respect," said Hem, "I am not ashamed of my countrymen. After she left I went in the routine way to the Medical Centre, but it has perhaps fifty exits, if you count unorthodox ones known to us students. I slipped up to the roof, slid down a drainpipe—sometimes it is advantage to be dark-skinned—then I jumped down into a lorry filled with sacks. It obligingly drove away."

"Jumped? How far?"

"Say, twenty feet."

"Hem! You might have been killed."

"No, I am that horse—how is he called—the horse with wings?"

"Pegasus. He is the poet's horse."

"Poet's donkey in this case." Hem laughed. "Then I came through our gap and hid in your sister's empty room. Come inside the bathroom. They will not see us there."

Una went in and closed the door.

"I had to come," said Hem.

"To find out about Ravi?"

"Ravi! To find out about you."

"I am—in one piece," said Una.

"Hush. Whisper."

"Tomorrow I won't be," said Una. "Tomorrow Edward will do as you said."

"I am sorry."

Una had started to shiver again and, "Now I have seen you are safe," said Hem, "I will go."

"Hem," said Una. "In Indian thought, a girl who isn't married—and has made love—is a whore, isn't she?"

"I have a Naniji too," said Hem, "who, if I said blasphemy—and I was a blasphemous boy—washed out my mouth with soap. We are in the bathroom. Do you want that I wash out yours?"

"I think, Hem," said Una, "you are the only person in Delhi I want to see again."

"I must go," said Hem hastily, "but wait, this is yours," and he held out a book.

"My *Elementary Mechanics*." Una looked at the forgotten book. "I won't need it."

"You will."

Una shook her head. "I have lost too much time."

"Poppycock," said Hem without sympathy. "I lost two years," and, Remember Mrs. Porter's little doll who wouldn't lie down, thought Una. Hem was like that doll.

"Hem," she said. "Will you tell me something? When they held that man down and threw acid into his eyes— Edward told me—it was Ravi who did it, wasn't it?"

"You should mind your own business," said Hem as he had said before.

"It is my business."

"It was long ago. We were stupid boys."

"But you went to prison."

"It is fashionable to be a jailbird—and I was acquitted."

"After a time—probably a terrible time—and Ravi was hiding as a gardener." Her face was hard as she said, "Have you ever heard, Hem, why a peacock gives those terrible screams? He has looked down and suddenly seen his feet. He had forgotten he had them because he was so busy admiring his train."

"Una, don't. Ravi is Ravi."

"Yes . . ." and she lifted those eyes, grown older now but, for all their unhappiness, still as candid. "That is the wonder. Well, I suppose," she tried to shrug, "anyone can have a baby; very few can write a poem."

Una was woken by a fierce cramp that made her whole body constrict. Have I got real dysentery? But it was followed by an aching pain that was familiar.

She was half-drugged with sleep. Had they put something in the milk that Ram had brought her? It had tasted of honey and Ram had stirred it as he put it down. She had thought she could not sleep, but sleep had come. Was Ravi in the room with his low chanted lullaby?

Nini, baba, nini
Roti . . .

I shall sing it to my baby but I can't remember the words. I must ask Ravi . . . but, of course, the hut was empty . . . empty. Half drifted into sleep, Una thought there was moonlight in the room; it seemed there had been moonlight all through this strange other-world time; surely there had been a moon when Alix went with Vikram: moonlight when she, Una, had stolen out to Ravi—"Read me your poems. . . ." "Then you must come to my hut to-night. . . ." The garden was filled with their whispered voices—she remembered the Budh Purnima moon at Agra. Had there been a moon when she bathed in the Ganges at Varanasi, or was it the light from the ghat? I was so hot then. Now she was shivering, but was it from cold or pain?

It was not a diarrhoea pain. Then why should she have it? I shouldn't have this sort of pain, thought Una, not for six or seven months. I am dreaming.

It was no dream. With the next cramp she heard a noise that brought her to reality; the sound of boots as someone moved to the edge of the veranda, cleared his throat and spat. Edward's melodramatic policeman! The moonlight was not from the moon but from the light left on for the guards on the veranda and the scene in the drawing-room seemed to come back. I screamed at Edward, thought Una, he shouted at me, then the pain was lost in the wonder of Alix. She, she Alix/Miss Lamont, took my part. For Alix to lose her temper with Edward was unthinkable, yet she had lost it. They quarrelled, thought Una in wonder, and suddenly it was honest. Though Edward was furious now, he must respect Alix, something Una guessed he had not done before. When Edward isn't angry, he is fair-minded, thought Una, but that will not save me; the anger would last well over the morning—when they are going to do . . . that . . . to me. That!

The cramp came again so that she rolled on the bed and had to bite her lip not to moan; then it went, leaving the pain and now she knew why it was familiar.

She dragged herself up from the bed and pulled the curtains closer to shut out the policeman and the veranda. In the bathroom, she turned on the light; yes, there was a stain on her pyjamas and, as she looked, a trickle of red ran down inside her thigh to her leg, an infinitesimal Ganges, but of blood: not heart's blood but womb blood which, for a woman, is far deeper and, like the river, taking these weeks and months away: beauty and ugliness: adoration, revulsion: cruelty and tenderness: suffering, well-being: misery, ecstasy, joy: Ravi and their baby. Una gave a sob. "So no one," she said aloud in the bathroom, "is going to have their way."

It was all ended in that little running stain.

The bonfires are out, wrote Hal. She had looked back in her diary to that long-ago afternoon in January. Now she wrote, *My affairs do drag me homeward,* and a tear splashed on the page. At the convent they were doing *The Winter's Tale;* again Hal had been chosen as Perdita—but I think I shall never play her. 'Homeward,' if you can call it home. Una was right; it was ignominious to be posted around like a parcel. *I am to be sent to Mother. I suppose some of this Una business has reached her—not by me this time—and she has threatened Dads. It is on condition I go to Miss Perry's school in Connecticut. School . . . school!* Hal's pen bit deep. *Plain living and high thinking once more.* Hal so much preferred high living and plain thinking. *When shall I see Vikram, my darling Vik again?* Another tear fell but Hal caught it. *I will see him again!* The pen bit deeper. *Dad's conference is transferred to Bangkok; he is going there with Alix, so we leave Delhi forever.* A whole spatter of tears. *Una has gone back to Cerne.* Then Hal wrote, *More amazement! Her gardener has won some tremendous prize for poetry. Then he wasn't only a gardener.*

In Shiraz Road Ganesh was showing the new young gardener how to take down the seed house; bamboos and mats had to be stored under cover or they would rot in the deluge of the monsoon. The new chota mali was eager and Ganesh was pleased at the deft way he rolled the mats, stacked poles, cleaned pans. "We will build it afresh in October," said Ganesh. "Another sahib is coming. Then I shall teach you how to sow the seeds."

FAWCETT CREST BESTSELLERS

THE GOLDEN UNICORN *Phyllis Whitney*	2-3104-6	$1.95
THE PEACOCK SPRING *Rumer Godden*	2-3105-4	$1.75
MAKING ENDS MEET *Barbara Howar*	2-3084-8	$1.95
STRANGER AT WILDINGS *Madeleine Brent*	2-3085-6	$1.95
THE TIME OF THE DRAGON *Dorothy Eden*	2-3059-7	$1.95
THE LYNMARA LEGACY *Catherine Gaskin*	2-3060-0	$1.95
THE GOLDEN RENDEZVOUS *Alistair MacLean*	2-3055-4	$1.75
TESTAMENT *David Morrell*	2-3033-3	$1.95
TRADING UP *Joan Lea*	2-3014-7	$1.95
HARRY'S GAME *Gerald Seymour*	2-3019-8	$1.95
THE SWORD AND THE SHADOW *Sylvia Thorpe*	2-2945-9	$1.50
IN THE BEGINNING *Chaim Potok*	2-2980-7	$1.95
THE ASSASSINS *Joyce Carol Oates*	2-3000-7	$2.25
LORD OF THE FAR ISLAND *Victoria Holt*	2-2874-6	$1.95
REBEL HEIRESS *Jane Aiken Hodge*	2-2960-2	$1.75
CIRCUS *Alistair MacLean*	2-2875-4	$1.95
CSARDAS *Diane Pearson*	2-2885-1	$1.95
WINNING THROUGH INTIMIDATION *Robert J. Ringer*	2-2836-3	$1.95
THE MASSACRE AT FALL CREEK *Jessamyn West*	C2771	$1.95
EDEN *Julie Ellis*	X2772	$1.75
CENTENNIAL *James A. Michener*	V2639	$2.75
LADY *Thomas Tryon*	C2592	$1.95

Send to: FAWCETT PUBLICATIONS, INC.
Mail Order Dept., P.O. Box 1014, Greenwich Conn. 06830

NAME

ADDRESS

CITY

STATE   ZIP

I enclose $_____, which includes total price of all books
ordered plus 50¢ for book postage and handling for the first
book and 25¢ for each additional. If my order is for five books or
more, I understand that Fawcett will pay all postage and handling.